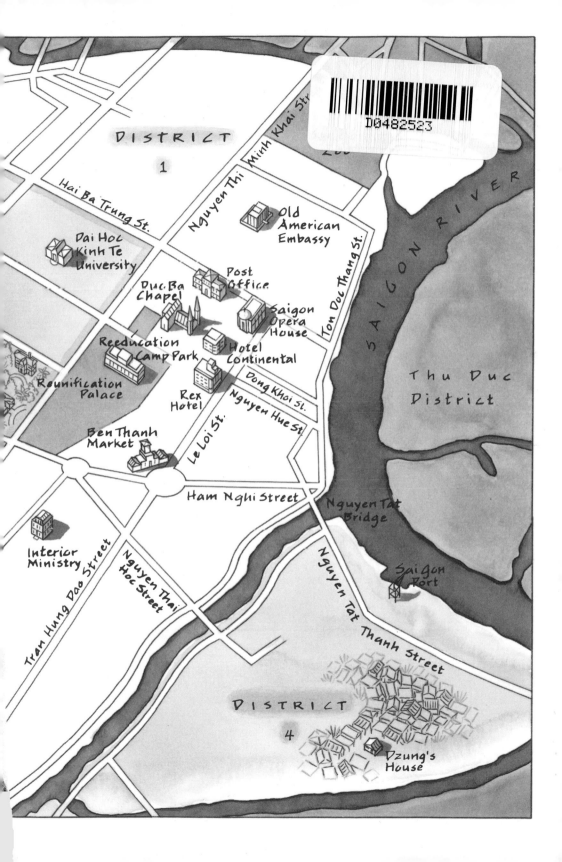

LOST SOLDIERS

LOST SOLDIERS

JAMES WEBB

BANTAM BOOKS

LOST SOLDIERS
A Bantam Book / September 2001

Grateful acknowledgment is make to the following for permission to quote from previously published material:

"What Was Lost" by W. B. Yeats. Reprinted in the United States with the permission of Scribner, a Division of Simon & Schuster, Inc., from *The Poems of W. B. Yeats: A New Edition,* edited by Richard J. Finneran. Copyright © 1940 by Georgie Yeats, copyright renewed © 1968 by Bertha Georgie Yeats, Michael Butler Yeats, and Anne Yeats. Reprinted in Canada with the permission of A. P. Watt Ltd on behalf of Michael B. Yeats.

The lines from "Mandalay" by Rudyard Kipling on page 324 are reprinted with permission of A. P. Watt Ltd on behalf of the National Trust for Places of Historic Interest or Natural Beauty.

BOOK DESIGN BY GLEN M. EDELSTEIN

Library of Congress Cataloging-in-Publication Data

Webb, James H.
Lost soldiers / James Webb.
p. cm.
ISBN 0-553-80214-3
1. Vietnamese Conflict, 1961–1975—Veterans—Fiction.
2. Americans—Vietnam—Fiction. 3. Deserters, Military—Fiction.
4. Vietnam—Fiction. I. Title.

PS3573.E1955 L6 2001
813'.54—dc21   2001025474

Published simultaneously in the United States and Canada

PRINTED IN THE UNITED STATES OF AMERICA

BVG   10 9 8 7 6 5 4 3 2 1

ACKNOWLEDGMENTS

A special thanks to Nita Taublib, Katie Hall, and Tracy Devine, who shared my passion for this book and made it happen.

And to my family, for enduring the odd world of a writer.

And to my many Vietnamese friends, both in Viet Nam and overseas, whose struggles, insights, hopes, and affection fueled these pages.

Arlington, Virginia
February 2001

What Was Lost

I sing what was lost and dread what was won,
I walk in a battle fought over again,
My king a lost king, and lost soldiers my men;
Feet to the Rising and Setting may run,
They always beat on the same small stone.

—WILLIAM BUTLER YEATS

LOST SOLDIERS

The Arabat, Moscow, Russia

A FAT, BRIGHTLY smiling woman in a tattered cloth coat stood on the landing where the steps came up from the subway, waving her hands into the air so that the puppies at her feet would dance. They were happy little dogs, eight in total, each one thick-furred and multicolored, of some unknown Arctic breed. The woman was trying to sell them to the tourists who were exiting from the subway to the street.

Anatolie Petrushinsky grunted cynically as he watched the well-dressed westerners move quickly past the woman. Not one of them so much as looked at her fuzzy little dogs. Foolish woman, he thought. Or maybe she has sold everything else already. But she would have done better to kill the puppies and make them into hats. For why would a German or an Englishman or especially an American want to bring a live dog home?

Petrushinsky stood on the curb thirty yards away, hunched inside an old army jacket. His grim, lined face was burnt from the cold. His own fur hat, which had been made in a rural village near Peredelkino out of rabbit skins, was folded down over his ears. He silently smoked a cigarette, masking his disgust as he scrutinized the tourists who were making their way along the street toward him. They emanated a conqueror's condescending arrogance, pausing here and there with an airy cheerfulness as they examined the paltry goods for sale.

Dozens of bedraggled vendors lined the curbside, making this section of the Arabat look like an odd, gigantic yard sale. Petrushinsky himself was holding a case filled with military trinkets. The case was rigged so that it folded out into a portable tray, hanging open just below his waist, its top part up against his chest and strapped around his neck. In contrast to those who owned the little shops behind him, he and the other curbside merchants were selling their goods without official licenses. The licenses were expensive, and difficult to obtain. If the police decided to conduct a raid he could snap the tray shut and quickly disappear inside the curling roads and vast blocks of apartments just behind him, where most police officers were too lazy and too afraid to follow.

What do they care, he thought. Pieces from my own army uniform. To sell away my pride I need a license, or at least to bribe the police officer? Petrushinsky hated what had happened in his country over the past ten years. There was no justice anymore, no nobility of purpose, indeed no Soviet Union. Only silly police shakedowns and a cannibalistic selling-off of one's own heritage. And every new morning another fucking game.

And so it has come to this, mused Petrushinsky as he huddled against the bitter cold. It is not enough that the CIA agent Gorbachev sold out our empire to the west. It is not enough that our government collapsed into a comical, corrupt anarchy run on the inside by the KGB and on the outside by a murderous mafia. It is not enough that our military, once the proudest in the world, occupier of more foreign territory than any army in history, is reduced to living in slums and suffering defeat at the hands of ragtag militias in places like Afghanistan and Chechnya. No, it is not even enough that two-thirds of the men in our country now die in a drunken stupor while still in their fifties, their very hearts polluted by the hopelessness of our new existence. Now I must survive by selling the emblems of our greatness, pieces of the uniform I wore with honor and pride, to the same slime who took our empire from us.

There were about twenty people in this latest group, strolling slowly in their threes and fours along the Arabat. Just down from him a dark-haired, fortyish woman in an elegant gray wool coat had stopped to bargain with a man who was selling antique dolls. A fur collar hugged her neck just below the ears, framing her face as if it were a winter halo. From her coat and the cut of her hair, Petrushinsky decided she was German. He found himself admiring her flawless complexion and the clean features of her face. When she smiled he fell in love with her just for an instant, his mind lost for that moment in a memory of a town near East Berlin.

Then he felt himself begin to hack. He could not stop it. In seconds he was coughing violently, his hands over his mouth. The endless cigarettes caused him to do this. And the vodka. And the cold. As he coughed he felt the woman's eyes on him. Turning, he saw that she was fighting back revulsion as she looked at his bluing face and his reddened, bark-hard hands. And in that instant he hated her.

I could have had you, he thought. Not too many years ago you would have been begging me to take you.

Four well-dressed men had stopped before him as he coughed. They elbowed each other, speaking quietly as they examined the buttons and medals in his tray. Their scrubbed faces and perfectly cut topcoats told him immediately that they were Americans. Three of them were older— from their slate-gray hair and etched faces perhaps in their fifties, but it was always so difficult to tell with Americans. The other one, a cherubic, animated man who smoked a pipe like an Englishman and seemed to be their escort, was considerably younger.

Petrushinsky could tell that they were speaking English, although he could not make any sense from their words. The younger man was pointing at him with an implied familiarity, and the three older men were now staring with fresh interest. Finally the younger man switched to Russian, speaking directly to Petrushinsky.

"We saw the tattoo on your hand when you were coughing," said the younger man. He had an accent so perfect that he might have been an academe. "I told my guests that you must have been a member of an elite airborne unit."

Involuntarily, Petrushinsky glanced down at the parachute that was tattooed on the back of his right hand, remembering for a moment the proud night that the tattoo gun had burned its image into him. Then he gazed back up at the four men who stood before him. Their eyes were bright, as if now viewing him with some vicarious camaraderie. From somewhere deep inside his spirit, a pride burst forth. We were as good as you, thought Petrushinsky. Maybe we were better than you.

"Yes," said Petrushinsky. "I was airborne, for many years. I know you are Americans. It may surprise you, but I served in Cuba, twice!"

The rotund younger man quickly laughed, translating the remarks for his three guests. Petrushinsky had now decided that the escort was probably an intelligence agent working out of the American Embassy and that his guests were visiting businessmen or perhaps government officials. Petrushinsky's remarks seemed to electrify the three older men. They spoke rapidly to one another for several seconds and then to their escort, as if ordering him to respond.

"These gentlemen are American businessmen," explained their escort. "But when they were younger, all three served in Viet Nam."

"I was in Viet Nam," answered Petrushinsky, determined not to be outdone. The shock that pulsed across the three men's faces when his words were translated filled Petrushinsky with a silent but gleeful pride. They began chattering, their eyes round with discovery, peering at him with an intense curiosity.

"When?" asked their escort.

"Many times. The first time, 1968. The last time, 1987."

The three men became even more intense as their guide translated for them. They spoke quickly, all at the same time, looking at one another as if on the edge of some profound discovery. Finally their guide translated another question for him.

"You were in Viet Nam in 1968? What were you doing?"

Petrushinsky shrugged nonchalantly, eyeing them as if they were stupid. What was I doing? What did they think I was doing? "I was a soldier!"

As the four Americans grew even more excited, a nervousness that bordered on nausea began to creep through Petrushinsky. He had not thought that such a casual boast would cause such an eruption of emotion. What was Viet Nam, after all? So many years ago. So much had happened since then. The war in Afghanistan, the emergence of the traitor Gorbachev, the collapse of the east, the drunken chaos of Yeltsin, the murderous, criminal shadow government, the folly of Chechnya. So much. What did it matter that he had been in Viet Nam?

"Where were you?" It was becoming overwhelming, an interrogation. The three men were asking him in English, leaning forward over his little tray, their voices tight with amazement and even disbelief, as their guide persistently quizzed him in Russian.

"What does it matter?" Petrushinsky finally muttered. "Soldiers go where they are told. I was in many places."

"No one has ever admitted there were Soviet soldiers in Viet Nam during the war! After the war, certainly. But during it? How many times were you there? What did you do?"

Petrushinsky stared in horror at their taut, incredulous faces, amazed at the reaction that had followed such a simple statement. He did not understand it, and now he deeply feared it. If he gave them any more answers, what would come next? Would they try to detain him and bring him to an American television camera? Would they call the police and request their assistance, causing his arrest for peddling without a license? Would they corral him and bring him to the American Embassy for further interrogation? Had he committed the breach of an oath he no longer even remembered?

No, he decided. There had never been an oath, because there had never been a need for one. There had never been journalists or probing, arrogant American businessmen or even the ability to ask such questions when the Soviet army was supreme. It was only now, after the army and the empire had been disgraced. He spoke fiercely now, startling them. "Why do you want to know all these things? Who are you? I ask you, why do you want to know?"

Quickly, he snapped his case shut and began walking away from them. One of the older men stepped forward as if to follow him, and Petrushinsky pointed at him, a threat. The man raised both hands as if pleading with him to be patient. And immediately Petrushinsky began running.

The four men's calling voices grew fainter, and then finally he could hear them no longer as he ran behind a row of shops. He turned onto a side street with more shops and other people lined against the curb, selling their pitiful bags of nothing. Across the street a fire had been lit inside a trash can, and a half dozen weather-beaten men were standing around it, warming themselves. My people, he thought, jogging past them. Soldiers who served the empire and today have nothing to look forward to but the bottle and an early death.

But he could not stop to be with them, not yet, not even for a moment to get warm. He disappeared inside a cluttered alleyway, still clutching his peddler's case. Maybe later he would come back. But now he kept on running.

CHAPTER ONE

Quang Nam Province, Viet Nam

"TYPHOON," SAID BRANDON Condley, his hard gray eyes expertly search-ing the bruised horizon.

It had been drizzling all morning, which was no surprise because actually it had been drizzling for weeks. But off to the east the real deal was rolling in from the South China Sea, having just wreaked havoc in the northern islands of the Philippines. Condley zipped his rain jacket all the way up underneath his throat as if to emphasize the coming storm, then pulled his worn baseball cap lower over his eyes. And finally, just to make the point that he did not really care, he laughed.

"Hey, Professor, Buddha's pissed. Welcome to the real Viet Nam!"

Hanson Muir stood like a dreamer ten feet in front of him, near the prow of the narrow wooden boat. The boat was struggling against the angry current of the chalky, swollen Thu Bon River, its two-cylinder motor putting like a loud lawn mower. Its bow yawed this way and that, smacking against odd flotsam and swirling eddies. The monsoon had come to central Viet Nam five weeks before. It had dropped a hundred inches of rain in two weeks and then settled into an intermittent drizzle that would last for months. The fog-shrouded, unending mountains to the west were still weeping tons of water every hour from it. The rivers and streams had outgrown their banks. The endless terraces of rice paddies that filled the valleys leading eastward to the sea were now hidden under vast lakes of rainwater, often indistinguishable from the rivers or even the sea itself. And along the tree-choked knolls and ridges in the middle of the paddies, hundreds of villages sat serenely above the water, isolated like ancient little islands.

"How much further, Brandon?"

Muir's posed stance made Condley laugh yet again. The brilliant scientist seemed to be imagining himself as a Viking marauder with his puffed chest and raised chin, one hand stroking his beard as the other held on to a railing. Hearing Condley laugh, he turned and caught the smaller man's amused expression.

"Having your fun, are you?"

"You look ridiculous, Professor."

"And it'll be even funnier if we drown, I suppose?"

"You won't drown. You're too fat to sink."

"I'm surveying the riverbanks," said Hanson defensively. "In the event I am required to swim ashore."

Condley laughed again. He knew this river. "I wouldn't give a nickel for you making it to shore if this boat splits in two."

"I thought you said I wouldn't drown."

"That doesn't mean I think you can swim."

"Your sense of humor leaves me weak."

"Then don't lose your grip, there."

Condley walked carefully toward the stern and caught the attention of the boat's owner. The tight-muscled little man, whose name was Tuan, was intently working the tiller of his creaky wooden craft while standing barefoot in a gathering pool of water. Three hours before, Tuan had seemed incurably happy when these two Americans had offered him forty dollars to take them upriver to the village of Ninh Phuoc and back. Now he had lost his smile. His narrow eyes squinted as he watched the clogged current. He was drenched and shivering, his rain jacket and shorts soaked all the way through.

"*Bao,*" said Condley, using the Vietnamese word for typhoon and pointing again toward the distant sea. "*Sap den! Phai khong?*"

Tuan glanced quickly up into the sky, then focused back on the dangers of the river. He tilted the rudder away from a swiftly moving log and then narrowly dodged the bloated carcass of a dead pig. "*Khong co sao,*" he answered. Condley could tell that a typhoon would never deter Tuan. Forty dollars was the equivalent of a month's wages, and the little boatmaster had already planned on how he was going to spend it. "*Di Ninh Phuoc di ve Danang, bon muoi do-lah, duoc, duoc.*"

"What did he say?" asked Hanson Muir.

"Roughly, he said, 'So fucking what?' The rain doesn't matter. He wants the money. He's a tough little bastard, I told you that."

"No, let's put this in character, Brandon. If you hired him, he's got to be the toughest little bastard in all of central Viet Nam, right? And by the time we finish this trip he'll have become a legend."

"He's already a legend, just for taking us," said Condley, secretly enjoying Muir's unease. "If we finish the trip, they'll erect a shrine in his honor."

Muir shrugged, nervously looking at the sky. "I take your point about the storm. Tell him we'll give him the money anyway. He didn't even look up at that cloud bank, you know."

"He was born here. He can smell a typhoon from fifty miles away." Condley waved the boatmaster on, laughing grimly. He loved the *nguoi trungs*, as they called the combative, tough people from Viet Nam's central mountain region. "The fucker's going to die for forty bucks."

"I told you, give him the money."

"Well, then you've got to deal with his pride. He's a *nguoi trung*, Professor. He'll never take a handout." Condley nudged Muir. "Are you sure you want to keep going?"

From the look on his flabby moon of a face, it was clear that Hanson Muir was not sure at all. The boat hit a half-submerged log, jarring them and knocking Muir sideways. The heavyset anthropologist held nervously to the boat railing and pushed his dirty eyeglasses back up his nose. Finally he sighed. "We're almost there, aren't we? If we return to Da Nang we've got to come back out here and do it all over again."

"If we keep going and then get back to Da Nang after the typhoon hits, we won't get out. The plane from Sai Gon won't even come in there. The entire airport area will be underwater. And if we get stuck in Ninh Phuoc during a typhoon, we might end up staying there till spring. The way the Taiwanese have been strip-logging up in those mountains, the root systems are almost gone. This whole region could become one giant mud slide."

Muir forced a grin, masking his fear. "I've always been tempted to take a Vietnamese wife."

"Trust me, you're not going to feel like settling down in Ninh Phuoc. If you want a wife, I'll find you one in Sai Gon."

"I was teasing. My present wife would object rather violently to being replaced, you know."

"No need for that," shrugged Condley. "The Vietnamese have always been polygamous. You can have as many wives as you can afford."

"Now *you're* teasing *me*."

"Actually, I'm not."

Muir rolled his eyes, obviously thinking of a retort, then let the notion go. Sai Gon was a long way away, but Ninh Phuoc was just up the river. If they could make it up the river. He gave Condley a questioning look. "You haven't really told me what to do or say when we get there."

"It depends on what they've got, Professor. If it's real, you can do your thing. If it's chitchat, just be nice. Make the people feel important."

"I'm a scientist. I'm not supposed to be nice."

Another dead pig floated past, and then off next to the shore a dead villager, spread-eagled and bloated, spinning in the rapid current. Muir swallowed hard, watching the body twirl past them. Condley nudged him, snapping him out of it. "When we get there, just watch me. Smile when I smile. Eat the rice when I eat the rice. Drink the tea when I drink the tea. Smoke the cigarette when they give you one."

"I don't smoke."

"You do now."

Condley's craggy face twinkled with secret happiness as the boat fought its way upriver. His shoes were squishy from the water in the boat and his fingers were crinkly from the rain. He feared the raw, surging power of Song Thu Bon, but at the same time he felt oddly content. The chalky river that ran from the mountains in Laos all the way to the sea just south of Da Nang was as comforting as an old friend. He had memories along its banks. Some of the memories were horrible. A few of them were even good. But all of them had meaning. And what was life if it brought you no meaning?

Muir had decided to ignore him. The brilliant academic had turned away from him now, studying the flotsam as if history itself were slapping and bumping along the gunwales. The old boat shuddered against the current, causing its boards to creak. Muir shifted his gaze from the river to the dangerous beauty of the mountains that now rose up fierce and shrouded on all sides. "Do you know where we are?"

Condley pulled out an old American tactical map he had kept from the war, carefully unfolding it. As a Marine thirty years before, he had laminated the map to protect it from the rains. It still bore black and red stains along its folds from where he had once used grease pencils to mark checkpoints for patrols and on-call targets for artillery. Turning it this way and that, he started matching the map to terrain features that rose up near the banks of the river. This was his area. He had walked every inch of it in another life, and neither he nor it had changed a whole lot since he'd left. Finally he held his finger on the map, showing Muir where they were.

"We're right here, Professor. That mountain over there is Nui Son Su. It was one of our key outposts on the edge of the Fifth Marines regimental headquarters in An Hoa. An Hoa is just behind the mountain. Or its ruins are, anyway. So that means we have two or three more turns in the river. The mountains will close in on us, then open up, then close in again—right here. And when they open up again, we'll be in Ninh Phuoc."

Muir looked upriver. Indeed, the mountains were assembling themselves through the rain-mist, pushing at the river from both sides. He gave off a little shiver as he stared into the gap. The current picked up, turning frothy as the river narrowed where it passed between the mountains. Condley watched Tuan, studying the boatmaster's face for clues and deciding from the little man's steadfast eyes that they were going to make it. Then for a long time he peered upriver through the rain, lost in memories.

Lots of memories. Years of them, clinging to the crags and standing deep inside old foxholes that still scarred the hillsides.

They broke through the pass and entered calmer, wider waters. Muir seemed to relax, his scientist's need for certainty calmed by Condley's map-reading skills. The river turned sharply to the left and Condley pointed to a high, steep mountain that rose more than a thousand feet up into the mist.

"That's Cua Tan," he said. "We're almost at Ninh Phuoc."

After Cua Tan the river's left bank opened into a valley that reached far to the east. Condley knew that the valley would eventually end in a huge canyon up against even higher mountains, a fiercely sharp range called the Que Sons. The Americans used to call the big box canyon the Antenna Valley. And at its entrance, just off the river, he could finally see the village of Ninh Phuoc.

"There it is," he said. "We made it."

Long time no see.

The boatmaster thankfully followed his directions and left the river's main current, navigating across the floodlands toward the village. "A badass place," said Condley as they approached the looming darkness of its tree lines. "Lots of people died in here. The NVA kept a division up in those mountains. We had a reinforced Marine regiment back in An Hoa. When they ran into each other it could fuck up your entire day."

Tuan didn't know ten words of English, but as he expertly worked the tiller he understood exactly what Condley was saying. He laughed, still shivering from the cold rain, and pointed toward the mountains.

"Da, truoc nay, co nhieu linh Bac dang kia." Tuan then slipped from Vietnamese into the mix of pidgin French and English still left over from the region's thirty years of war. "Boo-coo bang bang obah dare."

"Boo-coo," laughed Condley, repeating the murdered French phrase that had become so common in Viet Nam. "Boo-coo bang bang."

Quyen was waiting for them. The Vietnamese government's liaison officer was standing on the high, flat paddy dike that marked the outer edge of the village, dressed in gray slacks, a white shirt, and black leather shoes. His thick hair was matted by the rain. Dozens of drenched villagers stood along the dike with him, smiling and elbowing each other as if the boat's approach was grand entertainment. Condley waved to Quyen, calling to him. The whole village waved back, welcoming them.

The boat putted up to the edge of the dike, docking alongside it as if it were a pier. Tuan threw a rope to a group of laughing, screaming young boys, who immediately tied the boat up to a tree. The current was strong here, even away from the main path of the river, and Tuan's boat nudged gently prow-first against the mud of the dike, held fast by the flow of the water.

"Chao ong, Chao ong!"

Quyen greeted Condley with genuine happiness as the American stepped from the boat onto the muddy dike. The political officer had traveled to the village the day before in order to prepare the villagers for the meeting. Condley had worked with Quyen twice before, and he knew the young bureaucrat would be dying to go home. Quyen was a city boy, from Ha Noi in the north. In Da Nang two nights before, the locals had teased him that the villagers in the mountain hamlets off to the west were wild, of a different species, that drinking their water or their tea might make him sick, that some of their food might kill him, and that many of them even had tails. Quyen had half believed even the part about the tails.

"Ah, Mr. Condley, Mr. Muir," said Quyen. He smiled brightly, rubbing his hands in front of his dark, narrow face as if each of these Americans were holding up a Buddha to be prayed to. "It is my great pleasure to welcome you to Ninh Phuoc. Come with me, come with me."

The dank air and clinging mud of the village were like a welcoming remembrance. Ghosts walked beside Condley on the muddy trails, dirty and unshaven, burdened by helmets and packs and weapons, loping tiredly, all parts of their bodies half asleep while their eyes stayed bright with fear. The ghosts would always be there, young-faced and yearning, even as time itself erased the evidence of their passing. It was a burden rather than a talent that Condley could walk a village trail and be in two time zones at once, the past just as fresh as today.

Condley could smell cook fires and the twists of homegrown tobacco as he followed Quyen down the muddy path in the center of the village, the odors emanating from little shacks that were hidden down dark trails to his left and right. Children crowded round him and Muir, jabbering excitedly to one another, never having seen a Caucasian before this moment. They fingered the hair on his wrists. They touched his pale skin. They looked with wonder at his skylike, molten eyes. Suddenly Condley began teasing the children in Vietnamese, and they burst into collective, appreciative laughter.

He passed rows of flimsily built thatch homes, nearing the center of the village. The waterbulls were tethered in their stench-filled pens, lest they make a false step in the mud and be washed away by the river. Ugly little dogs barked and sniffed. Smiling, curious faces peeked out from shadowed doorways. It was all familiar. Nothing had changed except the war. And the knowledge that he was looking at it through the eyes of that which had already happened. But at least, he thought, already-happened was better than never-was.

Condley teased Muir as they walked the dark paths in the center of the ancient village. "You know how to say *dog* in Vietnamese, Hanson?"

"I suppose this is going to be funny."

"'Dinner.'"

"They don't really eat them."

"You know when we had 'wild deer' the other night in that restaurant in Da Nang?"

"I think I know what you're going to say."

"You had 'filet of mongrel dog.'"

"Why didn't you tell me?"

"I just did."

At the center of the village, Quyen halted before a larger, stone house. The house was covered by a corrugated tin roof, rather than the usual thatch. From its size, its tin roof, and the two sheds in the yard, Condley knew that this was where the village chief lived. Glass had not yet made its way to Ninh Phuoc. The house's window boards had been opened from the inside. As Condley caught up with Quyen he could see shadows moving underneath a single bare lightbulb that was hanging on a wire from the main room's ceiling.

"Electricity," said Condley. "Now, there's progress."

Quyen smiled, gesturing with an arm, indicating they should walk inside. "Yes," he said through his insistent happiness. "Electricity. Here in Ninh Phuoc, two years already!"

The village chief watched them carefully as they entered. The chief, a tough-looking man of about sixty, had arranged two small wooden tables at the center of his open-windowed entry room. A cracked porcelain pot was on one table, flanked by two small trays holding ten little teacups. The teacups were turned upside down on the trays. Next to the teacups on each tray was a pack of Vietnamese-brand cigarettes. To the chief's right, sitting on small wooden stools, were five old men. In other days they would have been called the village elders, but Condley knew that now, under the edicts of faraway Ha Noi, they were termed the village's People's Committee. To his left, sitting nervously by himself on another wooden stool, was a younger man of perhaps forty. An old calendar was on one wall behind them. On another wall were three certificates for military service, each with a picture of a smiling Ho Chi Minh and a communist flag.

"Le Xuan Minh," said Quyen officially, waving a hand toward the village chief. "And the People's Committee of Ninh Phuoc."

The seven men stood ceremoniously when Quyen ushered in the two Americans, wiping damp hands on their dirt-stained trousers. They had dressed up for the meeting, wearing long, gray-colored pants and long-sleeved cotton shirts, although their wide, powerful feet remained sockless in flip-flop sandals. They nodded perfunctorily when Condley shook their hands, each of them in turn holding his hand weakly, as if squeezing it would be a physical confrontation, and spoke softly to him in Vietnamese. Expectation filled their eyes, but they were patient and polite. Quyen had prepared them well.

"*Moi ong ngoi do,*" said the village chief, gesturing to the chairs.

"What do I do?" whispered Muir, suddenly nervous.

"Sit down and shut up," grinned Condley, never taking his eyes off his counterpart across the table.

Condley, Muir, and Quyen joined the village elders at the little table. An unsmiling young woman appeared from nowhere, dressed in black slacks and a peasant shirt, her long hair pulled back behind her ears. She did not even look at them as she silently poured tea from the porcelain pot into the cups. Le Xuan Minh ceremoniously took a cigarette and lit it with a wooden match, then offered the pack to Condley.

"*Da, cam on ong,*" said Condley, thanking him and taking a cigarette, then passing the pack to Muir. The heavyset scientist tottered uneasily atop his little stool, taking out a cigarette as delicately as if it were a stick of dynamite, and passed the pack on to the ever-smiling Quyen.

"The weather is terrible," began the village chief in Vietnamese, sipping his tea and dragging again from his cigarette. "But if you waited it would only get worse. So we thank you for coming to our village today."

Condley answered him with ritualistic politeness, speaking also in Vietnamese. "We are happy to be able to join you in your village, sir, and we deeply appreciate the goodwill you have shown to the American people by making this report to your government."

"He is not from our village," answered Le Xuan Minh as the village elders nodded. "It would be wrong for him to be kept forever with us."

"We very much appreciate your having kept him for so many years with your own people," answered Condley. "And it is right that he be returned."

"Surely he has a family in America," said Le Xuan Minh. "They will have missed him."

Quyen had grown increasingly nervous from the two men's immediate rapport. The political officer puffed mightily on his cigarette, then leaned across the table, interjecting himself between them. "The Vietnamese government has always worked very hard for complete cooperation on these issues," he said, making sure that both parties remembered where the ultimate power lay. "So you see, Mr. Condley, sometimes we have success."

Condley took an extralong drag on his own cigarette, the harsh local tobacco hurting his lungs. He frowned, playing with his teacup for a moment. Finally he cleared his throat, hesitating to make the obvious point. "So that I may make a full explanation to my authorities, I must ask you why it took so long to report this man, since he was buried in your village cemetery."

They were prepared for the question. In fact, Condley knew that was why Quyen had insisted on leaving for Ninh Phuoc by himself the day before. The village chief nodded to his elders before speaking, indicating that his comments were not merely his own.

"We did not find the body until the rains washed away part of the cemetery this year," said Le Xuan Minh. "It was in a family plot." He exchanged another deliberate glance with his elders, gaining nods of affirmation from them. Then all of them looked over at the younger man sitting separately from them. Finally Le Xuan Minh stubbed out his cigarette.

"This is Nguyen Hao," he said. "He buried your soldier among his ancestors when he was a little boy."

Hao remained silent, looking nervously at the others with what seemed to be great embarrassment. Finally he spoke. "I was twelve years old. We found him dead outside our house. My grandmother told me to bury him."

"Why didn't you report it?" Quyen asked the question with harsh tones, but Condley knew that the political officer had already rehearsed both the question and the answer with the beleaguered Hao. This was a Vietnamese version of Kabuki, an act designed to allow the government and the villagers and perhaps even the Americans to save face.

"Who would I talk to?" Hao grew defensive. "I was a boy. Soldiers from all sides constantly moved through our village. The Americans never came to ask about him. I could not go to the Americans. Both sides might shoot me. I was afraid."

"But what about later?" Quyen pressed him. "All the villages know that we have had an agreement with the Americans for many years. You are shaming our country when you hold back information. Your entire village loses face."

Hao looked at them all, this time with genuine fear. "I was afraid for my family, that the government would think we took sides in the war. And Mr. Quyen, sir, I say with great respect once again that no one ever asked about the dead American during the war. There was no fight in our village on the night he died. There was no crashing of a helicopter, no land mine explosion, no ambush. Soldiers moved through our village, both sides. Artillery always fell at night while we slept inside our family bunkers. We woke up and the American was lying dead on the trail outside our door. And my grandmother, sir, was the senior voice in our house. She told me to bury the soldier and to be quiet. We did not want any trouble, even then. She was the voice of the family and I must respect her."

A silence fell over the gathered men. The young woman reappeared with a second pot of tea, then slipped back into the darkness. Outside, the rain was falling harder. It was making little pops against the tin roof above them and they could hear it in the trees. The dogs were still yapping and the children were playing happily in the rain. Condley sipped fresh tea. He lit another cigarette. And finally enough time had passed that he could utter the ritual words of forgiveness.

"Mr. Quyen, Mr. Minh, I would like to say on behalf of my government that I hope no harm will come to this man. After all, his family committed an act of great kindness when they allowed our soldier to be buried among their ancestors. If they had not shown him this respect, we would not have been able to come here today and recover his remains. So I am deeply grateful to Mr. Hao for the actions he took as a young man. And if it is permissible, we would like to examine the remains and then take them back to America."

An audible, relieved sigh filled the dank room. The village elders moved almost in unison as they returned empty teacups to their trays and rose from their little stools. For the first time, Le Xuan Minh smiled, showing off a mouth full of snaggled, tobacco-stained teeth. He reached across the table, shaking Condley's hand.

"Mr. Hao is a good man. He meant no harm. His father died in the war. He was honored for battlefield bravery with a certificate personally signed by Ho Chi Minh."

"Mr. Hao is a very good man," answered Condley. "We will remember his kindnesses, and those of your entire village, to the dead soldier's family once we have identified the remains."

The remains were in a tin-roofed shed next to the village chief's house, wrapped inside an old American poncho. Once they reached the shed, the eight Vietnamese men stood respectfully off to one side as Condley and Muir moved to the poncho.

It was as if Muir had suddenly gone into a trance. He stood motionless in front of the remains, looking down at them with opaque eyes. He was breathing deeply. His meaty hands clenched into fists and then relaxed, then clenched again. Finally Condley nudged him.

"Are you okay, Professor?"

"This is the hardest part," said Muir, his eyes still on the poncho. "Touching it for the first time."

"Relax. It's dead."

"It's not an 'it.' "

"Then why did you call it an 'it'?"

"Let me say something about what we're looking at. Would you like to feel completely inconsequential, Brandon?"

"Frankly, no. I'd just like to get out of here."

The scientist was undeterred. It was as if anthropology were his religion and he were a high priest, and it was essential that a sermon be issued before he delved into the remains.

"We're looking at a mystery that's thirty years old. It might even confound us, just as so many others have as we've tried to piece together old bones and clumps of equipment to unravel the tragedies of the past. But do you know what thirty years is in the context of eternity, Brandon? Nothing. Nothing. Not even a drawn breath in the lungs of Father Time."

"They're waiting for us to do something, Professor. And a typhoon is getting ready to make you a permanent resident of Ninh Phuoc."

"I have my emotions," answered Muir. "Respect that."

Muir now obliged Condley by kneeling before the remains and starting to undo the torn and rotting poncho. "Did you know that eight hundred thousand years ago a meteor smashed into what is now Viet Nam, burning forests, throwing up fresh outcroppings of rock, and killing thousands of people? We can't find their remains, but we have been able to find the axes made from those rocks by the people who moved onto the land just after the meteor crashed. As well as the tektites from the meteor itself. Think of that. We can find the tools from almost a million years ago. We know just where the meteor hit. And yet we strain with difficulty to positively identify a man who died only thirty years ago."

It was raining harder. Condley was growing nervous. And, besides, after five years of "digs" he was used to Muir's emotions. "Well, give it a go, Professor. We've got a boat to catch."

Muir had calmed down. He was in his element now, all business as he carefully peeled back the old poncho and began to examine the stiff skeleton of a man dead nearly thirty years.

"It's in remarkable shape," mused the scientist as he considered the skeleton before him. "Definitely Caucasian—look here at the cheekbones and the structure of the teeth. I'm amazed we have a full skeleton instead of the isolated jaw here and femur there that we find in the crash sites. He's lucky they took such good care of him."

"He doesn't look that lucky to me."

Muir caught the irony of his comment. "Sorry, Brandon. It's the wages of being an anthropologist. I tend to think of them as . . . well, still existing, but merely in an altered state." He continued his intricate preliminary examination, leaning forward in the dark musty shed to get a closer look. "The cemetery must be mostly sand. That helped to preserve him. The jungle soil is so voracious that it even eats the teeth away in a remarkably short time. And look at this—"

Condley leaned forward also. Muir was holding a pair of dog tags that still remained on a chain. They had been around the dead man's neck. Condley whistled, amazed. "Positive ID. What a find. What service is he, Professor?"

"Army," answered Muir, squinting in the darkness. "Theodore

Deville. Specialist, Fourth Class. Blood type, O negative. Religion, no preference."

"Well, he's a Buddhist now, isn't he?"

"Show some respect, Condley. This is a comrade-in-arms."

Muir stood slowly, shifting his gaze from the skeleton to the leaden sky that showed through the shed's doorway. Along the pathway in front of them the children were gathering again, staring excitedly as if the two Americans were visitors from Mars.

"Let's get out of here."

Now Condley knelt next to the remains, beginning to fold them back inside the old poncho. "Roger that. I've seen absolutely no women in Ninh Phuoc that you should spend the winter with."

———

THE TRIP DOWNRIVER was quick and fun, like falling down the far edge of a roller coaster. The typhoon ended up stalling just off the coast, then turning north in late afternoon and heading inland toward Vinh. Condley made the flight to Sai Gon, leaving a depressed and disconcerted Muir in a leaking, broken-down old hangar at the Da Nang airport, where he was tasked by the American Embassy in Ha Noi to await a military aircraft. The Joint Task Force for Full Accounting had already summoned a cargo plane that would take the remains back to the Central Identification Lab in Hawaii, and Muir, who lived and worked in Hawaii, would accompany it.

"You bastard," grunted the bulky scientist as he shook Condley's hand to say good-bye. "I deserve at least one night of R and R for all my efforts."

"Take care of them bones, boy," joked Condley.

"That's my job."

"Exactly. You're the scientist. I'm just the tour guide."

Muir, ever the dramatist, came to a respectful version of attention as he looked over at the wrapped remains. "But let me remind you that these are not mere bones. Lying there inside that poncho is somebody's son, Brandon. Maybe someone's husband and father. Someone who served his country and lost his life in the process. An American hero, at this moment unrewarded for his sacrifice. We will have the honor of rendering him that award."

"Even if you don't get laid in Sai Gon."

"I didn't even want to do that. What's wrong? Why are you being so adamantly cynical, Brandon?"

"I don't know," answered Condley, staring pensively at the poncho that held the pile of bones. "I just keep wondering how he ended up in that village when Hao said there wasn't even a fight that night."

"Or why his hand is gone."

"What does that mean?"

"His left hand is off," said Muir, obviously intrigued. "It appears to have been severed cleanly, as if by a knife. Very strange, on a combat casualty."

"Maybe some villager souvenired it," mused Condley. "Or an NVA soldier. You know, like some of our guys used to cut off ears."

"A gruesome thought."

"It was a gruesome war."

"We will have that answer soon enough," said Muir. "Once we make a positive ID on Specialist Fourth Class Deville we will locate his family, his unit history, and his former comrades. And we will also find out not simply how he ended up in that village, but why they apparently did not go back to find him when he disappeared."

———————

A SHABBY LITTLE bus took Condley from the hangar to the airport terminal, built during the war by the Americans. Inside, he sipped filtered coffee in the same waiting room in which he had stood thirty years before as he prepared to board the giant Freedom Bird that would take him away from the war zone. The cracked pavement underneath his feet was the same. So was the huge mural on the wall depicting a waterfall somewhere in the Rocky Mountains and even the fake little pond just outside one window, cobbled with molded gravel and underneath a now-unworkable water fountain. All the same—the runway, all twelve thousand feet of it, built by the French in one war and expanded by the Americans in another, the sagging hangars, the crumbling revetments that once had housed scores of American combat aircraft. The mountains rose up like looming shadows to the west, and just beyond them had been the war. Literally thousands of battles had been fought within an easy helicopter ride from where Condley stood.

A French Airbus with a British pilot and a crew of gorgeous Vietnamese flight attendants took him back to Sai Gon. There were not a lot of people on the plane. Condley dozed fitfully at his window seat, exhausted from his journey to Ninh Phuoc and back. At one point he awakened as if from a nightmare, imagining that he had put Specialist Deville's remains in his hanging bag and wondering where the bag had gone. But finally he relaxed, looking out the window and remembering.

There wasn't a whole lot to remember. He hadn't done much with his life other than to live it. The war, first with the Marine Corps up north and then returning with the Agency west of Sai Gon and in Laos, and when it ended not knowing what to do. A year floating past as he traveled aimlessly through Australia, living off the sizable earnings of the war years, which he had never had the opportunity to spend. After that there was no sense going back home, anyway. Home hadn't been home for more than eight years. It had been too long, he had grown too untamable, and he had perfected skills for which there was very little demand in the States. His few short visits confirmed that the good jobs were taken and that the country was on its ass, paralyzed by endless and angry debates. So he had returned to Asia, sometimes with the Agency, at others on his own, pulling security work for American companies as they set up businesses in Thailand, Indonesia, and the Philippines. An easy life, devoid of ambition.

The years had blended into each other, a blur of dark-eyed women, warm turquoise oceans, and the smell of jasmine, smoke, and muck. He grew older, more cynical, less combative but somehow more confrontational. He drank less, ran slower, longed for old friends who wrote him at various post-office boxes and occasionally drifted through Bangkok or Manila and dragged him along on a two- or three-day binge of booze, friendly women, and old memories.

On rainy evenings as the typhoon winds rattled shutters on whatever hotel or house he happened to be occupying with whomever he had ended up with for that night, he might hear his mother in the whistling wind, wishing for him as she bewailed the unredeemable emptiness of his Asian fate. Now and then along the dirt roads and in the yeasty jungles of Indonesia and the Philippines he smelled the rot of dead carcasses and felt he could reach out and touch Hai and Dan and Thanh, Baker and King and McDowell, all friends he would have died for, but who instead were left violated and lifeless along the road that he himself still traveled. And always he would think of Mai, with her full lips and husky, teasing laugh, whom he had really loved and who had died because they hated her for loving him.

It was beery, painless, loveless, and so free he might have been falling through a warm sky, untouched and unencumbered. And then one morning he had stared into a brightly lit mirror and admitted that he had lost his youth. After that there had been questions. Sometimes he wished he had a wife. Sometimes he wondered if he did in fact have children. Sometimes he woke up in a panic, knowing that after all the dreams that once had mattered and the struggles that had in the end simply drained out the wishes and the hopes, after the years of trying to live without owing anybody anything, without playing the whore to any other man, he had finally comprehended that all of it added up to nothing more than a trick.

He'd spent twenty-five years trying to put salt on the tail of a mirage bird, or maybe an unrisen phoenix. Nothing had changed except his age. The whores may have sold out, but at least they had something to show for it.

In the early 1990s the "Bamboo Curtain" that had been imposed by Viet Nam's ruling communists in 1975 began to lift. The season of terror and darkness that followed the war was slowly receding. Foreigners were allowed to visit some areas of the country. And he began to dream of going back. What better place to return to, in a world where everything was lost, anyway? Sai Gon, where he might still take a five-dollar room in one of the flophouses of Pham Ngu Lao Street, float again on a band of raw emotion, no longer drearily certain of where the end might find him, no longer moribund with where the past had taken him.

Then, like some deus ex machina, the American government had delivered all that back to him. They needed a liaison officer to work with the Army's Central Identification Lab as it searched for the remains of those still listed as missing in action during the war. Someone who understood the culture and spoke Vietnamese. Someone who didn't mind lousy pay and frequent travel to the worst areas of the country. He'd jumped at it. So now he spent about half the year in Viet Nam and the other half in Hawaii. He'd even learned to like Hawaii, which had surprised him after spending most of the past thirty years in Asia.

He dozed again. In minutes a flight attendant awakened him, bringing him tea and a sandwich. As he ate, the plane suddenly descended from the high skies and settled toward the wide green paddies and the sluggish, curving rivers, and in one beat of his heart Condley felt that he was home again. Below him were earthly rhythms that had formed his adulthood. Merely seeing them brought him again into their cadences. In the last moments before the plane touched onto the runway at Tan Son Nhat, he looked out at abandoned military towers, the long rows of curved concrete parapets that had once housed dozens of American warplanes, the ruins of an old military hospital, the streams of thin brown people on motorbikes and bicycles, past and present mixing into a yeasty dynamism that jumped up at him from every face and tree.

Yes, he liked Hawaii, but he felt more at home in Sai Gon. He did not know why. He only knew that it was true. *Sai Gon*, Condley remembered from an old and happy song that spoke of the city's beauty and its carefree ways. *Dep lam.*

CHAPTER TWO

District Four, Sai Gon

UNDERNEATH THE OLD green mosquito net five feet away, the baby was crying again. Dzung lay next to his wife in the dark room on the square board that was their bed, forcing himself awake, studying her face and trying to think of what to do. It had rained all night, and although the water had stopped flowing along the floor of their small wooden shack, the wet remained behind. The water had awakened all the odors of the cramped and squalid neighborhood, filling their shack with the reminders of someone else's food, someone else's human waste, someone else's struggle. It had brought out a legion of mosquitoes and cockroaches as big as mice. It had actually made Dzung cold.

His wife's face was beautiful as she slept, smooth as a child's and framed in a swirl of tangled black hair. Dzung wanted to wait as long as he could before awakening her. He knew that when she awoke, her mouth would immediately tighten and her eyes would go distant and her tiny body would grow rigid with responsibilities that would not let up until she again was freed by sleep that evening. And yet the baby, now only two weeks old, was insistent, starving, demanding. His wife needed sleep. The baby needed his wife's breast. The burden of these two loyalties was too complicated. So Dzung stroked his wife's face and watched her sleep and waited for the problem to solve itself.

Dzung was remembering the first time he had seen her. It was hard to believe it had been fourteen years, during the time Sai Gon was only beginning to awaken from the darkest days of conquest or liberation, depending of course on one's perspective, just before the government announced the new change, *doi moi*.

He had been pedaling his *cyclo* along Hai Ba Trung Street just where it met the Sai Gon River. A new Soviet ship had docked near the old naval base just up the river, at the same spot the American ships used to dock and before them the French, and Dzung had been hoping to pick up a customer. She was standing on the road near a scraggly patch of grass where a pair of old French cannons still loomed over the water, also pointing toward the ship. She was holding a basket of mangoes, her circular straw *non la* hat tied underneath her chin with a bright yellow ribbon. The pink and yellow flowered pattern of her blouse and slacks excited him. It was a bold fashion statement. For nearly a decade the government had issued only black cloth at its garment stores. Sai Gon was emerging from a dark cocoon.

The tilt of her face and the sureness in the way she stood reminded him of a girl he had loved once, when he was much younger and such a thing as love had seemed more possible. She was looking at him so openly, so warmly that he knew she was not a Sai Gon girl, that she was in from the villages. She stood firmly, the mangoes under one arm, her small breasts rising toward him as she breathed, and she smiled as if she were actually happy to see him.

Somehow it made him imagine he was making love to her. Yes, like a memory. Hiding from the others, whispering and laughing and embracing as they stood lazily neck-deep in a warm pond with the water swirling and sucking against their bodies and the paddy dikes and high weeds surrounding them and the rain beating down and the smell of rotting soil and wet grass and lotus blossoms wafting over them. And the moon above them, shimmering like a mirage beyond the rain. And the sound of artillery, far in the distance. Or had it been thunder?

And so he had slowed his *cyclo,* pulling alongside her and teasing her.

"Where did you come from?" he asked.

"Bien Hoa," she answered, her smiling face telling him already that she liked him.

"*Nha que*, huh? A country girl. You came all this way to sell mango to a *Lien So*? The Russians eat nothing here in the city. They only drink. You should be bringing whiskey."

"My father doesn't grow whiskey," she had answered, surveying his thin frame. "Besides, why do you want to take them in your *cyclo*? They're as big as waterbulls."

He had shrugged, now standing close to her. "For the money I would pedal a waterbull all the way to hell."

"They don't have any money."

"Then why are we here?" Now they both had laughed. Dzung touched her hand and folded down the seat pad in his *cyclo*. "I'll tell you what," he said. "If you give me a mango, I'll take you wherever you want to go."

Her name was Tu. She was eleven years younger than Dzung and had seen the war only through a child's eyes. Slowly, with a delicacy that made him ache, she sliced the mango for him. And then she climbed into the seat. He drove her away on his *cyclo*, devouring the mango as he pedaled, pointing to this old building and that former hotel as they passed through the haunted, quiet streets of the dark days. He took her to the Ben Thanh market near the old abandoned railroad station and showed her how to sell her fruit. And by the time he left her at the crowded bus stop for her trip back to Bien Hoa, Dzung knew he would always love her.

She came into Sai Gon twice a week. From then on he would meet her at the bus station, taking her to the Ben Thanh market, hovering over her like a protective hawk while she sold off her father's fruit. Then they would spend hours as he pedaled her along the city streets, talking and laughing, sometimes even daring to trust each other and speak about the past.

Within a month he had traveled with her to the small village near Bien Hoa to meet her family. He brought her father a small dog in a wire cage and gave her mother a silk scarf a Cuban woman had dropped and abandoned on Dong Khoi Street one afternoon during a violent rainstorm. Then he apologized to them for coming by himself when tradition required that he bring his own family with him, assuring them he meant no disrespect but that all of his family was dead or missing from the war. Her father understood and judged Dzung to be an honest and industrious man. And in another two weeks they were married.

That was fourteen years ago. Now, five children later, she lay exhausted next to him, starting to stir from the wails of their newest child. Their nine-year-old daughter, Thuc, had crawled sleepily from another bed and picked up the baby. Still half asleep, Thuc was holding him in the dank darkness of the shack, rocking him back and forth, her toes digging into the mud of last night's rain as the baby sucked hungrily at her bare shoulder.

Looking at the two children together made Dzung feel deeply proud. There was so little one *cyclo* driver could do to bring harmony to the world, and yet Thuc's gentleness assured him that his life was a success. But Dzung was also somewhat worried. Thuc was beautiful, with her big round eyes and small triangular face. His daughter stroked the baby's back and head with a certainty that seemed inbred. Dzung would do anything for her, and Tu, and the other children. But there was so little he could do.

Tu was awake. She sat in the bed, taking the baby from Thuc and putting him to a breast. She smiled softly to Dzung, a reassurance that made him worry even more about her exhaustion. For her size she was incredibly strong, and she had never complained about their life. Over the years he had lost nearly everything, suffered the deaths and dislocations, the torture of not knowing whether family members were dead or alive, the cruel spite or perhaps the masked incompetence of the conquerors or liberators. But he knew that if he ever lost this one person, this woman who had married him and in whose arms he collapsed every night, he would want to lay down and die.

A good Vietnamese woman is tot nhat, he liked to brag in passable English or French to the foreign customers he sometimes would pedal through Sai Gon, *the best in the world. Beautiful, man,* dep qua. *They take care of you, love you till you can't let go.*

Their home had no doors. Shafts of sunlight poured into the front entranceway, lighting the inside of the shack. His two older sons began to stir on their boards near the opening. Outside, he could hear the neighborhood awakening, mothers calling to their children, small dogs yapping, pots clanking as the rice was being made. Odors moved toward him, smoke from the cook fires and cigarettes, dank memories of last night's rain, someone else's food. A motorbike started and soon passed along the narrow sidewalk that made a road between the shacks of District Four.

Dzung walked to the rear of the shack and then outside, standing on a small piece of mud that was his back porch. The mud sloped slightly, a natural streambed that passed between two other houses and then disappeared. The slope was filled with clutter, trash, and effluvium. Other houses pushed toward his from all sides. The sun was up, high and hot, and it had already begun to bake the mud.

Dzung stretched like a cat, scratching his chest and rubbing his face and head. He waved lazily to a neighbor. He squatted, making a cook fire. Then he dipped a bucket into the ceramic pot that held the family's water and put it over the fire. Lighting a cigarette, he took a deep drag and then measured out that morning's rice, pouring it into the bucket and stirring it while the water heated. And as the rice softened it filled Dzung with a sense of calm, an odd tranquillity.

Women's work, boiling rice. He often found that thought ironic. In the city, in peacetime, a man was laughed at if he cooked rice for his wife. And yet on the battlefield and in the reeducation camps it was the very symbol of manhood, that one could find and make his own meals, could provide for himself. In the cold and lonely mountains more than twenty years before, Dzung had become quite the envied epicure, knowing just which weeds could combine with the rice to make a gourmet stew.

The rice was cooked, fluffy and white, filling the bucket. As was his custom Dzung scooped out portions for each of his children, then for his wife, and finally for himself. They had no table. He handed the children their bowls and then carried his own, along with Tu's, to the bed, where she still sat in the shadows, feeding the baby. They ate quickly, silently, and without ceremony, holding the bowls just under their mouths and scooping the rice with quick movements of their chopsticks.

The neighborhood was now pulsing with noise and motion, as if the packed dirt underneath him and the thin walls around him had come alive. The sounds of the motorbikes passing and the two old grandmothers across the alley beginning their daily argument and the dogs forever yapping energized Dzung as well. He put on a stained white T-shirt and pair of baggy black trousers, found his old black baseball cap and his gray plastic flip-flop sandals, and waved good-bye to his family.

Outside the front doorway, he unlocked his *cyclo,* climbed onto its high seat, and set out for work.

It would take fifteen minutes to reach District One. Dzung pedaled along the narrow cracked concrete alley that fronted his home, waving to familiar faces squatting in the doorways. Then he turned onto a slightly larger road, bordered by tiny sidewalks that were filled with an interminable row of small tables and stools. Older men were gathered at most of the tables, drinking tea or beer, smoking their first cigarettes, and arguing about the past. They wore shorts and rubber sandals. Their hair was gray and their eyes were vacant and red. They had lost a war twenty-five years ago and after wounds, terror, humiliation, and reeducation, this was their final repayment: to sit idle in the squalid isolation of District Four, with no work permits, no permission to relocate, and nothing to look forward to but the long hot days of sitting and smoking and remembering.

He reached Nguyen Tat Thanh Street and turned left, heading toward a bridge that would take him into District One. Nguyen Tat Thanh, which bordered the Sai Gon River, was the major artery of District Four. Dzung found himself immediately lost in a swarm of vehicles, large and small: cars, trucks, motorbikes, bicycles, and *cyclos*, all mixed together in no particular lanes or order.

Dzung blended in with the flow, a wave of contentment rushing through him. He was at one with his *cyclo* now, his body swaying slightly side to side as he pedaled, his hands resting on the curved metal of the *cyclo*'s carriage as he maneuvered the vehicle in the traffic. Motorbikes sped past him, some holding whole families. Large trucks honked their horns and threw sand and dust into the heavy air. He passed another bicycle that had been mounted to a flatbed trailer, where two boys sat together in the driver's seat, their feet sharing the pedals on each side as they pushed a load of six pigs stacked onto the trailer. The pigs had been stuffed into individualized cylindrical baskets that froze them motionless. A yellow "meter taxi," new to Sai Gon, slipped in and out of the traffic, its driver hauling some well-heeled foreign customer. Dzung looked enviously at the taxi as it disappeared in front of him. It was his dream to someday own one.

On the old concrete bridge a small girl squatted, her heels on the curb and her trousers lowered as she defecated onto the road. Nearby, her mother sat languidly in the morning sun behind a small pushcart, from which she was selling drinks and pastries. A wiry dog trotted over to the little girl and sniffed curiously at her haunches as she continued to squat. The girl looked nervously behind her at the dog and began to cry. Twenty feet away, a British tourist snapped a picture of the girl and the dog. The girl's mother now stood and screamed an insult, then rushed toward the tourist. The tourist backed away, apologizing and protecting his camera. And in the time it took Dzung to pass them, they had all reached a smiling compromise when the tourist agreed to buy two cans of cola for what was obviously an exorbitant price.

Sai Gon, Sai Gon. Dzung laughed, watching the impish satisfaction on the woman's face as she pocketed the money and returned to her tiny stall. Everything had its price, especially forgiveness.

A beautiful butterfly landed for a moment on the *cyclo* seat, and Dzung's father entered his thoughts. Dzung felt immediately certain that the old man's soul had been carried to him on the butterfly's wings. His father had disappeared during a battle in the mountains of Laos thirty years before, when the division he was commanding had been surrounded and attacked by the North Vietnamese Army. Some had said his father was captured, others claimed he had been killed. Sometimes the uncertainty still bothered Dzung, but it no longer really mattered. His father was dead by now. Why else would he be visiting on the wings of the butterfly?

Swaying side to side as he pedaled the *cyclo*, Dzung began to sing. It was a song his father had taught him when he was a young boy, as they washed together in the shallows of the Han River among a row of beautiful fishing nets that in the morning drooped above the water on long poles like sails. His father would sing as they rinsed in the river and the fishing boats floated slowly past them and the pretty girls drove their bicycles along the nearby bridge, heading from Da Nang toward the salt-white beaches at My Khe. A long time ago, with his mother chewing betel nut, standing above the rice pot in their house up from the beach, and his grandmother smoking a twist of tobacco as she squatted comfortably on the porch, and his father now laughing and clutching him with thin but powerful arms, carrying him over one shoulder from the river back into the house. And his brothers playing along the road, young and still alive.

A long time ago, before he had lived enough to understand its meaning. And in his heart Dzung was happy, because he heard his father
singing also.

> We stood in front of our house and the scent of the
>   night air
> Brought the memory of a thousand years returning,
> The night so peaceful on the road where the young
>   men
> Came and went, offering their lives, their hearts filled
>   with love
> For this land. Now the moon hangs overhead, and
>   the winds
> Bring the scent not of flowers but of everything they
>   lost.

The butterfly departed, fluttering behind him, back toward the river.
For a moment Dzung felt abandoned, but finally he smiled again. It was
a good sign, his father coming to see him.

He turned right at the end of the bridge and pedaled toward Nguyen
Hue Street, home of the oldest and best hotels. *Cyclo* drivers fought jeal-
ously for their territory, stationing themselves every day at the same
street corner or office or hotel. For several years he had kept a waiting
place just across the street from the Rex Hotel, where during the war
years the Americans had housed mid-level military officers. The Rex was
well-remembered by foreigners and was almost always full. And the
right tourist might pay ten dollars simply for a slow tour of the historic
sights.

Yes, ten dollars, if they chose a *cyclo* over the motorbikes and taxis
that were crowding him out of his business. It could happen. And Dzung
felt very lucky today.

CHAPTER THREE

BRANDON CONDLEY LOVED Sai Gon. It was the museum of his own heart, a tortured and yet insistently happy city where along the streets his memories could once again race and dive amid the fecund ferment, the mangled but sly-eyed beggars, the crumbling old yellow French buildings now conquered and abused, the rivers muddy and eternal, the toothless *cyclo* drivers suborning him from the roadsides, the motorbikes loud and reckless, begging for the future, the never-ending stares, the measuring smiles, welcoming and wary, the con games of bright minds trapped inside dumb lives, the odd, funky food cooked on the streets, the black puddles on the sidewalks, wet from rain and urine and wash water thrown out of doorways, the stench of all that mixed together. In all an insistent beauty, pushing up through the muck of a fierce and dreadful past like Buddha's lotus, a beauty just as real as what his own past might have become, always pushing, insistent as a weed, fresh as the future.

It was six o'clock. Dusk hovered over the center of the city like a dark descending blanket, giving the lights of nearby hotels and shops a special glow. Condley walked up from his place near the river, passing the old Sai Gon Opera House as he headed toward Nguyen Hue Street. It was hot, even for Viet Nam. The gluey puddles of water gathered along the street smelled like other people's sweat.

In the small park across the street from the Rex Hotel he could see a half dozen *cyclo* drivers camped side by side on the seats of their cabs, chatting as they watched the hotel's entrance for possible customers. From a hundred yards away, Condley searched their clothing and baseball caps. He knew that business had not been good for the *cyclo* drivers lately. Even as they watched and waited, a steady stream of motorbikes, limousines, and taxis informed them of the inevitability of the future. They were stuck on their *cyclos*, offering up a quaintness that linked them to yesterday as tomorrow unraveled before their waiting eyes.

The park behind where the *cyclo* drivers lazed was dominated by a crude statue of Ho Chi Minh ministering to a small child. Its grounds were packed with perhaps the greatest mix of people one could find anywhere in Viet Nam. Vietnamese of all ages milled about as if at carnival. Some of them were young parents who had motorbiked from the outskirts of the city, mother and father and tiny children all packed onto one Honda, to buy their kids a balloon or a toy and let them play on the sidewalks and in the grass. Some of them were old, dressed in traditional *ao dai* clothes. Some were in groups, come to take pictures of themselves at the very center of everything that had always been Sai Gon. Foreigners of all color and stripe walked through the park, largely ignoring both the Vietnamese and those from countries other than their own. Japanese, Korean, French, British, overseas Chinese, and every now and then an American milled about, and even an occasional Russian in from a ship in Sai Gon Harbor or one of the oilers off Vung Tau.

Among the tourists the usual gang of local vendors, hustlers, and beggars plied their trade. A worn old man in a fading blue beret walked through the crowd, selling helium-filled balloons. A scarred, one-armed veteran with black powder burns on his face from some long-ago explosion stood at a curb, hawking an armload of toy helicopters he had made from Coca-Cola cans. A beaming, slick-haired young hustler wearing a gold necklace offered books of worthless Vietnamese stamps, his dancing, mischievous eyes promising a host of more delightful alternatives if the right deal could be made and the proper money changed hands. Young children danced in and out, insistently selling chewing gum, postcards, newspapers, and souvenir booklets. In front of Uncle Ho's statue a large wedding party had formed a wide reception line, and as the bride and groom laid a wreath at Uncle Ho's feet the ceremony was being filmed with a home video camera.

Situation normal, thought Condley, grinning madly as he crossed the street and made his way through the park. Even as he fought off the entreaties of a dozen hustlers, he did not take his eyes off the *cyclo* drivers. Noticing his searching stare, the drivers immediately alerted, and in an instant several of them recognized him. They jumped from their cabs and ran toward him, calling to him as a long-lost friend, waving and jabbering, their thin faces electric with friendship and even hope.

"Cong Ly! Hey, Cong Ly! Hey, *lau qua, lau qua!*"

Behind them, across the street, the doormen of the Rex Hotel watched with faintly muted disapproval as Condley indulged the *cyclo* drivers. The doormen did not like the *cyclo* drivers, even though they tolerated their presence. The reason was very complicated, unless one was Vietnamese, and then it was very simple. The doormen were in. They had jobs and protection. Their family histories were clean when it came to examining the past. The *cyclo* drivers were out. Many of them were former South Vietnamese Army soldiers. Others were the sons of former soldiers. In an unspoken but firm apartheid, they were blocked by their past from the benefits of whatever Viet Nam's future held.

It did no good to question this distinction, because everything else flowed from it, and if one questioned it he had to question everything else. But having shared their past, Condley felt a special need to recognize and in some odd, minimal way to protect the *cyclo* drivers. And so this welcoming celebration in front of the Rex Hotel whenever he returned to Sai Gon had become a great game among Condley and the drivers over the past five years.

They had collectively altered his name from Condley to Cong Ly, which pronounced correctly in Vietnamese meant "justice," a sobriquet now widely used by other Vietnamese who knew him. And he had nicknamed many of them as well, pronouncing their Vietnamese names in various ways that had given them his own characterizations of their personalities. In front of him just now were "Lazy," "Happy," "Tiger." And now, moving slowly from the rear with a quick, knowing wave of the hand, came "Fearless." Fearless was Dzung. And Dzung was Condley's best Vietnamese friend.

Condley was surrounded by them now. The suddenly energized *cyclo* drivers were speaking rapidly to him in Vietnamese as they caught him up on all the latest Sai Gon gossip. Across the street the doormen grumbled, and in the park many other tourists stared curiously as the drivers mobbed him. He had stopped walking, becoming ecstatic at their attention, laughing at their insistent antics, liberated by their very presence. Two young girls joined the group, pulling insistently at his hands, trying to sell him Wrigley's chewing gum and packs of picture postcards.

"Cong Ly! Cong Ly! You buy gum from me, you already promise!"

"Okay! Okay!"

He bought some gum, angering the little girl selling postcards. She pouted, slapping him playfully.

"Cong Ly, you *nguoi xau,* you told me okay before, now I sell you for ten thousand *dong, muoi ngan, muoi ngan*!"

"Muoi ngan mac qua!" he replied laughingly, telling her she was charging way too much and then giving her a dollar, half again as much, for her useless postcards.

The *cyclo* drivers laughed merrily, teasing him for being a sucker as the two girls ran away. As they chattered he looked at the narrow, hopeful faces, the broken and missing teeth, the dirty baseball caps, the eyes that read his every move with an intuitive exactness, the suborning invitations that he knew were all a part of their routine, a practiced and professional game. Each of them wanted to work for Condley, but they also knew that he would not hire any of them other than Dzung. In Sai Gon a *cyclo* driver was much more than a ride. Used properly, he was part valet, part protector, and part courier. Treated fairly, he was also fiercely loyal, but he expected loyalty in return.

Dzung waved perfunctorily again, a silly smile on his face, stepping forward and claiming his longtime client and friend. The others laughed, a few of them pushing Dzung away, keeping him behind them even though they knew that he was Condley's only choice.

"No, you take me, you take me! Dzung no good, Cong Ly! He lazy-y-y!"

But now Dzung was standing in front of Condley and the two grinned at each other as if they were brothers. Which in a way they were.

Just after his arrival in Sai Gon five years earlier, Condley had stood before a similar group of drivers, asking which one of them had been the best soldier during the war. And they had immediately turned to the serious-faced, tight-muscled little man, with a deference that had been palpable.

"Dzung," said one of the gathered drivers, pointing to the man as the others began to fall away, looking for someone else to haul. In English it sounded like "zoom." "He airborne soldier, many, many fights, many awards for bravery. His father was a general. He very smart, sir, already he study in the Vietnamese Military Academy at Da Lat. He do good job for you."

Dzung had stepped forward, wearing a shy and almost weary grin, and addressed him in English. "Yes, sir. I was soldier *Viet Nam Cong Hoa.*"

"Dzung?" Condley had smiled, tasting the name on his tongue and liking the man instantly. "*Dzung cam*, huh?" Condley's pronunciation changed the meaning to "Fearless," giving Dzung his nickname.

"Thank you, sir."

Dzung had stood before him with a kind of tragic openness, hands at his side, smiling self-consciously as if he were on the offering block, waiting for Condley to decide his fate. Condley had studied him as if he were indeed a horse for sale. Dzung's face was lined, from the years and the sun, so that his age could not be accurately measured. The baseball cap he wore on the back of his head, coupled with his nervous smile, took away much of his seriousness. In fact he had seemed somehow fragile, with his narrow shoulders and the thin legs shooting out from below trouser legs that were rolled up almost to his knees so he could pedal the *cyclo*. But Condley had known how tightly muscled most Vietnamese were. Dzung could pedal him from here to hell and never take a break.

"*Anh co phai di tu sau chien tranh khong?*" Condley had asked, wanting to know if Dzung had been sent to the infamous "reeducation camp" prisons run by the communists after the war.

"Oh, no," Dzung had answered carefully, playing a nervous game. "They send me back to *school.*" He continued to smile, obviously aware of the dangers of direct conversation with a foreigner on any subject that could be labeled political. "I study three years in the mountains after '75."

"Then you must be very smart." Condley had laughed, having picked up on Dzung's careful words.

"Oh, yes, sir," Dzung had said, offering the seat of his *cyclo* with a gesturing arm. "It was a very good school. They teach me many things. It's very good now, no problem. That why I give you such good *cyclo* ride."

"Then let's go."

Condley had hopped aboard. Dzung took a running start, pushing his *cyclo* and then jumping onto the seat, and pedaled off onto Nguyen Hue Street. He had turned left almost immediately onto Le Loi, where they joined the traffic flow of seemingly thousands of vehicles. And then he had leaned forward, speaking to Condley above the noise as he pedaled the *cyclo*.

"You tell me your name."

"*Cong Ly,*" Condley had said, Vietnamizing his surname as he had done so many times before, so many years ago, now falling completely into the rhythms of the city and the culture. He had then looked back and seen that Dzung was savoring his Vietnamese name—"Justice." Finally the *cyclo* driver had grinned widely, his face filled with a delicious happiness.

"Cong Ly," said Dzung. "You were here before '75? Maybe soldier, huh?"

"Six years, off and on."

"Six years? Oh, very good, sir. I know you love Viet Nam. I know."

"*Thuong nhieu qua,*" Condley had said. *Too much love.*

He had been suppressing it, but he could not hold it back any longer. It sat on him, pushing his head onto his chest: the memory of a hundred nights spent with Mai's lithe golden body pressed against him and her legs entwined around him and his lips tasting her long soft neck and her black hair falling onto his face like a gossamer veil as he kissed her and heard her whisper with delight and smelled the perfume she always wore in her hair and just below her ears. And of the morning when he returned to their little flat and felt his stomach sicken when she was not in the outer room to greet him and he realized that from upstairs he was hearing the echoing, empty sound of the shower water running, straight onto the floor like the patter of heavy rain, constant, without the interruption of a body scrubbing and rinsing underneath it. And then yelled up to her. And had known when she did not answer that she was dead.

"I love Viet Nam. I have missed Viet Nam very much."

Dzung had labored behind him, swaying gracefully side to side. "Where we go today, Cong Ly?"

The city and its traffic had been a swirling mist and the afternoon sun had beaten down on him and the dust and fumes had risen up to greet him and the *cyclo* had become a time cocoon, freezing him inside forever. And it had not mattered. "I don't know. You take me."

"Okay," Dzung had said, turning left toward the Sai Gon River. "I know. I know. I take you."

And Dzung had indeed known. On that first afternoon they had floated along inside the stream of traffic, passing old memories, new sights: the old naval bases now dilapidated and falling apart, some still occupied and used by the Vietnamese military, others being leveled to make room for new hotels; the wide streets dotted with French architecture along Ton Duc Thang Street near the Sai Gon Zoo; the American Embassy, its cylindrical, screened guard posts along the high white walls rusting and empty, the roof where the last U.S. helicopter took out the last load of Americans and South Vietnamese in 1975 a haunting monument to failure; the park near the center of the city that once had been a cemetery for thousands of South Vietnamese soldiers, whose graves had now disappeared underneath the conqueror's plow; the rising steeples and red bricks of the Duc Ba Chapel, built by the French across from the huge old post office in an area that once had marked the cultural center of the city; the ubiquitous new hotels and office buildings creeping up toward the sky, drowning out the landmarks of the past; the stark contrast of people traveling in Mercedes and others living curbside in front of downtown buildings. It had all washed over Condley, scoured him out, insulted and consoled him, and in an odd way made him whole.

Along the way people had watched him, waved to him, and smiled. Kids on bicycles had pulled up next to him, asking in broken English if he was American and then grinning in delight when he said yes. Women had embraced him nostalgically with their eyes, sitting on little plastic stools behind curbside stalls or driving Hondas near him in the traffic. Men, young and old, alternated between scrutinizing stares and welcoming, remembering grins, some calling out to him or holding up a finger and calling, "America Number One!" It had become his very own homecoming parade.

As they rode, he and Dzung had conversed, throwing together a mix of Vietnamese and English that became a workable, fluent vernacular. They talked about everything, working carefully to where they could speak frankly to each other about the past and then even about the present. Their dialogue was a careful recounting of facts, devoid of opinions, which in the wrong ears might become personally dangerous. And by the time Dzung reached behind him for the pull brake and brought the *cyclo* to a halt in front of the Rex Hotel, the two had become friends.

Condley had sought to pay him, but Dzung had refused. "No, no, Cong Ly. You pay me later. When you leave or maybe one week."

Condley had realized it was Dzung's way of keeping him as a customer. He had relented, but then slipped his new friend fifty thousand *dong*, the equivalent of five dollars. "Okay. But you buy your kids something. From me."

Dzung had nodded, pocketing the money, his warm brown eyes showing how deeply Condley's generosity had moved him. "We go tomorrow?"

"You're my main man, Dzung." Condley had patted him on a narrow shoulder. Even the mood had seemed to be a memory. "You're my limo driver. Wait for me every day, I pay you ten dollars."

And so it had been, every time Condley had returned to Sai Gon from wherever his job had taken him. He no longer stayed at the Rex Hotel, having found a smaller, cheaper, and more relaxed hotel several blocks away. So when he needed Dzung he would walk over to the Rex and claim him.

While Condley chatted with the others, Dzung had run across the street and fetched his *cyclo*. He now pushed it before him, dodging an arriving limousine as he made his way back to Condley. He climbed onto his seat, tested the pedals, and patted the chair in front of him, indicating that Condley should get in.

"Where we go now, Cong Ly?"

"You know the Kieu Hoa restaurant?"

Dzung began pedaling, fitting quickly into the flow of traffic. "Off Dien Bien Phu, I think. In District Three."

"I've never been there. They say it's owned by Nguyen Manh Khoa. You remember him from before, Dzung?"

"Oh, yes," said Dzung, growing quiet. In Sai Gon, "before" always meant before 1975, and when one talked about before 1975 it paid to be careful, even among friends. Condley looked over his shoulder and caught Dzung's knowing smile as he pedaled along Le Loi Street, looking for the right crossing street that would take them up to District Three.

"Nguyen Manh Khoa. He's a very famous man."

"A very famous man," agreed Dzung somewhat evasively. "I think."

"He used to be the Bob Dylan of South Viet Nam."

"I don't know Bob Dylan," chuckled Dzung, as always pretending innocence when Condley became too overtly political.

"You don't remember? I remember. He wrote and sang a lot of anti-war songs. He was against the old Sai Gon government. He sang about what he called 'the cultural genocide' committed against the Vietnamese people by the French and the Americans."

"I don't know, Cong Ly," grinned Dzung, weaving his way in and out of an unending swarm of bicycles and motorbikes and taxis. "Long time ago."

"The old government threw him into jail."

"I was only a soldier." In the midst of this thick traffic Condley had gone too far, and Dzung was going to say no more. Anyone listening to them could take down the license number on Dzung's *cyclo* and report their conversation to the authorities, even the smiling young schoolgirl coasting just next to them on her bicycle. Probably not, but the prospect was never certain, and that was how they kept control.

"They claimed he was a communist, but he said he was neutral. That the old government was corrupt, and the slaughter had gone on too long. He said."

"Maybe," shrugged Dzung, looking around him a bit nervously as he pedaled, wishing to be done with Condley's vocal speculation.

The air was terrible from Condley's perch on the *cyclo*, filled with dust and slick with fumes. It was growing dark, with an equatorial quickness that always stunned him. The traffic had thinned as they left District One. They passed a hospital and then a school. Dzung was laboring now, his body leaning side to side, putting extra weight against the pedals as he worked his *cyclo* uphill through the traffic. A few minutes later Dzung turned onto the wide boulevard of Dien Bien Phu. The *cyclo* coasted a bit, enabling him to breathe more easily. Almost alone on this stretch of road, Dzung finally nudged Condley, with what he knew was a subtle, laughing taunt.

"So why you like his restaurant?"

"I don't like his restaurant. But I have to make a report to Colonel Pham and he's eating there tonight."

"Colonel Pham," chided Dzung, unable to hold back any longer. "He no good, Cong Ly."

"He's okay."

"He VC," said Dzung, reverting to the term for the communists that was used during the war.

"Yeah," said Condley, "he's VC. But he's a good VC."

"VC no good, Cong Ly. You know that."

"He's okay, Dzung. I've worked with him for three years now." Dzung said nothing. "We found the body of an American soldier yesterday. In Quang Nam Province."

"Very good, sir."

"I am giving Colonel Pham the report."

"I am happy for you." Dzung paused a bit, thinking about it as he pedaled. "After you find all the Americans do you leave Viet Nam?"

Condley had never thought about that. "I don't know. Maybe."

"Then maybe you don't find them all."

Condley looked back and caught his friend grinning once again. He laughed, and then Dzung laughed too, in a way that only two former soldiers can laugh about the dead.

"They're pretty hard to find, Dzung."

"That's true, sir. Or else you would have found all of them already. So please take your time."

In the darkness Dzung turned suddenly into an alleyway that joined the boulevard. At the end of the tree-shrouded lane was an old French villa that had been turned into the Kieu Hoa restaurant. The Kieu Hoa was famous, one of the two or three most elaborate restaurants in all of Sai Gon. But Condley had to force back his bile as he dismounted from Dzung's *cyclo* and started for the door.

Some memories never die, as hard as we try to smile them away.

"Wait here?" asked Dzung, conscious of the hard stares he was receiving from the two black-uniformed valets who were more accustomed to arriving taxis and limousines than the antiquated *cyclos*.

Condley checked the faces of the well-fed young valets, then looked over at the near-emaciated frame of Dzung, now sitting nervously atop the *cyclo*. An irritation rankled him, never far from the surface when he was in Sai Gon. If things had gone differently in that long-ago war, this Da Lat–trained former officer who had served so well on the battlefield would probably be among those running the country.

But this was the way things had gone, and this was the world they all lived in. He handed Dzung ten thousand *dong,* which wouldn't buy a glass of water in the Kieu Hoa but was enough for a feast just down the road.

"Go eat. Come back and get me in an hour."

CHAPTER FOUR

CONDLEY'S MEMORY OF Khoa had fully returned by the time he walked into the Kieu Hoa restaurant and saw the former singer sitting at the bar. Khoa was dressed to perfection in a new tuxedo. His hair, now sprinkled with strands of silver, was still worn below his shoulders as before, although these days he pulled it stylishly back into a tight ponytail. His glasses were decidedly western, if not bought in Rome or Paris then certainly a competent Hong Kong rip-off.

The restaurant itself was spectacular. As he entered, Condley was amazed at its elegant furnishings, replete with textured-fabric furniture, French Impressionist paintings on the walls, and European classical music played by a live string quartet. A tuxedoed maître d' greeted him just inside the door. Other tuxedoed waiters walked rapidly to and fro, speaking variously in French and English as well as Vietnamese. A large, hand-calligraphied menu near the bar announced a varied and highly expensive fare of nouvelle French–Vietnamese cuisine. And the place was packed, mostly with well-dressed foreigners, with not an empty table.

As the maître d' greeted him, Condley's eyes met Khoa's. For a quick moment the former singer's gaze intensified, as if they might have once known each other. Then he caught a different kind of recognition in Condley's face and looked quickly away, feigning interest in the string quartet. Condley watched him for another moment and then allowed himself a knowing smile. "I'd say the old government was probably right," he said to himself.

"Excuse me, sir?" The maître d' seemed puzzled.

"Your boss has himself a very nice place."

"Yes, sir," answered the maître d', looking uncomfortably at Condley's casual shirt and at the sweat that stained it. "Thank you for the compliment. Can I help you, sir?"

At that moment Condley both resented and envied the young man who stood before him. He had been born after the war, or certainly toward the end of it. Manipulation, treachery, betrayal—all were irrelevant unless they kept him from finding a much-needed job, and clearly his own family history had helped him get this one. To such a man, Vietnamese history had no lingering internal markings, no justifiable divisions, no past acts that bore remembering, other than the unexplainable conduct of "puppets" such as Dzung. He had not been a part of the struggle. He brought nothing with him, no scars or memories that needed to be sorted out. Except, perhaps, those that were being carried by his family, and despite such scars, his family had won. So the rest could be forgotten, or at least never gone into. Vietnamese were simply Vietnamese, just as Germans were Germans or New Yorkers were New Yorkers. Some were heroes who were rewarded with good restaurants. And others were traitors who now drove *cyclos*.

"I'm looking for Colonel Pham."

"He is expecting you, sir?"

"Tell him Brandon Condley is waiting to see him."

"Oh, yes, of course," the young man said, obviously surprised that the ill-dressed man before him was the same person he had been told to await. "You are Mr. Condley?"

"I left my tuxedo in Honolulu," answered Condley, wearying of the false niceties. "It's in the backseat of my Mercedes."

"Yes, sir," answered the maître d', hiding his irritation behind a frozen smile. "Please follow me."

Colonel Pham was sitting near the back of the restaurant, at a table with three others, two of them Vietnamese women and one a well-dressed Caucasian man. From the cut of the man's gray silk three-button suit and the shaggy length of his hair, Condley could tell he was not American. One of the Vietnamese women was older, presumably the colonel's wife. The other woman's back was to him, but from her slimness and the way her long hair flowed so freely down her back, Condley knew she was younger, and probably the girlfriend or wife of the Caucasian man.

The colonel gestured to Condley as he approached, standing up to greet him and calling to a waiter for another chair. "Mister Condley," he said in Vietnamese. "Please join us."

The table was against the rear wall, underneath a spotlit reproduction of a Monet landscape of the Alps at Antibes. Condley approached it cautiously, studying the four people for clues so that he might understand the ambience that he was interrupting. For despite Colonel Pham's tight smile, it seemed that his approach was bringing a tension to the table.

Colonel Pham's formality was to be expected. Perhaps fifteen years older than Condley, the former Viet Cong soldier was rarely emotional in public and almost deceptively nondescript. Condley had learned that the colonel's controlled emotions were a camouflage that hid the kind of man whom in Asia too many Americans overlooked at their peril, and usually to their later regret. The colonel's teeth were stained from years of strong tobacco and poor dental hygiene. His glasses looked as if they had been bought forty years before. Several long strands of hair grew from a mole on his chin, just to the right of his mouth. His small, paw-like hands hung slightly in front of his thighs, as if he had spent so many years carrying weight on his back—pack and weapon and rice roll—that his shoulders and fingers were permanently curved. And he clearly did not belong in a suit. He wore it loosely and messily, the collar too big, the knot of the tie too fat, the shirtsleeves too long, making him appear ungainly and even more diminutive than he actually was.

But from the very first, Condley had picked up a sureness in the older man, a toughness that those who had not fought the war could never fully penetrate. Pham had made hard decisions, of the sort a mere businessman could never conceive. He had endured years in the jungle, conquering it and making it his friend. He had ordered soldiers to their deaths. He had killed people. And from the measuring look he and

Condley had always exchanged behind their smiles, it was clear that Pham had killed Americans.

Condley knew that Pham had always read his own face just as quickly. *Yes,* their eyes said to each other every time they met, *we both endured and we both killed. But that was then, and this is now. So where do we go from here?* In a way this knowledge gladdened both of them, giving them an odd but unbreakable bond. He and Pham shared a secret kinship. They knew the truth of the battlefield, a conviction so real and permeable that neither of them would ever need to mention it to the other.

"Chao Ong," said Condley, shaking the colonel's hand and moving to the chair the waiter had placed at the head of the table. Taking his seat at the colonel's elbow, for the first time he turned to the others.

"You have never met my wife," said the colonel in Vietnamese, gesturing formally to the older woman at the table. His very comment was a half-embarrassed admission that their relationship over the past three years had been cordial but never fully personal. "Her name is Tho."

"I am very glad to meet you," said Condley, nodding to the older woman from across the table.

The waiter magically appeared with a can of Tiger beer, pouring it slowly into a tall glass as Condley and the woman smiled carefully at each other. It was hard to read Pham's wife, who was gracious and at the same time very nervous, unsure of these elegant surroundings. She wore a simple black *ao dai* dress and kept her face neutral with a blank smile, but Condley could see that she was cataloging movements and looks just as thoroughly as he himself, all to be mulled over and analyzed later.

"And this is Francois Petain," continued Colonel Pham, gesturing to the man sitting at his left. "He does not understand my Vietnamese, so let me switch to French." Fluently, the colonel made an introduction to Petain in French. When he concluded, the Frenchman waved his hand carelessly in the air, smiling sardonically to Condley.

"So perhaps we should simply speak English, no? The colonel and his wife may have some problem, but Van and I speak it well."

There was a casualness in the way that Petain referred to the young woman sitting just next to Condley that spoke of possessiveness, as though he were used to making decisions for her. Condley studied the Frenchman as he reached his hand across the table toward him. Petain was in his late thirties, although his face and frame had already softened considerably from lack of exercise. He wore an expensive maroon silk tie, the knot casually loose at his neck. A top-of-the-line Cartier wrist-watch revealed itself as he reached an arm toward Condley, shaking hands. His handshake was soft, more from a dismissive air than a lack of strength.

They began an odd three-way conversation using a mix of English, French, and Vietnamese. "Mr. Petain is a businessman," said Colonel Pham in Vietnamese as the two men shook hands. "He lives most of the time in Tokyo but has been coming here very frequently of late." The way the colonel nodded and smiled as he mentioned Petain's frequent trips to Sai Gon clearly had some reference to the young woman at his side.

"What's your business?" asked Condley, retaking his seat.

"Perfume. I am the Asian president for Lanvin."

"Perfume?" Despite himself, Condley could not restrain a chuckle.

Petain's eyebrows arched. "People spend lots of money on perfume. So what is your problem with that?"

"They don't smell bad, Francois. They're hungry."

His answer brought a scathing frown from Petain but an immediate laugh from the young woman on his right.

"He's right, Francois! But I do love your perfume!"

Petain waved his hand as if dismissing Condley, then spoke as his eyes wandered around the restaurant. "What do Americans know about Viet Nam? They came in and blew it up with millions of bombs and then left. We French have been here for—what shall I say? Two hundred years or more."

Condley did not really care about the French one way or another, but at bottom he did not like this man. "As I recall, they kicked your asses out of here a couple wars ago."

The young woman laughed again, clearly delighted with the debate that had erupted without warning or even provocation between the two men. "Francois, I think he is quicker than you."

The colonel cleared his throat, as if half embarrassed yet again. "My daughter," he said, still speaking Vietnamese. Then he caught himself, becoming almost apologetic. "Actually my youngest daughter, because I have others. And because she is my youngest she is also spoiled. This is Van."

Daring finally to stare fully at Van, Condley saw that she had a raw and natural beauty. She appeared to be in her mid-twenties. Her face glowed from a reflection of the spotlight on the painting above the table. Her hair was pulled straight back from her face and cascaded freely down to the small of her back. She sat still and erect in her chair, her chin high and her hands held together on her lap. She was wearing a blue *ao dai* dress with white silk slacks. The dress split from ankle to waist along the sides, and through the gauzy translucent fabric he could see splendid firm long legs and hips outlined by the imprint of white bikini underwear. It caused him to marvel once again that a culture so subdued and modest could adopt such a subtly tantalizing traditional dress.

And she had an impish smile, a signal that beneath the demure exterior was a rebel. Her long face with its bright almond eyes and full smile caused her to radiate mischief.

Her English was accented but easily understood. "You're very funny, Mr. Condley," she said.

"Actually I was serious."

"One should never become too serious in Asia," tweaked Petain. "There is not enough room for it. It would eat away at your emotions."

"Okay, so tell me a good joke and let's all drink another bottle of pinot noir."

"Oh, you know how to pronounce French wine," goaded Petain. "Quite a surprise, since the waiter saw your costume and immediately brought you a cheap local beer."

"Yeah, he knew I wasn't French the minute I had the courtesy to speak to him in Vietnamese." Even as he said it Condley was surprised at the depth of his reaction to this man he did not know. Van laughed again, and her throaty chuckle spurred him on. "Sell them perfume and let them eat cake, huh? Didn't somebody French say that?"

"That's exactly what I mean," said Petain dismissively. "You have become too aggressive, over nothing."

"Testosterone does that."

"He's winning, Francois," teased Van delightedly.

"It is not a contest." Petain was thoroughly piqued.

Colonel Pham cleared his throat, regaining control of the conversation. He absently twirled the long hairs that grew out of the mole on his cheek. Condley knew that such hairs were considered a sign of wisdom, and to twirl them was to invoke strange powers. "Mr. Petain has been very kind to invite us to dinner tonight," said the colonel, still speaking only Vietnamese. The comment was a request that Condley cease his sarcasm.

Van leaned forward, as if taking his instructions. "And we are happy that you might join us, Mister Condley. So let me propose a toast? To friends."

They raised their glasses, clinking them together above the center of the table, a merriment that, if not false, was certainly forced and un- certain.

"To friends!" They took turns, saying it in three languages.

Condley studied the faces and the smiles as he touched each glass with his own. The colonel's sudden cheerfulness seemed in part to be a demand that Condley enjoy himself at the risk of losing face. Francois's cool eyes belied his smile, filled with denigration for the poorly dressed American. Mrs. Pham held her reserve, still studying everyone, and espe- cially studying Condley. And Van was ravishing and aglow, clearly taken with Condley's whole casual demeanor.

She touched glasses with him, smiling again. "My father has spoken about you before," she said in Vietnamese, as if wanting a private moment from Francois. "He says many good things about you. That you know Viet Nam. Some others only want to use Viet Nam."

"So why do you like him?" Condley was surprised at his own blunt- ness, even though they were speaking a language that Petain could not understand. From the corner of his eye Condley could tell that Van's mother had heard the question and was watching them.

"The French are so *elegant,*" Van said obliquely, mixing the French pronunciation of the word in with her Vietnamese. Petain smiled at her when she used the French word, certain that she was complimenting him. She smiled back at Petain for a quick moment and then spoke to Condley as if using code. "And he likes to buy me nice things. What's the matter with that? Don't you like nice things?"

"He seems to be an ass," said Condley, realizing once he spoke that his comment reeked of unnecessary jealousy.

"You're very reckless with your feelings," Van answered coyly, still speaking in Vietnamese. "Or at least with your words, no?" Then she looked over at the three waiters who were now descending on the table and switched to English. "Francois ordered the entire meal."

"So here it is," said Petain, as if he had created it himself.

The waiters quickly went about their work, laying out appetizers on each plate and six steaming, heaping dishes in the center of the table: seafood, crab, duck, beef, chicken, and pork, along with bowls of steamed rice, all prepared to perfection, to be shared family-style in the Vietnamese tradition. Another bottle of wine found its way to the iced canister next to Francois. He wrapped a towel around it and poured ceremoniously for the others and then for himself. At the same time he gestured toward the plates of food.

"Everyone, please! Really, help yourselves!"

Colonel Pham needed no further encouragement. He jumped onto the food, followed by the others, and began eating greedily, devoid of the etiquette Francois was carefully following. As Condley filled his plate he studied Van's mother. She caught his look and returned it with a courteous smile, then offered him the plate of beef. He took the plate, thanking her, and decided that he might perhaps draw her out and began speaking to her in Vietnamese.

"You are also from central Viet Nam?" he asked, knowing that the colonel himself had been born in Tam Ky, just south of Da Nang.

"Yes," she answered almost shyly, taking rice into a small bowl.

"You have other children?"

"I have eight children," she answered, glancing over to Van, who was talking earnestly with Francois. "Van is my baby." She looked now at Colonel Pham, perhaps for support, then back to her rice, as if attempting to end the discussion.

Condley continued, not having picked up on her unease. "Do your other children live near you?"

"Three are here," she said. "Two are in Da Nang." She blinked and Condley saw she was fighting with her emotions. "Three are dead."

Condley then comprehended that he had gone too far. In this new Viet Nam, any conversation, even any gesture, could bring back some scar from the past. He had relaxed too quickly after his exchange with Van, and now he knew why Colonel Pham had never brought him into their home.

"Two girls," she continued. "One boy." She had stopped all motion and was looking into her plate, hiding her tears in order to compose herself. Finally she looked back up at him, the tears gone and her face firm, and moved a hand through the air to simulate an airplane on an approach path, and finally threw the hand upward to indicate a bomb.

"Linh My. Ac lam," she said, continuing to look him directly in the eyes.

American soldiers. Wicked. It was from a memory, said for perhaps the millionth time in order to push away her grief. But to say it here, now, and to him was pointed, painful, even holding him somehow responsible.

It didn't make him feel that way. Instead, it brought back a swarm of similar memories to him as well. They spilled from the flash of anger in his eyes onto the table alongside hers, sightless, odorless, and yet palpable, even to her. Condley wanted to tell her that the bombings were probably careless but never intentional. He wanted her to hear of the cruelty and wickedness perpetrated by her husband's cohorts. Of his friend Thanh, captured by the enemy who then left pieces of his body in a dozen nearby villages as reminders of his misplaced loyalty. Of the two dozen villagers he had buried after they were ambushed and slaughtered inside a home for no reason except that they had come to a meeting sponsored by the Provincial government.

Most of all he wanted to tell her what it was like to discover the beautiful, innocent Mai lying cold and twisted on the bathroom floor with her throat slashed and the blood draining forever from her, every ounce of his own hope and happiness gurgling into the gutter along with the loud incessant stream of water from the shower. And how it felt to know that she had died for the sin of loving him.

But he could not. One story would beget another, until soon the whole war would be piled onto the table. It was over and it made no sense to continue it by fighting over who had been crueler or who had suffered the greatest loss. Her loss was overwhelming, total, irreplaceable. That was enough for him. And it had been caused by an American aircraft.

"Mrs. Pham, I am very sorry," he finally said. "If you will take me to temple, we will pray for your children together."

Her look gradually changed, from an angry, accusing sadness to mild disbelief and then to genuine respect. She regained her smile and slowly took his hand.

"My husband told me that you are a good man," she said.

"I mean it. I'll go if you will take me," said Condley, feeling cleansed by his own words.

"I will take you," she agreed.

"We will pray for all the dead."

"I will do that too," she said.

Condley glanced at the others. Colonel Pham nodded to him encouragingly, as if he had suddenly become family. Francois Petain was bored and distracted, his mind somewhere between Paris and Tokyo, fading fast from jet lag. The Frenchman looked down at his watch again, uncomfortable with this ugly business of war and loss and emotions.

But it was Van's look that struck him. She had stopped in the middle of serving Petain a portion of food. Petain's arm was touching her shoulder, as much an act of ownership as his earlier announcement that he and Van would both speak English. But her surprised, appreciative look told Condley that she fully understood his answer to her mother and the painful journey he had taken in his mind in order to reach it.

The string quartet was playing elegantly near the front of the restaurant. He heard Petain mention casually to Van that the piece was from Tchaikovsky. A young woman in a yellow silk *ao dai* came to the table selling roses. Petain bought one for Van and another one for her mother. They both thanked Petain appreciatively, and then both smiled almost secretly to Condley as Petain paid the flower girl.

Soon the food was gone and the wine bottle was empty. Petain looked at his watch yet again, ready to leave. Sensing the evening was finished, the colonel now turned to Condley. As always, they spoke in Vietnamese. "What is it that you have to report to me?"

"Yesterday we located the remains of an American soldier in Quang Nam Province. In Ninh Phuoc, along the Song Thu Bon west of Da Nang. He was buried during the war in a family plot in the village. We have the full skeleton, and also his dog tags."

The colonel nodded appreciatively, then frowned. "I find this very strange. Why did it take them so long to report him if they knew he was buried in their village?"

"They didn't know. The recent floods washed away part of the cemetery and they found the body. The man who buried the soldier had been afraid to report it. He'd buried him when he was a little boy. He found the body outside his family home one morning and his grandmother made him bury it."

Colonel Pham looked at Condley for another moment, digesting the report. "I don't know of another case like this. The Americans kept very careful records of when and where they lost their soldiers. There have been no reports from that area in Quang Nam."

"I agree with you," said Condley. "We're trying to find more information. Perhaps he was captured on a different battlefield in Quang Nam, or Quang Tin or even Quang Ngai, and died while your side was marching him to a camp back in the mountains. We have his name. Professor Muir will be contacting Washington and asking for an examination of his military records."

"Should our government announce this discovery?" asked the colonel.

"Not yet," said Condley. "I agree with you that there is something strange about this case."

Petain had paid the bill and now was standing. His eyes were on the door, signaling the maître d' to have the valet summon his limo. He checked his watch for the tenth time and again put his hand possessively on Van's shoulder. As Condley stood, Petain made a great display of reaching for his hand and shaking it dismissively.

"*Bonjour,* Mr. Condley. Good luck with all your skeletons."

"Yeah, well, I hope you sell a lot of perfume down there in District Four." Condley turned his back on Petain, leaning down to shake the hand of Tho, the wife of Colonel Pham. He spoke to her gently in Vietnamese. "Mrs. Pham, I will look forward to praying with you."

"You must come to our home very soon," she answered, her eyes then shifting to Van.

And as he walked out of the restaurant, Condley's last glance was at the mischievous grin of Van herself. Petain's hand was on her shoulder, but her eyes were on Condley.

———

DZUNG HAD DRUNK three beers. He teetered atop his *cyclo* as he steadily pedaled Condley back toward District One.

"So I gave you too much dinner allowance," teased Condley, noting Dzung's reddened face and neck and the wetness in his eyes.

"No, Cong Ly," laughed Dzung, his gaze now staring far away into the quiet darkness. "You gave me just the right dinner allowance. But I used it very badly!" He pedaled harder, working his way up a small hill, and now grew serious. "My little baby very sick, Cong Ly. Yesterday I take him to the hospital. They say they can do nothing for him."

"What's wrong with him?"

"He just sick," answered Dzung blandly, as if no further explanation were possible. They were nearing Condley's hotel. Dzung pulled on his brake, stopping the *cyclo*. "Maybe he die. My wife, she very sad. I can do nothing. So tonight I drink beer."

"I'm sorry, Dzung. If I can help, I will try."

"Thank you, Cong Ly. But you are not a doctor."

Condley jumped down from the *cyclo*, heading for the hotel's front door.

"Tomorrow?" asked Dzung somewhat dizzily, watching him depart.

"Eight o'clock," said Condley, waving good night. "Right here."

———

CONDLEY KEPT A permanent room in the Vien Dong Hotel, even though he spent more time in Hawaii than in Viet Nam. In his simply furnished room were a half dozen changes of clothes, a long shelf of books, a full medicine cabinet, a useless TV, and, incongruous with his normal style, a fax machine. He had arranged for the hotel to supply him with his own fax machine after numerous telephone messages from Hawaii had been boggled in translation by the well-meaning clerks who worked the front desk.

Condley knew that in reality the fax belonged to the Ministry of Post and Telecommunications and that the ministry monitored all his faxes, just as it monitored the faxes at all the hotels in Viet Nam. It hadn't mattered to him, since he knew that most of his telephone calls were also monitored, as were his comings and goings whenever he was in Sai Gon. The Vietnamese were the great spies of Asia, not only because they were masters at intuition but because they genuinely loved the game. With the game came revenge, and they especially loved revenge. They kept files on everyone, including on one another. He never acknowledged that he knew he was being monitored, and sometimes he sent bogus faxes just to play with the minds of the unseen agents off in some dank, ugly office who spent their days meticulously keeping his file. But it was helpful to know that the game was being played. Most Americans inside Viet Nam were oblivious to it, and thus at a constant disadvantage.

Somewhere in the middle of the night, Hanson Muir sent him a fax. He heard the machine go off as he slept but could not bring himself to read it until morning. It surprised him that Muir would have faxed him so quickly after arriving in Hawaii. But then he read the fax.

Saigon, we've got a problem. Or shall I say, BC phone home?

It was morning in Sai Gon but five in the afternoon in Hawaii when he called. Hanson Muir was just getting ready to leave for the night.

"So where have you been?" Muir asked when Condley said hello. "Off getting married again?"

"You're not allowed to be jealous, Hanson. Take what you can get and leave the rest of us alone."

"He's not an MIA," said Muir with a sudden bluntness.

"What are you talking about?"

"Our boy. The skeleton from your famous little village. The guy we risked our lives to bring home."

"Stop being dramatic, Professor. You loved that boat ride."

"Sure, about as much as I'd love riding a bicycle in an ice storm. I said he's not on anyone's list. He was never missing in action and he was never a prisoner of war."

"So what was he?"

"Brandon, I don't know what he was. He did exist. I mean, we have his dog tags. We've asked the Department of the Army to put a rush on pulling his file from the archives in St. Louis. I should have it in two days."

"So what do you want me to do?" asked Condley. He had been listening to the Professor, but mostly he was deciding what he was going to have for breakfast.

"Be back here in two days," said Muir. "I need your help. We have to talk about this."

CHAPTER FIVE

Hawaii

"COMING HERE IS always like visiting a hospital," said Brandon Condley as he entered the doorway to the Army's Central Identification Lab. "Except all the patients are already dead."

"An illusory distinction, if one is an anthropologist," assured Hanson Muir, shaking his partner's hand and ushering him inside. "They get excellent care here. And lots of individual attention."

Located in a corner of Hickam Air Force Base just outside Honolulu, the Central Identification Lab, Hawaii, also known by the acronym CILHI, was home to a few dozen soldiers, anthropologists, and scientists. Their principal mission was to identify American military personnel whose remains had been found after becoming missing in action during World War Two, Korea, and Viet Nam. They were also frequently brought in to help identify those who died in civilian disasters such as the crashes of commercial airliners.

The nondescript one-story lab did indeed look something like a medical clinic, with administrative offices and a conference room off to the left of its main entrance and a string of examining rooms off to the right. As Hanson Muir led Condley down a long corridor toward the room in which the remains from Ninh Phuoc were kept, they could look through glass windows into other rooms on their left and right and see numerous skeletons, laid out on white sheets atop rigs that resembled surgical gurneys. Many of these remains were actually partial skeletons, and some held only a few pieces of bone. But each gurney was nonetheless laid out carefully, with whatever bones that had been found placed in their proper anatomical locations.

"Look in here," said Hanson, stopping suddenly and opening a door into one of the examining rooms. "Come on in, Brandon. This will interest you."

Inside the room were a dozen gurneys, each holding a largely complete skeleton. Along the floor at the rear of the room were numerous other plastic bags, all carefully labeled with dates and a peculiar form of grid coordinates. The dirt-flecked skeletons were the color of copper. Rotting tatters of military uniforms still clung to some of them. On a nearby gurney Condley could see that the skull of one of them rested inside a rusting World War Two–style helmet.

As was his tendency, Professor Muir became immediately emotional when he surveyed the roomful of remains. His bearded chin lifted slightly and his eyes went distant, as if he were surveying an old battlefield.

"You were a Marine," said Muir. "Do you remember Carson's Raiders?"

"Every Marine remembers Carson's Raiders," said Condley, his own skin beginning to tingle as he stared across the room.

"Handpicked infantrymen," continued Muir. "Tough. They were the very best we had. In the summer of 1942, the Pacific campaign was in doubt. When our Marines landed at Guadalcanal on August 7th, the Raiders struck just across the channel at Tulagi, preventing Japanese reinforcements. A few days later Colonel Carson loaded 221 of his best troops into two submarines, the *Nautilus* and the *Argonaut*, and headed out for the Makin Atoll, many hundreds of miles away. You also remember Makin, Brandon?"

"Tarawa," said Condley instantly. "But the main battle at Tarawa wasn't for another year."

"Exactly. But at midnight on August 17th, 1942, the submarines surfaced off the Makin Atoll, dropping the Marines in landing boats over the side. And just before dawn, Carson landed his men on

Butaritari Island and surprised the Japanese Army garrison by attacking them on their own turf. The raid was an act of strategic deception, designed to discourage massive reinforcements on Guadalcanal. Strategically, for the good of the country, it made sense. But can you imagine what that was like for these two hundred men? Vastly outnumbered. Attacking the Japanese when they were hundreds of miles from any other American forces. No reliable maps that showed where the Japanese positions were on the island. No supporting arms other than a couple of six-inch guns mounted on the submarines themselves. They fought the Japanese through the day and into the darkness. By all accounts it was a vicious, confusing mess. They took casualties throughout the day, and then when they were pulling out, several of their boats were lost in the surf as they were returning to the submarines. In all, twenty-one Marines were left behind. Their remains were never recovered. Until now, that is."

Muir moved forward to the nearest gurney, looking down at the bones as if peering at a living Marine, one whom he in his competence was going to heal. "We always imagined that our casualties had been cremated, although the locals on the island have been telling us for decades that the Japanese buried the Marines in a mass grave at the edge of the island. We tried several times but never were able to find them. And finally, a few months ago, we did. Our people performed an archaeological dig, as if we were attempting to uncover some ancient city. We staked out the possible site, laid azimuths through it, and dug deep into the sand at various spots until finally we found a set of remains. After that, it was easy. And now comes the hard part, although I don't need to tell you it will be the most rewarding. We are going to identify every set of remains, Brandon. We are going to return these Marines to their loved ones."

Condley stood respectfully, his usual sarcasm fully in check in the presence of such certifiable heroes despite the nearly sixty years that had passed since their deaths. And he had no doubt that Hanson Muir and the others at CILHI would indeed identify the remains. First, they would pull the military files of all those who had perished in the famous raid. The starting point would be dental records, which on skeletal remains were as accurate as fingerprints, so long as a jaw had been recovered. Where dental records were not sufficient, the anthropologists and scientists could go to identifiable trauma on the skeletons that would have been present before the war, such as evidence of broken limbs. They could also narrow down the unknowns through one's height. And if they could find a maternal relative and a good sample from the skeletons, they could match DNA.

"We leave no one behind, Brandon," said Muir with his unending emotion. "I don't need to tell you that, you've lived it. I'm not a soldier and I've never been one. But I'm an American, and when I look across a room like this it makes me so proud that we are the way we are."

Sarcasm was Condley's best refuge from his own inner emotions, and he'd found his once again. "So what do you want me to do, salute?"

"Actually, that would be fine."

Condley thought about it, then came to a full attention and offered the retrieved heroes a slow, crisp Marine Corps salute.

"Thank you, Brandon."

"Don't thank me, I didn't salute you." He chuckled softly as Muir turned to leave the room. "But I'm proud as hell to salute them."

"Let the record show that Mr. Condley has a heart."

"So where are we keeping Specialist Deville?"

"He's right down here," said Muir, again leading Condley down the corridor.

The remains from Ninh Phuoc were on a gurney at the rear of the next room. Muir had carefully assembled the bones into a semblance of a skeleton but left them atop the rotting poncho. The dead man lay on his back, his skull facing the ceiling and his arms flat at his sides. Condley approached the gurney carefully, his mind exploding with odd images from the dark trails of the isolated village and the shed from which they had retrieved the remains. The lab was spotlessly clean and well-lit, but an aura seemed to rise above the bones, shimmering with sole-sucking mud, barking little dogs, bad tea, and dead, bloated pigs rushing past in the river's chalky current.

"I don't have his complete file yet," began Muir.

"You told me two days," teased Condley. "I busted my ass to get out of Sai Gon in time."

"You know the government, Brandon. Promises, promises. They're sending it out from St. Louis with a courier. It'll be here by tomorrow."

"A courier, huh? Like they don't have overnight mail anymore?"

Muir puffed up again, and Condley sensed that he was in for another patriotic speech. "We can't risk losing these files, Brandon."

"How about a computer? Can't they send you the data?"

"You can't e-mail dental records. And anyway, the file is thirty years old. Do you know how many million veterans there are? It hasn't been reduced to computer text."

"What you're saying is that somebody in St. Louis wants a few days R and R in Hawaii."

Muir allowed himself a small smile. "Why are you such a cynic? But you may be right. Partially, at least."

The huge scientist now looked at the remains, an unhidden revulsion creeping into his eyes and tightening his mouth. "But I had them fax me a few pages from his service records and give me a preliminary report over the phone. I've got some news for you. As I mentioned to you, Specialist Deville was never a POW or an MIA. In fact, I must confess that our earlier respect for him was misplaced. It seems our man was a deserter."

"*Your* earlier respect, you mean," corrected Condley. "I told you something was wrong about him."

"Yes, but did you ever think he'd be a deserter?"

"In Ninh Phuoc? No. That doesn't make any sense. The people I know of who deserted in-country stayed in Da Nang or Sai Gon. I'd say there were a couple thousand of them living in Sai Gon by the end of the war, and another few hundred in Da Nang. Usually it was a guy who maybe fell in love and ran away with his girlfriend or got into a fight with his first sergeant and ran away, period. Or got involved in the drug culture."

"Two out of three isn't bad," said Muir rather stiffly, picking up five pages of notes from a table next to the gurney. "Here's what I do have. Specialist Theodore Deville started out as an infantryman with the 199th Light Infantry Brigade, seeing extensive action in Tay Ninh Province west of Sai Gon during late 1966 and early 1967. Not a bad soldier, from all indications. Wounded in action. Received the Bronze Star and Army Commendation Medals for valor. In March 1967 he extended his tour in order to switch to a supply unit at Long Binh, just outside Sai Gon. Got involved with drugs. Was accused of being a dealer. In September 1967, while awaiting court-martial on the drug-dealing charges, he apparently killed the government's principal witness, who was a fellow soldier, and then disappeared. Last seen heading from Long Binh to Sai Gon, in what turned out to be a stolen jeep." Muir fixed

Condley with a steady, questioning gaze, his bushy eyebrows furrowed. "What am I missing here?"

"When was he buried in Ninh Phuoc?"

"What did they say? August 1971, I think."

"So you're missing four years. And Ninh Phuoc is a long, long way from Sai Gon."

"Particularly in the middle of a war, wouldn't you think?"

Condley laughed cynically. "I couldn't have gone a hundred meters outside my company perimeter by myself in that area without the risk of being killed. What the hell was this guy doing in Ninh Phuoc?"

"Other than dying, you mean?"

"Oh, *that*." He thought about it some more, staring at the bones that lay before them. "So what do we do with the remains of a deserter, Professor? We don't just wrap them up in the American flag and fly them back to Dover in a C-141, do we?"

"That, as they say, is above our pay grade." Muir's disdain was palpable as he surveyed the remains before them on the gurney. "We do our job, which is to make a positive identification. And then we turn the matter over to the powers-that-be."

"Stand by for a fucking parade, right up Pennsylvania Avenue."

"Stifle yourself, Condley."

"Another victim, coming home from Viet Nam."

"We do our job, they do theirs."

"I remember that drill. The way they do their job. I learned it about fifty-eight thousand dead guys ago."

"Fifty-eight thousand and one."

Condley grunted. He was beginning to feel claustrophobic. "Call me when you get his file. Hanging around him makes me sick."

Muir put a hand on Condley's shoulder, guiding him toward the door that led to the hallway. It was a fatherly gesture, from a man only five years older than he himself. But Muir, despite his flights of emotion, was far older in his soul than Condley.

"Get some rest, Brandon."

"Maybe." Condley knew what he needed, and he knew just where to find it. "If I'm not in my apartment, call me at Maria's."

CHAPTER SIX

"NEVER GET DRUNK before noon in the Philippines." Condley's perpetually sunburnt face was filtered by the bar's dim light, making him seem twenty years younger as he continued his fruitless lecture. "It's too hot. You get sick and then you get robbed."

Yes, this was Hawaii, but Maria's bar was in a heavily Filipino enclave just west of Honolulu that the locals called Little Manila. The four sailors sitting across from him were on their way to a deployment in the Philippines, so they had decided to drop in on the neighborhood for a little ethnic warm-up. And it was ten minutes to twelve. And they were already drunk.

The four weren't actually sailors. They were Navy SEALs, special-operations-capable fighters who trained to the edge of masochism and liked to fly around the world and blow things up. They had muscles right out of a bodybuilding magazine. Their faces carried an aura of untested invincibility. The biggest one, whom Condley had nicknamed "Statue" an hour before, now raised a finger into the air and made a circle, summoning the Filipina barmaid. Statue's huge biceps hung like a ham hock as he twirled his finger.

"Hey, Maria, one more round! Give our friend two."

"I'll take one more, then I'm done." Condley studied the huge man, then shook his head. "I'm telling you, Statue, Little Manila isn't San Diego. You're taking your life in your hands getting drunk around here."

Maria winked sleepily at Condley as she placed a new bottle of San Miguel in front of him. "Brandon Condley, you got one more beer."

"Sweet Maria. My little Dulcinea."

She touched the back of his hand, giving him a smile filled with old memories and new promises. He smiled back. She was almost like a wife, except that he did not live with her and she slept with other men for a living. Truth to tell, he had actually been married to Maria for about five minutes a few years before so that she could get her green card and follow him from Manila after he'd been hired for the CILHI job. The marriage had been a perfunctory courtesy, like leaving a large tip for someone after years of outstanding service. And the divorce had been just as perfunctory as the marriage. Condley remained proud that neither the divorce nor the marriage got in the way of their friendship, because he genuinely liked Maria. He knew the tones of her voice and all the secret movements of her body. She was as comfortable to him as the bed he slept in as a child. She idly stroked the back of his hand for another second, then walked to the rear of the bar and continued wiping empty tables.

The sailors were the only other customers in the bar. Condley toyed with the beer bottle as he almost insolently continued to eye Statue and his shipmates. Condensation from the hot dank air had made a quick puddle on the bar. He absently drew little circles in the puddle. Finally he raised the bottle in a mock toast.

"You guys do steroids?"

The SEALs had noticed Condley's faded Marine Corps tattoo when he walked into the bar an hour before and had bought him one drink and then another. But now they laughed loudly and elbowed one another, sharing a secret joke or maybe a kind contempt. Condley persisted, eyeing the squared muscles of their chests and the large deltoids that flared out of their loose-hung, sleeveless T-shirts.

"No, really. When I was in the Marines we worked out like crazy and none of us got bulked up like that. Got to be steroids. Does your skipper know? I mean, they don't actually allow you to do that, do they? That shit'll tear you to pieces in a few years. You're going to be walking around on canes, calling for a nurse to help you pump up your dick so you can get laid."

Statue's main sidekick, a squared-off, no-neck slab of muscle just taller than a dwarf, scratched a new tattoo and shook his head unbelievingly at Condley. "You really were a Marine? In the Nam, huh? Come on. What the hell happened, they put your body through a shrinking machine when you got back?"

The other three laughed uproariously, as if No Neck were a stand-up comedian. Then they drained huge gulps of beer straight from their bottles. Some trainer or maybe officer had taught them that they were royalty, fit to come down from the mountain every now and then to mingle among the mortals.

Condley laughed with them. It seemed to disconcert them. Then he leaned around the bar and stared at their feet. "How many pairs of running shoes do you guys own? I'll bet you've got a different pair for beach running, road running, sidewalk running, cross-country running. I'll bet you've got a special pair you spit-shine for goddamn *inspection*. That is, if you still spit-shine shoes in today's kiss-ass, aerobic Navy."

"Yeah, we got running shoes," said Black Goliath, now deciding to directly taunt Condley. "When's the last time your narrow ass ran a mile, Home?"

"Last time I ran further than a hundred feet was when somebody was shooting at me, trying to kill me dead."

"In the Nam?"

"Hell, no. Right here in Honolulu. A very unhappy guy. He thought I was in the rack with his wife. They can shoot you for that in Hawaii, you know. At least that's what they tell me."

"Were you?"

"In the rack with his wife? Not when he was trying to kill me."

Condley watched them carefully as they elbowed one another again, raising their beers to him in an approving toast. It had become a standoff of disbelief. They were trying to decide if he'd really been a Marine, and he was trying to decide if they could fight.

"Sorry. You guys look too pretty, like some kind of recruiting poster. Did they send you to modeling class? I know you've been to all the right schools—SCUBA school, Ranger school, Airborne school. But do they teach you how to take pain? Do they mess with your *minds*?" He grunted, a dismissal. "Probably kiss your ass every payday, thank you for taking their money."

"Why, you want to fight, old man?" Black Goliath laughed, giving off a look that bordered on pity.

"I'll give you a hint, Goliath. If I was going to fight you, you'd be the last one to know. You wouldn't find out until the knife was sliding along your throat."

Statue seemed mystified by Condley's unbending composure. He peered boozily at Condley, his huge head waving from side to side as if buttressed by a gentle, changing wind. "Any one of us could beat the fuck out of you."

"I'm a lot meaner than you think."

Grinning, Statue made just the slightest move toward Condley. Before he made it off his bar stool, a banana knife had appeared from nowhere and was making a dimple in his throat. Surprised, Statue turned slowly to see sweet Maria, her feet apart like a boxer, pressing the knife forward.

"No fights in my bar," said Maria. "And you don't ever hurt my lovely Brandon. He is my prince."

Statue's arms were up in the air, his hands open in surrender. Condley laughed quietly, dropping his own banana knife onto the bar. "Could have come from over here just as easy, Statue. Forget what they taught you in all that aerobic training. This is a fucked-up world we live in and people don't like to be pushed around."

Maria pulled away her knife and started laughing. "I can hook off my jab too," she said, shadowboxing for him and proving it, throwing a jab toward his stomach and coming up with a quick hook that just grazed his chin. Then Statue started laughing. Within seconds they were all best friends. Maria's banana knife and quick hands had magically brought them closer together. After five beers the reddening strawberry on Statue's throat was a treasured little prize.

Statue sat back down and slapped Condley on the back. "What do you do, man?"

"I'm a bone picker," said Condley.

"What does that mean?" asked Black Goliath.

"I go wherever they tell me to go and do whatever they tell me to do.

Yesterday I was in Viet Nam, now I'm here, tomorrow I may be in Borneo. Picking up bones."

"You're a spook!" No Neck sounded triumphant, as if he had finally solved a puzzle.

"I did that once, a long time ago. But I am now totally legit. I find the bones of dead heroes and I bury them. That's it. Mostly in Viet Nam."

"Sorry about that. Sounds boring as shit, man," said Black Goliath.

They grew quiet, as if embarrassed for him. Maria finished wiping the tables and now walked lazily to the jukebox and punched in a dozen numbers.

"It has its moments," said Condley, absently watching Maria at the jukebox. "And it keeps me in Asia. I like that."

The front door opened, causing a flash of hot sunlight to intrude on their retreat, bringing with it fresh smells of a city cooking in its own noonday juices. Whoever was at the door had thought twice about it and quickly retreated back onto the street. The jukebox suddenly surrounded their reverie with a blast of drum-pounding disco music.

"I hate beer," said Statue. "It's like a thousand little flies buzzing in my stomach. And every one of them wants out."

Condley kept watching them. They were growing uneasy under his stare. The heat and the beer had made them woozy. They were in their early twenties, but now they looked like children acting out a grown-up game of war and bravado. Finally he smiled. It was as close to feeling paternal as he could come.

"You'll change. Just wait. You stay long enough in Asia and it takes over. It doesn't have any answers, and after a while you stop asking for them. That's what I like about it and that's what I hate about it. In the States everything is, 'What's the bottom line?' There isn't any bottom line in Asia. There's always one more paragraph, two more choices. The problem is, none of the choices are for good, because tomorrow there's a different reason and maybe it totally contradicts today."

He was enjoying the confusion his words were bringing to their faces. "Try Java. I was there for six months once, on a security job for an oil company. In Java they tell the story of a fruit called the *simalakana*. It kills your mother if you eat it. It kills your father if you don't. That's Asia. Get it? You look at something and it's clear as a bell. Just a little problem, right? But no matter what you do, you may end up paying.

And you see as much or as little of what's in front of you as you dare to. If you see too much, you kill your friends. If you see too little, you kill yourself. *Simalakana."*

"Semilock on your what?" No Neck, the tough little bastard, had come up for air. He grinned triumphantly at his joke as the other three laughed again.

"On your brain, No Neck. If you had one."

They didn't have the slightest idea what he was talking about. They'd gone through tough training and they were physically hard. Somebody had convinced them that they could run through a brick wall if it came down to it. But they didn't have any idea what was on the other side of the wall. Maybe a fifty-foot drop-off. Maybe the mayor, with the key to the city. Maybe somebody sitting in an easy chair, waiting to shoot them. Who the hell knew?

"I'll tell you what, let me buy *you* a round. How's that? Are you up to it?"

"The ancient veteran, not to be confused with the ancient mariner, who at least rhymed, is buying us a round," said the fourth SEAL slowly, looking at the others. Condley had nicknamed this man Plato because he didn't talk very much and seemed to weigh his words when he did speak. Condley hadn't decided whether Plato was extremely drunk or extremely smart.

"That is, if you can hang with me for one more round?"

"Hell, yeah," said Statue. "If you're up to it, we're up to it."

"Right," said No Neck.

"I hate to take the man's money," said Black Goliath. "But if you feel like you gotta do it, go ahead."

Condley stood up and walked toward the front door. Statue called to him. "Where you going? The head's over here, man."

"I don't need to take a leak."

"You buying us a drink or what?"

Condley smiled mischievously. "Don't go away."

The sun was white-hot, right out of hell, and the street was filled with garbage. Rotten banana peels made a stinking little pile near the curb, black in their ferment. Flies were everywhere, like smoke. A new green Mercedes was parked next to the curb. Maria had bought it from the money she made whoring and running the bar, which she now owned outright. Across the street a boom box was blaring disco music from inside an apartment. The windows and curtains of the apartment were pulled up, revealing three young women who were awakening from morning naps after a night of dancing and turning tricks for Maria. One of the girls waved automatically to Condley as she stretched away her nap. An old woman slept between two trees in the garden outside the apartment, having made a makeshift hammock out of a set of sheets. That would be Maria's mother, who managed the apartment on behalf of her upwardly mobile, well-invested madam of a daughter. Near the tent, a small boy lay dozing on a wooden bench, as ignorant of the noise and rot and flies as a languid dog. That would be Maria's nephew, recently arrived from the real Manila under the Immigration and Naturalization Service's famous family-reunification plan.

Condley saw it all but took none of it in. In a way he had created the whole scene before him by enabling the ever-industrious Maria to obtain her green card. But that had been several years ago. Now it was simply a midday view of Little Manila, hardly as nice as Waikiki but a whole lot healthier than the Philippines. Sometimes it was pretty, often it was ugly, and every day it changed. So it didn't do any good to think about it.

Finally he saw the *balut* vendor. Condley called to the frail, sandaled old man. "Hey, hey! *Baluts!* You gimme five!"

The old man trotted immediately toward Condley, balancing a tray full of duck eggs on a strap that went over one shoulder. Condley waved him on, turning back toward the bar.

"This way!"

The four young SEALs had not moved from their seats. Their bottles of San Miguel sat empty before them as they awaited Condley's free round. They peered curiously at the *balut* vendor, who smilingly urged each of them to take one of the eggs.

"What the fuck, over?" No Neck fingered his egg, mimicking an old military phrase for confusion in combat.

"You never had a *balut*?" Condley cracked the top of his egg-shell, holding the rest of the egg like a shot glass, just below his chin. "Gentlemen"—he raised the egg, as if offering a toast—"to your success in combat."

They followed Condley's lead, cracking the top of the egg. Then all four froze, peering inside the shell. Plato looked back up at Condley, his eyes gone hollow. He swallowed hard and licked around the edges of his lips.

"There's a baby duck in there."

"Well, not quite. Another three or four days it would have been. Cheers, guys." Condley downed the *balut*. The placenta squirted inside his mouth as he chewed the full-grown embryo. Finally he swallowed and raised the eggshell in another mock toast.

"Good protein. Kind of like oysters, huh? Go ahead. This is a Navy tradition! I made a toast to your *future*. So, down the hatch. What's the matter, you need some salt?"

The four young men looked at one another again, sharing a secret dread. Statue went first, tipping his *balut* into his mouth and then delicately mulling it around with his tongue, as if he had just inserted a hot rock. Black Goliath followed suit, followed by No Neck.

Plato stared at the other three, then ran toward the head. Condley heard him retching as he reached the toilet. Black Goliath walked quickly to the front door. In the shaft of bright light that followed the opening of the door, Condley saw Black Goliath spit his *balut* into the street and then stand at the curb, spitting and spitting. Statue attempted to swallow, and then puked onto the floor.

No Neck, the little bastard, was smiling comfortably as he finished chewing the *balut*. He swallowed with satisfaction.

"Not bad," said No Neck.

"The perfect warm-up for a pro-life rally," answered Condley, warming to No Neck.

"I think it would go on a pizza," said No Neck.

"*Shut up*, man," said Statue. He was on his knees now. Maria had begun screaming and clucking her tongue as she trotted toward him with a bucket and a mop. "Just shut the hell up."

"Pepperoni, unborn baby duck, and provolone," said No Neck, who now waved toward the *balut* vendor. "I'll take another one."

Condley patted No Neck on one of his beefy shoulders as he waved good-bye to the others. "I like you, man. You're sick."

———————

A GRAY CHEVROLET with government license plates was parked in front of Macy's Apartments, where Condley paid five hundred dollars a month for an efficiency unit. As Condley approached the car, a red-faced man stepped out of the passenger door and pointed toward him. The man's eyes were commanding, electric with anticipation. He was wearing a gray polyester suit, a heavily striped shirt, and a loud red tie. He was in his mid-thirties and was overweight. And from the bulge underneath his left shoulder Condley could tell he was carrying. The man stepped in front of Condley, blocking the sidewalk.

"Okay, I give up. What'd I do?"

"Nothing," said the man.

"Then get out of my way."

"You've got to come with me."

"Who the hell are you—Dick Tracy?"

The man reached inside his coat pocket and showed Condley a Naval Investigative Service badge. "You're Brandon Condley, right? The general wants to see you."

"Give me a break. I never even met Hillary Clinton." Condley noticed a small grin beginning to work on the NIS man's face. He shrugged. "Okay, we had a beer together, but that was it. I mean, she was married and I wasn't ready to make a commitment. And, anyway, it was a long time ago."

"They told me you were a total wiseass," said the agent.

"Oh, they did, huh? Who is 'they'? You got a file on me?"

"We keep a file on everybody who's important, Condley. Which means we wouldn't waste any paper on *you*."

A small crowd had gathered on the street, watching the two. The agent seemed increasingly nervous. Condley gestured toward the car.

"They know you're a cop, driving a white-bread shitbox like that. You're affecting my reputation, as they say in the press."

"Don't worry. Nobody's going to write a story about you."

"Unless I get shot. You guys drive around town in these marked cars and everywhere you stop you leave bad will. Bad will, man! Look at these people! Now they think I'm in the mob or maybe the CIA, either that or they think I'm important and are now deciding they'll rob my ass whenever you leave. So thanks a lot, dickhead."

"You're a very hard man to find."

"Not if you know where to look."

"If you ever answered your phone this would've been a lot easier."

"That's why I use caller ID. So when I see a government number I know it's somebody trying to interfere with my First Amendment right of free association. And besides, I've been out of the country." Condley sighed knowingly. "Why does he want to see me?"

"Because he needs your advice."

"I don't think so." Condley sighed again. Then he brushed past the agent, on his way inside Macy's Apartments.

"Where are you going?"

"Well, if you're taking me to see the general, at least let me brush my fucking teeth."

CHAPTER SEVEN

CONDLEY AND DICK Tracy drove slowly through the city, heading for the interstate highway that would take them toward Pearl Harbor. It began to rain, a brief, warm squall in from the sea. The car stopped at a traffic light. Condley watched from the window as a beautiful little girl whose eyes seemed to take up half her face led an old blind man from car to car, asking for money. She peered at him from one inch away through the window, jerking her head upward slightly, an urgent, almost seductive gesture. Her face dripped water from the rain. Her eyes were demanding, even condemning, and for a moment he wanted to climb out of the car and save her. The light changed. As the car inched slowly forward, her face changed to disgust, and she flipped him the bird. Condley found himself laughing merrily.

"Tough little girl," he said. "She ought to take that blind guy and open up a franchise in Sai Gon."

"You're a heartless asshole," said Dick Tracy, his car splashing another pedestrian as they drove away.

"What's heartless about wanting to see a little girl succeed?"

"Don't you have any feelings for the blind guy?"

"You're right," agreed Condley. "He'd never make as much money in Sai Gon, there's too much competition."

Dick Tracy decided to ignore him. Soon the car turned right, and in minutes they were on the interstate. The agent could no longer hold back his curiosity. He eyed Condley, then probed him as they drove. "What the hell advice does the general think he needs from you?"

"I manage his investment accounts. I'm a clandestine agent for Merrill Lynch. He invests heavily in foreign governments. China is high on his list."

"You're loopy. You talk in circles."

"No, I talk in sentences. So stay out of my brain."

"I'll do that, Condley. I doubt it's a very orderly place to visit anyway."

To their front and then to their left as they drove along the interstate Condley could now see Pearl Harbor, majestic in its memories. He was still sentimental enough to remember the great, tragic battle that began World War Two and the millions of American servicemen who had poured from gray ships tied up at its piers over the past century on their way into and out of Asia. Pearl Harbor was a touchstone, and in a way a wailing wall. It dredged up a panoply of unconnected memories. And it made him glad that the general had decided to shanghai him for an afternoon.

"He thinks I saved his life," said Condley.

"Who?"

"The general."

"What happened?"

"It doesn't matter. Shit happens in wars."

"The war? That was a long time ago."

"Not when you're still alive."

The rainsquall ended. A grand rainbow streaked the sky above Pearl Harbor. The car kept driving, stuck in a mass of traffic, then turned right and headed up a steep hill toward Halawa Heights. Within minutes they reached a gatehouse and passed a Marine sentry, who waved the government car onto the base. Dick Tracy then drove past a complex of huge boxy old buildings that were the headquarters for the four-star admiral who commanded the American forces in the Pacific.

"The general's office is at Camp Smith," said Condley absently, wanting Dick Tracy to know that he'd been there before.

"He's meeting you at his house."

"So I guess he wants social advice."

"I'm not privy to the general's thinking," said Dick Tracy with all the stiff formality that a GS-9 civil servant could muster. "But after meeting you my guess is that he wants to make sure you don't embarrass him in front of a whole lot of people."

"You're hurting my feelings, you know. Remind me to never save your fucking life."

"That's what I mean," said Dick Tracy. "What kind of a man would go out of the way to insult his own military escort?"

"You're not military and you're not my escort. You're more like a nightmare version of somebody's parole officer."

"I rest my case," said Dick Tracy. "That's exactly what I mean. I fucking rest my case."

As he drove, Dick Tracy pulled out a cell phone from his jacket pocket and punched in some numbers with his thumb. Finally someone answered. "This is Combs," he said. "We're a couple minutes out." He punched the END button on his cell phone and put it away. "The general's been in meetings," he announced to Condley. "It'll be about fifteen minutes."

They were driving along a street lined with old, sprawling frame homes. The homes had been on Halawa Heights since before World War Two but had been frequently refurbished and were meticulously well-kept. The highest-ranking officers in the Pacific Command lived in them. In a few minutes the car slowed in front of one of them. A sign was posted in the manicured yard:

LIEUTENANT GENERAL WAYNE DUNCAN, USMC
COMMANDING GENERAL FLEET MARINE FORCES PACIFIC

The car spun into a circular driveway and stopped underneath a covered portico. Dick Tracy stepped out of the car and moved to Condley's side, opening his door so that he could escort him to the front door of the house.

"You're here for lunch," reminded Dick Tracy as they walked toward the house.

"I already ate two *baluts*."

"You really are loopy. Those things are foul. I wouldn't want to be inside your intestines right now."

"You're insulting the eating habits of an ancient Asian culture. I should report you to the diversity police."

"I *am* the police," reminded Dick Tracy.

"Have you ever had a *balut*?"

"I smelled one once."

Dick Tracy rang the doorbell, all the while carefully watching Condley as if he might soon bolt. A servant opened the double doors and Dick Tracy nudged Condley forward, waving good-bye and declining to enter the house himself. Condley stepped onto a shining teak entrance-way. It was so cool inside that he began to shiver. The servant, who was a Navy steward dressed in a white coat and black trousers, gestured toward the living room.

"Would you like a drink, sir?"

"I'll take a San Miguel."

He heard a noise off to his left, and then a woman's voice. "Maybe you'd like a Heineken?"

He turned and saw the woman, who was descending a stairway. She was about his age, firm and athletic but tense-looking around her eyes and mouth, as if she were expecting him to attack her or break all her dishes. Her hand was on the outer rail. She was wearing a red silk dress, far too nice for a lunch at home. She looked mildly disappointed when she saw him, her eyes lingering on his rumpled shirt and faded blue jeans as if his clothes emanated a bad odor. But then she recovered, perfectly feigning happiness.

"We have every kind of beer."

"San Miguel is fine," he said. "Beer isn't worth drinking unless you can taste the rust."

She laughed. Once her face relaxed he could tell that she was unpretentious, and he decided that he liked her. "The infamous Brandon Condley," she said with tentative fondness. "Or shall I say, the legend?"

"You better stick with infamous. Look, I don't think I can stay for lunch."

"Of course you can! Wayne will be here any second. I'm Maureen."

He shook her hand and joined her at a small table that had already been set for three people. The servant brought him his beer and he drained most of it in one large gulp. She was studying him with a curiosity born of a hundred stories told through the decades until reality and imagination had fused into an impossibly complicated and mildly cartoonish persona.

Brandon Condley, still on patrol, passing checkpoint infinity . . .

"Wayne said you never did, actually, come back from Viet Nam. Not in the way the others did. That you've stayed in Asia all these years. What is it that you've done out there?"

Music dominated the room, a compact-disc collection of classical strings. The servant entered from the kitchen, carrying a silver tray covered with succulent, elegantly prepared beef and vegetable appetizers. Condley picked at the appetizers, relaxing into the music and deciding to enjoy this moment of fairly exquisite living. The day's quotient of beer had settled into him with a joyous glow.

"Usually I just sell Bibles."

Maureen scrutinized his face even more intently, looking for some hidden significance or an indication that he was making a joke. Condley winked, nodding meaningfully. She nodded back, dropping her gaze and smiling as if accepting it.

"Bibles," she said.

"Right," said Condley. He grinned, raising a finger into the air and winking at Maureen again as the servant poured her a glass of wine. "Luke, chapter five, verse seventeen. It's what got me started and it hasn't let me down." He had no idea what Luke five, verse seventeen, said, but he figured that Maureen would probably check it out before she went to bed that night.

"Do you sell many?" asked Maureen.

"In the Philippines I've done real well. Truckloads of them. It's a Catholic country. Everybody wants a Bible."

"Yes. But they don't have any money."

"They've always got money for the Church." Condley appraised the floor-to-ceiling bookcases on a nearby wall and the wealth of artifacts the Duncans had collected over their years of traveling. "If you were in the Philippines they'd sneak in here and steal those antiques, then use the money to buy my Bibles." He winked again. "So you see, what you're doing, what I'm doing, it all interconnects—politics, international security, commerce, crime, the Bible. Religion is a very powerful force."

"But you don't . . . actually represent the Church," insisted Maureen patiently, now smirking at him with thinly veiled disbelief. Her eyes then lifted, staring past Condley. Behind them he heard the front door open again and then quickly close.

"I don't need to represent the Church directly," said Condley. "I have my connections in that capacity, but the Bible is its own church."

"Quit lying to my wife!"

He turned his head. Wayne Duncan was standing just behind him, his hands on his hips, grinning madly. Suddenly the general put his huge hands on Condley's shoulders and began bouncing him up and down in his chair. "Maureen, don't believe a word that comes out of this cracker's mouth!"

"Be careful," howled Condley, straining to rise from the chair as Duncan kept bouncing him. "You're being sacrilegious, and besides, you're going to break my shoulders!"

"Condley, you always were a sorry son of a bitch! Tell her you lied, you little prick!"

Condley was getting whipped, but he was laughing. He felt happy and young again, fighting like this with Wayne Duncan. "All right, I lied! Did you want me telling your wife I hunted people down and blew them away before they gave me this job poking around in the dirt for bones?"

"I already did, you idiot!" Duncan quit pounding him, and they shook hands. "Good to see you, *Lieutenant*."

"Skipper," said Condley fondly. Their handshake was firm and as exuberant as the general's shoulder-crunching welcome. "What's the idea, dragging me off the street?"

"I reserve the right to kidnap you at any time. It was in the small print of your commissioning oath. Have a seat. Let's eat."

General Duncan took the third chair at the table. With the wave of his hand the servant appeared, bringing him an iced tea, followed by a second servant who carried a tray with three plates of food. The plates were covered by the kind of metal lids that were often found on hotel room-service food. The servant set the plates delicately onto the table before each of them and lifted off the metal lids one at a time, revealing a pretty fine meal of beef stroganoff and mixed vegetables.

As the plates arrived, Condley watched the etched face of his longtime friend and then let his eyes drop down to the eight rows of ribbons on Duncan's chest. He was remembering all the months they were together before, when it had been too hot to eat during the day and too dangerous to cook over a little tin stove made of a punctured C-ration can at night. They'd both lost twenty pounds very quickly, even before Condley caught hookworms from the wormy water and lost ten more.

Duncan was a fighter, one of the best company commanders of that long-ago war. And he had been smart enough and smooth enough and lucky enough over the ensuing years to have made it past all the wickets, the little traps in the promotion process where the gunfighters so often fell prey to the shrewdness of accomplished staff officers. Not only to make general officer, but to have commanded a division after that, then a Marine Expeditionary Force, and now all of the Marine Corps forces in the entire Pacific.

"So I can swear in front of your wife?"

Maureen laughed throatily, fully relaxed now that Duncan had arrived. "I taught high school for twenty years, Mr. Condley. I don't think there's much you can do that would surprise me."

"Don't give him a challenge!" roared General Duncan, his face afire with memories. "The boy has a very active imagination. Believe me, Maureen, he could surprise you." He softened, slapping Condley on a shoulder. "It's good to see you, even if I did have to arrest you in order to buy you lunch."

"Nice place you've got here," teased Condley as the servants again disappeared. "Kind of reminds me of *Gone With the Wind*. Do the slaves turn back your bed at night? Leave a little mint on your pillow?"

"Actually the mess attendants are here in your honor," said Duncan dryly. "I fragged them from the flag mess for a VIP lunch."

And finally Condley could hold it back no longer. "Skipper, what do you want? I haven't had food like this in years."

"I want you to enjoy a good meal," said the general. "And we'll talk when we're done."

They had a merry little lunch. Duncan and his wife told Condley all about their three children and where each one of them was working now that they had finished college. They talked about their assignments over the course of Duncan's long career, the tours at the Pentagon and at Camp Lejeune, the years on the NATO staff in Europe, his unaccompanied deployments to Okinawa and the Mediterranean, and his most recent tour back on Okinawa as commanding general. They asked Condley about his lost decades in east Asia, glancing secretly at each other when he tried to make sense of his wanderings and to justify his panorama of bad choices, their faces tight with a pathos that informed him that he had indeed been the subject of many conversations. Brandon Condley, said the general to his wife through the flecking of his eyes and the small lift of their brows, could have been a great one. But he had cared too much, tried too hard, and in the end had lost not only the bubble but his very future.

Sort of like the way I look at Dzung, he decided, not happy with the analogy but accepting that it was probably true.

Finally lunch was over. Maureen stood, her face now warm with what he knew was a fond familiarity and a sweet kind of sadness, and delicately shook his hand.

"Brandon, it's been great to meet you after all these years. Unfortunately, I have an officers' wives' reception that I'm hosting this afternoon, so I need to go."

And then it was just him and Duncan sitting at the little table, chewing on fresh-baked cookies and drinking tea. The general was gathering himself, Condley could tell as he watched Duncan take in a deep, preparatory breath. Then he stood, motioning toward the nearby sitting area.

"Come on over here. I've got something to show you."

As Condley moved to the black, soft-leather sofa, the general walked back to the front entrance and retrieved a manila envelope from where he had left it on a table near the door. Then Duncan eased into a leather chair just next to him, plopping the manila envelope onto the coffee table in front of them.

"I've been following the message traffic on this—what the hell do you call it? It's not a body, and I don't want to just say it's a skeleton, because that sounds like Halloween. The dead guy you found out in Quang Nam Province."

"Why don't we just call him the deserter," said Condley acidly.

"Right," said the general. "How about the *dead* deserter?"

"How about—" Condley was going to trump the general with the perfect epithet for the dead scumbag he had found in Ninh Phuoc, but for some reason he lost interest in the middle of a thought. Who cared? "Never mind. It was a long time ago. And he's dead."

"No," said Duncan. "Let's mind. Why don't we just decide to give a shit for a few minutes here?" The general leaned toward him and took a deep breath, his eyes going wide and hard. "I remember this guy."

"What?"

"I remember him." Now Duncan reached inside the manila envelope and began pulling out several papers.

"So you're the reason we didn't have the file when I was at CILHI this morning."

"I had them bring it to me first," said the general. "Your scientist buddy has the whole file now, but I wanted to burn some copies."

"Isn't this a little below your pay grade, Skipper? Don't you have a Marine Corps to run?"

"This is personal," said Duncan. He measured Condley as he held the papers in his hand. "When I saw the first piece of message traffic it bothered me but I couldn't understand why. I mean, I kept thinking about it, and every time I thought about it I was pissed off. And then I was getting pissed off at myself for being pissed off. I was waking myself up in the middle of the night and then making myself go back to sleep by saying just what you were saying. That it was a long time ago, and besides, he's dead. But after a few days a little light turned on in my brain. Sometimes that happens, you know. We've got so much data stored up there once we reach our age that it takes longer for the computer between our ears to sift through it. I mean, how many gigabytes of garbage does it have to process before it reaches 1969 and then the Que Son Mountains? But finally I started remembering. It was the name. Deville. You don't forget a name like that, not after what he did. Because if you pronounce it a little differently it comes out as 'devil.'"

"I'm not tracking with you," said Condley, mystified by the general's tirade. "I've got no idea what you're talking about."

"He personally killed two of our Marines. I saw him."

The general took an eight-by-ten photograph from the papers and dropped it onto the coffee table. The picture was a standard boot-camp photo from Deville's service record book that had been enlarged and computer-enhanced. A very young Theodore Deville stared stoically back at them. His eyes were fearless, dark and brooding, daring the camera to hit him with its best shot. This was not someone who had come to the Army from the nurturing bosom of Chevy Chase or Beverly Hills.

"June 24, 1969," continued Duncan. "I remember because it was my mother's birthday."

"Salt and Pepper," said Condley quietly, mesmerized by the memory and by the photo itself.

"In this case," said the general, "why don't we just stick with Salt."

Condley sat back in the sofa, stunned into silence. It was washing over him, just as he knew it had chilled General Duncan in the middle of whichever long night the realization had come to him as well. The betrayal he hadn't wanted to believe, much less remember. The nightmare that could be avoided only by constant motion or by going to sleep. The place in his mind where even now he didn't want to go.

The hot, canopied jungle and the parched eyes of his forty-man platoon as it climbed three thousand feet up the steep, rock-strewn slopes, machete-hacking their way through the canopy with sixty pounds of gear on their backs, trying to link up with another Marine company that had been surrounded for three days in the caves and brittle ridges of the mountain's crest. The hand grenades suddenly bouncing down the slopes toward them, a cacophony of terror and blood as dozens of them clicked and careened from rock to rock, exploding at their feet and in the air. Cringing in the cleavage of the rocks to avoid the shrapnel, trying to find a target up the slope to shoot back at. Then seeing two men standing behind a boulder on the crest, no more than fifty feet above them, one black, the other white, both wearing jungle utilities and carrying American M-14 rifles. Condley thinking that he might have read the map wrong, so that his platoon had walked into an outpost from the company they were trying to save. A Marine near Condley thinking the same thing, standing and waving at the two, yelling at them to cease fire, only to be shot immediately by both of them. Both of them. From fifty feet away. No mistake. The Marine crumpling over, dead. And then the whole ridgeline above them opening up with steady fire from a North Vietnamese Army ambush.

A very close, very effective, very bloody ambush.

And later on writing and then trashing the letter that he knew he could never bring himself to mail. *Dear Mrs. Smith. Your son was shot by a white man and a black man who were leading a North Vietnamese unit in an ambush along the crease of two Marine Corps rifle companies in the Que Son Mountains. I am deeply sorry. I don't know who they were. And I cannot think of a more ironic ending to a more ironic war.*

Salt and Pepper. It had not been the first reported incident. They all had heard of these two men before. Some said they were an eastern European and a Cuban, operating as advisers to their North Vietnamese allies. Others said they were American turncoats. Some said there were several such teams. But one thing had become reasonably certain after the ambush of June 24, 1969. This one, this Salt, was American.

"You're sure this is the guy?" asked Condley softly.

"I probably didn't tell you this before," said General Duncan. "There was so much going on, I mean, who has the time to focus on last week or even yesterday when you're getting your ass shot off in combat? But when we rotated out of the mountains back to the regimental rear, the Office of Naval Intelligence sent an investigator out to An Hoa to interview me. I brought in a machine gunner from second platoon who had shot the white guy in the leg from a ridgeline on your right, maybe thirty feet away. We set up a little interview room in the company office. The ONI guy had a book of missing American servicemen. It was all very official. The ONI guy swore the gunner in and interviewed him, and then he walked him through the picture book. When he flipped over the page to where Deville's picture was, the gunner damn near shit in his mess gear. 'Him!' he said. 'Are you positive,' says the ONI guy. 'This is a very serious charge.' And my guy says, 'Positive. I'll never forget the motherfucker's face as long as I live.'

"We wrote up a statement." General Duncan dropped another paper onto the table. It was a photocopy of a faded hand-typed statement. "So when I saw the name in the message traffic the other day, I finally knew for sure that the gunner had been right. I had them pull this out of the ONI archives too, just in case somebody would think I was losing the bubble and fantasizing. It's the report from An Hoa."

Condley quickly read the paper, in which one Corporal Dustin Richards on 1 July, 1969, had identified the white turncoat in the incident of 24 June, 1969, as Specialist Theodore Deville, absent without leave 5 September, 1967, declared a deserter 5 December, 1967, whereabouts unknown.

"So where's Pepper?" asked Condley, working to regain his offhand cynicism. "I remember him."

"Let's just focus on Salt here for a minute," said Duncan. "How are we going to report finding this guy to the media? We can't say he was an MIA, because he's never been on any list of those reported missing. I suppose we could just say he's a deserter and let it go at that, but then are we doing our duty? On the other hand, if we make the allegation that he was a turncoat, can we really back it up? If we try and then fall on our asses, how stupid will we look? We'll be accused by the media of being vindictive, opening up an old war wound without justification. And what about his family? And even more important, if we start refighting the war, dwelling on the past, what's going to happen with the cooperation of the Vietnamese government on future digs?"

"What about the two dead Marines?"

"Well, what about them?" replied the general. "I've thought about that. Is it going to do their memories any good by announcing all these years later that they were killed by American deserters? At least now their families can have a clean picture of what it was like for them to die. Fighting the enemy is heroic. Getting shot by a turncoat is sickening. And think of the negative way so many Americans look at the guys who fought in Viet Nam anyway. Great story, huh? Americans shooting other Americans in Viet Nam, as if it wasn't enough that Americans were rubbing their own soldiers' faces in shit when they got home."

Finally Duncan threw his hands up in the air, leaning back against his chair. "Look, I'm not trying to put this all back in a box. If I were, I wouldn't have asked for the file in the first place. I want to do the right thing. But I just don't know what the right thing is. We need to think this through. That's why I had them run you down and bring you here to my house."

"So what do you want me to do, Skipper?"

"Take that asshole back to Ninh Phuoc and bury him again." The general slowly smiled. "Just kidding."

Duncan stood and began pacing, his hands clasped behind his back and his face lowered in thought. "You're a shit magnet, you know that, Condley? It was the same in combat. Some other platoon commanders could take your same patrol route and come back without a shot being fired. But you, no. You've got to go find the assholes, even if it means digging them out of bunkers, rooting them out from whatever rice paddy dike they've decided to hide behind, shaking them out of the fucking trees. You find shit, and shit finds you."

Condley grinned, deciding to take Duncan's blustering as a compliment. "Actually, sir, I've always sort of looked upon myself as the ultimate agent of truth. Kind of like Don Quixote. I was blessed with a natural curiosity. I like to think that I find shit because it's supposed to be found. If you want to find it, send me in. If you don't want to find it, send somebody else."

"Life's that fucking simple, huh?" said General Duncan, still pacing. "That's easy for you to say, because you don't have to make the hard decisions."

"What's so hard about this?"

"I doubt you even see the problem."

"Actually, I don't see the problem," said Condley. "We shot the fucker in 1969 but he got away. Somebody else shot him in 1971 and hit the bull's-eye. A nice, happy ending. All the rest is somebody's mill drill, except now you're a fucking general and you've had your lobotomy, so you're thinking like a politician."

Duncan stopped pacing and turned on him. His face was growing red with a gathering fury, as if he were going to attack Condley right where he sat. Despite himself, Condley squirmed on the couch. He respected Wayne Duncan more than anyone on earth, and he knew that at some level the feeling was mutual. Fighting Duncan would be interesting, he thought, but also pretty depressing.

And then the general started to laugh. He walked to the couch and slapped Condley on the shoulder, an act of forgiveness. "I needed to hear somebody tell me that," he said. "That's why I had them go get you. You're right. The truth is its own liberation. We tell it straight. Let the bow-ties in the Pentagon sort it out."

Condley wasn't laughing, though. He was thinking about what Duncan had just said about him, because it also was the truth. He'd been a shit magnet for thirty years. He had a nose for it, and it wasn't ever going to stop.

"So what about Pepper, Skipper?"

"What about him?"

"Do you still give a damn or not?"

General Duncan stood above him, looking down and shaking his head with a mix of admiration and dread. "What's on your mind, Condley?"

"I don't know yet."

"All right," said the general. "All right, all right. Look, I'm not your boss on this. And running down turncoats isn't in your job description anyway."

"It would give me great pleasure to find him, though."

General Duncan shook his head and smiled. Part of his smile was admiration, and part of it was whimsical, even nostalgic. "I think I just created a monster."

"No, sir," said Condley. "You did that in 1969."

CHAPTER EIGHT

"WE HAVE A problem," growled a visibly irritated Hanson Muir as Condley walked into his office at the CILHI headquarters.

Muir's office reminded Condley of an ill-kept attic in a very old house. The rotund professor sat like a lost child behind a huge oak desk that was covered with a mass of unorganized papers. In fact, his entire office was littered with papers. Professional periodicals were piled like plates in several corners of the room, having been collected over the years but never shelved. Newspaper editions that had run favorite articles were stacked near one chair. The chair itself was littered with copies of other articles. The professor's shelves were cluttered as well, a disorganized array of fossils, rocks, old pieces of wood, Asian cultural souvenirs, and dozens of pictures, mostly of his family and of himself on various digs.

And besides that, he was wearing a trippy, multicolored luau shirt. "What tourist from Indiana did you have to mug so you could steal that shirt, Professor?" asked Condley, taking a seat on top of the copied pages.

"My wife bought it for me. It was an anniversary present."

"Does she hate you that much?"

"She bought me two. And as a matter of fact she is from Indiana and you know it. So what's your point?"

"What did you give her, a free ticket to a Don Ho concert?"

"You know, Brandon, I've decided that you're some kind of a low-end elitist. I happen to like Don Ho. And at least I have a wife."

Condley threw both of his hands up into the air in mock surrender. "Whooee. Low-end elitist, I like that. And no wife to buy me luau shirts. Boy, you've got me there."

"I said we've got a problem, Brandon."

"I know," said Condley. "I just spent the afternoon with General Duncan. He had your files."

"I know he had the files. But I have them now. And you don't know the half of it." Muir was fingering an old, thick folder that Condley immediately recognized as someone's military file.

"I know our boy Deville was more than a deserter," said Condley. "That he might have been a turncoat."

"Definitely a turncoat, in my opinion." Muir was flipping through the pages of the military folder, looking for a marked page. "And a murderer." Muir glanced over at Condley. "Do you remember when I told you that he was wanted for killing a fellow soldier in Long Binh? The man who was going to testify against him in his court-martial?" Muir found the page. "Well, guess what. After he killed the man he cut off his hand."

"Pretty sick."

"Yes," said Muir. "Pretty sick."

"And then somebody cut off Deville's hand," said Condley. "Were they wearing black raincoats back then? Was this an initiation into some secret Gothic society?"

"Actually," said Muir, "somebody didn't cut off Deville's hand."

"You said he didn't have a hand."

"I said the remains we recovered didn't have a hand."

Muir held Condley's gaze for several seconds as the reality of what he had just said sank in. Finally Condley whistled softly, shaking his head. "I guess you're right. I don't know shit."

"You know *some* information about Specialist Deville," corrected the burly professor. "But you don't know very much at all about the remains we recovered in Ninh Phuoc."

"Are you positive?"

Muir gave Condley a look of mild exasperation. "Brandon, I am a scientist. Certain areas of anthropology are exact. Which is to say that yes, to the extent that medical records are accurate, I am positive. The remains that we have in the lab are not those of Theodore Deville."

Muir rose from his swivel chair and picked up the military file from his desk. "Let me show you what I mean."

In minutes the two were standing in the lab, next to the gurney that held the remains of the body they had brought back from Ninh Phuoc. Muir was coolly clinical now, in his element as he compared the information in Specialist Deville's medical files with the specimen on the gurney.

"First and foremost, we have the teeth. In a properly matched set of remains, they are as conclusive as fingerprints on a dead body. We are lucky in this case to have a full set of the . . ." Muir hesitated for a moment. "What are we going to call this man now? We don't have a name or a circumstance."

"Try 'victim,' Professor."

"Definitely the victim," said Muir. "The severed hand indicates that he was very likely murdered. So. We have a full set of the victim's teeth. And we also have Specialist Deville's dental file."

Muir took out a small metal pointer from his shirt pocket, expanding it like a car antenna, then opened the dental file to where it displayed a chart of Deville's teeth. As he spoke, he used the pointer to compare the file with the victim's skull. "Deville had fillings on eight teeth. Here, here, here, and all along here. The victim had only three fillings. Look here. And on those teeth, there are no markings in Deville's dental file. See? End of story. Case closed. The only reason to pursue it further is in the event, by some incredible accident, we have the wrong dental file. Probability, far less than one percent. But just to be sure, I looked at the medical side."

Muir flipped a few pages in the folder, then again held it near the victim's remains. "Deville fractured his left femur in a motorcycle accident when he was a teenager." The pointer went to the victim's left femur. "You'd be able to see the imprint of that fracture on the bone. Nothing here. And actually this man—this victim—is from my calculations about two inches shorter than Deville. Again, case closed. This is not Deville."

"You're sure you have the right file, Professor?"

"His name is all over it, on every page. There's no mistake here. And think about the hand, Brandon. Could the amputation of two hands be an accident? It's what we like to call a signature. And you know whose signature it is. I'm telling you, these remains are not Deville."

"So the only thing that matches is the dog tags."

"That's it," said the professor. "So ask yourself. Why would Specialist Deville kill this man and leave him behind wearing his own dog tags?"

"Because he wanted whoever found the body to think that he was dead."

"Exactly. And why would he want us to think that?"

"Because he wanted out," said Condley. It all made perfect sense now. "He deserted because he wanted to avoid a court-martial. But he didn't want to stay in Viet Nam no matter what the hell he was doing up there in the Que Son Mountains. And how do you get out of Viet Nam when you're a deserter, when there's a war on, and the American military controls all the flights? You can't be Specialist Theodore Deville. You have to be somebody else."

"Somebody they're going to allow onto an airplane," said Muir.

"He killed the guy, figuring the body would be so decomposed by the time they found it that they would assume it was him, and then stole the man's identity," said Condley.

For the first time in a long time Condley felt genuinely spooked as he looked down at the skeleton on the gurney. The dirt of Ninh Phuoc, crusting the sheets of a lab in Hawaii. The moldy old poncho, like a memento that had crossed a time warp. The sand-blanched, copper-colored bones. The skull without a face. The teeth that did not match. The leg that had never been broken. The hand that was not there. The name they did not know, stolen along with his life by a man who was nothing if not ruthlessly audacious.

"Who is he? Excuse me, Professor, I'm sounding like you. Who *was* he? And how the hell did Deville find him up in the Que Son Mountains, in the village of Ninh Phuoc?"

"Better yet," said Muir, "where's Deville?"

"Well, okay. Both."

"Right," said Muir. "Both."

Condley could not help but notice that the normally emotional scientist had become coolly clinical, at the very moment that he himself was trembling with an anger that he found difficult to control. Deville's treachery and savagery had awakened an animal inside him that he thought had died a quarter century before. A blood lust was rising in him that he knew would not be quenched unless he found Deville. He realized that, oddly, he was prepared to risk everything, and even to die, in order to bring Deville to justice. Not that he planned to die.

"He's still alive, Professor. I can feel it."

"We have some avenues of approach," said Muir. "On both counts, actually. I've asked that the FBI do a nationwide fingerprint search on Deville. If he's been involved in any activity in the United States that requires a fingerprint, no matter what false identity he's using, they'll be able to start running him down, or possibly already have. I'm not optimistic on that count, but it's a start. Within the next few days we'll also have a computer-imaged photo that will show what Deville should look like today. We'll get that out to the right people. With respect to our unfortunate friend here, I'm pulling in all the files of those still listed either as missing in action or as deserters inside Viet Nam. A whole new category, that. I hadn't thought much about the deserters before. And we've got a few things to work with in order to narrow down our search."

Muir took out his pointer again, his manner indeed professorial, and began touching the remains as he spoke. "Brown hair—a few tufts were still inside the poncho. Definitely Caucasian, from the cheekbones and the set of the jaw. He was, I'd say, about five foot nine inches tall. Clear indications of a damaged right shoulder, probably from repeated trauma. And look at this . . ." Muir touched the skeleton at the very top of the spinal column, where the neck met the skull. "See how worn this vertebra is?"

"I'll take your word for it."

"No, look right here. See? It's a bit shiny, as if it's gone through a good bit of trauma. Possibly a bad car accident, but my guess is that he was an athlete who played hard at contact sports that repeatedly caused blows to the head. Boxing, perhaps, given his size. The damaged shoulder would go with that diagnosis. There's also some formative arthritis on the upper vertebrae, which is unusual for a younger man and would confirm that suspicion. And look at these ridges on his teeth." Muir's pointer ran along the molars at the back of the skull.

"Yeah," said Condley, seething. "Just look at that."

"They're worn far beyond what one might expect in a young man. This suggests a coarse diet, of the sort that might be found more often in rural America. Appalachia, perhaps."

Muir ceremoniously closed the pointer. "We'll find him."

"You mean you'll find out who he was," corrected Condley. "Then find out what the fuck he was doing in the Que Son Mountains. And while you're doing that I'll find Deville."

"How do you propose to do that, Brandon?"

"I don't know yet." A thought crossed his mind. "Maybe if we find out about this guy it will lead us to Deville. Especially if we can find out what they were doing together. Who knows, maybe he was a turncoat too."

"Possibly," mused Muir. "But logic tells me that he wasn't. Why switch places with someone just as bad off as you are?"

"You're right." Condley looked at the man's remains with a renewed sobriety. "If we knew where they met, or what they were doing, maybe there's an intersection that can help us backtrack to Deville. He did steal the guy's identity."

"For a while, possibly. But if he were smart enough to steal this man's identity, you can assume that Deville was also smart enough to take on a new one as soon as he escaped."

Condley marveled at the scientist's demeanor as they walked back toward his office. "Why are you so calm about all this, Professor?"

"Because it's all come down to science, Brandon. We have our variables. We have computers. We have good people working on the problem. It gives the whole issue the kind of certainty that I enjoy."

"It may be science to you—"

"I know," interrupted the huge, garrulous Muir. He patted Condley on the shoulder as they walked. "For you it's personal. So may I remind you as your friend? Don't let your emotions get the better of you, Brandon. If you do find this man, you can't afford to make a mistake."

"Them," corrected Condley.

"Them? I don't understand what you mean."

"There's two of them."

CHAPTER NINE

Sai Gon

THE NOONDAY SUN faded quickly, disappearing behind a bank of ugly gray clouds. An eerie darkness covered the city, as sudden as an eclipse. And then the sky opened up with a windless torrent of rain.

In front of the Rex Hotel the sidewalks emptied in a matter of seconds as hustlers, hawkers, and beggars scurried into covered alleyways or huddled under tarps, while tourists headed into street cafés or back to their hotels. Along the streets the *cyclo* drivers pulled poncholike rain jackets over their heads and buttoned up their passengers inside windowless canvas flaps. The covered *cyclos* looked like dark, oversize baby buggies as they navigated through puddles and avoided the splashing traffic of cars and motorbikes.

A few blocks away, across the street from the shabby little Vien Dong Hotel, Dzung sat in his own *cyclo* cab underneath a large shade tree. He had pulled the canopy around the cab and snapped himself inside as soon as it had started raining. His knees were up to his chin to avoid the torrent. His eyes were faraway. The rain pattered all around him, cold on the canvas of the canopy.

Trapped in his little bubble, Dzung felt strangely free. He thought for a long time about the way the rain had smelled, musty and alive, where it mixed with the river behind the porch of his childhood home, and then of the young foreigner who yesterday rode with him for an hour and did not pay him, and finally of how every day his smallest child faded further from him, slowly, slowly dying. But he could change none of these things. So mostly he thought of how pure and safe he felt inside the canopy as the rain washed over and around him.

Cong Ly was back. A taxi had taken him to the hotel from Tan Son Nhat airport late last night. The word had gotten out on the street early that morning, passed along among the hustlers and *cyclo* drivers, letting Dzung know that his well-paying friend was once again in Sai Gon. And so Dzung had posted himself across from Condley's hotel three hours before, on duty just as surely as if he were standing watch in a foxhole during the war.

Finally the rain left the city, with the same suddenness that had marked its arrival. The sky brightened and the sun began to bake the streets. The cars and motorbikes drove endlessly by, splashing through fresh puddles. The hustlers and the hawkers emerged from their hide-outs, calling and laughing to one another, comparing how deeply they had been soaked. Dzung unbuttoned his canopy and folded it back as if emerging from a cocoon. Then he sat again on the seat and lit a cigarette, silently watching and waiting.

In a few minutes he saw a small commotion at the hotel's front door. It was Condley, joking playfully with the doorman. Dzung brightened, tossing away his cigarette and jumping down from his perch on the *cyclo*. He waved happily, with the bright face of a small child.

"Cong Ly! Cong Ly!"

"Hey, Dzung! *Manh khoe khong?*"

"*Da, khoe! Khoe!*" said Dzung, letting Condley know that things were fine. For otherwise, where would one begin?

Condley crossed the street, shaking his hand and slapping him on a narrowing shoulder. Dzung reversed the seat on his *cyclo*, patting it to indicate that it was dry, and gestured for Condley to climb aboard.

"Where we go today, Cong Ly?"

"I have to take a taxi." Dzung's face fell noticeably, as if he had just been fired. "Only for a little while," said Condley. "I have to go to Thu Duc. Too far for you!"

"I can take you to Thu Duc!"

"No, on your *cyclo* that would take at least an hour each way. I need to be there very soon."

Dzung nodded, accepting the limitations of his *cyclo*. "Why you go Thu Duc, Cong Ly?"

"I go to the golf course at Binh Trieu."

Dzung started laughing. "Binh Trieu golf course no good, Cong Ly, you know that."

The Binh Trieu golf course was a well-known joke in Sai Gon. Just across the Sai Gon River in the district of Thu Duc, a Taiwanese consortium had built two large golf courses, replete with upscale clubhouses. Since almost no Vietnamese could afford equipment, club dues, or fairway fees, the logic behind the investment had centered on providing recreation for foreigners, particularly the Japanese, whose passion for the sport, they had reasoned, would bring in loads of tourists. But few Japanese traveled to Viet Nam on pleasure rather than business, and golf, for all its usual seductiveness, was not going to lure them, at least not in Sai Gon. The cool, mountainous area around Da Lat, perhaps. But Sai Gon's weather, which cycled between an unbearable oven heat and torrential rains, was not a fit for those who wished to spend three hours outdoors hitting little white balls along alternately parched or soaked fairways.

The business had failed. The Taiwanese company had departed, leaving the golf course and its facilities to its Vietnamese partner, which was in reality an umbrella company run by the government. And these days, as it rather forlornly awaited the prospect of a new investor, the government kept the golf course and its clubhouse open for the use of its higher-ranking officials.

"I don't play golf," said Condley. "This is business."

"You meet Colonel Pham there. I know, I know." Dzung started laughing again. "He stupid, walking outside all day in the sun!"

"He thinks it's fun," said Condley.

"That's why he is stupid. You know, Cong Ly, sometimes I don't understand, so please tell me again. How did the VC win the war?"

Condley grinned. It was an old joke, more true than either of them really would like to admit. "They didn't understand that they were beaten."

Across the street the doorman waved at Condley, holding open the door to a waiting taxi. Condley nudged Dzung again as he headed back toward the hotel. "Maybe three hours, okay?"

"*Ba tieng dong ho,*" agreed Dzung, reluctantly walking back underneath the shade tree and again climbing onto the seat of his *cyclo*.

VIET NAM'S SCORCHING heat, sudden rains, and mosquito-infested wetlands did not make it an ideal place to play golf, but you could never explain that to Colonel Pham. No one used the Binh Trieu golf course more regularly than Pham. The former Viet Cong officer had developed an intense passion for the sport that matched his former enthusiasm for soldiering. Hardly a day passed without the colonel having played at least nine holes. He played in all but the heaviest of rains. He played in even the worst heat.

In reality he was terrible at the game, except for a dead-eye ability to putt. But a thrill glazed the colonel's eyes every time he talked of golf. Secretly, Brandon Condley believed that golf was the metaphor for much of what Colonel Pham had fought for, or maybe merely against. For as he traipsed carefree and timeless along the fairways, the former Viet Cong soldier could imagine that he was part of a larger world. A world where people whiled away the hours in idleness and had no need for toil. Where smacking a silly little ball and having drinks on a terrace afterward while watching a satellite TV channel was evidence that he had risen above the beggars and the toilers. Where—yes, it was true—he had a bit of payback, a taste of the life of those playboy capitalists he had spent so many years trying to kill.

Condley had an ulterior motive in meeting the colonel at the golf course instead of in his office. Certain discussions were permissible in Pham's office, and others were dangerous, no matter how innocently begun. Talking in the office about policies that already existed was safe. Asking questions in the presence of other, ever-listening ears about matters that had happened in the past, and particularly policies that had existed before the fall of South Viet Nam in 1975, was an application for reprisal.

The colonel was on the fifth hole, almost alone on the course as he readied to tee off in the boiling sun. He was wearing tan slacks, a patterned golf shirt, and white athletic shoes. On his head, incongruously, was a green

North Vietnamese Army pith helmet. As Condley approached, Colonel Pham waved casually to him, then took his shot. The ball arched lazily for a while, then landed in a puddle about seventy yards down the middle of the fairway. Its location seemed to please Pham greatly. He smiled as the ball rolled a few more feet, holding on to the top of his pith helmet with one hand and urging the ball forward with a little body English. Then he sighed, putting his three wood inside his golf bag and slinging it over a shoulder.

"Nice shot, Colonel," said Condley in Vietnamese. He was already sweating profusely as he reached Pham. They shook hands briefly, then the colonel set off down the fairway toward his ball.

The colonel was into his game, staring intently down the flat, straight fairway that only a few years before had been a rice paddy. "What club do you think I should use?"

"I've got no idea," answered Condley, walking alongside him. "I've never played a game of golf in my life."

"I thought everyone in America likes golf."

"No, sir. Some do, some don't. If I was going to waste three hours I'd rather just go fishing."

"Fishing!" laughed Colonel Pham. "In Viet Nam the women go fishing."

"I'll take a woman fishing any day of the week," grinned Condley. "As long as she makes my lunch and baits my hooks."

"But you told me your ancestors are from Scotland." One of the colonel's greatest fascinations, now that he had come to know his former enemy, was that almost all Americans could trace their ancestry to another country.

They began to cross a puddle on the fairway that was the size of a basketball court, compliments of the earlier rain shower. Condley's head was baking through his baseball cap and his shoes were thoroughly soaked, but still the colonel plodded on. In the middle of the puddle Condley could see the colonel's golf ball. "There's your ball, Colonel. Yes, you're right. My ancestors were from Scotland and Ireland, mostly."

Colonel Pham's face took on a new excitement. "But you see, golf was invented in Scotland. It is their national sport, so you should love it!"

"For some it is." Condley smiled as they reached the ball. "But for my people golf is a diversion. Fighting is their national sport. It's our tradition, even in America. We call it 'the redneck way.' "

"Redneck?" The colonel seemed confused.

"Red. Neck." Condley pointed to the back of his neck. "It's our culture. The Scots–Irish in America. Because we work with our hands, the upper classes always looked down on us. They call us rednecks because our necks get red working in the sun. And fighting is our sport. Not golf."

"Boxing?"

"Not all the time. Sometimes just fighting." Condley shrugged slyly. "Any kind of fighting. Fighting in a war, fighting in a bar, fighting with your friend, fighting with your boss, fighting with your wife."

"So you are like the Vietnamese," said the colonel. "Golf and fighting, very good!" They both laughed. He was standing over his ball now, trying to figure out which club to use. Condley's comments had amused him greatly. He loved to hear stories about America, and Condley knew that later on he would retell them to his associates, probably with great embellishment.

"So, I think the three iron," decided Colonel Pham.

"I don't even know what a three iron is. If it was up to me I'd put that ball in my pocket and walk it all the way to the clubhouse."

The colonel pulled out a three iron and took a mighty swing. The club splashed in the water just before it hit the ball, taking away the power of the swing, and the ball rolled forward another fifty yards or so. Pham swore under his breath, putting the club back into his golf bag, and marched forward yet again. Following him, Condley secretly checked his watch.

The colonel caught his gesture and smiled. "You are in a hurry?"

"Colonel, you are my trusted colleague, so I will tell you the truth. You are a very slow golf player. Very dedicated, but very slow."

"Then it is time for me to take a break, yes?" Colonel Pham stopped walking, giving Condley a quick, knowing look and then reaching inside his golf bag for his liter of bottled water. "You're just back from Hawaii? You have some good news, I hope?"

"Well, not exactly."

"So that's why you found me here instead of in my office."

They traded wry grins that were so similar one might have thought they were brain twins. Both of them possessed razorlike intuitive skills that had been fiercely honed on the kind of battlefield where detecting a bent grass blade or a broken tree branch was often the difference between living and dying. That they had been on opposite sides only sharpened their ability to read each other's intentions. So there was little room for hypocrisy or cant between them.

"There are very few places to speak privately in Viet Nam," said Condley.

"A golf course on a hot day," laughed Colonel Pham.

"I have a sensitive matter, on which I would like to ask your advice."

"So, he was not a battlefield casualty," said the colonel, studying Condley's face for further clues. "Or you would be very happy to report the identification of his remains."

"We don't even know that much," said Condley, choosing his words carefully. "We still don't know who he was. But we are trying to solve a curious mystery. All we know for sure is that he was wearing the dog tags of another man when he was found."

"Maybe they were going steady," teased the colonel. "Don't they trade rings and necklaces in America?"

"Actually I was thinking they might have had a mix-up getting dressed in the dark," answered Condley dryly.

"You were a good soldier," said Pham, laughing. "You know how to fight without getting mad." He took a long pull from his bottle of water, pleased that he knew enough about Americans to have made his little joke. "Why do men wear necklaces and earrings in your country, Mister Condley? It reflects a certain insecurity, I think."

"Freedom, Colonel."

"Freedom? What do you mean?"

"Like playing golf in the rain."

Colonel Pham tilted back his pith helmet, nodding his head with appreciation. "Doing foolish things that make you happy."

"If you want to."

"Choosing to be foolish. So that is your definition of freedom."

"No, it is one aspect of it."

"You always talk in circles," announced the colonel, indicating that their frivolities were done. "In your last life I think you were a politician. What can you tell me about these bones?"

"We don't know about the bones, but our scientists will soon find out. The dog tags belong to a soldier who was a murderer and a deserter,

Colonel. And there's another problem. We have evidence that he was fighting for your side."

The colonel watched him carefully. "Half of your country was fighting for our side," he said, delighting in another minor provocation.

"Not by killing our Marines."

For the first time Colonel Pham lost his jaunty air. "You are sure?"

"We are positive."

"Is he still alive?"

"We don't know yet. I think he is, though. He apparently killed this man in order to take his identity. He was hoping the body would be found and the Americans would assume he was dead, so they would stop looking for him. But the war ended, and they didn't find the body either. We don't know where he went. If he's still alive he could be living anywhere. Even here."

Condley took out an envelope from his trouser pocket and handed it to Colonel Pham. "We are not talking about this publicly. We are not looking for a confrontation with the Vietnamese government. But we intend to find him. His personal information is inside this envelope. Maybe you can bring me some news about . . . how he helped your government and if they know where he went."

"This will be difficult," said the colonel, choosing his own words very carefully. "I know of no such cases."

"That's why I came here to see you. I must ask you personally, because I am confused. Can you tell me what usually happened to the Americans who fought for your side after the war ended?"

"I know of no such Americans." Colonel Pham had stiffened into an abrupt formality. Condley sensed that his posture was driven more by bureaucratic fear than any sort of anger. "Mister Condley, I must remind you that it is the position of our government that there are no Americans from the war who are still alive in Viet Nam."

"I'm only asking for your advice, Colonel. The question is for my personal education." Condley studied the colonel's face carefully, looking for clues. "And I have another question, because my memory troubles me. When I left Viet Nam at the end of the war, there were a few thousand American deserters living in Sai Gon and another five hundred or so living in Da Nang. Can you help me discover what happened to them?"

Colonel Pham lifted his chin, his face becoming intransigent. "As you know, I spent the war in the mountains. I know nothing of what happened here in the city during those times. But there were no living Americans in Ho Chi Minh City at the end of the war! I am sure of this!"

"All of them got out before your side took over? Every one of them? Where would they have gone so quickly?" Condley sensed the hopelessness of pursuing the matter further, at least at that moment. "Excuse me, Colonel, you are an honest man and I am not questioning your word. I am merely trying to think through this problem, so that I can advise my government."

A small smile crept onto Colonel Pham's face. A negotiation that could cause both of them serious trouble was taking place behind their friendly banter. Pham was wordlessly thanking Condley for not pursuing the matter to the point where either of them would lose face. "I have no idea who was in Ho Chi Minh City before April 30, 1975, but I have had many discussions inside our government since I started working on the issue of Americans who remain missing in action. I can tell you that there has never been a report of Americans anywhere in Viet Nam from that date forward, Mister Condley. So we must help your government solve the problem in a more constructive manner."

"Except for Garwood."

The name of a famous turncoat deserter hung between them like a bad dream that would not die. Garwood, a former Marine who had aided the enemy, had suddenly surfaced in Viet Nam several years after the war, asking to go home. Watching Pham's face, Condley knew that he had subtly trapped the colonel. Pham had two choices. He could either take the bait and admit that others might have remained in Viet Nam, which was most likely the truth, or seize upon Condley's offhand statement to end the discussion.

"You are right," said the colonel. "Except for Garwood. A very strange man, Garwood. We did not know what to do with him because for a long time he did not want to leave."

"And the others?"

"What about the others?"

"They wanted to leave?"

"There were no others, Mister Condley."

Pham took another drink and then put away his bottle of water. He was thinking, avoiding Condley's waiting gaze, his eyes searching forward to where the ball had landed a few minutes before. Finally he nodded, as if agreeing with some unknown counselor. "All right, I will be honest with you, because after many years of working with you I trust you. I know what I am supposed to say, but in reality I do not know the answer to these questions. I will try to help you. I will ask the question inside my government." He turned to Condley now. "But please understand, it must be approached very carefully."

"Thank you, Colonel. We don't want an incident, but I have a duty to investigate the matter."

"Carefully, Mister Condley."

"Carefully. But thoroughly."

"I will do my best. You know that."

"You have always helped me more than I deserve, Colonel. That I know."

Colonel Pham regained his smile, satisfied that he and Condley had recovered their normal rapport. "My wife is waiting for you. She was very moved by your offer to go to temple."

Condley smiled graciously, knowing that the colonel's invitation was an indication that their relationship had not been hurt by his questions. "I would be happy to pray with her at any time."

"Then you can come to our house later this afternoon?"

"It would be my honor."

"Van will be there." Colonel Pham searched Condley's face expertly as he made his announcement and found exactly what he had been looking for. "She liked you very much."

"She is a very beautiful woman."

"Her French friend Mr. Petain hates you."

"Then he should learn to control his emotions."

The colonel laughed at that. "Yes," he said, with an irony that informed Condley they shared the same view of Petain. "One should never waste his emotions in Asia, should he?"

"What else is left for the French in Asia besides emotions?" Condley checked his watch. "May I come at five o'clock?"

"My daughter is very spoiled, you know."

"Beautiful women deserve to be spoiled, Colonel."

"In your country, perhaps."

"It's the freedom thing again."

"Perhaps, but you said freedom is for being foolish. She's not foolish. Only spoiled."

"Yes, but I think she is beautiful enough to make other people do foolish things."

The colonel laughed, scrutinizing Condley's face once more. Again seeing what he wanted to find, he gave Condley a small wave and took out another iron. "I have to finish my game. See you at five o'clock!"

CHAPTER TEN

DZUNG SAT FORLORNLY in his *cyclo*, smoking cigarette after cigarette and reading through that day's edition of the popular newspaper *Tuoi Tre*. Every now and then he would glance up at the midday traffic, looking for the meter taxi that would announce Condley's return from Thu Duc. Having been starved for information during the years in the reeducation camps and the other years of near-total news blackouts, Dzung was an avid, even voracious reader. And being the product of a culture that had endured centuries of dominance and hidden resistance, like most Vietnamese he found great pleasure in looking past the surface of each story to guess which reality was being contorted for the benefit of the governing powers. Reading what was said, Dzung was very good at knowing what was not being said. And as always he felt a huge lament that he could not find a way to tell the communists how to fix the country's problems. For even on this isolated Dong Du Street sidewalk, Dzung knew how and where they could be finding answers.

But I am *gia*, he thought again. An old Viet Nam Cong Hoa soldier, never to be listened to or trusted.

A half block away, a muscled but toothless vendor named Truong had set up two vertical stalls filled with maps and books and T-shirts and was awaiting the tourists who might pass him on an afternoon stroll. On Dzung's other side, amid the garbage and the muck from that morning's rain, a sad and shriveled old woman who still refused to tell him her name was peddling rice cakes and just-warmed noodles to a stream of hungry street people. A cat continually licked the old woman's feet. Two puppies she was fattening for sale devoured leftovers that she dumped in puddles just off the curb.

Gloom covered Dzung's face. He had been waiting for Condley all day, and his thoughts were overwhelming him. He studied his own bare feet, impervious to the usual array of hustlers and cretins as they came and went. Hai, the one-armed, one-eyed beggar, walked up, pulling briefly at Dzung's sleeve, hoping for a few hundred *dong* for lunch. Hai had stepped on a mine as a communist soldier in Cambodia in 1985 but begged from western tourists by telling them he had been blown up in "America's" war. Dzung ignored Hai, who quickly moved down the street toward other targets.

Others flitted past Dzung, carrying out their daily routines. Old Ba Thuc, shriveled and hunchbacked, nodded as she shuffled silently by, sweeping last night's trash from the damp and treacly gutter with a waist-high, loose-bristled broom. Two tough street urchins pulled a flatbed wagon along the broken sidewalk, heading for the fertile begging grounds at the intersection of Le Loi and Nguyen Hue Streets. Their rented passenger was a hapless quadriplegic lying facedown on the wagon's boards, his bone-thin arms and legs twisted behind him like pretzels. Delicate, moon-eyed little Ahn, sent onto the street every afternoon by her mother with a ream of no-win lottery tickets and a book of worthless stamps, tried to tease him out of his misery. Then, when he did not respond, the angel-faced child cursed him fluently for half a block as she retreated.

But Dzung did not care. He was sad, afraid, portentous, living under a pall. The cars and motorbikes drove by, their noxious fumes wafting over him. To Dzung, the gasoline odors smelled like money, opportunity, even freedom. Condley was at Thu Duc in a car. He knew that the American rode on his *cyclo* purely out of loyalty, that if it had not been for their friendship Condley would be driving himself in a car or on a motorbike while in Sai Gon. True, Dzung was just as loyal, looking after

Condley and always listening among the gossipmongers on the street for news that might affect his friend's fortunes. But for some reason, he felt a change coming. Condley would not ride like this forever. And without Condley's generous salary of ten dollars a day, his life might become impossible.

And there was another problem that would not go away. Slowly, as if exploring, Dzung put a hand at the center of his chest and felt his heart beating. Then he tried to imagine what it would be like if his heart suddenly stopped, forever. Would his baby know when that happened? Would he panic in his mind, even though he could not move? Or would it be a merciful and swift deliverance?

He had no right to question fate. These things happened. He had been a good son, a good husband, and a good father, so it could not be a punishment. And it did no good to grow bitter over that which one could not control. But what would be so terrible if the great god Chua, or his messenger the temple-master Phat, granted the little boy a reprieve?

Finally the meter taxi arrived, dropping Condley off in front of the Vien Dong Hotel. An energy lifted the American's face as he paid the taxi driver and headed across the street toward Dzung. It was the energy that had caused Dzung to worry. All the years before, Condley had seemed much like Dzung himself: lost and poetic, living neither in the past nor the future, skimming by on the raw power of Sai Gon's daily roar. Condley had been along for the ride, here because there was no better place to go. But in all that time he had gone into nothing too deeply. There had been women, but never for longer than a few days. There had been friends, but none with whom he shared even the emotions of the past. Other than Dzung himself.

Something had happened. Perhaps in Da Nang. Perhaps in the Kieu Hoa restaurant the week before. Perhaps back in Hawaii. But Condley had gone through a subtle change, and with his piercing insight Dzung felt that his friend was slowly drifting away.

As always, Dzung jumped down from his *cyclo* and waved happily to Condley. "Where we go, Cong Ly?"

Condley pointed toward the hotel. An excitement lifted his voice. "I'll come back in one hour. Then we go to Colonel Pham's house."

"We go his house?" Dzung tried to hide his amazement.

"One hour!"

"You never go his house, Cong Ly. He VC."

"He's a good VC, Dzung."

"There no good VC. VC no good, Cong Ly, you know that."

Condley stopped for a moment, making himself focus in on the confused and increasingly stubborn face of his longtime friend. Finally he patted Dzung on a shoulder. "Dzung. This is very important to me. I'm your friend. Trust me."

Dzung held Condley's eyes for several seconds, then regained a weaker version of his normal smile. "I am old Cong Hoa soldier, Cong Ly. We always trust the Americans, even in 1975. You know that."

It was a bitter shot, and Condley knew it as he watched Dzung walk back across the street toward his *cyclo*. And both of them were still stinging from it when he returned an hour later.

———

DZUNG PEDALED CONDLEY up Hai Ba Trung to Dien Bien Phu Street. It was a long journey through dense, noxious traffic. Dzung was sweating heavily. He did not seem happy. In fact, for the first time ever, Dzung seemed to be in a sulk. Condley, on the other hand, could barely restrain his excitement.

It was December, the month of *chap ma*, a time to look after the resting places of the dead. Only then could the living enjoy the New Year's celebration of *Tet* that would follow. The Vietnamese cared for family above government and on a par with God. In fact, dead family members became deities, worshiped and indulged by the living, looked to for advice and often for consolation. In Viet Nam the ghosts were never far away. And after decades of struggle, there were a lot of ghosts.

To be invited to the Phams' house at such a time had a deeply personal meaning. And from the colonel's parting comments, Condley sensed that Van herself had played a role in his invitation. Twice Condley had attempted to ask Dzung's advice about visiting Pham's house during *chap ma*, and both times Dzung had declined to give it, telling him only that each family was different and that Condley should watch and listen to Mrs. Pham.

Condley had known Dzung might be offended by this visit, but he was surprised at the depth of his friend's resistance. He decided on a different tack as a way to reassure Dzung of his loyalty, something he had been thinking about for some time.

"Dzung," he said as they left the madness of Dien Bien Phu and took a narrow, quieter street. "I'm thinking about buying a car."

Dzung seemed startled at first. He wiped sweat off his face with a casual, practiced move of one shoulder, pushing his shirt into his eyes. Then he regained the smile that had become his lifelong, postwar mask, the face that saved his face.

"Very good, sir. The street too loud, too hot for you!"

"Too slow," said Condley as they pushed along toward yet another side street.

"Yes, sir," agreed Dzung, swaying side to side as he navigated old potholes. "I am very slow. *Cham qua*. And you are a very important man now."

"Some days I need to go to Bien Hoa. And then maybe after that Thanh Da or even Vung Tau. I can't do that in a *cyclo*."

"Very good, sir."

Dzung's eyes were faraway, lost for a moment in the memory of a village outside Bien Hoa where he had brought gifts of a dog and a scarf and helped Tu's father rethatch a roof before asking for his blessing on their marriage. The concrete well on the packed dirt pathway outside their home brought the whole village as much water as it could use. Her family had grown rice and manioc and mangoes in the lush, flat fields. It was a good life. He had taken that from her, to the squalor of District Four. And now even this was going to disappear.

"Maybe sometime you still need me," he said hopefully. "I still take you, maybe at night?"

"I want you to drive," said Condley.

"Drive, sir?" asked Dzung, looking quickly at the road in front of them. "I am driving, sir. Drive where?"

"I want you to drive my car!"

A *car*? Dzung's face went flush with the thought of it. "Oh, thank you, sir, but they will not give me a license."

"You drove before '75, right?"

"Yes, sir. I drove jeep, truck, no problem. But I am old Cong Hoa."

Condley looked up to him, smiling with delight. "I will take care of it."

Dzung could not believe it. "The government will not allow it, sir. I know that."

"I'll call in a chit with Colonel Pham."

"Call in a chit?"

"I will get the car, maybe soon. After that I will take you on driving lessons. Then you'll be my driver."

"You are sure of this?"

"Yes!"

A surge of pride and anticipation lifted Dzung in his chair, empowering his tired legs. A car. "Thank you, Cong Ly. I will do good work for you."

Dzung turned onto a smaller street. Nearby, the sun cooked the juices of a pile of garbage, filling Condley's senses with the odor of decaying bananas, making him think in an odd way of Manila. Then suddenly in the laughing scream of a young boy he remembered the naked children of Guadalcanal, brown as raisins, their frizzed hair bleached with streaks of blond, calling to him in a village that had no electricity and no road. Such cycles were his karma, just as in Manila and Guadalcanal he had never stopped thinking of Viet Nam.

They made false turns, hit dead ends, maneuvered around randomly parked cars, piles of sand and gravel in front of old walled homes. Crowds of young kids were playing soccer or throwing their plastic flip-flop shoes at cola cans as they laughed and chattered in the street. Old Sai Gon, District Three, block after block of small villas and upscale homes left over from the French and then the Americans, confiscated from the wealthier Vietnamese who fled more than two decades before, taken over as the spoils of war by those who had served the other side.

Home to Colonel Pham. But enemy territory to a man like Dzung.

Condley sat in the *cyclo,* searching house numbers painted on the outer walls. Finally he found it. As Dzung halted the *cyclo* he stiffened, setting his face in an unmovable stubbornness, his voice for the first time in Condley's memory growing hard and even bitter.

"This place no good. I don't wait here, Cong Ly."

"You want to come back later?"

"I go see my baby. I don't wait here, I don't come back."

Dzung's normally impassive face grew taut and even more lined as he glanced toward Colonel Pham's home. The war, his lost family, the misery of the camps, the future he might have had, the different country he might have had a hand in leading, all flickered like dim explosions in the twitching of his eyes. "*Xin loi,* Cong Ly, I very sorry. VC, *khong thich,* number ten. I know, I know. No good. I go now."

"Hieu," said Condley. *I understand.* He gave Dzung ten thousand *dong.* "You bring your baby something from me."

He was very nervous as he approached the closed yard of the old villa. Mrs. Pham was waiting on the front terrace, dressed in a black *ao dai.* She turned sharply as he creaked open the gate and stepped inside, betraying her own nervousness. He smiled gamely, walking to her and offering a bouquet of flowers.

"Chao Ba Tho."

"Da, chao Ong."

She melted a bit, smiling her thanks and immediately looking around for a vase in which to put them. Then she opened the front door, bowing slightly and welcoming him inside.

It was cool inside, quiet except for the sound of children playing on the street, unlit except by sunlight through the open windows. The ceramic tiles on the floor were still damp from the morning's sudden rain. A portrait of Ho Chi Minh hung prominently on the living-room wall. On either side were several citations, military awards given to Colonel Pham. The house smelled of musk and food, but over their odors he caught a whiff of perfume. The perfume made him think of Van and then, oddly, of Francois.

The merchant of aromas. He gives her nice things.

Mrs. Pham led him to a small table. At the table he sat in a wooden chair. She sat across from him and poured some tea. A quiet tension passed between them. She had a way of watching him without fully looking at him. Every movement of his hands and feet was being evaluated, as was every bodily shift, even the way he drank his tea. He avoided staring at her as he sipped the tea, allowing her to inspect him.

Finally he set the teacup back onto its saucer and smiled again to her. She smiled back, warm and real, revealing blackened teeth. Somehow he had passed her test. Looking fully at her for the first time he could see the beauty that had carried over into Van and the strength that had no doubt held the family together through the years of war. Her eyes twinkled. Her skin was still smooth and unblemished. When she closed her full lips to self-consciously cover her betel-nut-stained teeth, he could peer so far into her face that he saw all the moments of her life mixed together. And he knew that she was kind.

"You have been very busy," she finally said in Vietnamese.

"My boss needed me," he answered, struggling for a moment to find the right Vietnamese words. "I was in Hawaii until last night." He smiled self-consciously, knowing somehow that he could speak to her from his heart. "You make me feel very shy."

She gave off an immediate, involuntary, girlish giggle, straightening in her chair and waving a hand at him, as if it had never occurred to her that she might have held this power over his emotions. "You're so strong," she said. "I'm only an old woman."

"I am nervous to be at your family altar," he answered.

Her face warmed with genuine affection. She stood and offered him her hand. "You are a very special guest," she said. "We are honored."

He took her hand and she grasped his, firmly and without hesitation, removing any doubts that she had fully accepted him. They walked together around a corner to another wall. The wall and a table in front of it were covered with pictures. At the center of the table was a hand-painted porcelain jar filled with sand.

She began explaining the pictures, introducing him to the ancestors, beginning with the oldest. An eerie calm crept over him as he saw the faces of her and Colonel Pham's grandparents, parents, sisters, and brothers. In the often stoic poses of old black and white photographs and the changing styles of clothes he saw the grief-racked journey of an unbending people. Without industry, their thousand-year love of education suppressed by French colonials, their people then starved and bludgeoned by the Japanese, who could fault the lust for independence that launched them on another thirty years of war? Condley knew that he and Colonel Pham would never agree on the exact reasons the war had been fought. But the faces on the wall told him that somehow it had been inevitable.

Two young men stared at him with lifted chins and proud eyes, wearing military uniforms. "*Bo doi,*" she said. It was his former enemy's word for what he and others simply had called Viet Cong. "My brother, Pham's brother."

Another young man smiled from an old school photograph, not allowed a military uniform even at his family altar. She pointed to the picture, glancing hesitantly at Condley as if she were trying to choose new words. "*Anh trai.*" My older brother. "*Nguy,*" she said at first, using the word for traitor. Then she relented, calling him the more respected term the South Vietnamese Army had used for its soldiers. "*Bo binh, Viet Nam Cong Hoa.*"

Her three dead children looked up from the table, next to the jar of sand. It was a group picture. Two doe-eyed little girls were hugging each other on what looked like a beach. They were laughing as a mischievous older boy grabbed them from behind, squeezing them into each other. She pointed, then said nothing.

Condley found that his arm was on her shoulder. For one elongated second he squeezed her into his chest and pressed his face into the top of her head. She smelled like soap and *pho,* an oddly moving combination of the present and the past.

He had brought a dozen joss sticks. He gave her half. Automatically she held them in a bundle with both hands, in front of her chest. He struck a large match, holding it under her joss sticks until they began to glow, then held his own sticks in one hand over the flame until they also were lit.

They stood silently side by side, holding the joss sticks in their palms just below their chins, their shoulders touching but separate now, repeating a ceremony that dated thousands of years, communing only with the ancestors. Outside on the street, the children called to one another again. Behind him he thought he heard scraping on concrete stairs. The sweet smoke from the joss sticks curled into the air, their odors invading his memory. He bowed once to the altar, then moved the joss sticks six times in his flattened hands, four long movements, down to his waist, then two short ones just underneath his chin. And then he placed the still-burning sticks into the sand-filled jar.

She had done likewise. They stood silently now, surrounded by the curling smoke and the presence of the dead, communicating with the spirits, listening to them. He went dreamy in his mind, not the least bit embarrassed as he spoke without words to her ancestors. He hoped they were at peace, that they would protect their family and bring peace to other families. He remembered Mai and asked them to make peace with her and her family.

Through the heavy joss smoke he smelled the perfume again. When he turned around, Van and her father were standing behind him. She smiled at him, looking stunning in a pair of blue jeans and a bright red pullover blouse. The old colonel was staring intently at Condley with a totally different look than his jaunty teasing at the golf course. He was fighting back his emotions, as if it were too much to comprehend that

Condley's presence had brought such tranquillity to the face of his own wife.

Finally he stepped forward and stuck out his thick paw of a hand, nodding brusquely. "*Chao Ong,* Cong Ly."

"We'll go to temple with you," said Van, her eyes thanking him more than he deserved. "If it's okay?"

CHAPTER ELEVEN

THEY TOOK TWO motorbikes. Colonel Pham drove his wife. Behind them, Condley rode on the back of Van's new Honda. She wove expertly through the obstacles in the side streets. He teased her for wearing a pair of elbow-length white gloves and a yellow handkerchief over her face to protect her skin from the bad air and the sun. The insides of his thighs pressed against her hips as he struggled to stay on the motorbike through pothole bumps and weaving turns. When they reached a wider road and picked up speed, her hair whipped and caressed his face. People on the sidewalks and in the traffic stared at him and Van with curiosity and faint disapproval. But she was alive, laughing and turning against him as she maneuvered the motorbike, teasing him for not trusting her driving. And by the time they reached the temple his hands felt like they belonged on her waist.

The temple sat back from the street, behind a yellow plaster wall. Old banyan trees and crumbling sidewalks marked its outer yard. Its gates were closed. Van drove through a narrow break in the wall meant for pedestrians and parked her motorbike in the yard itself. The temple seemed ancient, the curling dragons on its rooftops derivative of Chinese architecture, while the Buddhist symbols and several gargoyles were reminiscent of parts of India. This intermingling of the two grand Asian cultures here at the very seat of their beliefs reminded him again why Viet Nam had once been labeled Indochina.

He and Van walked together toward the temple's door, where her parents already were waiting. Her nearness, and the long minutes he had spent with his arms around her as they rode along the city streets, made this journey seem somehow symbolic: the temple, high and yellow and ornate; her parents, waiting at its doors; she herself, dressed modern but striding slowly with an eternal grace toward an ancient task.

A monk in a flowing brown robe met them at the temple door, accompanied by a gray-robed nun. Each of their heads had been shaved bald. The nun seemed old enough to have been Colonel Pham's mother. She pressed her hands together in front of her face when they entered the temple, greeting them, and then walked away toward one side of the altar, where a large cymbal hung from the ceiling.

They followed the monk to the altar, standing just behind him. A huge gold Buddha towered over them, flanked by flowers, brass bowls, and plates filled with fresh fruit. The monk lit another bundle of joss sticks. Then he moved them up and down, just as Condley and Mrs. Pham had done at the family altar, and placed them in a larger jar at the Buddha's feet. The monk stood for a long time at the altar, praying to the Buddha. Then he walked off to their left, kneeling on the floor in front of a hollow wooden drum.

Colonel Pham stepped forward, bowing his head before the Buddha. Condley, Van, and Mrs. Pham remained just behind him. It was now their time to pray. He found himself at first talking to Mai, telling her that he was sorry for everything, even for loving her, but especially for having been away when they came to kill her, that he had killed them back for her and had refused to love anyone else, but that it might be different now if she would only help him. Then he talked to his friends, Vietnamese and American, those who had died alongside him, the others who had died because he had left. Then finally he talked to the six years' worth of people he had killed.

His hand brushed against Van's leg. She reached out without looking and took it, wrapping a fist around one finger. He looked over at her hand, and then up to her face. She was done praying. And she smiled.

Colonel Pham finished last, stepping back to join Condley and the two women. Condley had no doubt the old soldier had prayed through a much longer list. They all sat cross-legged on the cool tile floor. The nun banged the cymbal with a mallet, two short gongs and then a long, lingering one that ran through Condley like the aching sadness of the past. Off to one side the monk began striking the wooden drum, the *go mo*, in a quick insistent rhythm that was soon matched by his high-pitched chanting.

They joined him, chanting the *kinh cau sieu*, a prayer asking peace for the dead, reading with him from booklets on the floor. Joss smoke wound its way like morning fog down from the altar. The *go mo* struck a hollow, haunting cadence that seemed to echo from inside Condley's heart. They chanted together, their words blending until they were at one with each other, inseparable, linked to the *go mo* and the altar and the millions whose spirits swarmed among them, dead by bombs and guns and man.

And then it was over. Condley embraced Mrs. Pham. Colonel Pham came to him and shook his hand. They gave their thanks to the monk, who spoke rapidly to them about their spiritual duties, and to the nun, who folded her hands once more underneath her chin and bowed. Within minutes the colonel and his wife had gone.

Condley lingered for a moment outside the temple, then dropped twenty dollars through the slit in a contribution box. It was supposed to be a secret, his own personal expression of thanks, but Van was waiting at the bottom of the temple steps and she saw.

"Why do you care so much, Cong Ly?"

Her question surprised him, because in truth he had never thought about it. "Because it gives me peace," he finally said.

"Can I take you back?"

"That's okay," he answered. "I'll find a *cyclo*."

She laughed merrily, as if he confused her. "You're the only American in Sai Gon who still uses a *cyclo*."

"I'm not in a hurry. And they need the money."

"So, give one of them the money and ride with me."

He could not trust the openness in her delicious, smiling face. She was unlike the other Vietnamese women with whom he had flirted and played since his return, deeper and yet somehow more free. There were no games in her smile, and yet there was no promise either. She clearly did not need him. And so he remained merely confused.

"Where's Francois?"

"He is in Tokyo." She raised her chin, casually tossing her hair. "This is not about Francois. We are fighting, anyway."

"Now, there's a line."

"What does that mean, 'there's a line'?"

"Your dad told me you're spoiled."

"Sometimes." She grew serious. "But this is—I don't know how to say it. Watching you with my mother made me feel very—" She searched for an English phrase and could not find it. *"Cam dong,"* she said, using a peculiarly Vietnamese expression meaning that she was moved inside her heart.

"Your mother is wonderful," he said, feeling awkward standing in the dusky temple yard.

"She likes you very much. And my father respects you as a soldier. I find it very odd." She was peering quizzically up into his eyes. "But somehow it makes me happy."

"Somehow it makes me sad."

He felt exhausted, empty. He gave her a small wave and started to walk across the outer yard toward the break in the wall that they had driven through a half hour before. Behind him he heard her motorbike start, and then she was next to him, driving slowly, dragging her feet along to keep with his pace.

"Get on my bike, Cong Ly! It's okay!"

He looked up. Her smile was natural, inviting. He decided that she really did like him.

"I don't think so."

He reached the wall and walked onto the sidewalk that bordered the busy street. She was still next to him. People were staring again but she did not seem to notice. She kept smiling, waiting, asking.

"You're afraid of the way I drive?"

"No."

"You're afraid of me?"

He stopped walking and faced her. She was very near, standing as she straddled the idling motorbike. Her elbow-length gloves were on but she had not yet covered her face with the handkerchief. Compromising, he took the handkerchief from her and held it up to her face.

"Yeah, I guess I am. You make me remember things."

"Another girl?" She took back the handkerchief, smiling teasingly, not wanting her face covered yet.

"A little bit. A long time ago. But she died. And her family was on the other side."

She shrugged, unconcerned. "You should forget the war."

"The communists killed her."

"I don't want to know that."

"They killed her because of me."

"Too many stories." She touched him on the face with one long finger, as if she were going to scold him. "We just prayed, Cong Ly. You're free. We're all free." And then she patted the seat of her motorbike. "I'm a very good driver!"

"You're hurting someone's business!"

She gave him a sharp look, her mouth curled into an impish smile. "Give me one dollar. Come on, one dollar!"

He hesitated for a moment, mildly confused, then gave her a dollar. She gunned her motorbike to the edge of the street, calling to the nearest lazing *cyclo* driver and giving him a series of instructions. Both of them laughed, staring back at Condley. Then she handed the old man a dollar, and he pedaled off into the dense traffic.

"There!" she said happily, returning to his side. "You have hired him for one hour! Now get on my bike!"

He did not ask her to park the motorbike once they reached the hotel or to pay the doorman five thousand *dong* to take care of it. He did not invite her to dinner in the hotel's small restaurant where they sat for hours, laughing and teasing each other as they shared a half dozen samples from the menu. But as he watched her talk and laugh and tease, a part of him that he had thought was dead slowly stirred from its slumber, daring itself to reawaken.

"I have to tell you about her," he finally said, toying with a beer and carefully watching Van's face.

"No," she pouted. "The war is over, Cong Ly. I don't want to know."

"Not about how she died. About why I loved her. And who she was. And what she wanted. It's not right to forget that, in the same breath that we try to forget a war."

"I think you've turned her death into your prison," said Van, with a look that bordered on jealousy.

"The first time I saw her, she was leaving the grounds of Sai Gon University, dressed in a white *ao dai*, riding a bicycle. They had a little club there, run by the Vietnamese–American Society. I was twenty-three. I had just come to Sai Gon from Da Nang. I had never seen anyone so beautiful. I said hello. She was surprised that I spoke Vietnamese. And it stunned me that she liked me. For almost a year, whenever I was in Sai Gon I would wait for her every afternoon in a small café just outside the university. We would drink coffee and she would practice her English. After a year she gained the courage to bring me home to meet her parents. Her father's family had moved from Ha Noi in 1954 after the country was divided. Her mother's family had moved from Hue. She was studying to be a lawyer. They had already decided that she would marry a doctor from another Ha Noi family. But she didn't. She went with me. And for three more years she loved me. And who was I? I don't know why she fell in love with me."

"Because you would take her to America," teased Van, trying to again lighten his mood.

"That frightened her," shrugged Condley.

"Her parents let you marry?"

"No," said Condley. "They let her love me, as long as they didn't have to recognize that we were in love. She finished school and they let her have an apartment. It was our apartment. I paid for it. When I was in Sai Gon we lived together. But when they spoke to their friends, it was only about her studies and her work, as if I were not a part of her life. They hoped that she would lose her fascination with the American. Or that the American would finally grow tired of Viet Nam and go home. And once either of those things happened they would have won, without losing face. Since they'd never recognized that we were together, they could reinvent those years in the eyes of the proper Vietnamese doctor or businessman who would be her husband. Save her face. Regrow her virginity. Allow her a proper life, with properly Vietnamese kids."

"Did they blame you when she was killed?"

"Of course," said Condley. "Because if it was not for me, she never would have died. And you know something? If it wasn't for her, I might not have stayed. So in a way, we did it to each other." He watched her face, wondering if he should say it. "I was a very good fighter, Van. The war is over but I have no qualms in telling you that. They couldn't catch me, your father's friends. They couldn't kill me. And so they went after her. I lived, but in the end they killed my heart."

"That is sad. But I cannot believe your heart is dead. Why are you telling me this?"

"Because I never stop thinking about it. She had the courage to love me, and yet in her own way she never betrayed her family either. She took care of us both. It wasn't a perfect solution, but the burden was always on her. And then she bore my burden as well. She wasn't a soldier. They never should have killed her."

"Do you hate my father for that?"

"No." Condley finished his beer. "I respect your father."

"You confuse me, Cong Ly."

"It's very simple if you think about it."

"Anyway, I'm not like her." Van shrugged almost casually when she said it, as if she were tossing away the past with the quiet movement of her shoulders.

"It's not fair, I know," he said. "But some things that you do remind me of her. Your laugh. The way you dismiss problems by making fun of them. Or maybe it was just the peace I felt when we left the temple."

Her eyes caressed him. She smiled, making her offer seem as natural as the simple touching of a hand. "Would you like to make love to me?"

"No," he said carefully. "I think that would hurt."

"Because of Francois?"

"No."

"Because you don't like me?"

"No." He watched her dancing eyes. "Because I'm afraid I do like you."

The restaurant had closed. Its weary owner watched them impatiently, wishing to clean their table and go home. Condley stood, walking her outside to her motorbike. As they reached the bike, she stopped for a moment, looking into his face as if he were a puzzle to be figured out.

"It's nice that you didn't want to," she finally said.

"I did want to."

"Then it's nice that you didn't. I would have felt bad afterward."

"I'll see you again?"

"Yes. Of course."

"When?"

She watched him for a long time, as if she were waiting for him to come to her and at least kiss her good-bye. Her eyes were laughing, though, and her smile was filled with satisfaction. "Don't tell anyone we were together tonight," she finally said. "I'm still with Francois."

"He buys you nice things," he said.

"Yes! He is so *elegant*! He's a better man than you think, Francois. But when he doesn't get his way he pouts like a little boy. I'm not sure I want to marry him."

"Does he want to marry you?"

"Of course."

She scanned the darkened streets, starting the engine on her motorbike. Impishly, she turned to him and gave him a wave. And then like a memory she was gone.

CHAPTER TWELVE

THE JET LAG finally claimed him. Condley crashed and burned once inside his room, falling into a deep and dreamless sleep. Just before dawn the traffic started on the street below his window, a steady stream of motorbikes that would not relent until well into the evening. The sounds of the whiny motors and the high-pitched little horns rarely stirred him, having become as normal as the surf near someone's beach house. But in his exhaustion he had not dropped the blinds, and the gray light pouring through his windows awakened him.

Sitting up and looking outside, he noticed that he had received a fax. It was from Hanson Muir, terse and coded as always.

> Am arriving Tan Son Nhat 0600 tomorrow morning.
> Meet me at the Rex Hotel for breakfast, 0800.
> Strange news. I think we might find some Pepper in
> the mountains?

CONDLEY FELT MORE comfortable in the cavernous rooftop restaurant of the Rex Hotel than anywhere else in Sai Gon. For several years he had taken most of his meals in the restaurant, which a generation before had been the dining hall for hundreds of American officers stationed in Sai Gon.

The hotel's elevator opened to an outdoor terrace. Just above his head, a familiar caged bird was cooing. The smiling, bowing young doorman recognized Condley instantly, greeting him in Vietnamese and ushering him into the dark old dining room. He stood for a moment, adjusting his eyes to the room's dim light, searching past stands of ugly tropical plants and over the faces of perhaps thirty scattered guests, looking for Hanson Muir. Given its size, the place seemed almost empty. Finally the professor waved to him from a far corner.

An aged, blue-suited waiter had already walked up to him, greeting him with the familiarity of a favorite uncle. Condley and the old man, whose name was Vo, had become friends years before. Vo had been a barber on an American military base during the war. He had also been a spy for the communists and had been given a lifetime-tenured job in the restaurant as a reward for his service. Vo was a sly old possum. His tragic look and emaciated frame belied his continuing ability to listen in and report on the conversations of important foreigners.

All part of the game, chuckled Condley as he greeted Vo in Vietnamese. "Hello, Uncle Vo! I'm looking for my friend."

Vo showed Condley to Muir's table, speaking with a humble voice that was as soft as a church usher's. "Good morning, Cong Ly. We don't see you very much anymore."

"You see me all the time, Vo. Everywhere I go."

"Ah, Cong Ly. You are such a funny man."

"That's because Sai Gon makes me so happy! The government takes care of me. It makes sure that I am never really alone." The two men shared a secret, knowing smile as Condley reached Muir's table.

It was eight o'clock, straight up and down. Muir was sitting near a window, sipping on filtered coffee and eating an omelette. He was wearing tan Bermuda shorts, Nike running shoes with white calf-length socks, and another one of his ostentatious luau shirts. He checked his watch, nodding approvingly as if evaluating or perhaps merely establishing Condley's promptness. "Very impressive, Brandon. You're never on time in Hawaii."

"I'm never on time in Viet Nam either. But you've got me curious."

Muir chuckled, enjoying the mystery. "Well, I told you I deserved at least a day of R and R in Sai Gon."

"Did you have to bring that shirt? You look idiotic, Professor."

"And I suppose you think you're a model for Calvin Klein?"

Condley fingered his old T-shirt, looking down at his faded jeans. "I dress like this for a reason. Half the people on the street are going to laugh at you. And the other half are going to try and rob you."

"Ah, yes," said Hanson sarcastically. "The mean streets of Sai Gon."

"You make the wrong people mad around here and your life's worth maybe twenty bucks."

"They'd never touch an American, you know that. You're always so melodramatic, Brandon."

"Have you heard of the Hai Phong gangs? Go ahead, piss somebody off, Professor, and try going for a walk by yourself at night."

Condley took a seat, quickly ordering an omelette, a sliced mango, and coffee from the waiting Vo. Watching the old waiter shuffle toward the kitchen, he nodded to Muir, casually stealing a piece of his French bread. "Don't talk business in front of that guy. He's a spy."

Muir chuckled indulgently, folding his arms across his vast chest so that they rested on his ample belly. He looked as if he felt sorry for Condley. "Murder on the street. Octogenarian spies in the restaurants. Oh, my, you live a fantastic life, don't you?"

"Okay, don't believe me. But why do you think they always try to put American government people in this hotel?"

"We stay here because the Rex gives us a good rate. And there's a certain nostalgia to the place, wouldn't you say? Sometimes I feel ghosts from the war."

"Did you leave any papers laying out in your room? Half of the bell-boys work for the Interior Ministry."

"Oh, Brandon, we've got to get you a vacation."

"One night a couple years ago I was talking on the phone to some-one back in Hawaii and I couldn't hear him. It was about two in the morning. The second time I told him I couldn't hear him, somebody turned the phone up so loud that his voice came out of the speaker on the wall."

Muir shrugged condescendingly, enjoying his little provocation.

"The operator was helping you out, Brandon. I know they're clever, but let's face it. We're hardly the CIA. We're out here looking for dead people. We're just not that interesting!"

"Oh, we are interesting, at least to them. How do you think a voice on the phone came out of a speaker on the wall that's supposed to be rigged for radio music? Trust me, Professor, I do know my former trade. And we're not talking about finding bodies in the boonies anymore. We're talking about Salt and Pepper. I can tell from talking to Colonel Pham that this one scares them. So be careful."

Muir finally laughed. "I'm smarter about these things than you give me credit for. Why do you think I flew here instead of talking to you about it on the phone?"

"Because you wanted some R and R in Sai Gon." Condley took another piece of Muir's bread. "Speaking of which, I almost got married last night."

Muir rubbed his beard, his thick hand masking a very jealous smile. "You get married a lot, Brandon."

"No, actually the marriage business has been kind of slow for quite a while. Or maybe I've slowed down. And the Interior Ministry does watch me, you know."

"I would think by now they have a complete folder, wouldn't you? What difference would a few more lovely ladies make?"

"Well, I have to assume her dad reads the reports, given that he's our government counterpart."

The burly scientist could not restrain his amusement. "Colonel Pham? Oh, no, Brandon. He has a daughter?"

"He has a daughter like Ho Chi Minh has a mausoleum."

"Wait a minute," laughed Muir. "You lost me on that analogy."

"Well, I never said I was a poet."

"Ho Chi Minh doesn't have anything. He's dead. I can confirm that. I've been to the mausoleum."

"Yeah, but have you done the DNA?"

"What?"

"How do you know that's really Uncle Ho? Did you match the dental file?"

"Didn't he have false teeth?"

"Not so loud, you're talking about somebody's version of God." Condley laughed, sensing that Muir was fighting to focus after his long flight. "Okay, forget the mausoleum. She's beautiful, Professor. Oh, man, I really don't know why, but I came very close to losing it."

"Of course you know why. You're a pig."

Condley laughed again, this time at himself. "All right, I do know why. But I hope the colonel doesn't feel like he lost face when he reads the morning reports and finds out I was hanging with his daughter."

"We need him," said Muir, becoming serious. "He's been the easiest official to deal with, and I sense we might be getting some resistance if we proceed as I'm about to recommend."

"He's doing some checking for me," said Condley. "I had a long talk with him yesterday."

"Just before you took advantage of his daughter?"

"I said almost," joked Condley. Then he thought better of it. "Look, I'm sorry I told you that. But he kind of had a hand in it. At least he seemed to like the idea of us getting to know each other."

"In the Biblical sense?"

"Buddhists don't have Bibles. Anyway, she seems to be different. Very straight up. I could get in trouble if I let myself."

Muir sipped the last of his coffee, his moonful face breaking into a knowing grin. "Oh, God, I can't believe it. Brandon Condley, of all people! You just said the magic words. It's all over. The next thing you know you'll be wearing luau shirts."

"She'd be more likely to try and put me inside a Givenchy suit with a silk shirt and a paisley tie. All right, enough. Stop bottom-feeding, Professor. If you want a house mouse I can get you one."

"Nice recovery, but you're blushing, Brandon."

"I'm always sunburnt. I was on a fucking golf course yesterday!"

"Excellent response!" The professor waved a huge hand into the air, a declaration of victory. "Because I'm your friend, I'll leave you alone for now."

Condley checked his watch. "So, why am I here?"

Muir frowned, regaining his focus. "We have a serious problem, and we need to move quickly on it. That's why I flew out here last night." He watched Condley's face for a moment, anticipating the next question. "We need to move quickly because I did assume that you had some words with Colonel Pham and that this situation would make its way rather quickly up the government food chain. It could be embarrassing for them if we discover that they've harbored collaborators after repeatedly denying it. It could even inflame relations after all these years. And if they have any indication that we're on the track of these two men, they'll anticipate us and remove the evidence."

"So now we're into evidence?"

"I have a tip," said Muir. "A very good one."

"Deville?"

"No, nothing on him," answered Muir. "No fingerprint matches in the States at all. We're sending agents to his old hometown to see if we can backtrack, but so far we've got a total blank. My guess is that he never returned home, or even to the States at all."

"The . . . victim?"

"We've put St. Louis on full priority. They're pulling the files on every unresolved missing-in-action and deserter case and looking for a match. Once they get into the files it should be a fairly quick process. He's got to be Caucasian, early twenties as of 1971, five foot nine inches, brown hair. That narrows down the search already. From there we go to the fillings in his dental records. Three fillings or less, which in itself is kind of unusual. There can't be more than a handful of people matching those indicators, so we should have an answer very soon. Perhaps within days."

Professor Muir's eyes lit up. "An odd thing here—one of my colleagues was looking at the skull the other day and he swears that these don't look like American fillings. Something about the materials and the way the drilling seems to have been done. It could be just another indication that the victim was from a pretty backward rural area, in the same manner as his worn teeth indicate a rougher diet. But it also could mean that he isn't even an American. Fancy that."

"Maybe Deville killed an eastern European adviser," said Condley. "If there was such a thing. Think of the irony in that. A turncoat actually killing a commie in order to get out of Viet Nam."

"That would surprise me as well," said Muir. "What good would it have done him? If he killed one of their advisers he would have been in deep trouble with them, so how could he have gotten out of, say, Ha Noi with their help? The only place they could have sent him was to another communist country, and I can't imagine him being welcomed there if he'd just killed an eastern-bloc soldier. And he couldn't have gotten out of the country from one of our airports in Sai Gon or Da Nang with the passport of an eastern European soldier who wasn't even supposed to be in Viet Nam in the first place."

The old waiter shuffled up, carrying a tray of food, so emaciated and expressionless that it seemed he might keel over and die with every step. Condley winked at Muir when Vo approached, and the two remained silent as he slowly placed Condley's breakfast on the table. Then Condley dug hungrily into his omelette.

"So you think you've got Pepper in the mountains," he said through a mouthful of food.

"This might be a coincidence, but I'm inclined to think it isn't." Muir sipped some coffee, looking around them and growing more intense. "I have another colleague who was sent out to investigate a reported sighting of an American a few years ago, up in the mountains near where we picked up the remains."

"The Que Son Mountains?"

"Yes!" said Muir excitedly. "The Que Son Mountains. But you know how these things go. They had to file a request and then receive clearance from province and district authorities. And then once the clearance was given, it took a full day to get up to the actual place. All told, from the time he put in the request to the time he showed up in the village it was something like five days. Plenty of time for the locals to, as they say, police the crime scene. Needless to say, he didn't find an American."

Condley was almost finished with his omelette. He grunted. "You came all the way here to tell me that?"

"Brandon," said Muir huffily. "I would not waste the government's money in such a manner. What he did see were black children. It was an accident. As they started back toward Da Nang, a group of local children came out along the road, calling to them and waving to them. There were two half-black children. He estimated both were under the age of ten. He said they were trying to hide behind the trees at the rear of the other kids, as if it were all a game. But he's certain they were half-black. Dark. Not as if they were the grandkids of someone who had been here during the war. This is a very remote village. Where there are half-black kids there is a black dad. And if there is a dad, why were they hiding him? I mean, clearly, if he's having kids he's hardly incarcerated."

"Pepper," said Condley.

Muir nodded. "I'd say from the location, which is not that far from the incident that happened to you and your Marines, and also not far from where we found our . . . victim, that there is a very good chance of it."

"But we've got the same problem, only now it's an order of magnitude worse," said Condley, knowing he was stating the obvious. "They'll never let us back there."

"Unless Pham takes responsibility."

Condley grunted, unimpressed. "For what? If he takes responsibility for our conduct, that means he's guaranteeing that we won't do anything to hurt the government or they can send his own ass off to jail. That's what taking responsibility is all about in this system: You volunteer to be the scapegoat if things go wrong. Which also means he'll do everything he can to keep us from finding anything, even if he personally goes with us on the trip. And if we do find something—which I intend to do—and they hold him accountable, we've just screwed our best friend in the whole Vietnamese government."

"Yes," said Muir, smiling with satisfaction. "Not to mention the father of your girlfriend, with whom you are now fully enamored."

"Professor, now you're hurting my feelings."

"Let the record show that Brandon Condley has feelings."

"Anyway, she's not my girlfriend. She's engaged to a Frog."

"Sorry about that."

Condley grinned slyly. "Pass on your condolences to the Frog."

"For now," said Muir, not losing his own smile. "Anyway, I thought about the situation with the colonel. But we can empower him, so that if we find something their government gets the credit. And if that happens, he wins."

"Now, there's a baby-boomer concept," laughed Condley. "You want to *empower* a communist government official. Have you taken a look around here lately, Professor? I hate to break this to you, but they pretty much have all the power they want."

"Slow down, Brandon. Listen to me. We empower him in the media. We can arrange it so that it's his discovery, not ours. We tell him the story is going to come out sooner or later anyway because my colleague back in Hawaii heard about the Deville situation and is preparing a report. We tell him that the Vietnamese government has the ability to preempt a very nasty set of questions that will soon be coming their way from the international media. We also guarantee that we'll support the Vietnamese government's version of the story. Which will be that the Que Son Mountains are so remote, and their inhabitants so primitive, that it was impossible to make the determination before now, anyway. That Pepper has simply been living up there with a bunch of Montagnards, hiding from everyone, including their government. So Colonel Pham, or his boss if he wants, becomes the hero, instead of the Vietnamese being the villains."

"What about the fact that Pepper was a turncoat?"

"We tell him we don't know anything about that." Muir looked hard at Condley, his face bright with challenge. "Do we? I mean, truthfully, isn't it a fact? We don't even know who he is."

"Yet," said Condley, meeting the professor's stare.

"Exactly," answered Muir. "Yet. And if something comes out later, well, that's later. If the media asks, the answer is that the Viets didn't know and we didn't know. All we have right now—that is, all we think we have, because even this isn't certain—is an American in the mountains that they're going to help us find. At least, we think he's an American."

"You're pretty smart," said Condley.

Muir grinned with satisfaction, folding his thick hands together on his heavy belly so that he looked like a contented Buddha. "Distance from the problem does have its advantages."

The old waiter crept apologetically up to the table and handed Condley a grocery bag filled with bread. Then he refilled Condley's coffee, quietly leaving the tab before he disappeared. Professor Muir glanced at the bag as he signed for the meal.

"What are you doing with that bread?"

A tantalizing grin crept over Condley's face. "Want to meet some interesting people? Some of them are women."

Muir's eyebrows arched quickly, giving away his interest as he stood up. "Well, I'm here on business."

"We've got several hours before we can meet with Colonel Pham. It's a golf morning."

Now Muir was smiling with an unconcealed, delicious anticipation. "The real Sai Gon?"

"The Sai Gon you've never seen."

Outside the restaurant, two gray-suited Japanese businessmen marched out of the elevator, followed by an older French couple dressed in almost identical baggy shorts and flowered shirts. The Japanese ignored them. The French couple looked at the two as if their presence in Sai Gon were a rude intrusion on their own antique, Francophone possession. Condley stepped inside the elevator and immediately pressed the button for the ground floor. Muir jumped in just as the doors were closing.

As the elevator descended, Condley found himself staring at a metal sign bolted to the wall next to the door. The sign said *Nippon Elevator Company.* Someone had scratched *Nippon* out with a room key or a knife. In Viet Nam it could have been anyone: Vietnamese, French, Aussies, Brits, Singaporeans, Koreans, even Americans. No one liked Nippon in Viet Nam, and maybe no one ever had. Underneath the sign was a metal screen covering a little loudspeaker. In Japan it probably serenaded passengers with elevator music, but in Viet Nam it no doubt listened as well as transmitted. That didn't surprise him either. Even Muir would never fully believe it, but Vietnamese intelligence agents listened everywhere; on the street, in the bars, on the phones, even in your own room if they wanted to. And what better place to gain business intelligence than to listen inside the elevator of the famed Rex Hotel?

Someone had scratched up the loudspeaker too. Amused, Condley took out a key and scratched it some more.

"What are you doing?"

"Saying hello to Comrade Nguyen."

"As I said, Brandon, I think you need a vacation."

The elevator reached the lobby. Condley stepped out, nodding to the uniformed elevator attendant and heading toward the front door. The lobby was filled with suitcases and jabbering French people, a tour group noisily checking out of the hotel. As they neared the outer door Muir finally grabbed him by the shoulder, halting him for a moment.

"Where are we going?"

"Sightseeing."

CHAPTER THIRTEEN

DZUNG WAS LAZING in his *cyclo* in the park just across the street from the Rex. He bolted upright when he saw Condley walk out of the hotel, then waved with the innocent happiness of a young boy. In seconds he had jumped to the ground and pulled the *cyclo* into the street, ready to depart.

Striding toward him with Muir in tow, Condley pointed to a second *cyclo* driver, calling to him in Vietnamese. When he reached Dzung, Condley put an arm around a reluctant, visibly addled Muir, introducing him. *"Anh trai,"* he said, pretending that Muir was his older brother. "Hanson."

"Hanson? Oh, very good," said Dzung happily, watching Condley climb into the *cyclo*.

Condley pointed to the second *cyclo*. "Get in, Hanson."

Muir swallowed, his eyes going wild with uncertainty. "Brandon, I don't mean to be rude, but this is not my thing. It's hot, it's dirty. My stomach isn't doing too well anyway." He checked his watch again, as if it were a security blanket. "Let's take a car. I'll pay."

"You'll pay anyway. Get in." Condley smiled easily. "You don't want to take a taxi where we're going."

Muir climbed hesitantly aboard. His voice revealed his unease. "Where are we going?"

"The real Sai Gon, Professor."

Dzung pushed out into the traffic, crossing Le Loi Street, and soon was pedaling smoothly, comfortably, swaying side to side with the rhythm that allowed him to work his back muscles into the pedals. He leaned over Condley's shoulder.

"Where we go today, Cong Ly?"

"We go to District Four."

Dzung laughed excitedly, as if the thought were madness. He called rapidly to the other *cyclo* driver, whose name was Luong, and they chatted quickly as they made their way along Nguyen Hue Street. Then he leaned over Condley's shoulder again.

"District Four no good."

"You live in District Four."

"Yes, sir. I live in District Four."

"Then District Four is good."

Dzung laughed again, exchanging glances with Luong. "Oh, thank you, sir, but District Four is very bad. Here in Sai Gon we say, if you want a nice house go to District Three. If you want good hotel, go to District One. If you want to die, go to District Four."

Muir had been leaning forward in his seat in the other *cyclo*, trying to follow Dzung's heavily accented English despite the distance and the traffic noise. Now he called to Condley. "What did he say about dying?"

"He wasn't talking about dying," lied Condley, turning around and watching his suffering, sweating friend as the *cyclos* wove their way along patched roads. He shouted over the noise of honking cars and droning motorbikes. "He said 'dining.' District Four's got a lot of good restaurants."

"Oh," said Muir uncertainly, checking his watch again and blinking exhaust fumes out of his eyes. "Well, we already ate." Muir thought about it some more. "Then why'd he say it was bad?"

"Because he knew we already ate."

"I don't believe you, Brandon."

Just in front of them two motorbikes collided in the heavy traffic, sending their occupants spinning and sliding along the pavement. One, an older man wearing a worn brown army officer's hat, whose fixed, stoic glare reminded Condley immediately of Colonel Pham, struggled to his feet and walked scraped and bleeding back to his bike. Picking it up, he drove away without so much as a word as blood dripped from his forehead and fingers. The other, a thin young man dressed in a flowing white shirt, lay motionless on the pavement, apparently out cold. The rear wheel of his motorbike still raced nearby as two pedestrians began to drag him out of the traffic, which had hardly slowed its incessant pace.

"Too many *Hon Da*," noted Dzung philosophically.

"I need to call Hawaii," moaned Muir, checking his watch.

"They'll be there when we get back," laughed Condley. "If you make it back."

Muir was sweating profusely, even more heavily than Luong, who was transporting him with the power of his thin, churning legs. "You know, Brandon, the reason I'll never trust you is that you really, honestly don't give a damn! If something happened to us you'd probably think it was *cool*! It'd show you had . . . *balls*."

"Relax, Professor. I've been out here a long time and I haven't died once."

"You're only making me more nervous. We're heading out of the city. Where are we going? I really don't need this. We have a very important job to do over the next few days."

Condley looked back to Dzung, grinning conspiratorially and speaking in Vietnamese. "My brother's afraid."

Now Dzung's face changed. Once publicly admitted, Muir's fear became personal to him, a matter of his own responsibility and honor. He took control, as surely as if this were a combat mission a whole lifetime before. He angled his *cyclo* closer to Luong's and moved just ahead of Muir, so that he was now looking down directly at him.

"Mister Hanson! Sir!" Muir looked up at him, and Dzung waved one arm into the air as he pedaled. "No problem. I know, I know. *Khong co sao*. It's okay. You go by yourself, maybe some problem. You my customer, Cong Ly he my good friend."

"Are you sure?"

Dzung spoke rapidly to Luong, who now leaned over and patted Muir reassuringly on a shoulder. "No problem!"

Muir was unconvinced. He called over to Condley. "Why should I trust them?"

Condley chuckled, comfortable on his *cyclo* throne. "Because if you don't you'll *really* have a problem." He searched Muir's reddened, sweating face as the traffic sped past them and noticed how tightly his hands gripped the side rails of the *cyclo*. For all his education, for all his competence, Muir was petrified simply to be out unprotected along the seedy edges of the city. "Calm down, Professor. If you ever double clutch out here you're in trouble."

"What does that mean?"

"You trust the people you're supposed to trust and you fight the people you're supposed to fight. And if you show no fear you're the king."

"King of what? *This?* Brandon, you're irresponsible." Muir mulled that, then let it go without further thought. He stared out at the chaotic clutter of renewal and decay existing side by side along the streets and at the river of traffic that surrounded them. They reached a major intersection and his head continually turned this way and that, registering his amazement as a blend of trucks, cars, motorbikes, motorized platforms, bicycles, and *cyclos* mixed together at vastly different speeds, not even always heading in the same direction. The two *cyclo* drivers deftly maneuvered them through the mass, managing a slow left turn as they picked up the road to District Four.

Professor Muir put a hand over his nose, trying not to breathe the mix of dust and exhaust fumes that had enveloped them. "I feel like I'm going to be sick. Do you actually think this is fun?"

Condley leaned back, glorying in it. "It's more than fun. It's life."

Muir touched his clothes where the dust was settling on his sweat. "Not my life, Brandon! Fun is an evening at the Outrigger restaurant with good friends, having a wonderful wine, watching the most beautiful hula dancer in the world, with Waikiki Beach as my personal backdrop. That's fun. This is . . . this is unnecessary! Unlike our little trip to Ninh Phuoc, which was a service to our country. It's voyeuristic! It's meddling in someone else's catastrophe! I don't need it."

"Yeah, you do. You need it."

"I didn't come to Sai Gon for this."

Condley shook his head with false concern. "Relax, I'm going to introduce you to some women."

Muir looked ahead toward a decaying bridge choked with slow-moving traffic. "Do you know what my wife would think if I were killed in some Sai Gon bordello?"

Condley pointed back at Dzung, who was pedaling up the slight hill with a steady, pendulumlike rhythm that informed his hidden strength. "You're not going to get hurt. This is one tough little guy. I guarantee."

"What's in it for him?" Muir leaned toward Condley, speaking softly, almost conspiratorially. "They could take us down by the river and strip us clean and leave us dead. No one would ever know the difference."

"Oh," laughed Condley, enjoying himself immensely. "Now you're worried about it! I thought you said it would never happen in Sai Gon."

"Okay, I lied."

District Four was an island, separated from Sai Gon by a few tawdry bridges. In 1975 the victorious communists had relocated thousands of former South Vietnamese soldiers and their families into the district, reasoning that if they ever tried to revolt they could be quickly contained by putting soldiers on the bridges. Over the years the population inside the district had swollen, even as basics such as water and electricity had slowly been allowed to atrophy.

"Welcome to District Four, Professor."

The crumbling sidewalks on the Nguyen Tat Thanh bridge were crowded with human effluvium from the district on the other side. Small unwashed children played in the dirt behind tiny stalls. Women sat listlessly on straw mats at the stalls, selling drips of gasoline from glass bottles, cigarettes from little display cases, soft drinks, stale bread, whatever might work to whomever might care. The water below was stagnant, choked with waste and trash. On the far end of the bridge, a gathering of patched-plywood shanties spilled out on poles above the water. The morning's attempt at laundry hung below the eaves of tin and canvas rooftops that were held unconvincingly in place by loose slats of wood and thin old bicycle tires. Near the shanties a few small boats with roofs and walls of straw were moored in the mud, home to those who could not afford a shack.

Muir gulped as they finished crossing the bridge, staring into District Four and swallowing back his fear. "What's here?"

"The people we left behind."

Nguyen Tat Thanh Street teemed with heavy traffic. It actually cut through the district, past Sai Gon's main port, off to the left a few hundred meters in front of them, and over another bridge that headed south out of Sai Gon. Nguyen Tat Thanh was Ho Chi Minh's true name, the one he had used when he had sailed from the port for France, hoping for a position in the colonial civil service and ending up a revolutionary. The unending slums of the district itself bordered the road on the right.

Dzung leaned over to Condley. *"Anh muon di dau?"* he asked. *Where to?*

Condley answered in Vietnamese, not wanting Muir to understand. "Into the district. On a smaller road," he said.

Dzung laughed again, his way of telling Condley that he was both nervous and excited. He stretched high in his seat as he looked for an opening in the traffic and chattered back and forth with Luong. Then they turned right, onto a narrower road.

The whole world slowed down in the time it took them to turn the corner. Cars and trucks immediately all but disappeared, giving way to bicycles, motorbikes, *cyclos,* and square carts filled with bricks or wood pulled along the road by sweating, bare-chested men on foot. Just off the curbs dozens of *cyclo* drivers sat idly in their vehicles, baking in the sun and watching with careful eyes as they passed. Tiny shops lined the sidewalks, little businesses with houses overhead that offered bicycle repairs, meals of rice or the staple soups *chao* and *pho,* spare parts salvaged from dead vehicles and appliances, rolls of fabric for making clothes at home.

Along one stretch a small market had gathered, offering food that would not have made the quality cut at better places such as the Ben Thanh market in District One. Dozens of women squatted in the road behind open baskets of rice, piles of dragonfruit, mangoes, durians, and custard apples, clumps of tiny overripe bananas, small wire cages containing dazed-looking puppies and bird-size chickens, metal trays piled high with crab and other shellfish, rows of fresh fish laid along the pavement, a dozen white ducks huddled in a circle around a water bowl. The road was potholed and rough, wet with spilled juices. Flies swarmed from the raw fish up to their faces. The stench was overwhelming.

"That's rather picturesque," said Muir bravely, swatting away flies and swallowing back his revulsion at the odor. "I should have brought my camera."

Condley turned back to Dzung, speaking again in Vietnamese. "A smaller road."

Dzung turned, into what appeared to be an alley. The world changed again, growing instantly more remote. The two-story buildings closed off the sun, pressing toward them from both sides like weeds on a jungle trail. Groups of older men sat next to the street on their plastic chairs underneath small umbrellas that announced their definition of a side-walk café. They drank their tea or beer, smoked their cigarettes, and stared with surprise as the two Americans passed them.

Condley relaxed into it, overwhelmed by memories. This was his Viet Nam, as real as the villages in the countryside, and free of the hus-tling, false-faced striving of District One. Sad, whining music rode the stagnant air from a half dozen different windows, competing for their melancholy embrace. The odors of cook-pot steam and cigarette smoke, the brack of old food and human waste, the sweet perfume of joss sticks burning at someone's family altar, all mixed together with the smell of his own sweat until he was inside it, carried away by it, a part of it.

Barefoot children ran in and out of darkened homes, watching them and calling excitedly to one another. Women stood idly in the doorways, gazing at them with piqued curiosity, many smiling through the gauzy filter of old memories. Young men stiffened, some smiling, others raising their chins, their eyes growing hot with undefinable defiance, a sense of invasion. They were all near enough to feel, close enough to reach out and touch, and in many of their faces Condley could see the temptation to do just that.

A shirtless, ageless man in shorts and plastic sandals smiled at Dzung from one little table, where he was nursing a glass of tea and dragging on a cigarette. Deep red burn scars covered half his face and much of his chest. Shrapnel had cupped away part of one calf muscle. Old scratches of tattoos garnished his forearms. He waved comfortably to Dzung. Dzung called to him and waved back, then leaned forward to Condley.

"My friend. Airborne soldier, very good! He fight for my father, five years."

The *cyclos* shook and clattered along the broken concrete road. It was so narrow that they could no longer travel side by side. Condley heard Muir call nervously from behind him.

"Brandon, honestly, I have to call Hawaii before the office closes. Shouldn't we be getting back?"

Children were following them, some calling out to them. "Hello!

Hello! What's your name?" Condley waved back, to their delight answering in Vietnamese. They had become a chattering, laughing entourage.

Condley turned back to Dzung. "Is your house far away?"

Dzung smiled, moved by the honor Condley was about to bring to his family. "Close." He hesitated for a moment, knowing that in the tradition he should offer but afraid of losing face if he had misunderstood Condley's intentions. "Cong Ly, you come my house? I show you my new baby."

"*Duoc,*" answered Condley. "I would like that."

Dzung again called to Luong, his voice now electric with excitement. In less than a block they turned once more, the trail of children merrily following them, and were on the broken concrete lane that led to Dzung's home. After another thirty yards Dzung suddenly stopped, dismounting from his *cyclo.*

"My house," he said, smiling shyly and gesturing to Condley's left toward a dark entranceway that held no door.

Condley climbed out of his seat and tested his legs after the jouncing ride. He pushed through a flock of chattering children, making his way to Muir, twenty feet behind. An even larger crowd was gathering as Dzung's whole neighborhood poured into the narrow alleyway. The older people with memories of the past stared incredulously, as if Condley and Muir had washed up on an isolated beach.

Muir clung to the rails of his *cyclo,* viewing the crowd as a dangerous mob. Condley reached him, pulling an arm and patting him on the shoulder.

"Easy, big fellow. These are our people."

"I feel very alone," said Muir warily, succumbing to Condley's pressure and beginning to climb down from the *cyclo.*

Dzung stepped forward. He had read Muir's fear and also the curiosity in the eyes of many of his neighbors. Now he waved his hands into the air, calming them. "*Di choi,*" he said reassuringly. "*Choi, choi, an thua gi,*" meaning that the two had come for pleasure, not politics or other life-threatening pastimes.

"*Nguoi My? Nguoi My?*" they kept asking, daring to believe but still unsure whether the two were Americans.

"Yes, we're Americans," Condley answered in Vietnamese, drawing an explosion of laughter and praise for speaking their language.

The older people were even more excited than the children. The two
frail old women who lived across from Dzung made their way to Muir's
side. They were twinlike, dressed almost identically in worn cotton
blouses and black silk slacks. Their gray-white hair was pulled back
tightly into similar buns. They smoked from the same pack of cigarettes.
Their rheumy eyes held mutual memories from American visits of long
ago.

"Lau qua!" one fairly screamed. Her wide smile revealed blackened,
betel-nut-stained teeth as she uttered the traditional Vietnamese greeting
of *Too much time has passed.* Her exuberance caused the crowd again to
laugh and cheer.

Her housemate, not to be outdone, now moved against Muir and
embraced him. He stood stiffly, transfixed by confusion as the crowd
cheered her on. *"Co vo Viet Nam chua?"* she asked, rubbing his arm up
and down fondly as the others laughed merrily.

"Roi, roi," answered Condley, causing them to laugh and cheer
some more.

Muir towered like Gulliver above the boisterous crowd, fighting
back his fear. "What did she say?"

"She asked if you have a Vietnamese wife yet," said Condley nonchalantly. Two children were pulling softly at the hairs on his arm,
examining their length and color. "See? I told you I'd introduce you to
some Vietnamese women!"

Dzung stood at the doorway to his house, filled with pride, gesturing
as he invited them in. Muir appeared stranded. The two old women kept
fawning over him. A half dozen children were examining him, pulling at
his arms and even experimentally touching the leather on his shoes.
Condley called to Dzung, pointing at the old women.

"Are they the oldest, Dzung?"

"Yes, sir," Dzung answered, his nodding smile showing that he knew
what was to follow.

Condley reached into the bag he had been carrying since leaving the
Rex's restaurant and gave each of them a loaf of French bread. "I'm
sorry, it is really nothing," he said with the humility expected when giving a gift in Viet Nam. They clutched the bread as if it were treasure,
immediately abandoning the hapless Muir. Then Condley followed
Dzung through the doorway into his home.

A tall, wide wooden shelf broke the entrance to the shack, the equivalent of both door and wall that offered Dzung's family some privacy from the street. On top of the shelf was a sand bowl with a half dozen burnt joss sticks sticking up like spent candles on a tiny cake. Around the bowl were nine pictures, most of them young men, some in military uniforms. At the center of this family shrine were old pictures of a man and woman. They sat formally next to each other in traditional *ao dais*, staring at the camera with dignified, solemn expressions. Condley knew from his earlier conversations that the pictures around the shrine were all that was left of Dzung's family.

"*Cha, me,*" said Dzung with quiet pride as he pointed to the older pictures, indicating they were of his mother and father.

Condley heard the uncertain wails of a tiny infant from behind the wall and followed Dzung inside. The home was dark, narrow, cluttered. Its ceiling was so low that Condley had to bend his head once inside. Other than three wooden beds, its furnishings included only two small stools. On one bed a little boy was sleeping in the stifling heat, curled into the fetal position. Just behind the wall itself, underneath a drab mosquito net, lay Dzung's wife and newest child.

"My wife," said Dzung almost hopefully. His eyes moved constantly behind his smile, studying Condley and then Muir for clues. "Baby."

"How many children do you have?" asked Muir, his head moving this way and that as he absorbed the surroundings of Dzung's home. Despite its squalor, Muir seemed to view the tiny room as an oasis, a refuge from the turmoil outside.

"Five already," smiled Dzung. He looked over at his wife and then quietly added a personal, secret boast. "I am very good fucker."

Even Professor Muir laughed at that, although his eyes betrayed a slight discomfort with Dzung's crudity.

The heat was oppressive, making the air dank and moldy. Condley walked slowly to the bed. Dzung's wife, Tu, was smiling bravely, but he could feel her exhaustion as certainly as he felt the heat. She slowly lifted the mosquito net, holding her newest child up for him to see. He touched the baby's head, stroking it and smiling back to her. The smile required conscious effort, a quiet repudiation of his anger. The baby was naked, thin and listless, covered with a mild rash. He looked as if he might die at any moment.

As he stroked the baby's tiny head, its dark, listless eyes watched him, and in the fastness of their gaze its struggle came alive. It was as if an electric current had run between them, causing him to feel the infant's hopeless and fading energy. All the tragedies of the war and its aftermath grabbed him fiercely at that moment, up from the past, in from these paltry surroundings, out like a lion from his heart. He felt angry and helpless.

"Dzung!" he finally said. "This baby needs to be in a hospital. I will help you. I don't care what it costs."

"He was there, Cong Ly." Dzung was smiling but his eyes showed his own unease. "They gave me pills for him. He just sick."

"He's very sick. We need to do something."

"Cong Ly. This is Viet Nam. We give him the pills."

Despite his misgivings Condley knew that Dzung was right. There was nothing else that could be done, and to say anything further would cause his friend to lose face. The best he could do was to self-consciously reach into his paper bag and offer Tu the last three pieces of bread.

"Dzung does very good work for me," he told her in Vietnamese.

She was gracious, and when her eyes lit up Condley could understand what Dzung had meant when he boasted of her beauty. "You are his good friend," she said, taking the bread slowly, her movements exaggerated by her weariness. *"Cam on ong, cam on rat nhieu."*

Condley straightened back up and discovered Muir standing just next to him. Muir seemed even more addled than before, as if he were struggling with what he was seeing but not wanting even to see it.

"Classic cultural regression," pronounced Muir, as if standing before a college lecture hall. "Socioeconomic inversion, actually. Not a rare phenomenon when revolutions occur. We saw it in the Soviet Union, obviously, with the disappearance of royalty after 1917 and the doing away of the upper classes. Here the communists did it to those who had any connections with the French or the Americans. They were at the top until the war was lost, and suddenly they had nothing. This is a largely Buddhist land and consequently I hesitate to quote the Bible, but shall we merely say that the last shall be first and the first shall be last?"

"Stop it, Professor. I really don't need one of those 'I just found a pile of bones' kind of speeches." Condley grabbed the professor's shoulders, speaking quietly from only a few inches away. "How do we help them? I'm no fucking politician. What do we do, Professor? What do we do?"

Dzung approached them. *"Phai di,"* he said to Condley, a note of urgency in his recommendation that they now leave.

Condley nudged Muir toward the doorway. "If we don't get out of here there's going to be a riot outside."

"Troublemakers?" Muir hedged, facing the overwhelming crowd that now was peering curiously into Dzung's house.

"No." Condley stepped in front of Muir and pushed his way toward the *cyclo*. "They're too happy."

————————

THE GATHERED CROWD waved and cheered them on as the *cyclos* rattled and clattered away from Dzung's house. The men at their tables and the women in the doorways in the next road were no longer surprised by their presence, offering them friendly but perfunctory waves as they passed. The small shops and eating places of the side street seemed tamer, more cosmopolitan after the narrow alleyways in the heart of the district. Nguyen Tat Thanh Street and even the cluttered ugliness of the bridge that took them back into District One offered a measure of openness and hope. And the busy boulevard of Nguyen Hue Street with its mix of ferment and growth might just as well have been Manhattan.

Muir was quiet and ponderous on the way back, even seeming to relax into the bouncing *cyclo* seat. Condley was lost in his own reverie, a deep frustration fed by the stark image of Dzung's new child, rash-covered and too frail to cry. Along Nguyen Hue Street the two rode side by side. Finally Muir reached some resolution. He called to Condley over the noise of the traffic.

"We can't save everyone, Brandon."

"We can't save anyone."

"Then why did you take me back there?"

"They needed a good laugh, Professor. They never saw an orange luau shirt before."

"You're a rogue, Brandon, but in a way you're a saint."

"Don't get carried away. I've killed a lot of people."

"More than you've saved?"

"Give me a few minutes. I haven't done the balance sheets on that one."

"Well, let me answer for you."

"Be careful, Professor, you've never seen me in action."

"I just did. And it was brilliant. Almost Christlike in its power and simple humility, Brandon. Brilliant."

Muir eyed him carefully, letting that thought sink in. Finally he slapped the side rails of the *cyclo* as if they were the arms of his desk chair back in Hawaii. "You're on a mission. I can see why this is so much more than bones to you."

"I'm going to get Dzung out of there," said Condley. "I'm buying a car, and I'm making him my driver. And then we're going to start a little business. When he's not driving me, I'm going to let him hire the car out and drive other people. He'll start making some real money, then he can ask for a better place to live."

"You make me feel quite humble."

Condley grinned. "Then I guess it's the perfect time to ask you for a loan?"

"Talk to my accountant," laughed the rotund scientist. He grew serious as they neared the Rex Hotel. "May I ask you a question? I admit to being somewhat confused, Brandon. Clearly, you hate what happened to Dzung, and yet you have no problem with Colonel Pham, who as we know is out there playing golf while these people suffer. Or—shall I be blunt? Possibly making love to his daughter?"

Condley thought for a moment, his mind buried in the past that had caught him up all those years ago and forever changed him. Then he shrugged casually. "I believe in God. Does that surprise you? And so I ask myself, why did He take me on this journey? Why did I wander through Asia for all those years, never fitting back in with my own people, never at ease with them anymore, in those false little kingdoms where they spend their days clutching their fragile idols of money and false power? And why was I led back here—simply to be swallowed up in bitterness, or to again become obsessed with death? I don't think so. Maybe something good was supposed to come out of it. Something new. A birth? Maybe a birth that looks like a death. The death of the old, and the birth of the new. I have a certain power, Professor. Let's call it the power of the uninvolved. I can talk to both sides, and both sides can talk to me."

"It seems to me you're very involved."

"Not when it comes to payback. If you're not Vietnamese they don't really keep you on their score sheet."

They had reached the hotel. Professor Muir watched Condley with a stunned respect as he climbed down from the *cyclo*. "I've never heard you speak so profoundly, Brandon. It's almost scary to know you've been hiding that kind of intelligence from me for so long."

Condley waved good-bye to Dzung as they crossed the street and walked toward the hotel's entrance, then he turned to Muir. "People talk a lot more freely in front of you when they think you're dumb."

"What about Salt and Pepper?"

Condley now laughed coldly, his skylike eyes growing molten once again. "That's different, Professor. They killed Marines. That's the American score sheet. And it's all about payback."

CHAPTER FOURTEEN

ACROSS FROM THE Rex Hotel, Dzung sat comfortably in his *cyclo* seat, smoking a cigarette and finishing his newspaper. Cong Ly and his friend had departed very early in the morning, saying only that they were traveling to the north. It was always like that with Cong Ly, mused the wiry *cyclo* driver as he flipped a page and continued to read. The American would disappear for a week or sometimes longer, never clearly saying where he was going or even what he was doing, and then return just as abruptly, filled with such a mix of exuberance and pathos that he could not help but touch Dzung's heart.

Twenty yards away, across the street and down the sidewalk, a younger man braked his Honda to a halt and parked it among a long row of motorbikes. With his uncanny antenna, Dzung immediately sensed that the younger man was watching him as he took a ticket stub from the attendant who looked after the parked motorbikes. The unsmiling younger man pocketed the ticket stub and began walking toward Dzung. He had piercing eyes and a thin, gangsterlike mustache that drooped along the sides of his mouth. He was well-dressed, in dark gray slacks and a white shirt. And he was wearing leather shoes instead of sandals, which told Dzung that he was either a government official or a businessman.

The younger man crossed the street and stopped near Dzung's *cyclo*. He lit a cigarette, surveying Dzung with an increasing arrogance, as if he were preparing to make an attack. A sudden, knowing tension filled Dzung as he rested under the younger man's gaze. He ignored the man, continuing to read his newspaper, but every instinct in his body told him that for some reason he was in trouble.

Finally the man flicked his cigarette butt so that it bounced off the rear wheel of Dzung's *cyclo*. Dzung looked down at the still-burning cigarette, which had landed near his feet. Then he looked over at the man. Their eyes locked for several seconds. Dzung's expression did not change, but his insides were now humming with anticipation, as if he were just about to walk into an ambush during the war.

Dzung was not alone in his quick trepidation. The mood among all the usual hawkers, peddlers, and drivers across from the Rex had changed abruptly in the space of a few seconds. The two *cyclo* drivers who had been lounging next to Dzung jumped nervously from their seats and walked into the park behind them. Others watched from a careful distance. Feeling their stares, Dzung knew that he had only one choice, unless he were to become a pitiful beggar in front of his friends after all these years of insult and abuse. He climbed out of his cab and picked up the cigarette butt. Then he examined it as if it were a relic, or perhaps a piece of evidence.

"You are a very wasteful man," said Dzung.

"Wasteful?" The man snorted, his chin lowered onto his chest like a dog protecting its throat.

"You wasted half a cigarette," continued Dzung. "Maybe you have so much money that you can burn it."

"Like the Americans?" The man folded his arms, his eyes hot.

"Here, finish it." Dzung tossed the cigarette back at the man. It landed at his feet. "You don't like Americans? Maybe you think the Russians were better."

"I hate them all," said the man. "I don't need them. I make good money from Vietnamese."

"That's how you and I are different," shrugged Dzung. "You, with your new motorbike and your fancy leather shoes. I don't make good money from Vietnamese."

"You worked for the Americans before. You fought for them." It was an accusation, even a damnation.

"You know a lot about me already," said Dzung. "Who are you?"

"My name is Nghiem Le Manh," he answered. "That's all you need to know for now."

"Well, Manh, I didn't work for the Americans before," said Dzung. "I fought for my country."

"*Nguy.*" Manh spat the word out. It was a slur used by the communists against the people who had supported the old Sai Gon government. "*Phan quoc,*" he continued, calling Dzung a traitor to his country.

The words were sadly familiar to Dzung, echoing like a jail gong through his memory, bringing with them the smell of jungle camps and the sounds of people slowly, slowly dying. He shrugged nonchalantly, now knowing with certainty that Manh worked for the government and that for some reason the younger man had been sent to harass or threaten or even arrest him.

"What do you even know about it?" mused Dzung, flicking the end of his own cigarette into the street. "It was a very long time ago, Manh. Were you even born then?"

"It's not your place to question me," answered Manh. "I am not the one on trial."

On trial. The world closed around Dzung as he stood staring at this young man who had appeared from nowhere. The sky descended and the street rose up and the buildings pressed toward him until he seemed to be peering at Manh from inside a box, or maybe a cage. Yes, thought Dzung, a cage. He knew this drill. He sighed, yielding to it. Nothing could change it, nothing at all.

"What do you want, Manh?"

Manh handed him a business card. "Report to this address. I will talk to you there." He wheeled back around, crossing the street and paying two thousand *dong* to the fierce, ugly man who had tended his motorbike. And then he sped off into the morning traffic.

DZUNG WALKED SLOWLY up dozens of wide stone steps, looking into the cavern of the ancient headquarters built by French colonialists a century before. The steps were worn in the middle, rounded at their edges from a million such journeys that had preceded him, step by agonizing step. He reached the top and opened a heavy door, walking slowly inside. As the door closed behind him, he found himself in a dank, dark lobby, sealed off from the energy and motion of Sai Gon's mad streets as if he had just entered a tomb. He could not remember the last time the world had gone so quiet.

He stood motionless in the high-ceilinged old lobby, squinching his eyes to adjust to the sudden darkness. Finally he noticed a uniformed guard sitting at a desk in the center of the room. The guard waved him over without saying a word. Dzung just as silently handed the guard his government identity card, along with the card that Nghiem Le Manh had given him. There was no need to converse. Both of them knew the drill.

"Room 212," the guard finally said, pointing lazily toward a nearby stairwell and then ignoring him.

He began climbing the steps toward Room 212. The flopping of his sandals echoed in the silence. The building emanated an odor that itself was foreign, a mix of dust and mildew, as if the closed-windowed, European structure had been slowly conquered over the years by Sai Gon's ferment and humidity and rot. The walls and ceiling were a dull, ugly greenish-blue, the paint so old that the dirt and mold on the walls was palpable.

The second floor seemed empty, just as eerily quiet as the lobby. Each office door was shut. No one moved along the hallways. He could hear no voices behind the office doors. No telephones were ringing. The only sound that broke the silence as he searched for Room 212 was the occasional whirring of an air conditioner. He had not felt an air conditioner in at least twenty-five years, other than the occasional gusts from the doorways of the Rex Hotel. He was already beginning to tremble slightly from the cold.

He reached Room 212 and stood before the door for several seconds, composing himself. Finally he took a deep breath and walked inside. Manh was alone in the small, stark room, waiting for him, sitting behind a cluttered desk. On the wall just behind him were three pictures of the ruins of Angkor Wat, no doubt a souvenir of Manh's military service during the decade that the Vietnamese occupied Cambodia. Other than the three pictures, the room was as barren as a prison cell.

"You are late," said Manh, lighting a cigarette. He held his cigarette all the way down between his first two fingers next to the palm, and pushed his palm against his chin when he took a drag. He looked as though he had copied his smoking style from the villain in an old movie, in order to make him look mysterious.

"I had a customer," answered Dzung blandly. "One hour, one dollar. I needed the money."

"When you are summoned by the Interior Ministry you are expected to report immediately," said Manh. "Or maybe you think your time is more valuable than mine?"

"You are paid a salary either way," shrugged Dzung. "What else do you have planned today, other than interrogating me?"

Manh's eyebrows lifted, as if he were confirming an unspoken suspicion. "Your records from the camps indicate that you are frequently insolent."

"It was only an hour," sighed Dzung, knowing what was coming. "I made ten thousand *dong*. Not even a dollar, actually. Not enough to buy shoelaces for your pretty leather shoes."

Manh stiffened in his chair, an indication that the formalities were over. "You should not be speaking to me like this!" He touched the telephone on his desk, a threat. "Your attitude disturbs me. It indicates that you learned very little in the camps. I can have you sent back with one phone call. Do you doubt that?"

Dzung forced a conciliatory smile. The Game had begun, and he was very adept at playing it. "Then let me apologize, Manh. I know that if I were to show you disrespect I would be insulting the revolution. And I have come to terms with the revolution."

Manh seemed immediately pleased. He stubbed his cigarette into the ashtray, then lit another one as he flipped through the hundreds of pages that Dzung knew made up his own personal file.

"You are smart," said Manh, indulging Dzung. "You went to college."

"Da Lat," smiled Dzung with small irony. His face lit up with a passion that was more a remembrance than an actual emotion, a dim light from long ago. "It was an excellent education. Very good training.

Tactics. Leadership. Engineering. English. That's why I make such a good *cyclo* driver."

"Yes," said Manh, knowing Dzung was being sarcastic. Da Lat had produced the old regime's best military leaders. Its graduates were despised by the communist government. "So we are both very smart. And after reading your file I am even willing to admit this, Dzung. You are probably smarter than I am."

A pulse of defiance charged through Dzung, despite his position of forced humility. He couldn't hold it back. He smiled. "How would I know, Manh? Perhaps you should show me your file. But you know that many people on the street believe those who work for the government are stupid."

"A predictable answer, given your history," said Manh, fighting to hold back his anger. "That is your problem. So much intelligence, and so little common sense."

"I had common sense or I would not have survived in combat," answered Dzung. "Then for almost four years your interrogators kept repeating that I had been stupid to oppose the revolution, and they re-educated me. So maybe all the lectures by the stupid propagandists took away my common sense."

"Be careful," warned Manh, tapping the phone.

Dzung was still smiling, but he spoke without a trace of sarcasm as he watched the Interior Ministry official's face. "Oh, it was a wonderful education, Manh! Nothing like the boring classrooms of Da Lat! Clearing minefields by hand and planting thousands of trees out in the wilderness. Eating bugs because there was no meat. Living in the mountains like we were some lost and hopeless tribe, never hearing a radio or reading a newspaper or seeing the people we loved, until most of the people we loved were either dead or had disappeared. Four years, listening to the gong man, the pit-bull man, the gun man, the propaganda man, the loudspeaker man, until my brain was so overloaded with nonsense that it emptied all the garbage out into the jungle, just the way you vomit when you have eaten too much food. All of it, left behind me in the camps. That is what happened to my second education, the education that was supposed to erase my education. But it helped me become more intelligent. It cleansed my mind and focused it, don't you see?"

"You must speak more carefully," warned Manh. "I am trying to help you when I say this. You should be showing me respect. If you knew how quickly I could lock you up you would be very afraid of the things you are saying."

"Afraid of what? You are a powerful man, so maybe you know fear, but do you know what courage is?" Memories washed over Dzung until the calm in his face resonated, penetrating even the depths of Manh's dark threat. "Courage and honor, respect and even pity, justice and, yes, you may not like for me to say it, but let me use the word—love? Do you know these words, Manh? A love for your children, so deep that you would die for them? Or maybe a love of justice, so pure that it demands that you speak out? These are the feelings that push the world forward. And what are they to you but words? What have you learned in the government schools that taught you how to hate and to interrogate? The honor of defending a failed revolution? Justice measured by a bribe? The love of retribution? Sometimes I pity you, and then I wish I could show you what could have been. Or what might have been. Or even what could be."

"I have lost my patience with you," answered Manh, repulsed by Dzung's rhetoric and looking to regain control of the interrogation. "You end up talking nonsense that no normal Vietnamese can understand. You are dangerous."

"Maybe I read too much, or perhaps I simply think too much," said Dzung. He had lost his smile. He knew that he had certainly said too much and that Manh would very likely make him pay for his careless words. But there was no point in stopping without finishing his thought. "Or maybe I have been through too much. But this I know: Courage did not save us, and fear will not protect us. So you're wrong to think I would ever be afraid, not anymore. The truth is, I've lost all my fear. But I've lost all my hate too. I've lost them both. Can you understand that, Manh?"

"Enough of this, I have a job to do," said Manh with crisp formality.

"I accept that," said Dzung. "And I do not hate you for it. In fact, I think I pity you."

Manh stubbed out his cigarette, becoming adamant. "For the last time, I am warning you! Do not talk to me like that! I have a task to perform, and you are a part of this task. I will hear no more lectures from the *nguy* enemy soldier who is so smart that he lives without water in District Four with too many children and a baby who is dying. Oh, yes, Dzung, I know all about you. And your puppet-general father. And especially your friendship with the former American soldier and intelligence operative who now pretends to be looking for the bones of dead veterans as he makes his way around our country and reports to his superiors on how to begin some new aggression. And I will have no more comments about the revolution or the war, in which I would like to point out my father gave his life. Yes, when I was a young boy! So talk to me about love and being willing to die for your children, and complain all you want about the camps, but you are still alive. And you will either listen to me and cooperate with me or you will be taken away for further political instruction. I have the authority to make this decision. It would not be subject to review until you are reevaluated in the prison camps. And such a reevaluation can take a very long time."

"I am sorry about your father," said Dzung, reading the loss in Manh's usually fierce face.

"It was a long time ago," shrugged Manh, recovering.

"I miss my own father every day."

"Your father was a traitor."

"I loved him. So did his soldiers. He talks to me frequently. That's how I know he died."

"We are not here to talk about your father."

"So why did you bring me here?" Dzung spoke quietly now, his mood deflated by the slow realization that he had just come within a few words of being marched away to the oblivion of another prison. "What did I do?"

"You have become suspicious," said Manh simply, as if the answer was in the word itself. "You want a license to operate a business. Where are you going to get the money for a license? And a car. Why should the American buy a car for you? What great skill do you have to offer, what connections with important people, what family history? We have many who suffered greatly during the war, who served proudly on behalf of the revolution, who still have nothing. Why should we allow an enemy soldier to move ahead of them? And I must ask something vitally important, Dzung. Your future hangs on it. What is it that has put all of these things into motion, just at the moment your American friend is probing too deeply into the past?"

Dzung looked at the floor, confused and disappointed. "I have no knowledge of what Cong Ly does. He is my customer for a very long time. I take him places when he is not working. I don't even know what his work is. He is generous. A good man."

"Cong Ly! Cong Ly!" Manh spat the words out. "All of you have perverted his name as if you are speaking code, twisting his very image into that of justice! Is he asking you to help him?"

"I am serious, I don't even know what he does, except that he looks for bones," answered Dzung. "He told me he would buy a car and that we could have a business. That when we made money I could move my family out of District Four, maybe to Song Be."

"The government tells you when you have permission to move. Not an American spy."

"We were talking only of possibilities," answered Dzung quietly. His mood had irreversibly sunk, because he was beginning to understand. He had tried to warn Cong Ly, and he knew now that the whole scheme had been hopeless. Not only hopeless, but destructive, summoning up the magnifying glass of the Interior Ministry's intrinsic paranoia.

"We do not understand this man." Manh was peering intensely at Dzung, as if he were asking a question. "We have followed him for years. We listen to him. We watch him. And still we do not know him."

We do not know him. Instinctively, Dzung knew that an offer had just been placed before him, one that was negotiable if he chose to accept it, and even promising if he was careful. Despite himself, he felt an odd thrill. It was his first moment of power in more than two decades. And just as quickly he felt a tightening in his throat and a roll of nausea deep inside his stomach. For if he chose to negotiate he could not stop. And if he began and then negotiated badly, either he or Condley would certainly lose.

"I know him only as a man," said Dzung. Compromising, he decided to tell Manh secrets that the government certainly already knew. "He spent many years in Viet Nam during the war. He was in love with a Vietnamese woman who died. He believes she was killed by people from your side."

Manh's dark eyes flashed. He suddenly smiled, as if welcoming Dzung into his home. And Dzung knew that the negotiation had begun. "We know that. Has he remained bitter?"

"He loves Viet Nam," shrugged Dzung. "He is like us, I think. He knows that to love our country is to experience tragedy."

"We do not believe he is so pure. Does he also love Colonel Pham's daughter, then?"

"I know nothing of that. He respects Colonel Pham."

"Why is he obsessed with the story of the Americans who were once missing in the mountains of Quang Nam Province?"

"I told you, Manh, he never mentions where he goes or what he does when he is not in Ho Chi Minh City. I know nothing of that."

Manh grunted, unconvinced. "He is your friend for many years and you know nothing of what he does? Don't you find that strange? Most Americans are like little children. They want you to know everything. They constantly need approval."

"He is very Vietnamese, Manh. Like an older brother. Sometimes he acts foolishly but he believes he is taking care of me."

"And why would he do that, for someone like you?" Manh's face was filled with a befuddled curiosity. "Yesterday he goes to District Four and passes out loaves of bread to your neighbors. Is this not an odd thing, meant to encourage unrest? The day before that he is with Colonel Pham and his wife at temple. That night he is with their daughter at his hotel. Today he is with Colonel Pham in Quang Nam Province, searching for the answers to a story that might embarrass the revolution. Colonel Pham speaks favorably of him and has offered to take responsibility for his actions. But Colonel Pham is getting old, and perhaps his daughter cares for this man. Perhaps the colonel has lost his judgment. Condley claims that he had no connection with American authorities for many years before coming back to Viet Nam, but why would he stay in Asia, and why would he come back here? I must tell you, he has all the mannerisms of a highly trained agent."

Dzung found himself shrugging helplessly. "You must believe me. I do not know."

Manh eyed Dzung shrewdly for several seconds, measuring him. "You would like to move out of District Four, though. Would you not?"

"Of course I would like to move," said Dzung. "Even the cockroaches and the rats dream of escaping District Four."

"And to take care of your family?"

The question was too pointed. A bomb exploded inside Dzung's brain. "What do you want, Manh?"

Manh ignored Dzung for a moment, returning to his thick file, flipping studiously through the pages to emphasize the point he was about to make. Finally he looked up to Dzung, giving him a sly smile. "You were a skilled marksman when you were a soldier."

"I was qualified as an instructor in many weapons."

"Do you like to shoot?"

"It's been a very long time." The reality of what Manh was putting before him crept up Dzung's spine on soft little scorpion's feet, causing him to suddenly shiver.

"Why are you trembling?" asked Manh.

"I am not used to air conditioners."

"Of course," said Manh. Then he closed Dzung's file, setting it to one side of his desk as if done with it. "I'm going to take you shooting. Just an hour or so a day. Report here every morning at seven o'clock. I will have you back at the Rex Hotel in time for you to begin working as usual."

"What do you want me to shoot?"

"Targets," said Manh. "To improve your skills."

"Why?"

"Because it has been decided that you will do it."

"It has been a long time," said Dzung carefully. "What if I don't want to shoot anymore?"

"You do want to take care of your family, don't you?"

"What if I'm no good?"

"You are a natural shot. An expert. It is in your files." Manh lit another cigarette, his dark eyes dancing mischievously. And then he waved a hand, dismissing Dzung for the day. "I will see you tomorrow morning. And when the time comes, you will know why."

CHAPTER FIFTEEN

Quang Nam Province

THEY DROVE SOUTH from Da Nang toward Que Son on Highway 1, a narrow, often broken road that was euphemistically named the National Highway. Colonel Pham sat in the front seat of the new Toyota sport-utility vehicle, next to a driver who had been hired along with the car itself in Da Nang. Condley and Hanson Muir sat in the back, quietly conversing with each other. The car crossed low bridges and made its way through a dozen noisy, cluttered little villages that in another life Condley had known with an intimate certainty. Traffic was thick, dominated by bicycles, motorbikes, and very old trucks, many of them creaking, repainted American military "six-bys" left over from the war.

The Toyota's driver, whose name was Ngoc, was in his late thirties. Whenever they were out of Colonel Pham's earshot, Ngoc would grin conspiratorially to Condley and speak to him in the pidgin English that the children of Quang Nam had used with the Marines during the war.

"Hey, Honcho, you souvenir me boo-coo chop chop, numbah one, huh?"

Conversing in their odd idiom, Condley and the driver would laugh together as if they were long-lost friends. But as soon as the colonel reappeared, the driver would immediately lose both his smile and his voice, worried that Colonel Pham would disapprove and report him for being overly familiar with the Americans. Now, as they made their way toward Que Son, Ngoc the driver stared straight ahead at the road, unsmiling and unflinching, as if he were both deaf and mute.

Colonel Pham would never understand, but Ngoc and his childhood friends secretly loved Americans. Except in the worst areas further out from Da Nang, the children had always crowded around the American perimeters during the war. They had chosen special friends among the Marines and whiled away the lonely, boring hours with them, helping them wash at village wells, joking with them, playing cards, competing for their favors and for rewards of food, cigarettes, and chewing gum, even mourning the ones who were killed or wounded. True, many of the children gave information to the other side about Marine gun positions, morale, and casualties. But they still remembered the Americans with an intimate, knowing fondness that all the propaganda since the war could never erase.

It took an hour to drive the twenty miles to Que Son. The rivers were swollen underneath the bridges. The rice paddies on all sides of them were lush and wet. The slate-gray sky was reflected in the paddy water and the rivers until the water and the eastern sky connected seamlessly, with only little dots of villages among the glassy paddies to mark the horizon. To the west the distant mountains were masked by a bank of dense low clouds that huddled just above the ground like fog. And at the edges of almost every village they passed the soldiers' cemeteries.

The ornate cemeteries for the communist soldiers who died during the war were among the few new structures along the road. They were clearly visible from the car, expansive reminders of the cost the communists had paid for their victory. Their entrances were usually the same: a stone gateway with a sign overhead—*Nghia Trang Liet Si*—and above the sign a gold star affixed to a circular red plate. Row after row of white gravestones filled the cemeteries, many with red stars on their fronts, reflecting the loss of hundreds upon hundreds of local soldiers even here among the midsize villages. A garish pinnacle stood at the center of most cemeteries, with either a primitive, heroic sculpture or a large communist symbol. Frequently, Ho Chi Minh's rallying slogan appeared at this pinnacle: *Doc Lap va Tu Do—Independence and Freedom.*

Hanson Muir had nudged Condley when they passed the first vast cemetery, reading the words above the gate. "What do those words mean?"

"*Nghia Trang Liet Si. The Resting Place of Heroes,* Professor."

"A lot of heroes," grunted Muir.

"Anybody who doesn't believe the body count from the war can go add them up now." Condley's eyes scanned a thousand graves in one village cemetery as the Toyota chugged along the highway. "Their side, anyway. They plowed under our guys."

"What was that, Brandon?"

"Our guys. The ARVN soldiers. The communists plowed the ARVN cemeteries under after the war."

The thought seemed to fascinate the huge, cerebral anthropologist, who brooded over it as they passed cemetery after cemetery. Finally, as was his wont, Muir gave a little speech. "The reason is terrible but simple, Brandon. Guglielmo Ferrero wrote about it more than a century ago in his book *Principles of Power,* referring to the leaders of the French Revolution: *The more blood they shed the more they needed to believe in their principles as absolutes. Only the absolutes might still absolve them in their own eyes and sustain their desperate energy.*" He gave Condley one of his ceremonial nods, his eyes off into the horizon. "I'm rather proud I remembered that. It was a direct quote."

"You need to watch more TV," grunted Condley.

"I'm drawn to timeless thoughts," said Muir. "They elevate me from the mundanity of my own life."

"Well, I tried to introduce you to some interesting women back there in District Four."

Muir laughed aloud. "Speaking of antiquities?"

"Just your style, Professor. A living, walking bone dig."

"Call me odd, Brandon, but there's a fascination in being able to measure what's around you against the context of history. And that's what we're seeing. They erect grand monuments at the same time they plow under the ARVN cemeteries. The Romans plowed salt through the soil of Carthage, so that nothing would ever grow there again. Why did they do that? Same principle. Here, the more the communist leaders went to the people and demanded their sacrifices, the greater their burden of proof became that their cause was not simply just, but sacred. A hundred thousand, two hundred thousand, eight hundred thousand, a million—every dead son another warning that if they were not right, if they did not prevail, they would join history's black pages as the slaughterers of their own people. And so every communist soldier's death has become a hero's, elevated to the point of a national religion, while every anticommunist death was traitorous, evil, and without justification. Plow them under. Erase them from history before some new generation comes along and starts thinking otherwise."

Just past the little town of Dien Ban the road was undergoing an emergency repair. They slowed, watching bent and filthy men and women fitting rocks into place by hand, one by one. Tar was being heated in fifty-gallon barrels at the roadside, under an open flame, and then poured from buckets onto the rocks. The workers wore long-sleeved shirts and the cylindrical straw *non la* hats usually found in the countryside. Their faces were wrapped in bandannas to keep the smoke and tar out of their lungs.

"Isn't that amazing," muttered Muir, watching them. "Individually the people have so much energy, so much resilience. And yet nationally they are so incredibly inept. A brick at a time, a bucket of tar at a time, to fix the national highway. Look at that! One American road crew would have that job done in an hour."

"But they make great cemeteries, don't they, Professor?"

"What's that?"

"Cemeteries. And monuments to themselves. While the cities and the highways fall to shit."

Muir chuckled softly, watching Condley's strained face with a gentle patience. "Oh, sometimes I forget, Brandon. I see all of this as predictable, a matter of history playing itself out almost beyond anyone's control. And you're always looking for answers."

At Thang Binh they left the beaten two-lane highway, heading west into a valley along a crumbling asphalt road. The recent rains had washed out the road in several places. Ngoc the driver cursed mightily as he shifted into four-wheel drive. Colonel Pham turned to Condley, smiling and shrugging his apology. They passed little villages, their crude houses built up against the road, interspersed with narrow stands of trees planted decades before on both sides of the road by forced laborers from the reeducation camps.

Staring at the row of trees, Condley thought again of a younger

Dzung, fresh from the battlefield, planting saplings under the watchful eyes of those he once had fought. Had he been here twenty years before?

The sights became predictable again. Young children stood in front of the houses, many naked from the waist down, waving and calling to the car as it passed. Hopeful vendors sat behind weathered little stalls, offering soft drinks, water, and local fruits. An old one-legged woman struggled slowly along the roadside, pulling a cow behind her as she worked a crutch with her other hand. At one point they halted for a young man who was herding a hundred little ducklings across the road, walking behind them and keeping them together by tapping a twenty-foot pole from side to side.

Across the valley to their north, the Que Son Mountains rose from the mists, the wet fog cascading down their slopes like huge, rolling balls of cotton. Muir pointed quizzically at the steep blue mountains. Noticing his gaze, Condley answered his unspoken question.

"The Que Sons, Professor. We're on the eastern end of the mountains, opposite from Ninh Phuoc. Maybe fifteen miles away."

"Only fifteen miles? Not exactly the Himalayas, are they?"

"The major mountain ranges run north to south in a huge belt, from here all the way into Laos," explained Condley. "The Que Sons are like a thumb pointing east toward the coast. That's why they were so much trouble for us during the war. The North Vietnamese could hump in from Laos along the mountains under a double-canopy jungle and position base camps within a few miles of the coast. They could come down very quickly when they wanted to attack, but it was hell taking it to them in the mountains when they wanted to defend."

"And Salt and Pepper operated with them from these base camps," reasoned Muir.

"Maybe Salt and Pepper," shrugged Condley, staring up at the rugged blue peaks. "Maybe many Salts and many Peppers."

Colonel Pham had been reticent since joining them at the airport in Sai Gon and had not spoken at all since leaving Da Nang. As they neared the center of the small town of Que Son he seemed to awaken. Looking intensely to their front, he tapped the driver on an arm, directing him to halt at the edge of the road in front of a boxy cement building that housed the Que Son District Headquarters.

Just outside the building, two squat, hard-looking little men were waiting for them underneath a huge red communist flag. The car stopped right next to the two men. Colonel Pham burst from it, leaving Condley and Muir still inside, and began an intense discussion with the district government officials. Watching the older man's sudden vigor, an enormous respect washed over Condley.

"He's taking no prisoners," mused Condley.

"Excuse me," asked Muir, "but aren't they on the same side?"

"Not on this one. This is sort of like 'you bet your life' for Colonel Pham, Professor. That's why he came up here with us. Ha Noi wasn't happy about our request, and he's on the hook personally if things go wrong. If we embarrass the government, he loses big face. If we were hiding a second agenda that's more explosive, he can count on either retiring or going to jail. So he's got to help us and at the same time not lose face with them."

"What's he saying?" asked Muir as the two caught bits and pieces of the conversation from inside the car.

"Basically, he's telling them he's in charge," said Condley. "And that he wants the no-bullshit, exact fucking truth."

"*Da,* honcho obah dare!" laughed Ngoc the driver, pointing at Colonel Pham. "VC *khong thich*, say America numbah fuckin' ten!"

"What does he mean, number ten?" Muir seemed confused.

"Number one is the best," chuckled Condley. "So use your imagination."

"Numbah fuckin' ten *thousand*," decided Ngoc, laughing greatly as he watched the three men conduct their intense debate. Then suddenly he retreated inside his mask, staring straight ahead again as Colonel Pham climbed back into the car.

"*Di theo duong nay!*" said the colonel firmly, pointing straight ahead, and Ngoc immediately pulled back onto the road. Looking behind him, Condley saw that the two men were following them in another four-wheel-drive vehicle.

The colonel remained silent for several minutes as they took the road through Que Son and back into the countryside. His tension was palpable. For a moment Condley regretted having put him into such a dilemma. Then finally Colonel Pham turned back to Condley. His face was determined, his eyes bright with challenge. He gave Condley an ironic but victorious grin.

"They have something to show us," said the colonel, speaking in Vietnamese. "But they will want a reward."

"Do they have the guy?"

"One step at a time, Cong Ly. They have something valuable. How much they have might depend on how big a reward they receive."

"What kind of reward?"

"Five thousand dollars. Maybe more."

"Five thousand dollars?" Condley choked back a laugh. "That's fifteen years of income for somebody living back here."

"It would not only go to them," said the colonel. "As you know, there are many people who would be paid. For them, maybe only ten or twenty dollars."

"Big problem, Colonel! We don't pay bribes!"

"Not a bribe!" said Colonel Pham. "In your country you have what they call a contract. What you get depends on what you give. Am I right?"

"Services," grinned Condley, beginning to understand. "They provide a service, and they are paid for the value of that service."

"*Dung roi!*" exclaimed the colonel. *Exactly.*

"They have to show us first."

"That might be difficult," said the colonel. "Because once they show us, the service has been performed whether they're paid or not."

"They can always work with Ha Noi to deny me an exit visa if I don't follow through."

Colonel Pham laughed at that. "You don't want to leave anyway. At least that's what my youngest daughter tells me."

It was the first time he had mentioned Van. Condley grinned stupidly, fighting back an immediate nervousness, and he could tell that the ever-astute colonel was reading his forced smile perfectly. "Sooner or later I will leave, Colonel."

"Maybe to Hawaii?"

Another knowing smile. Given their shared cynicism regarding Francois Petain, Condley decided to take both remarks as compliments, even as an encouragement. "Maybe to Hawaii, maybe to Da Lat." The colonel laughed warmly at that, as if it were confirming some secret expectation.

"I should show you Da Lat sometime, Cong Ly."

"Okay, Colonel. And I'll show you Hawaii."

"I would like that. You could buy me a shirt like Professor Muir's. Then maybe people would think I'm a Filipino."

Condley grew serious. "Please tell them we're not trying to trick them. But it really depends on what they have."

"I think you will be happy with what they have," said the colonel. "But there has been some resistance to this idea. If you want success you should make sure that they are happy too."

The driver in the car behind them began beeping his horn, little staccato blasts, again and again. Ngoc slowed, allowing the second car to pass them. After that they followed the second car along steadily worsening roads as it headed up into the mountains. An hour passed. Asphalt gave way to gravel. Gravel gave way to mud. Ngoc cursed and muttered to himself as he fishtailed and slid through vast puddles, ugly craters, and endless washboard gullies. The mountains closed around them and still they climbed. Finally, on a ridgeline two thousand feet above Que Son, the lead car halted. Ngoc pulled up just behind it and turned off the engine.

The narrow road was cutting through a saddle in the mountains. To their right and left, huge crags rose steeply, their peaks lost in the insistent mist. Straight ahead, the road fell down the mountains into a wide, waterous valley. It was so quiet they could hear one another breathe. And stepping out of the car into the silence, Condley fell like a rock into the past.

Hanson Muir had walked around the car to join him. The professor stretched mightily, trying to shake the kinks from the long ride. "Do you have your map, Brandon? The old one from the war?"

"I don't need it." Condley pointed knowingly down into the valley. "That's Antenna Valley. Ninh Phuoc is about five miles from here."

"Amazing," said Muir, straining to see that far. "Beautiful, isn't it? I've never breathed air so clean. And it's just . . . right there! It seems like another lifetime that we were in Ninh Phuoc, doesn't it?"

Condley did not hear him. Nor did he merely see the mountains. At that moment he was inside them, almost a part of them. He stared coolly up both steep slopes, measuring their crags and the tangled jungle foliage, wondering where the trails might open up to reinforced caves or ambush-ready clearings, trying to decide how he would either attack or bypass them and along which rock-strewn ridge he might place his defensive perimeter for the night. It was happening again, the brain trick that he neither desired nor understood. The war was all over him, more real than the thought of pressing into the mountains with three former enemies and this well-meaning but permanently naive scientist who believed the world's answers turned on the riddles found in bones.

"Ninh Phuoc's an easy hike from here. The Marine base at An Hoa isn't far away either." He pointed expertly. "Right over there, see the bend in the far river? And Que Son is just down the mountain behind us. Great place for an NVA base camp, huh, Professor?"

"If you say so," said Muir. "Personally, I find it unbearably primitive."

In front of the other car, Colonel Pham and the two district officials were arguing again. Muir watched them quizzically. "They're not happy with this, are they?"

"I think we need to let them talk with Andrew Jackson."

"Are you speaking in code?"

"Loan me forty dollars and I'll demonstrate."

Muir smiled slowly, getting it. He took out his wallet and handed Condley two twenty-dollar bills. "Can I put this on my expense account?"

"Absolutely, Professor. You didn't notice, but we had a late breakfast in Que Son."

"For forty dollars it must have been a feast."

"We killed a whole pig, didn't we?"

Muir grinned. "What did we do with the other thirty-nine dollars?"

"Orange juice is expensive out here."

Condley approached the three men. They ceased their discussion as he neared, the two government officials eyeing him with unmuted suspicion. He nodded deferentially to Colonel Pham, recognizing his role as the leader of their little delegation, then shook hands with each of the government officials and spoke to them in Vietnamese.

"Good morning, gentlemen. I'm sorry that I didn't get a chance to introduce myself before. On behalf of the United States government, I would like to express my deep appreciation for your assistance today. I know that our request has caused many inconveniences in your busy and understaffed headquarters, as well as additional costs for such items as fuel for your vehicle. When we're finished with this expedition I will work very carefully with you to fill out the necessary forms for a full reimbursement from my government, including"—he raised his eyebrows a bit, as if telling them a secret—"certain administrative expenses, depending on the success of our mission."

The two officials nodded somberly to Pham upon hearing those words but still remained silent. Condley continued, handing each of them a twenty-dollar bill. "For now, since I do not want you to have incurred any expenses from your own pockets, please accept these small payments to cover the costs for the trip this morning."

They silently accepted the bills, the equivalent of a month's pay for each of them. Pocketing the money, they glanced quickly at each other and then at Colonel Pham, a signal that the bickering was over. Finally they nodded grimly to Condley, an indication that they were ready to proceed, and began walking toward a thin, muddy trail that disappeared inside the foliage of the mountain on the eastern side of the road.

Colonel Pham gave Condley a secret wink, pulling him aside and speaking quietly before they began to follow the two men. "They are both former Viet Cong soldiers. Their families suffered greatly during the war. You must understand that they are not yet over their bitterness. They wish to speak to you only through me. But they have their orders, so they must cooperate. And your little gift was helpful. Go ahead, follow them. They have some information you will find interesting. This way. It's not too far."

"So much for the pure flame of the revolution," teased Muir as he began walking behind Condley and Colonel Pham.

"Greed is its very own philosophy, Professor."

"Another little toll booth on the road toward fulfillment."

Condley chuckled. "If you're going to get screwed, you may as well get kissed."

They trudged up the narrow, muddy trail behind the two tough former soldiers, fighting rocks and brush as they made their way toward the fog-shrouded crest of the mountain. The cooling effect of the recent monsoon was kind to them as they struggled up the slope. If they had been forced to make this trek during the dry months, it would have been so punishing that Hanson Muir and possibly even Colonel Pham would have succumbed to a blistering tropical heat.

In front of them, a rickety wooden footbridge connected two peaks above a rushing stream. Reaching the bridge, they crossed it slowly, one man at a time. The water in the gorge below was as clear as glass, pouring over piles of rocks and churning into froth as the stream made tight turns. Looking upstream as he walked across the little bridge, Condley recognized a pile of huge, distant boulders. To Condley's trained eye such rocks and boulders had their own signatures, particularly around streambeds. In his other life they had provided important landmarks when he was navigating his platoon underneath the blanketlike jungle canopy.

And Condley had no doubt that he knew those rocks. He had waded knee-deep up the same stream a lifetime ago as his company bypassed a piece of jungle too thick to hack through with machetes. The very jungle on the ridge just below his feet. In June 1969.

Reaching the far side of the bridge, he called to Muir, who was now crossing it. "I've been here before, Professor."

"I know, Brandon," teased Muir, panting greatly as he walked toward him. "I saw your initials carved on the bridge."

"There wasn't any bridge. And the road back there didn't exist either."

"So they didn't drive you up here in a car?"

"I remember the rocks. If you follow that streambed to the other side of them you'll find the ambush site."

"My best guess is that you'll drown if you try to walk in that stream."

Then and now. Now and then. The professor was right. He was living in two worlds again. "In December, maybe, but it was late June. The dry season. There wasn't as much water in it. It was knee-deep, refreshing. We filled our canteens in the stream as we walked. It looked so pure. Later on, half of us caught shrimp fever."

Muir reached him. They paused for a moment, catching their breath. "The rocks are telling you all this?"

"Bones talk to you. Why can't rocks talk to me?"

"I'm fine with that, Brandon. Really. It makes perfect sense."

"Liar."

Muir laughed, his chest heaving as he drew in huge gulps of air. "Yes, I am. But only on irrelevant issues."

"Rocks are very relevant in the mountains."

"See? I'm not very good at it, am I?"

The two district government officials started climbing again. They followed the trail for another fifty meters until it suddenly leveled off, reaching a plateau. The two tough little men stopped for a moment, looking back with satisfaction at Colonel Pham, Condley, and Muir, who was still breathing deeply as he recovered from the climb. Then one of them pointed toward the jungle on the right side of the trail, and they disappeared into the foliage.

"They could have saved us a lot of trouble by bringing this fellow down the mountain and meeting us on the road," sighed Muir, walking reluctantly up the trail.

Condley's antennae were working too, but for a different reason. "Who's going to take this guy into custody, assuming they actually deliver him to us? It's a long way back down this mountain, and I don't see him going quietly."

"A scary thought," said Professor Muir nervously. He gave Condley an uncomfortable smile. "As you know, Brandon, I get involved only after they've decomposed."

They followed Colonel Pham and the others down a narrow passage that had been recently cut through an immense tangle of leaves and vines, as if just for them. The jungle swallowed them as they walked. Thick, reaching trees blocked the light above them. The vines pushed in all around them. It appeared they were moving through a clinging green tunnel, from which there was no clear entrance or exit.

"Is this what it was like during the war?" asked Muir.

"Try cutting the trail yourself," laughed Condley. "With fifty pounds of gear on your back and somebody waiting to kill you at the other end."

After a hundred meters the jungle just as suddenly ended, and they stepped from the vines into a wide, grassy clearing. The five men stood at the edge of the clearing for a moment, uniformly exhausted. They breathed heavily, nodding warily to one another as they rubbed the scratches on their arms and faces, having developed an odd camaraderie through their little ordeal. And then Colonel Pham nudged Condley, pointing across the clearing as if offering him a personal gift.

"They are coming now. Prepare yourself. You will have only one opportunity to convince them."

"Convince them of what, Colonel?"

"That this is important. And that you are sincere. These are mountain people, Cong Ly. They know nothing since the war."

In the distance several dogs were barking, and now they heard children's voices. As Condley looked across the clearing he could see a hundred people emerging from the far trees and walking toward them. A collective, expectant electricity seemed to pulse through them as they walked. They were of all ages. They wore the coarse blue or black pajamas and conical straw *non la* hats of rural Viet Nam. The little yellow dogs chased among them, yapping at their feet.

"The village is not far from here," said Colonel Pham, as if explaining their eerie approach. "We are not invited there. Not yet."

Hanson Muir's mouth was agape, his eyes transfixed on the villagers. "Brandon, look. There they are."

Condley followed Muir's gaze. Walking toward them, mixed among the native villagers, were several half black children.

The district government officials waved to Colonel Pham and began to walk forward. Condley, Muir, and Colonel Pham followed them to the center of the clearing. They were immediately surrounded by the excited villagers. For several minutes it was impossible to speak. The villagers curiously inspected them, talking to one another about them as if they were frozen statues in a museum. They touched their clothing and their hair and ran their fingers along their skin, conversing in such a thick, slurred rural dialect that Condley had great difficulty understanding their words.

"I thought one of our search teams visited them before," said Condley in a near-whisper, eyeing the half-black children among them and remembering his conversation with Professor Muir at the Rex Hotel.

"No," grunted the colonel. "I will be honest with you, because I made them explain this. They brought that search team to a different place. Another village, nearer to the road, where the black American did not live. The children from this village heard about the visit and some of them went down there to spy on the foreigners. The children were playing. Your people saw them only by accident."

A thin, bent-legged old man with a wispy white beard, obviously the village chief, moved to the front of the villagers, leaning on a cane as he walked. He wore gray shorts and a faded green soldier's shirt. He had a serious, etched face. Even at his advanced age his eyes burned brightly with a discerning curiosity. He stared at Condley and then Muir for a long time, saying nothing. And then finally he turned to Colonel Pham.

"We have nothing for them," he said, turning his palms upside down in a helpless gesture as his clever eyes danced on Pham's face.

Another negotiation, thought Condley wearily, giving Hanson Muir a secret, cynical glance. Another little toll booth.

"What do they want, Colonel?"

The villagers erupted in surprised laughter, recognizing for the first time that Condley spoke Vietnamese. The old man's face brightened momentarily, and he addressed Condley.

"We want nothing. Only to be left alone."

"We were told that you had something to give us."

The old man shrugged again, as if helpless. "They came here and they asked me. But the black American has been dead for three years. Why do you bother us?"

Condley glanced at the two former soldiers who had guided them to this improbable spot. They were smirking at him from the back of the crowd now, seeming to enjoy the awkwardness of the moment. They did not know that a part of him was secretly rejoicing in this knowledge, for it meant that there would be no physical struggle with a deserter who did not want to go home.

"It doesn't matter that he's dead," said Condley. "We will be happy to collect his remains."

"He became a part of this village," insisted the old man. "He married one of my nieces. He is buried in a family plot. His remains should stay here, with his family."

"It is very important for us to identify him," said Condley. "We are trying to solve a matter left over from the war."

"The war has been over for a very long time," said the old man as the rest of the villagers nodded their affirmation. "What difference can it possibly make?"

"He must be identified," repeated Condley. Watching the old man's face a long moment, he decided to take a different tack. "So that his American family can have peace."

"We know nothing about his American family. We do not even know his American name," said the village chief. "He gave himself a Vietnamese name. And so we called him Nguyen My Den."

"Nguyen My Den?" Condley could not restrain a laugh. The dead deserter either had a great sense of humor or very little imagination, having named himself Nguyen the Black American. "Anyway, we don't need his American name. If you gave us his American name we would still have to examine his remains. He could have made up an American name, just as he made up a Vietnamese name. We identify people through their bones," he said. "And especially their teeth."

"What good does it do, anyway?" asked the old man. "He came to our side during the war and he stayed here after the war. He was not embarrassed by this. He did not want to go back to your country. It would insult our family if you took him from us."

"Then why did you agree to meet with us?"

The old man shrugged absently, nodding toward the nearby government officials. "Because they told us to."

Condley was stumped. He paused for a moment, looking to Colonel Pham for help. The colonel shook his head, as if there were nothing he could do. "*Shit,*" mumbled Condley, feeling oddly betrayed. "Just *shit.*"

"What's he saying?" asked Muir.

"Pepper's been dead for three years, but they're not going to give us his remains because he's a part of the family now. He's not an American anymore. They don't give a shit about the war."

"All we need is his skull," said Muir calmly, stepping up next to Condley. "The skull. Tell him we want to borrow it."

"You're a genius, Professor."

"As I said, distance from a problem has its benefits. And if you would please hurry up, I'd like to be very distant from this one."

Condley patted Muir on the back, nodding now to the village chief. "My partner is a very distinguished American scientist. He has offered a solution, which I hope you will consider. We would like to borrow the head of the dead American, so that his family in the United States can examine his teeth and know for certain that he is dead. You can keep the rest of his remains here in your village. And once we identify him, we will return the head to you."

The village chief glanced at the two government officials, then into the faces of his fellow villagers, looking for dissent. Finding none, he nodded.

"All right. We will rent the head to you for five thousand dollars."

"*Five thousand dollars?*"

"For the head," said the old man. "The body would be more. And only if you return it. Nguyen My Den is not American anymore. His head belongs here in my village."

"Who's a genius?" muttered Muir as Condley translated the old man's reply. Condley looked wryly at his partner, and then over to Colonel Pham, who had broken into an amused smile.

Gotcha.

And as Condley followed the old man and his entourage toward the village, he was sure he heard the colonel laugh.

CHAPTER SIXTEEN

Sai Gon

"THIS IS A Heckler and Koch P7," said Nghiem Le Manh, taking a small black pistol from the shooting stand and holding it in front of Dzung. "It was manufactured in Germany. For many years the West German commandos used it as their weapon of choice."

Staring at the beautifully crafted pistol, Dzung could not resist a small jibe. "So much for the revolution, if you want me to shoot an inferior capitalist weapon."

"This is not politics," shrugged Manh. "The Germans are the masters of weapons. Did you know they actually designed the AK-47 rifle? Oh, yes. Take a look at their STG-44 infantry rifle from World War Two. The Russian Kalishnikov stole the design."

"For the good of the revolution," said Dzung dryly.

"I told you, I don't like the Russians either," replied Manh. "Anyway, you will love shooting this pistol. If you are like I am, Dzung, and from your files we do seem to have this in common, shooting this weapon will make your heart sing." And then he smiled, raising his eyebrows as if he were letting Dzung in on a secret. "Besides, if you were ever caught with a pistol, it would not be good for the revolution if it was traceable to the government, would it?"

"Manh, let's be practical. You would never turn me loose on my *cyclo* with a pistol."

"Of course I would." Manh grinned widely now, enjoying the surprised look on Dzung's face. "I know you perfectly, Dzung. I have carefully studied every page of your file. I have talked with the political officers who supervised you during your reeducation. I have had you watched, on the street and even at your home. You are obsessed with the love of your family. It is your great strength and it is your tragic weakness. You will do nothing to hurt your family. And if your family is at risk, you will do anything to save them. So if I gave you this pistol and told you to show it to no one and to use it only when you were ordered to do so, you would obey me. Because if you did not obey me, your family would suffer. How many people could you shoot with seven bullets? Not enough to destroy the revolution. Only enough to destroy yourself and your family."

Dzung searched Manh's face, accepting the truth of what the Interior Ministry agent had just said. "What do you want me to do?"

"For now, learn to shoot the weapon. Enjoy yourself."

Manh became officious, standing next to Dzung and pointing out the characteristics of the pistol. "This is a nine-millimeter pistol. The magazine holds eight bullets, but we always load only seven, to preserve the tension in its spring. You are probably remembering the American forty-five-caliber pistol, which was very complicated and very unsafe, even though it had several different safeties. Remember? The grip safety, the thumb safety, the slide lock, and still the forty-five killed people accidentally all the time. There is only one safety on this pistol, the squeeze safety, but it is completely effective. That means that you must squeeze the grip when you want to shoot a bullet, or the pistol will not fire. Very simple. Very German."

There were a half dozen loaded magazines on the shooting table. Manh picked up one of them, pushing it upward inside the pistol's grip as he kept it carefully pointed downrange. A host of memories clogged Dzung's mind as he watched Manh load the pistol and release the slide, arming it with a bullet in the chamber. It was amazing to him how easily he regained the memories and even the panache of a quarter century before.

"I was born to do this, Manh. You should know that."

"I do know that," said Manh simply. He handed Dzung the pistol, giving the *cyclo* driver a taunting grin. "So go ahead, Dzung, shoot me. You can, you know. No one would be able to stop you from doing it."

Dzung grinned also, looking up and down the empty firing line of the shooting range and then back at Manh. The Interior Ministry agent was indeed correct that Dzung could kill him with ease at that moment. But both of them knew that Manh had the ultimate defense against such action, greater than any bullet-proof vest or indeed any gun. For if Dzung shot Manh he would never make it out of the shooting range, much less back to his home. And even if Dzung was given the gun and later shot Manh on the street, there would be no place for him to hide. And even if he found a place to hide, some of his family would be marched off to prison, and all of them would suffer for the rest of their lives whenever they tried to find a job or a school or a house. Nor would they ever be allowed to emigrate away from such misery. The whole country would become their jail, to set an example for the others, because shooting Manh would be a crime against the revolution.

"Bang," said Dzung, pointing the pistol for a moment at Manh's head.

Manh did not even flinch. "Go ahead. Get all of the anger out of your system." And then he lit a cigarette, watching Dzung as if he were sitting in a spectator section, far away.

Dzung toyed with the pistol for a while, admiring its sleek design and testing the squeeze mechanism on its grip. The pistol felt immediately comfortable in his hands. Without coaching, he spaced his feet sideways and apart, as if in a boxer's stance. Then he raised his right arm until it was straight, pulling his left hand into the pistol to steady his grasp, and looked for a moment through the sights, lining up the dot of the front site exactly with the two dots of the rear sights.

"It is a beautiful weapon, Manh."

"Go ahead," said Manh. "Shoot it."

Twenty-five meters away, Manh had set up three circular metal targets. The pie-plate targets stood atop metal stands. Two of them were chest-high, while the one in the center was head-high. Dzung took careful aim at the center target and slowly squeezed off a round. The pistol exploded and the center pie plate immediately pinged loudly, rocking on its base.

"You are very good," said Manh. "First shot, dead center."

"I am better than good, Manh."

"Prove it."

Dzung squeezed off the other six rounds, firing quickly and putting two bullets onto each of the targets. A thrill raced through him as he fired. This was the ultimate empowerment. For a second he allowed himself a wild fantasy, that every *cyclo* driver in Sai Gon might be armed with one of these sleek pistols, so that they might all fire at once until Manh and every one of his fellow government officials were dead. And then he laughed, this time at himself. Most of them would probably miss anyway. Weapons had been his talent, all those years ago. Most of the others, even the former soldiers, had probably never fired a pistol in their lives.

"Excellent!" Manh smiled, taking Dzung's laughter as an expression of simple enjoyment. "Go ahead," he said. "Fire another magazine if you like."

Dzung ejected the spent magazine, marveling at the engineering of the pistol, and popped a fresh one into the receiver. He squeezed the grip, which automatically brought the slide forward, loading a bullet into the chamber, and fired off all seven rounds within five seconds, pinging all three targets once again.

"Perfect!" said Manh.

"Firing a pistol is as natural to me as breathing," said Dzung.

"What are you thinking?" asked Manh.

Dzung masked his seriousness with a small grin. "I'm wondering again how we lost the war."

"History was not with you," laughed Manh, his smile curling up behind his drooping mustache. "So get over it, and keep shooting."

Dzung dropped the second magazine from the pistol, reaching for another full one. "Why am I doing this, Manh? Who do you want me to kill?"

"Today, no one," answered Manh. "And besides, you are not ready, Dzung. We have much preparation to do. This is only familiarization. Once you are completely comfortable with the pistol we will put you through a combat course."

"A combat course? I was in combat for seven years," said Dzung. "Seven years, Manh! What are you going to teach me about combat?"

"You won't be using this weapon on a battlefield," said Manh. "You must learn to shoot quickly, from only a few meters away. And then if you wish to save yourself, you must learn to get rid of the pistol and disappear without being caught."

Manh's comments washed over Dzung like a sudden, cold rain. Shooting a pistol on a firing range was a novelty, even fun. Going into combat was as natural as waking up and cooking rice. But killing someone on the street at the direction of the very government that hated him, and then escaping without being caught, was beyond his ability to comprehend. And what then? Would they allow him to disappear back into the anonymity of his *cyclo* trade? Would they catch him and charge him anyway, having set him up as a scapegoat for the same crime they forced him to commit? And if they didn't charge him for the crime, what would they want him to do next?

"I am not the person to kill someone like that, Manh."

"Not yet," said Manh, finishing his cigarette and tossing it toward the targets. "But we will teach you."

"There's nothing about this that you can teach me." Dzung emptied the third magazine into the pie plates effortlessly, almost without looking. Seven shots, five seconds, seven hits. "Are you sure you want me to have a pistol? You're taking a risk, Manh."

Manh grunted, unconcerned. "You are as predictable as the rains."

Dzung turned casually toward the young Interior Ministry official, letting the barrel of the pistol rest just underneath Manh's chin. "Check my file. I have a very bad attitude."

Manh grinned coolly back, not the least bit intimidated. "Yes, but you will never let your family down. We know you, Dzung. We are not foolish in these matters. So, keep shooting. You have a great deal to learn, and not much time."

CHAPTER SEVENTEEN

Hawaii

THE SKULL OF Nguyen the Black American lay on a clean sheet at the top end of its own gurney, as if awaiting the arrival of Prince Hamlet, who might pick it up and stare moonfully into its dirt-crusted recesses. Or perhaps, thought Condley a little more cynically, the members of the Central Identification Lab, Hawaii, actually believed that someday the rest of Pepper's remains would magically appear from the harsh village with no name far toward the peaks of the Que Son Mountains and cover the entire gurney with ribs and vertebrae and femurs and patellae, all the missing, irrelevant evidence that might allow him to picture the dead man more clearly.

"I hate his guts," he said flatly. "That is, if he still had any guts." He was wishing that Nguyen the Black American might come alive just for a moment so that he might kill him properly instead of allowing him the luxury of a simple, peaceful death.

"Behold Alphonse no-middle-name Smith," said Professor Hanson Muir, reading with his characteristic flourish from five pages of summary notes. "Born April 27, 1948, in Chicago, Illinois. Father unknown.

Mother presently unlocatable and probably not still alive. Nine and a half years of schooling. Enlisted in the Marine Corps on September 5, 1966. Arrived in Da Nang on March 21, 1967, where he was assigned to the Force Logistics Command."

"You're telling me this guy was a supply pogue from FLC?" interrupted Condley unbelievingly. "That this so-called badass was a rear-echelon puke who spent his days stacking boxes of skivvies in a warehouse?"

"According to his records."

"How'd he ever end up leading NVA patrols?"

Muir chuckled ironically, looking up for a moment from his notes. "Don't you always like to boast that every Marine is a rifleman?"

Condley grunted, amazed. "The closest the FLC guys got to combat was loading ammo and C-rations onto the convoy trucks."

"Well, it appears he made up for it when he joined the other side, doesn't it?" Muir began reading again. "Where was I? Okay, here. Commanding officer's nonjudicial punishment, 11 September, 1967, for the offense of disrespect to a noncommissioned officer. Ten days' confinement and loss of pay. Special court-martial, 14 November, 1967, for being absent without leave for twenty-seven days. From these notes it seems he was apprehended while trying to live permanently in the transient barracks at the R and R Center in Da Nang."

"Not a bad choice if you're going to run away from your unit," mused Condley grudgingly. "The officers in charge see you walking around and think you're in from the bush, on your way to Hong Kong or Bangkok or Singapore. You don't have to show any R and R orders to eat in the mess hall, so you get three hot meals a day for free. Find yourself an unassigned cot in the barracks after everybody goes to bed at night, so you have a place to sleep. There are new faces every day coming in and out from R and R, and no permanent occupants in the barracks, so who's going to finger you for being AWOL?"

"Yes," answered Muir. "I never realized there were so many ways to disappear inside a combat zone. But anyway, they finally caught him."

"Maybe he forgot to get a haircut," joked Condley.

"Indeed," laughed Professor Muir. "After twenty-seven days you may be right. So our man was reduced to private, with forfeiture of all pay and allowances, and sentenced to two months in the Third Marine Amphibious Force brig, Da Nang. His next offense: commanding officer's nonjudicial punishment, 15 April, 1968, for disrespect to a non-commissioned officer. Fifteen days' confinement, loss of all pay and privileges. Next offense, or shall I say the final straw: absent without leave, 6 May, 1968, never seen or heard from again, whereabouts unknown."

"He probably disappeared inside Dogpatch at that point," mused Condley, remembering the thicket of tin-roofed shacks near the First Marine Division headquarters where hundreds of errant Marines once hid. "That's where they ended up when they fell in love."

"Really?" said Muir, amazed at Condley's instant certainty. "If it was that logical, and if they believed he was in this Dogpatch, why didn't they just go in and get him?"

"Picture an inner-city neighborhood where everybody is carrying an M-16, Professor. Would you want to be the one to go in there and get him? War is hell, but intramural firefights are definitely a bitch. The MPs tried to sweep through Dogpatch every now and then, but there were a few hundred guys in there with weapons who knew they were heading for jail and then a bad paper discharge if they were caught. Not to mention that they'd be leaving their honeys behind, probably forever. The shacks were packed close together and the alleyways were about five feet wide. I was in Da Nang once when the generals tried to send the MPs in. It sounded like the battle for Hue City for about an hour, then the MPs called it a day. Can you blame them? Those were trained soldiers and Marines in there. They may have gone AWOL, but they did know how to fight."

Muir stroked his full beard. "The generals knew where they were, and they just let them stay?"

"If they came out they could be grabbed. But how'd you like to write the letter to the family of a Marine killed fighting the great battle of Dogpatch?" Condley grinned ironically, composing it in his head. "Dear Mrs. Evans. I regret to inform you that your son died in a valiant effort to capture a group of soldiers and fellow Marines who left their posts and were shacked up with their girlfriends in a ghetto inside the city of Da Nang."

"All right, I take your point." Muir shrugged, returning to his pages. "So here it is. Final entry, classified as a deserter on 5 August, 1968." He looked up again. "Another question, Brandon?"

"You mean, do I have one?"

"No, I do." Muir seemed slightly puzzled. "Weren't Marines sent to

Viet Nam for thirteen-month tours? How can he still be there in May, 1968, when his tour should have ended in April?"

"Ah, but brig time doesn't count on your tour, Professor. If it did, half of the malingerers in Viet Nam would have figured out a way to get themselves locked up until the clock ran out and they could be sent home. Think about it. What's a few months' jail time compared to living in the mud, drinking wormy water, and getting your ass shot off?"

"So, on to Dogpatch," mused Professor Muir, intrigued with the irony of it all. "Marvelous. A place to run to, inside the combat zone. Let's call it the poor man's Canada."

"Not to mention Cho Lon in Sai Gon, where our friend Deville first disappeared," said Condley. "And don't forget the Que Son Mountains."

"No, we shall definitely not forget the Que Sons." Muir held up an eight-by-eleven-inch photograph of the late Private Smith. "Does this man look familiar?"

Condley stared at the picture for several seconds, his insides tightening around a futile agony. The bulky neck, the thick shoulders, the rounded face, all leapt tragically out at him from the old photograph. No, he thought. It could not be a coincidence, particularly since this man's bones were found so close to the ambush site itself. "That's him."

"You're sure?"

"I'm sure."

"Can you testify to that under oath?"

"Yeah."

"In the papers? In court? In front of a congressional hearing?"

Muir continued to hold the photograph in front of his face. Doubts clouded Condley's anger as he stared at the blank young face of a man who, despite all the later disrespect and rebellion, at least had stepped forward those years ago and offered to serve his country before going bad. Unlike with Deville, there had been no positive identification of Pepper after that long-ago ambush, only reports that the other attacker had been black. Could he now provide it with certainty, based on quick glimpses during the madness of combat more than thirty years before? What if there was someone else after all, someone who got away, even a Cuban adviser? What if Alphonse Smith's greatest crime was indeed merely having fallen in love and abandoned his post, then drifting up into the mountains to live harmlessly in a remote village?

"Is this Pepper?" asked Professor Muir, relentless in his objectivity.

"Yes, Professor, that is Pepper."

"You're absolutely positive?"

Finally Condley threw his hands up into the air. "Look, I know it's him, okay? But how can I be absolutely positive, like I've got some strand of DNA under a microscope, when I'm staring at a thirty-year-old picture and a fucking skull?"

"Well, you have to be, Brandon, if we're going to take this forward. *Probably* isn't good enough. Probably doesn't work in a court of law. Not when we are condemning a dead man to an eternity of retribution."

Condley sighed, suddenly deflated. "Okay. Enough of this shit. I mean, I know that's him. I have no doubt. But you're right."

"I'm sorry, Brandon." Muir lowered the picture, putting it back into the manila folder where he kept the pages from Smith's record books.

"So what do we have now, Professor? What are we taking forward from here? Answer me that."

Muir pondered the skull. "For the sake of public consumption, all we have is a deserter who ran up into the mountains and hid for thirty years until he died. An interesting two-day story if the media did obtain the facts from us and then decided to print a story on them, but not exactly a modern-day Benedict Arnold. We are looking at a lost soul who eluded American and Vietnamese authorities in order to live out the remainder of his life up in the mountains. That's it. Unless some famous producer wanted to turn him into a hero and make a movie about him. You know, sacrificing his country to be with the woman he loved."

"Don't say that too loud, Professor. The thought scares me."

Muir shrugged, touching the skull. "He lost five teeth. I almost feel sorry for the fellow."

"I'm not exactly shedding any tears here. You didn't see him when he was busy shooting my Marines."

"Well, now you're the one who's right." Muir let out a breath. "I'm sorry I said that, Brandon. I must have sounded like one of those whiners who gather outside the courtroom when a hardened criminal is being tried for murder. Consider the poor man's deprived childhood, and that he fell in with the wrong crowd, and got involved with a woman, and was scarred by the cruel military process when they made him do a little time for insubordination. Poor fellow. He was entitled to a few ambushes to help balance out his psyche, wasn't he?"

"So we're both right, Professor. How comforting to our fucking egos. And we haven't solved a thing."

The remains from Ninh Phuoc rested on another gurney thirty feet away from where they stood. Muir nodded toward them. "Don't be so pessimistic, Brandon. We've solved a lot, no matter that none of it does us any good just yet. We do know who Salt is, even if we can't find him anywhere in the known universe. We don't know who the poor fellow is that he murdered, but we have his remains, and sooner or later science will prevail. And we have Pepper, or at least we have his head, with a positive identification from the dental records. So there may come a time—perhaps when we find Salt—that we can obtain a confession and implicate this man as well."

"What are the odds on that?" Condley glared malevolently at Pepper's skull. "That fucking head cost me five thousand dollars too."

"I've filed a request for reimbursement. I'm sure they'll pay you back. It was a judgment call and you certainly were within the regulations."

"I'll tell you what, Professor. If they don't reimburse me for that skull it's mine. I'm taking it home and turning it into an ashtray." He paused. "Maybe a urinal."

"It's an important piece of evidence."

Condley emanated a bland, cynical disgust. "Evidence for what? Do you think anybody in our government even wants to find out the answer to this question? Who's going to pick off that scab, huh? If he were alive they'd have to face the truth of what he did, but the man is dead."

"We could always convince the village chief to buy it back from us. A reimbursement of sorts, what do you think?"

"Now, there's a laugh. First of all, I doubt the village got more than a hundred bucks out of the deal once everyone along the government food chain took their cuts. And second, I'd be surprised if the old man really cares one way or the other about Nguyen the Black American's head. They're great entrepreneurs, the Vietnamese. They'll sell you anything. But they aren't into buying things back."

Muir held up his hands in mock surrender. "Just kidding, Brandon. But we will file a report on all of these findings, so don't think the matter will be pasted over by the bureaucracy." Muir now gave him an empathetic look. "You've already had a small revenge, don't you think? I mean, you're standing there looking at his skull. He's not in the mountains, gloating over yours."

Condley grunted, gazing absently at the skull and then over to the remains of the man killed by the elusive Deville. Despite himself he felt oddly attached to both sets of remains, as if he and they had been rubbed into the same earth so fiercely and so completely that the dirt inalterably connected them, however bitterly. Mud brothers, he thought. Sharers of a truth that could never be defined by the labels that had been created by outsiders. After all, what tiny fraction of America had ever even seen that nasty, vicious little corner of the war, that corridor of terror and sorrow that had so devoured the few who had?

"I'd like to know one thing about him, Professor. Only one thing." He thought about that and reconsidered. "No, maybe two. The first is whether he really believed in what he was fighting for when he shot my Marines. Because if he did, whether I like it or not a part of me has to respect him. I mean, that makes him a soldier, doing his duty as he understood it."

"And the second?"

"Did he use any information that he gained as a Marine in order to help the other side? Because if he didn't, he was just accepting the risk of the battlefield. Taking it as he found it, just like we did."

Muir pursed his lips, watching Condley's face. His words now danced delicately, as if Condley's emotions were like a balloon about to burst. "And what do you think about that, Brandon?"

"This guy was nothing. He was a supply pogue. What the hell did he know about the battlefield?" Condley thought about that for another moment, remembering again the first few seconds of the ambush all those years ago, and suddenly changed his mind. "No, Professor, I can't go with that. He and Deville were wearing American uniforms and carrying American M-14s. He shot one of my men who thought we'd stumbled into an American unit. Good people are dead because their first instinct was to protect the lives of what they thought were two fellow Americans. I can't slide on that. No forgiveness."

Without even deciding, Condley found himself sauntering slowly toward the lab's doorway. Muir chased him with yet another question.

"What about Deville?"

He stopped walking and turned toward Hanson Muir. "Deville's in a class by himself. He's not only a turncoat, he's a murderer. He killed a man in cold blood and ran from the Army. He killed another man in cold blood and ran from the Viet Cong. There's no honor there. Pepper was a scumbag but at least what he did was on the battlefield, and at least he stayed with the other side after the war. Can't you see the difference? Pepper was a treasonous asshole, but Deville is downright evil."

"Calm down, Brandon."

"I am calm," muttered Condley. "But let me make you a promise, Professor. I'm going to find that motherfucker. And if he's still alive I'm going to kill him."

"Not a very good career move, I'd say."

"Well, hey, let's hear it for my brilliant career. What'll they do, send me to Viet Nam?"

"Think jail, Brandon. Think jail very hard. Homicide has that effect on certain juries."

"The possibility of jail is why Deville is never going to see a jury."

"I was talking about you."

"If I find him I will do him, Professor. And if I do him, no one will ever know."

"Unless I tell them?"

"Who said I'm going to tell you?"

Condley headed again for the door, and Muir called again to him. "Where are you going now?"

"To get laid."

"Where can I reach you?"

Condley opened the door, not even looking back. "Where do I usually get laid?"

"That's hard to keep track of, actually," said Hanson Muir with a laugh. "Maybe when we get back to Viet Nam I can check with Colonel Pham."

CHAPTER EIGHTEEN

MARIA LOVED WAIKIKI Beach. It matched her dream of what America should be. Outrageously dressed people from all over the world, of every age, physical description, and social class, walked elbow to elbow along the parklike sidewalks, played games on small stretches of grass, or lay motionless on towels along the beach as if they were fish sticks, baking in an oven. The hot, swirling air reeked wonderfully of tropical flowers and suntan oil. The turquoise ocean was pristine and majestic. Its far horizon reinforced the romantic isolation of this island paradise, and its near waves were dotted with the timeless image of young surfers waiting for the perfect wave. Elegant hotel complexes filled with shops and restaurants sprawled along the beach, sending cool wafts of perfumed air toward the water, mixed with tinkles of laughter from happy tourists sitting at the outdoor bars.

Oh, Hawaii, oh, America, Maria's dark, dancing eyes proclaimed happily each time she spent an afternoon on Waikiki. Play station for the universe. A land of boundless beauty, glorious excess, conspicuous waste, unapologetic fatness, shameless exhibitionism, and delicious anonymity.

They had parked her green Mercedes in a lot just off Ala Moana Park. Now Maria and Condley walked side by side on the walkway behind the Hilton Hawaiian Village, heading slowly along Hotel Row toward the distant beauty of Diamond Head. Green was Maria's favorite color. She was wearing her finest chartreuse thong bikini, which not only displayed her supple, muscular legs and ample curves but also was a showcase for the bright gold and green butterfly that was tattooed on her left buttock. Her long black hair was pulled tight and twisted into a knot on top of her head. Maria knew she looked regal with her killer bikini, her two-hundred-dollar Serengeti sunglasses, and her million-dollar body. She glowed with pride as she strode past the glassy stares and listened to the secret whimpers of idle, dreaming men who looked up from their beach towels or halted their volleyball games to watch her pass.

"Brandon," she almost whispered, her face happy and playfully distracted. "Do you think they think we're married?"

"Well, I guess we were," mumbled Condley, who himself cared little for strolling in the hot sun among thousands of broiling, coconut-oiled strangers. "For a few minutes, anyway."

His answer seemed to make her happier still. She took his hand for a while as they walked, showing him off as her possession. He played the game just to keep her happy, his face emotionless and his eyes faraway, staring past the hotels and the beaches toward the haunting crags of Diamond Head. His mind was as removed as his gaze. He felt sullen in the midst of all this opulence, oppressed by old memories of this same beach, memories that now stretched back more than thirty years to the first time he had visited it, hard-bodied and wide-eyed on the way into his first tour of combat in Viet Nam. And irritated by other more recent thoughts, the swirling uncertainties and muted disappointments that would not go away.

"You should have worn a bathing suit," insisted Maria, glancing at the ever-present blue jeans and T-shirt that seemed to comprise Condley's modern-day uniform.

"I burn like a lobster, Maria. Who needs that? If you want cancer bad enough, go smoke a Marlboro."

They neared a loud, packed beachside bar. Inside, the patrons were drinking and laughing as they watched a basketball game on four wall-mounted TVs. "Will you buy me a piña colada?"

Despite himself, he snorted. "Haven't you had enough of bars?"

His casual dismissals were landing on her ears as sharp rebukes. She suddenly let go of his hand. Now she frowned at him. "You're not being nice today."

"When is the last time I was nice?"

She thought about it for a moment and then took his hand again, changing her tactics as they strolled through a stretch of ankle-deep sand. "You're always nice. I wouldn't even be here if you weren't so nice."

"I wasn't being nice. You were just smarter than I was. What the hell did I know about green cards?"

"Yeah, but you got me one. That was nice."

Condley allowed himself a small smile, squeezing her hand a little to show her he wasn't really mad. They walked from the beach back to the sidewalk. Off to their left was a park where the old Fort DeRussy bunga-lows had once bordered the beach. The bungalows, built by the Army to house recuperating casualties from the Pacific battles of World War Two, had been a favorite R and R spot for the American military for a full generation after that.

The mind trick worked even on the beach in Hawaii. Ghosts haunted Condley as he passed the park. In his mind the bungalows were still there, low and shabby. Young men with new tattoos and fresh scars from battle strolled the beach uncertainly with teenage wives or girl-friends, trying to find and mend their brains with a week on Waikiki before flying directly back into combat. Yes, that had really happened, and why didn't anybody care enough to remember?

At the edge of the park a brick-brown young man with ten tattoos and hair as wild as a lion's mane offered to take a picture of them with his parrot. Condley absently waved off the man, who then squeezed his bird's legs, a secret command, until it began to curse them.

"Fuck you," squawked the pissed-off parrot as they walked away. "Fuck you. Fuck you."

Condley finally laughed, flipping off the parrot, and then gave Maria an apologetic look. "Sorry I'm a jerk. Some things are bother-ing me."

She thought about that for a moment, eyeing him shrewdly. "Brandon, you are my prince. I would give anything to see you happy. But you are a very emotional man. You have too much emotion, really. That's why you hide it with your silly jokes and waste it with all your fighting."

"Well, here I go again."

"What, Brandon?"

"I can't talk about it."

"You always say that."

"Then it must be true."

They neared the old hotels at the center of Waikiki's most famous stretch of beach. Looking at them and remembering his early days on Oahu, Condley was overwhelmed with a sudden undefinable nostalgia, and on top of it a sense of hopelessness. Life moved on. Kids were born and grew up, parents grew old and died. Beaches and cities and civilizations rearranged themselves to meet the new needs of the future. But Brandon Condley still puttered along, now passing checkpoint infinity on the road to nowhere in particular.

Maria watched him carefully, seeking clues in his averted gaze. "You want to have the final conversation. You don't want to be around me anymore. You're moving to Viet Nam. You're not coming back, is that right, Brandon?"

"I can't even see tomorrow, and you're talking about next week?" He put an arm around her shoulder, pulling her into him for a moment as they walked, a gesture of reassurance. It seemed impossible, but he really did care for this woman who had gathered up the best assets God had given her and turned them into a successful business, however publicly deplored. "I just need to go see somebody."

"A different woman?"

"It's not a woman, Maria. Why does everything have to be about another woman? It's business."

"Your business is dead people. Dead people can wait until tomorrow."

"It's important."

She sagged a little as they walked. "I took the whole day off just for you, Brandon."

"Then come with me."

"Where do you want to go?"

"Have you ever met a Marine Corps general?"

She brightened, a devilish smile growing on her beautiful face. "I think I knew a few. Before they were generals, anyway."

————————

As Maria's Mercedes approached Halawa Heights's main gate, the corporal standing duty stepped from his sentry box into the road, putting up a hand and halting the car. Condley dutifully flashed his government ID card from the driver's window, but by then the young Marine was not looking at him anymore. He had gone into a hypnotic trance, unable to restrain his dumbfounded eyes from traveling all along Maria's lithe, bikini-clad frame. And just to rub it in, she waved cheerily to the young man, taking off her sunglasses for a moment and giving him a playful wink.

"Corporal, stop slobbering on my Mercedes." Condley's hand was still dangling outside the window as he continued to hold his ID card up for the sentry's inspection.

"Sorry, sir." The embarrassed corporal shook his head like a dog snapping water out of its ears. He leaned forward, checking Condley's identification. "You have business at Cinc Pac Fleet, sir?"

"I'm from CILHI," answered Condley with just the right tone of mystery in his voice. "We're here on an MIA case." The sentry nodded knowingly, returning Condley's ID card. To his surprise, Condley handed the young man one of Maria's business cards in exchange. "If you like what you're looking at, they're open seven days a week. Bring a friend."

The corporal checked the card, looking hungrily back at Maria, and put it into a trouser pocket. "She works there?"

"She is the proprietor of this fine establishment," said Condley dryly. "But she's got lots of highly talented employees with, shall we say, equally admirable assets."

"I'll be there Friday night," said the grinning corporal.

"If you're coming on Friday bring lots of friends. The SEALs think they own the place."

The corporal gave them a secret thumbs-up as he waved them through the gate. Driving inside the headquarters compound, Condley glanced casually at Maria, feigning anger. "I should get a tip, pimping for you."

"Don't say you're pimping for me, Brandon. You hurt my feelings. And, anyway, I don't do that anymore."

He gave her a teasing glance. "No kidding? I seem to remember having done it about three hours ago."

She held her chin high, looking airily out the window. "Not for money, not anymore. Except for you, I've been a virgin now for almost three years."

Her comment startled him. "You're not turning tricks?"

"Except for you." Her eyes flashed as they navigated past perfectly manicured lawns. "I have my green card, and we've already been married. So why should I lie?"

The thought that sweet Maria was actually being faithful to him after all these years of uncomplicated friendship made him suddenly nervous. It was as if a different woman were sitting next to him, and he did not know what to do about it. "You changed the rules without telling me. Why'd you do that?"

"Brandon!" She laughed, taken with the notion that her newfound semivirginity brought with it a subtle power. "I didn't change anything. I just don't see anyone but you that I would like to have sex with."

He thought about that for a moment. "But if you did, you would?"

"What are you talking about?"

He gave her an earnest look, as if somehow his own freedom were now at risk. "If you did see someone you wanted to sleep with, you would. I mean, you don't feel . . ." He couldn't finish the thought. "Okay. What I mean is, you can't put this on me. It's not my fault. I didn't do anything to make you act this way."

She seemed touched. Her sharp, doll-like face melted a bit and her huge eyes made her look for that moment like a child. "That was so sweet."

"That's not the answer I was looking for, Maria."

"Yes, it was."

They were nearing General Wayne Duncan's house. For the first time he became aware of how Maureen Duncan might receive them. "I, ah, kind of wish you weren't wearing that thong."

She looked down at herself, seeing nothing to be ashamed of, and then shrugged. "I have a sarong in my bag."

He parked the car and walked around to the passenger side, opening the door for Maria. Standing next to the car, she took a multicolored wraparound dress from her bag and pulled it around herself.

"Not bad." He smiled.

"Admit it, Brandon. I look like a princess."

Maureen Duncan stood in the open doorway as they walked toward her, having seen them pull up at the curb in front of her house. Condley relaxed immediately, seeing that Maureen herself was dripping with sweat, dressed in spandex running shorts and a sports bra. She leaned against the doorway now, her arms folded underneath her breasts. She was grinning expectantly, more amused than surprised by their sudden appearance and by Maria's decision to dress herself in public.

"Well, Brandon Condley," she said in an amused, soft Southern drawl. "You look like you could use some Gatorade."

CHAPTER NINETEEN

"THAT ONE. THERE. Recognize him?"

Condley grinned mischievously, watching Maria's expression as General Wayne Duncan stormed through the front door. She turned in her chair and surveyed Duncan carefully as he headed through the living room toward the back veranda, where Condley and Maria now sat with Maureen under a yellow sun umbrella at a large round picnic table.

Duncan grew increasingly nervous under Maria's bold and playful gaze. She faced him, her glass of iced tea held just below her chin and her crossed legs aimed directly at his approach, and took off her sunglasses, getting a better look. When her sunglasses came off, the general froze, looking from Maria to Maureen and then to Condley.

"I don't think so," said Maria finally.

"What is this?" blustered Duncan.

"Oh, Skipper, you're a lucky man."

Duncan gave his wife a quick, nervous glance and then took a deep breath, rising to his full height. "Maureen, I have *never*—"

"Just kidding, Skipper." Condley rose and took the general's hand as the two women laughed merrily. "This is Maria. We were married once. So stay away from my stuff."

"Hi, Maria, sorry you ended up with this underachieving troll, however temporarily." Duncan crushed Condley's palm in his larger grasp, then slapped him on a shoulder. "You little shit, you're lucky you're not dead."

"I'm not pulling you away from any important golf games, am I?"

"All my golf games are important." Duncan laughed, settling his large, muscular frame into the fourth chair at the table. He was carrying a sealed manila envelope, and now he put it on the table as Maureen poured him a glass of iced tea. "I've been looking for you, actually. So let's call this a summoning of the minds from outer space."

"That's where you'd have to find me. I'm pretty elusive these days. They started up a Dick Tracy watch in my neighborhood. Whenever a polyester suit comes within a block of my apartment an alarm goes off."

"Agent Combs told me you were being uncooperative. That's why I sent you a brain wave." Duncan fingered the manila envelope tentatively. "How'd it go with that skull you brought back? That was a true Brandon Condley moment, paying five thousand bucks to rent a dead head from a bunch of mountain tribesmen. It even made the Cinc Pac staff briefings."

"Don't blow my cover, General! But if Cinc Pac knows about it, maybe you can get me reimbursed."

"Yeah, and what account do they use to reimburse you for renting skulls?" The general chuckled some more, shaking his head from side to side. "Anyway, was it Pepper?"

"I know it's him," said Condley, feeling the hopeless anger surge again. "But Professor Muir says there's no way to prove it."

"He's probably right." Duncan drained his tea in large gulps, then set the glass back onto the table, where Maureen automatically refilled it. "We never got a positive ID on him before. Even with eyewitnesses it might be impossible to walk the cat back thirty years. Unless we can find someone who actually knew him and can testify that he was indeed the guy."

"So you found somebody who can do that?"

"I've been following something," said Duncan quietly. He drained the second glass of iced tea and then nodded to Maureen. "Will you ladies excuse us for a few minutes?"

Maureen nodded back, accustomed to the necessity of being excluded from conversations that contained classified information. She stood, smiling to Maria and gesturing toward the house. "How'd you like to see my, ah . . . oh, I don't know, my—"

"Kitchen?" said Maria helpfully, playfully joining the intrigue.

"Kitchen. Absolutely." Maureen picked up the tea pitcher and headed toward the sliding glass door that led inside. "O . . . kay, we'll be going to the kitchen now," she said lightly.

Duncan watched them disappear, taking a long, full look at Maria's departing frame. "What's *that* all about?"

"We were walking the beach." Condley shrugged. "And I must have got your call."

"I'm surprised my message made it through all the static."

"That kind of static I'm used to. Getting satellite pings from the fifth dimension is kind of new. What'd you guys do, implant a microchip in my butt when I was wounded?" Condley watched Duncan carefully, enjoying his obvious distraction. "You've been long at sea, Skipper."

"No," he laughed. "I just appreciate your . . . versatility, that's all."

"Hey, I'm all about diversity. I was way ahead of the government on that."

"Speaking of government." Duncan picked up the manila envelope, now growing earnest. "Call it instinct, but I think I've got something here."

"Pepper?"

"I can't say yet." The general opened the envelope, pulling out a sheaf of papers. "I had my G-2 staff start keywording *Viet Nam* into all the intelligence traffic. Quietly, just to see what came up. They've been marking the reports for me, and I just take them in bundles and read them either at night or when I'm traveling. I didn't even tell them why I'm doing it. And most of it's junk, anyway. But not all of it. And you know how it goes. Wherever there's a pile of horseshit, sooner or later you're going to find a pony."

Duncan handed a dozen sheets of paper to Condley. "You can't take these with you, because they're classified, and I doubt somehow you have a safe in your apartment."

"In the neighborhood where I live I'm lucky I even have a fucking bed in my apartment."

"My point exactly. But I want you to read them. And I want you to remember a name: Petrushinsky. Anatolie Petrushinsky. Actually, I'm going to write that down for you before you leave."

"Anatolie Petrushinsky." Condley tried the name, rolling it on his tongue. "Got it. Russian?"

"Lives in Moscow." Duncan took a deep breath, speaking carefully, never having been given to wild speculation. "I have good reason to believe he may have known Salt and Pepper. It's a long shot, but if I had to put money on it I'd actually give good odds."

Condley read the pages voraciously as the general continued to talk. "Skip Rogers, a political officer from our embassy in Moscow, bumped into this guy at a street market in an area called the Arabat. He was selling off some of his old Soviet military badges. I've met Rogers before. Not a bad guy. Was a Marine before he went over to the Agency. He's a little like you, Condley, only a lot younger and more, shall we say, urbane. After he left the Corps he started smoking a pipe, reading a lot, and using big words. Bottom line is, I trust him. Anyway, Rogers was escorting some American businessmen who'd served in Viet Nam during the war and as a matter of conversation told Petrushinsky that they were veterans. Petrushinsky kind of puffed up and responded that he'd spent a lot of time in Viet Nam as well, but when they tried to engage him in a longer conversation he ran away. Rogers, ever dutiful, wrote a little summary of the encounter for the files. After I read his initial report I sent him a message asking if he could follow up on the guy. I mean, this is news, right? Nobody's ever admitted there were Russian soldiers in Viet Nam during the war. And Rogers has worked up a pretty interesting profile, not the least of which is that Petrushinsky has at various times bragged to his fellow veterans that he served as a so-called 'observer' in the mountains near Da Nang. We can't get to him, though. He won't talk to us, and we can hardly make him. And the Russkies don't like us very much these days, so there's no chance of getting their government to cooperate with us. Not on this issue, anyway. What are they going to do, help us prove they've been lying about the level of their involvement in Viet Nam for thirty years?"

"Great stuff," said Condley, finishing his perusal of the papers. "I like this Rogers, even if he's joined the tweedy crowd. Skipper, can you sanitize these pages for me?" He held the papers out as if he were weighing them. "I've got a few ideas. But I need an unclassified version with the important information on it, in a way that I could use it and still not compromise our sources."

"That's easy to do," said Duncan, taking the papers back and putting them inside the envelope. He relaxed now and suddenly winked, nodding toward the inside of his house. "That's a fine-looking woman, Condley. Exotic, huh? A little wild, though. You married her?"

"Don't pay any attention to that. It was more like a friendly date."

"You're losing me here."

"Forget it."

"Are you in love with her?"

"There's only one woman I've ever really loved."

Duncan softened, watching the jolt of pain that still was able to find its way into Condley's skylike eyes after all the years. "Brandon, let me give you a small piece of advice. It wasn't your fault that Mai died. She made her choices too, just like we all did. So it's okay to fall in love with somebody else. She wouldn't mind. In fact, I'm sure she'd want you to. And quite frankly, you're running out of time."

"I've had a lot of time to think about it. And maybe I just don't want to be in love with anybody else."

"Everybody wants to be in love."

Condley found himself chuckling softly. "Is this Mad Dog Duncan talking to me like that? The guy who once told me he was so horny he'd fuck a mud fence? For a minute I thought I was listening to a country song."

"It's true," insisted Duncan. "We learn that as we grow older."

"All of us? What did you do, take a survey?"

"I just worry about you sometimes, Brandon."

"I'm fine, Skipper. And right now what I'd really love more than anything would be to finish this fucking case." Condley stood, shaking the general's hand. "I'm out of here in a day or two. Maybe you can have Dick Tracy drive the sanitized version of these reports over to CILHI?"

"Easy to do," said Duncan, standing also and walking with Condley toward the house.

"Nice fellow," said Condley.

"He doesn't think you're very nice."

"Well, he's right," shrugged Condley as Duncan slid open the glass doors and walked into his living room. "I mean, he's nice and I'm not."

"Sorry if I pushed too far, Brandon. I care about you."

"You can say anything you want. You're closer than family, you know. We bled together. Not many people can say that."

"Deville's still alive." The general said it with such simple conviction that Condley knew it must be true. "I don't know where he is. There's not a trace of him anywhere. But he's too smart to be dead."

"I'm going to find him."

"I know you are," said Duncan.

"And then I'm probably going to kill him. If I get the chance, anyway."

"I know you will," said the general again. "But I have this fucking *job,* Brandon. Congress can call me to testify at any time. The President can summon me to the White House. *The Washington Post* can call me in the middle of the night with a series of questions. And *60 Minutes* can show up on my doorstep with the cameras rolling. Do you get the point?"

"Not really," said Condley, standing in the front hallway and waiting for Maria to join him from the kitchen.

"You're an employee of the United States government. And you've been assisted by government officials"—Duncan cleared his throat, holding Condley's eyes in his own like a vise—"including a certain general officer in the United States Marine Corps, although there's no official record of that at the moment. And it would definitely be the position of the United States government that if this individual were locatable and still alive, he should be turned over to the custody of the appropriate federal agency, where he might be interrogated, tried in a court of law, and provided all the normal protections of the Constitution of the United States of America."

"And made a fucking media hero along the way," said Condley, not hiding his bitterness.

"Probably."

"With the movie of his life story on HBO."

Maria and Maureen were in the hallway now, walking toward them with a curious, shared amusement.

"Highly likely."

"So what's your point, Skipper?" Condley spat the words out, defiantly holding the general's gaze.

"My point?" asked Duncan, glancing for a moment at the two women who had now joined them. "My point is, I'd love to see you, shall we say, *succeed*. Just don't tell me about it until after I retire."

CHAPTER TWENTY

HANSON MUIR SEEMED almost uncontrollably happy as Condley sauntered into his office the next morning. He put a ham-hock fist into the
air when he saw his grizzled, craggy partner, a gesture of glorious victory, and nearly jumped out of his chair in his enthusiasm.

"I've been looking for you, Brandon!"

"What the hell are you doing wearing a tie?" asked Condley as he
stepped inside Muir's office.

Muir looked down at the huge, flowery tie that hung from his neck
and rested awkwardly on his stomach, having forgotten in all his excitement that he'd dressed up that morning. "Well, it's been years since I've
worn one."

"And?"

"And I thought it would be fun. What's the matter with that?"

"A tie in Hawaii? You look very, very dumb."

Hanson Muir fingered his tie tentatively. "I rather liked it. And
you're not the person I'd be going to for advice on how to dress, anyway.
Brandon, enough of this. I've got incredible news."

"So do I," said Condley, dumping a pile of old newspapers off one of Muir's chairs and taking a seat. "I may have a breakthrough."

"Well, I'm sure I do," said Muir. He picked up a stack of photocopied pages from his desk and held them in front of Condley's face. "Would you believe we're going to Australia?"

"Try Russia," countered Condley. "I've got a full report coming over to us right now."

"What's in Russia? What are you talking about?" Muir seemed suddenly unsure of his own information.

Condley leaned back in his chair, nodding toward Muir's stack of papers. "No, you first."

"All right," said Muir. He brightened, grinning conspiratorially. "I'm talking about the young gentleman in the other room."

"You have a visitor?"

"On the gurney. In the poncho, with his hand cut off by some poor sick psychotic. Our little friend from Ninh Phuoc." Muir stroked his beard, appearing unusually professorial. "I decided to try a different theory. Rather than continuing to focus on the files of American servicemen who never came home, which was getting us exactly nowhere, I decided to go back into the news accounts of Viet Nam at the time our boy was murdered. Not only the battles, but everything that came out of the place. They put a researcher on it for us in Washington. She just spent her entire Christmas holiday split between the Pentagon and the Library of Congress, going through the archives of every newspaper we could think of, reading all the little items that never made it to the front page, anytime the word *Viet Nam* popped up. Suffice it to say, she's become quite an expert on Viet Nam in the year 1971. Not to mention very bitter toward me for ruining her holiday."

"So," said Condley, moving his hands in circles to urge Muir forward. "After all that, you ended up in Australia?"

"Yes!" said Muir, his face animated with discovery. He held up a page, as if presenting evidence. "First she found a small item in the old *Pacific Stars and Stripes*." Now he held up another. "That led her to *The Bangkok Post*, which had printed another little story." And now he held up perhaps a dozen pages. "Which led us to a flurry of small stories in the Australian press that went on for a couple of weeks, before the issue finally died its own death, if you'll forgive the pun. I think we have our man, Brandon."

"Let me see what you've got."

"It's a simple story," said Muir, enjoying the mystery he had pro-
voked. "His name is Mathew Larkin. Or was. He was a photographer
based in Sai Gon who worked as a stringer for several smaller
Australian papers. Every now and then he sold some photos to the wire
services, especially AP and UPI. By all accounts a bit of a wild man. He
left Sai Gon in July 1971, after telling a few associates that he'd made
secret contact with the VC and was going to do an exclusive photo
shoot with some of their units in action up in I Corps. All very hush-
hush. The VC apparently arranged to take him out of the city in the
middle of the night, on his way to destinations unknown, and he was
never heard from again. When he wasn't back within a month, people
started worrying, hence the newspaper stories. When he hadn't shown
up by Christmas, it was assumed he'd died, and everybody went about
their usual business. I mean, he was crazy, he took a big risk, and he
lost, that's basically the way they played it in the papers. The VC never
acknowledged anything, not even that he'd been with them. That was
their policy, anyway. To speak about the matter would have opened
them up to questions about a whole array of issues, including who
their contacts were inside Sai Gon. And that was that."

"A little pimple on the ass of a very long war," grunted Condley.

Muir held up a copy of a photograph of the long-departed Mathew
Larkin. "Look like anyone else you know?"

"That's Deville. That's our boy," said Condley with a flat certainty,
looking at the photo. "It's him."

"No, actually, it's not. Larkin's a little blonder, a little shorter," said
Muir. "But good enough for a black and white passport photo, if Deville
wanted to use it to flee the country, no? I mean, how close are they going
to look at someone's passport when he's boarding a plane at Tan Son
Nhat airport in the middle of a war?"

"Bold stroke," said Condley grudgingly, his skin tingling with goose
bumps as he contemplated the photo and thought of Deville. "If nothing
else I'll give him credit for guts. Some photographer who looks like his
little brother shows up in the jungle, and he knows if he's ever going to
get out of Viet Nam he needs to move fast, kill this guy and steal his
identity. And he does it. The man is an evil genius."

"Indeed," agreed Muir. "As for Larkin, he apparently grew up in
western Australia, which explains the somewhat primitive fillings in his

teeth. I've been trying to find out exactly where, so we can do a positive ID on him."

"Can't you just send for his files?"

Muir shook his head slowly, folding his arms over his chest. "This isn't like calling the Department of Defense and giving them a name so they can trace down a man's files, Brandon. There aren't any centralized medical records in Australia. Mathew Larkin was never, to our best knowledge, in the Australian military. We've got to find out where he lived, and if we're lucky we'll either find his family or a medical facility that for some reason still might have his dental records. At this point, if there aren't any medical records available, we may have to try a DNA match with family members. If there still are family members."

"It seems pretty obvious he's the guy."

"That's not good enough," said Muir. "It's 'pretty obvious' Pepper was Pepper, too." He raised a finger into the air as if lecturing an elementary classroom. " 'Pretty obvious' allows us to proceed forward, so that we might become, quote, 'absolutely positive.' "

"Fuck it, he's dead," grunted Condley. "Let the Aussies figure it out."

"Brandon, you're hopeless." Muir picked up a sealed manila envelope from his desk, holding it out for Condley. "By the way, another fellow wearing a tie dropped in this morning, leaving this for you." Muir read from a business card. "Special Agent Combs?"

"Dick Tracy," laughed Condley.

"He seemed very agitated that you weren't here yet. In fact, he said some things about you that weren't very nice."

"Yeah, but they were probably true."

Muir thought about that and shrugged. "You're right. They were."

"He wasn't supposed to give that to anyone but me."

"Yes," said Muir, reading now from the labeling on the envelope. "In fact it does say, *Eyes Only Brandon Condley,* on the envelope."

"I suppose I could get him fired for that. But he already knows I'm an asshole, so why bother?"

"Strange that he would give it to me," mused Muir. "But I guess I look trustworthy."

"It must have been the tie."

"Anyway, I didn't open it." Muir handed the envelope to Condley, slowly breaking into a smile. "Anything good inside?"

"Dirty pictures," said Condley, breaking the seal of the envelope with a pen. "They've been following you and your wife." The envelope was open now. Condley pulled out the pages General Duncan had sent him and quickly examined them. Ever cautious in such matters, the general had printed them out on plain white paper, without a letterhead or other notations that might be easily traceable. The information that had been in the classified documents was now carefully sanitized to remove notations that were either too sensitive regarding methods or too specific regarding the identities of informants inside Russia. But all the essentials remained, including the name and address of the mysterious Anatolie Petrushinsky.

"Spot on!" said Condley, in a rare moment of true enthusiasm.

"The Russia thing?"

"We've got a contact point inside Russia who apparently used to operate as an adviser in the Que Son Mountains. There's a strong chance he would have known Salt and Pepper both. He may be the only hope we have of actually putting a trail on Deville."

"A Russian in the Que Son Mountains?"

"Looks like."

"Well," said Muir in his booming voice. "We should be able to clear this up pretty quickly."

"Except that he apparently won't talk, and the Russian government isn't exactly excited about making him. In fact, the more we pressure him or them, the more likely he's going to disappear. So the only hope is to kind of swoop in on him and catch him off balance."

"Brandon," sighed Hanson Muir. "Let me remind you that our job is to find bones and identify them. Bones. On old battlefields. Not to ambush live Russians in Moscow or live Devilles wherever he may be."

"We're trying to identify remains, Professor. Anatolie Petrushinsky may hold definitive information regarding the activities of what's-his-name, the guy whose skull I own—"

"Rent," corrected Professor Muir.

"*Own*," emphasized Condley. "Unless the government decides to pay me back, I'm keeping that bad boy hostage."

"Oh, whatever," said Muir, knowing where Condley was taking this line of reasoning. "Alphonse no-middle-name Smith."

"Exactly. Petrushinsky might even be able to confirm Smith's activities, as well as possibly being able to tell us something about these other two. So we go see him."

"You don't need me in Moscow. You go. After you come with me to Australia."

"Well, I don't want you in Moscow, but why do you need me in Australia?"

"I'm not the man to go thousands of miles away and interview live people by myself. I lack the finesse. You said it yourself. I'm better when they're dead. Besides," Muir said invitingly, "if Matt Larkin was from Australia, it makes sense that Deville may have headed into Australia when he escaped from Viet Nam."

Condley's eyes lit up immediately. "Okay, I'll go."

"And I don't want you to be searching for Deville by yourself. Anywhere you go where Deville might be, I go too, Brandon."

"That could seriously cramp my style, Professor. And it could also scare the shit out of you."

"You're not going to kill that man, unless it's in self-defense." Muir said it flatly, but with a powerful conviction that surprised Condley.

"What difference does it make?"

"Murder is not in your job description."

Condley sighed, shaking his head and staring at the pictures on Muir's wall for several seconds. All the people in the pictures were happy. Muir's life, in fact, was happy. He had immeasurable respect for the dead but he had never heard the actual, horrible sounds of death, the gurgling of lungs filling up with blood, the crack and whump of combat, the running of a shower in an upstairs bathroom where a woman was lying with her limbs in utter disarray, her throat cut with such ferocity that only a few threads of skin on the back of her neck kept her from having been decapitated. Death came with an odd purity to the gentle Professor Muir, in bleached bones that awaited identification and after that a hero's burial, replete with a spotlessly clean flag.

"I'm not going to murder him, Professor."

"Do I have your word on that?"

"I might execute him, if I get a clean shot. But that's different."

"I'm not going to let you do either. Because there's another reason, Brandon, one that transcends your anger and your thirst for revenge. Wouldn't you like to interrogate this man? Don't you want to know how he escaped from the American military, how he made contact with the enemy, and what he did for the other side? Not to mention how he again escaped from them, assuming that he did? Or maybe they even helped him kill Larkin, what do you think of that? And maybe he still works for them. Whatever the truth is, doesn't history deserve to know?"

"He killed two of my Marines. He betrayed everything I and a lot of others believed in, at a time when we were being humiliated even in our own country for believing in anything. History is for guys like you, Professor. I want my moment. One on one. Me and him. And I don't give a rat's ass about preserving his options to be interviewed in the media and sell his memoirs. I couldn't care less about that."

"Well, a lot of other people will. Sure, a few of the media divas will try to make him a hero. But this is a side of the war we know nothing about. I for one would like to know the entire story."

"That's because you're a typical American pervert, wanting to feed off the stories that come in on CNN so you think you're really alive."

Muir stiffened, a rare moment of rebuke. "That was gratuitous, Brandon. I've taken my risks with you in some very nasty places."

"I'm sorry, Professor, you're right about that." Condley broke from his semitrance and stared at Muir. "This is a great argument we're having, but aren't we a little ahead of ourselves, anyway? First, we have to find him. And after that we have to, shall we say, cause him to be apprehended. And this is not a stupid man."

"Indeed, he's not." Muir casually fingered some papers on his desk, thinking hard. "But why would this fellow in Moscow even consider talking to us?"

"To me, that is," said Condley. "He'll talk because Colonel Pham is going to help us."

"Colonel Pham?" Muir seemed incredulous. "Why do you think Colonel Pham would—or even *can*—help us in Moscow?"

"He lived in Moscow after the war," answered Condley. "I caught him talking Russian with one of his Interior Ministry pals one day. He seemed pretty fluent. When I asked him about it he told me he'd spent a few years there as a so-called 'student' in the late seventies, and you don't get sent there by Ha Noi unless you have some kind of pull in the Vietnamese government. He knows Moscow; he speaks Russian."

"That was more than twenty years ago. You saw how little power he has, just by watching him try to help us up in the Que Sons."

Condley stroked his chin judiciously, his eyes faraway. "Maybe,

maybe not. I thought that too, at the beginning of our trip. But did you see his smile when they stuck me for the five thousand dollars? The colonel knows how to play both sides. We have no idea what he was really doing with us in the Que Sons. It all could have been an act. He's a very clever man."

"Precisely, Brandon. That's another thing. I'm not sure I'd trust him with this piece of information. It could be volatile."

Condley shrugged, his eyes burning with challenge. "I just have a feeling he'll help us. If nothing else, why would he turn down a free trip for a sentimental journey back to his old stomping grounds?"

"You want to take him *with* you?"

"You got any better ideas?"

"Except for this Mathew Larkin business, I don't have any ideas at all." The two stared at each other for several seconds, and then finally Professor Muir nodded, folding his arms across his chest. "Come with me to Australia. I'll come back here while you're in Moscow. I'd be in the way there, and my paperwork is piling up anyway."

"Amazing, isn't it?" Condley picked up the manila folder. "Some sick, treasonous deserter named Deville meets an Aussie photographer who had a wild hair up his ass and ran off to do a story on the VC, then murders him on a muddy trail in Ninh Phuoc—*Ninh Phuoc*, a scabby little village that doesn't even have an outdoor toilet—and we end up on paid vacations to Australia and Russia."

"Now, didn't I tell you that anthropology was an exciting profession?" laughed Hanson Muir. "I rest my case."

CHAPTER TWENTY-ONE

Sai Gon

DZUNG'S *CYCLO* CLATTERED slowly along the broken concrete alleyway a few blocks from his house. The *cyclo* swayed in the pavement's gullies and Dzung swayed with it, side to side, leaning and muttering as he pedaled, urging his carriage along as if it were a tired old horse headed for its stall. It had been a long and disappointing day, nine hours of pedaling after his usual morning session at the firing range with Manh. And all for just under fifty thousand *dong*, less than five dollars.

Dzung's feet moved steadily on the pedals, almost robotically, requiring neither thought nor conscious action on his part. He was exhausted, ready to fall immediately into bed when he reached his shanty of a home. But as he pedaled past one house and looked into the open windows of its front room, Dzung's body immediately became electric with an unwanted, dreadful certainty. Quoc, his eldest child, was not at his usual position against one inside wall. And Dzung knew something was seriously wrong.

Nguyen Van Tam, once an ARVN soldier, now a shoemaker, lived two blocks away from Dzung's house along the same crumbling alley.

The dimly lit front room of Tam's two-story concrete house was the District Four equivalent of a factory floor. Lacking even benches and chairs, a half dozen local workers spent their days sitting on the floor against a wall, chatting and smoking cigarettes as they cut patterns from synthetic leather. The patterns were then taken upstairs, where Tam and his wife formed them and sewed them into shoes. Twice a week Tam took his shoes to the Ben Thanh and Sai Gon markets, selling them for four thousand *dong,* or about forty cents.

Quoc had begun working for Tam three years before, when he turned ten. Little Quoc worked eight hours a day. He learned fast and worked hard, cutting fabric insoles, for which Tam paid him five thousand *dong* a day. Quoc was deeply proud of his employment and frequently bought the family extra water and rice. A responsible, serious child who bore the sorrows of his father as a personal burden, Quoc had never missed a day of work.

But now Quoc was not inside. When Dzung pedaled slowly past and looked beyond the open doorway for his son, the others in Tam's front room stopped talking. One of them waved perfunctorily, then returned to cutting an insole. The others avoided his eyes.

He did not want to, but Dzung continued to pedal down the familiar broken sidewalk, feeling his legs move ever more slowly as he neared his home. He clutched the handrails on his *cyclo.* He squeezed his eyes together. He shook his head. He stared up at the hot and cloudless sky. But it did no good. There were no answers. He was pulled like a magnet to his wife and children even as he wanted more than almost anything to avoid the sad sight that he knew awaited him.

Paralysis, that was his karma, propelled by the inevitability of suffering. Going home would hurt, but staying away would kill him. And so the only thing that was left was to keep pushing the pedals of the *cyclo* until some outside force intervened, deciding what should happen next.

His daughter Thuc was crying, a mix of bewilderment and sorrow. He heard her long before he maneuvered his *cyclo* around a narrow bend and saw her standing on the sidewalk outside their home. She appeared so small in the middle of the concrete, almost infantile, with one hand pulling at her lower lip as she stared bleakly inside the house. As he neared her it was hard for him to comprehend that she was really even nine years old. And yet the look on her face told him she would never be young again.

The baby had given Thuc her first faint glimpse of adulthood. How many mornings had her little brother sucked hungrily at her shoulder as she stood barefoot next to the bed, her toes crimped into the dirt, cradling and loving him so her mother could have another five minutes of sleep?

She saw Dzung and ran toward him on the cracked pavement. Her small triangle of a face was desperate. Her arms were outstretched. Her eyes told him she wanted him to make this go away, that she needed to be a baby again. He stopped the *cyclo* and picked her up, kissing the tears out of her eyes and clutching her to him. He was rocking her now, and she began to bawl.

He did not know what else to do. That seemed always to be his curse. So he tried to do everything all at once. He held her in one arm, kissing and consoling her as he pulled the *cyclo* out of the narrow roadway with his free arm and then locked it. He stood next to the house, holding her close to him for another long moment, trying to calm her. He angrily waved away the old women from across the lane, who now peered out of their upstairs windows with their rheumy, remembering eyes. And finally he carried Thuc with him into the house.

His son Quoc was standing alone just inside the doorway, next to the shelf unit that blocked the view from the road. Quoc's small hands were clenched into fists. His head was bowed, as if he were fighting off his own indecision. Yes, thought Dzung, walking up to his oldest son and putting his free hand on the boy's back. He's like me. He'll always be like me. When bad things happen he wants to do too many things. And so he stands there doing nothing.

More wailing came from the other side of the shelf unit. Dzung did not want to go any further into the house. He began to take another step forward; Thuc, clutching his neck, crying louder, caused him to halt. Standing for another moment with Thuc in his arms, he nestled Quoc's head against his chest.

"Come, son," he said to Quoc, pressing the boy in the small of his back as he moved into the house. "Your mother needs us."

His wife, Tu, saw him and stopped wailing. Her eyes embraced him with sadness as she sat motionless on the edge of their bed. Her face was wan with exhaustion. Her arms hung limply around Vong and Hao, the two middle children. Vong, the daughter who was eleven, sat numbly on

Tu's lap. Hao, the younger son, stood as Dzung entered, and walked over and clutched his leg.

"The baby is dead," said Hao.

On the bed the mosquito net was drawn up toward the ceiling. His wife had never lost a child but she knew the traditions, the proprieties, all the little, intricate, mandatory ceremonies that drove their culture, even when there was no money, even now at the point of death. She had put down a clean straw mat and a white cloth over that. The baby was lying on the white cloth, dressed in pale-blue cotton pajamas. Underneath his head was a pad made of thin white linen. A white handkerchief had been placed over his face.

Little Thuc looked at her dead baby brother's corpse and suddenly began screaming again. Dzung rocked her for a few more seconds and then carefully handed her to Quoc. She was almost too big for Quoc to hold, but the young boy who in his heart was already a man managed to clutch her to him. Quoc patted her almost mechanically on the back, his face a terrible mix of confusion and duty.

I must have been very bad in my last life, thought Dzung as he silently moved forward to embrace his wife.

At that moment he missed his father more deeply than at any time in his life. And he found himself wondering if his mother might somehow still be alive. So many things had happened since those young days on the sandy banks of the Han River just outside Da Nang with his father walking and singing in the fields among the mulberry bushes and his mother at the cook pot, watching from the house on the road just up the rugged, red-clay hill. And his grandmother looking after him, with her twist of tobacco always dangling low from her lips, beneath her chin. And his brothers, like sentries at the edge of the far road, waiting. And then in the time it takes to say good-bye, all of them together gone like chaff blown by a sudden wind, off to be soldiers, refugees, prisoners, corpses, ghosts.

So many things, so many people gone. But no tragedy could have prepared him for staring at his own dead child.

His wife eased little Vong from her lap, leaving the young girl on the bed, and walked over to Dzung, embracing him. They said nothing, for there was nothing left to say. A ritual as old and deep as the culture that spawned them drove them instead to action.

As the children sniffled and watched, Dzung and Tu began moving silently through their home, as if propelled by unseen commands. Dzung found a small rice bowl and filled it with uncooked rice, placing it just above the baby's head. His wife boiled an egg and put it on a plate next to the rice bowl, along with a small mound of salt. They lit two white candles, placing one above each of the baby's shoulders. Dzung brought three joss sticks, lighting them in a candle's flame and placing them into the bowl of rice. The three joss sticks glowed in the dim, ever-darkening room, filling it with sweet, sad smoke, a wispy fog over their tiny dead son.

His wife moved to the small family altar at the house's entrance, where she lit two red candles. Dzung joined her there with three more joss sticks, again lighting them in the candles' flame. The joss sticks always came in threes when a family member died: one for heaven, one for earth, one for hell. He placed them in the sand jar at the center of the altar, and then he and Tu clasped their hands, moved them six times, and prayed.

To a lost child, dead of bad hygiene and disease.

To a new ancestor, protector, and adviser.

To themselves, trapped by fate, bound by love, grieving with four children in this waterless, mud-filled hovel somewhere between heaven and hell.

Little Thuc was crying again, clinging to Dzung's knees. Hao, now again the youngest living child, had walked over and buried his head into his mother's waist. Quoc, so much like Dzung himself, was again motionless, paralyzed by his very energy. And Vong still sat limply on the bed next to the dead baby, her eyes shut tightly as if to remove her from this scene of massive sorrow.

The narrow road in front of their home was beginning to fill with onlookers, the curious and the kind, mostly neighbors who soon would offer condolences and who tomorrow might bring small portions of rice and cakes as a gesture of their sympathy.

Suddenly it all overwhelmed Dzung, making him think for the first time in his life that he might go mad. The eyes of his neighbors, the wailing of his children, the sweet smoke and the glowing candles, everything his senses touched seemed to pour their memories inside him like some hot and bitter brine. They finished praying and Dzung felt he was swelling up with anguish, as if he might soon burst like a balloon from his toes to the top of his head and leak his hopelessness onto the packed-dirt floor until his ability to endure was completely gone.

At that moment only Quoc's steadfast eyes saved him, loyal and inquiring. Their very gaze infused him again with dignity. Quoc wanted him to do something. His eyes told Dzung that there was indeed a tomorrow, and that only he could take them there.

It was a massive thought after twenty-five years of hopelessness, that he might find a way to prevent this moment from happening again. And it bordered on the impossible to think that he could ever bring his family a future, one that was more than a grinding, daily battle to endure, one crowned with hope and possibilities. But Quoc's eyes told him that he must try—indeed, that if he did not try, he was betraying his own blood into eternity.

A quiet agony propelled Dzung forward. He called again to Quoc as he pushed his way through the onlookers outside his door and began to unlock his *cyclo*.

"Take care of your mother. Boil the rice."

It was nearly six o'clock. He had to hurry.

His neighbors watched him departing with querulous, disapproving faces. He ignored them as he guided the *cyclo* through them and jumped onto his seat, pedaling away. Little Thuc howled behind him, running onto the concrete and watching him leave. He pushed hard on the pedals, driving too fast along the narrow alleyways, ringing the small bell on the *cyclo* handle when he negotiated the tighter turns. Children and small dogs raced out of his way. Old men called to him to be careful as they sat at their small plastic-table thrones with their cigarettes and beer and tea. Young men laughed and pointed, viewing his recklessness as wild abandon rather than a suffocating grief.

On the main roads the traffic serenaded him with its very chaos. Its noxious fumes were like a drug that calmed him. Yes, this was normalcy, more than a decade of it now, he in the middle of this frantic churning, this massive, elemental striving, pushing the pedals, feeling his chest heave and his body sweat, the sun baking down on him and the fumes burning his eyes. Pushing toward something, pedaling away from something, waiting for Buddha to stop laughing long enough to allow him a real destination.

But now there was a destination. He wondered at his own audacity as he made the turns and headed toward it. On the surface of it, he had no leverage, none. He had nothing at all to bargain away, and he had nothing more to offer than what they knew they already had. He could not refuse to carry out Manh's orders if and when the time came. The implicit threat of harm to his family was already the guarantor of that. They could cause the trigger to be pulled at their target, and pulled well. But there was one intangible that they never could demand, and which he had never believed he would offer.

His loyalty.

In the dark, cool lobby of the Interior Ministry building, the small-faced guard was sitting with a grand self-importance behind his wide old French-made desk, smoking a cigarette, guarding his precious few hundred square feet of tomblike emptiness as if it were heaven's very door. As Dzung entered the lobby, the guard waved commandingly, summoning him to the desk, ever scowling, ever stupid, thinking nothing had changed. But everything had changed. Dzung burst past him, ignoring the usual mandatory, humiliating courtesies, and started up the now-familiar flight of moldy old stairs. The guard rose from his chair in protest, but Dzung froze his motion with a threatening finger and violent eyes.

"Stay where you are, frog. He's waiting for me. Room 212. I don't have any time for you today."

Inside Room 212 Manh was sitting behind his desk, smoking a cigarette and looking casually across the room. He jolted upright when Dzung burst through his door. Dzung walked inside and stood in front of Manh's desk, heaving with exhaustion, his face racked with tragedy, trying to gather the composure to speak. And then he noticed a woman of about his age sitting in the chair where Manh had first interrogated him. She was well-dressed and plump, too well-dressed and too plump to be living inside Viet Nam. From her clothes, her haircut, and the heavy jewelry on her wrists and fingers, it was clear she was an overseas Vietnamese, probably back from France or America for a visit. And she and Manh were comfortable with each other, even intimate, although in a nonsexual way, as if they had enjoyed a long and prosperous business relationship.

Or political partnership, thought Dzung as his eyes moved carefully from one to the other. Was this woman one of the Interior Ministry's many foreign agents, back in Sai Gon under a tourist visa to give them information about the political activities of Vietnamese living overseas?

"What are you doing here?" asked Manh harshly, recovering from his initial surprise. "Why didn't you knock? Who do you think you are?"

Dzung felt the woman's eyes on him as she slowly inspected him from the plastic sandals on his unwashed feet to the old baseball cap that covered his rough-cut hair. Following her eyes, he became acutely conscious of his sweat-stained, faded clothes and the gaps between his teeth. And of her obvious opulence, gained from a life in another country, even as she reported on those who had escaped the sad, misguided system that kept him and others in bare feet with their broken teeth and dead children.

"You must go outside until I'm finished," ordered Manh, ignoring the woman and speaking directly to Dzung. "I tell you, I am in a meeting. You wait outside!"

Dzung stubbornly held his ground, standing halfway between Manh and his overseas informant, suddenly shivering from the whirring coolness of the air conditioner as he alternated his gaze from one to the other. "I'm not leaving until we have spoken privately, Manh. Until I am satisfied. Check my file. I can be very persistent."

"Excuse me," said the woman. She rose quickly from the chair and began walking toward the door. "I am sorry. It is time for me to go. Good night." And she was gone, the door clicking quietly behind her as she pulled it closed.

For a long moment Dzung and Manh stared quietly at each other, neither of them moving from where they sat or stood. Above Dzung's head the air conditioner whirred, bringing the only sound into the room and causing him again to shiver.

"You forget yourself. Remember your family." Manh fairly blurted the words, causing Dzung to tremble with rage.

"Yes, my family, Manh. I am remembering my family. I am trying to take care of my family, which now stands together in our luxury home in District Four as it watches over the dead body of my baby. He is properly attended to, all decked out with the appropriate linens. The egg has been cooked. Are you surprised we had the money to buy it? We have lit the candles and the joss sticks. His soul has passed to join the ancestors. Yes. And I am remembering my family."

"I am sorry," Manh finally said, stubbing out his cigarette as he dropped his eyes. "I am truly sorry."

"I need your help," said Dzung, his chest still heaving. "It is a simple thing, but you are the only one who can do it."

"What do you want?"

"You are using me, Manh. You are going to use me for something evil. Evil but very important to you. And so if it is important to you, this means I am somehow valuable. To the revolution."

Manh watched him carefully, rocking back in his chair and taking out another cigarette. It was clear to him that, despite Dzung's deep grief, he was opening up a new negotiation. "Perhaps," he said.

"You know my weakness."

Manh lit the cigarette, holding it far down between his fingers like his old gangster heroes as he pulled it away from his mouth. "We know everything about you."

"Then you know I keep my word."

"Yes."

"Then I will give you my word." Dzung's face had become deeply lined over the past two hours, as if someone had drawn cobwebs around his eyes and along his cheeks. He stepped toward Manh. "Give me a cigarette."

Manh took a cigarette from his pack and gave it to Dzung, then held out his lighter while Dzung lit it. Dzung inhaled deeply, calming himself. He took off his cap and waved a hand through his hair.

"My family is more important to me than my life. They are dying, Manh. They have no future." Manh said nothing. He already knew that, remembered Dzung. It was in the files. "If that is how you control me, then that is how you must reward me."

"What do you want?"

"I want my baby to be buried in Bien Hoa, with my wife's family, not alone in District Four. I want you to help me take my family there, for the burial ceremony."

"We can do that," said Manh. "But you should think clearly, Dzung. You don't want the others to know you are working with us. It could be dangerous to you."

"Or maybe to you?" answered Dzung immediately. "After I have served your purposes and am disposed of, or perhaps killed, will they know you were behind my actions?"

"We don't care," said Manh. "Why should we care about that? What would they do to us? We can always deny our involvement. We can reinvent your history with the sweep of a pen. Who would challenge us? But I promise you this, Dzung. If you are successful, we will not betray you. We will have no need to. The matter will be over. It will pass into history as a random act. A freak occurrence. An unsolved mystery."

"What do you want me to do?"

"When the time comes you will know."

"But you admit it is for the good of the revolution."

"We only act for the good of the revolution."

"Then you must also promise to take care of my family."

"How?" asked Manh. "To do what?"

"I fought on the wrong side in the war. I accept my fate. But if I am going to serve the cause of the revolution, then the revolution should forgive my family. They should have a future. Just like yours."

"I will look into it."

"No. You must promise me."

"I am only one small frog in a very big pond," said Manh, stroking his mustache and eyeing Dzung shrewdly. "But you make sense. I promise you I will argue for you."

"I accept your promise," said Dzung, finally, relaxing into a slump that announced the depth of his sorrow. He put out the cigarette and rubbed his hands over his face, squeezing back the tears he would never allow Manh or any other government official to see. "And so I will give you my word. When the time comes, you have no need to question my loyalty. If you promise to take care of my family no matter what happens to me, I will do it. And I will succeed."

Manh rose from his chair and moved to Dzung, standing in front of him for a moment and then reaching out to take his hand. He shook Dzung's hand firmly, for a long time, and then formally took it inside both of his, as if welcoming him into a new and deep friendship.

"We will take care of your family, Dzung. I promise you. Better things will happen. You will see."

"No matter what happens to me," insisted Dzung.

"No matter what happens to you."

THE NEXT MORNING an unmarked white van drove far into the bowels of District Four. Its driver announced to Dzung's neighbors that he was from the Bien Hoa People's Committee and had been sent to take

Dzung's family and their deceased child to a burial ceremony in Bien Hoa in accordance with the new government policy to encourage "family reunification after death."

Dzung carried the baby in his arms as he and his family followed the driver down the alleyway for several blocks, where the van was parked on a wider road. He sat in the front seat of the van, across from the driver. His wife, Tu, and the children sat in the two back rows of seats, amazed at their first automobile ride and the feel of air-conditioning on their skin. The baby was placed in its rear compartment just behind the third row of seats.

The driver announced that he was taking them to a small village just outside Bien Hoa, where the baby would be buried in Tu's family cemetery. A representative of the People's Committee would be present at the burial. Tu's entire family had been notified and were waiting at the burial ground for their arrival. Courtesy, said the driver again, of the new government policy that favored the reunification of families after death.

The traffic was very heavy. They listened to sad music on the cassette player just above the radio. Manh was nowhere to be seen, but to Dzung his presence was as real as the music, as permeating as the cool air that washed over them from the vents inside the van. And from that moment forward Dzung knew the deal was sealed. He could never again question the uses to which he would be put. He had made the offer, and Manh's superiors had accepted it.

CHAPTER TWENTY-TWO

Exmouth, Australia

FROM PERTH THEY flew eight hundred miles due north, over vast, empty deserts and ledges of dust-covered, craggy mountains. The sea was always just to the west, cobalt blue, as endless and as empty as the sky. Below them, a stringlike, hopeless road paralleled the coastline, connecting occasional little towns that appeared to be more like frontier outposts than modern living centers. Herds of wild horses vectored this way and that like schools of fish as the twin-engine aircraft passed over them, and then a throng of donkeys, and after that a valley full of ostriches and mobs of jackrabbits, thousands of them seeming to pile on top of one another as they scrambled away from the sudden noise. Halfway to Exmouth, Condley was certain he saw the silhouettes of camels loping ghostlike through the shadowed, powdery ridges. It was the wildest and most eerily empty terrain he had ever seen.

Finally they reached the northeast corner of the continent, where a peninsula jutted out for another twenty miles into the first beginnings of the Indian Ocean. Above the sea the aircraft bounced like a kite from a sudden burst of wind, then dove quickly, finding a narrow strip of

runway among the dust-filled weeds of the peninsula, where it barked
and skittered to a halt.

"Exmouth," said the fleshy-faced, balding pilot, consciously checking his watch as he called to them from his seat. "I guess three hours will
do it before we turn around?"

"Four hours at the most," called Hanson Muir, unbuckling his seat
belt and clutching his briefcase. "As far as I can tell, there are only two
people we can talk to in this town."

"You call that a town, mate?" The pilot chuckled, shutting down the
engines. He pointed to the small shack that housed the runway's operations facility. Just next to it was a gas pump. Other than the operations
shack, a dusty, shrub-filled emptiness surrounded them for what seemed
to be miles in every direction. "I'm going to refuel, and I'll wait for you
in the operations shack. And no offense, you hear, but my price goes up
if you get me stuck here overnight."

A pimply, forlorn-looking sailor was waiting for them at the end of
the runway where the aircraft had shut down. The reed-thin young man
was standing next to a white U.S. Navy staff car, incongruous in this
wilderness. A neck-high barbed-wire fence, built to keep large animals
off the tarmac, marked the outer boundaries of the runway. As Condley
walked toward the car he saw five wild horses grazing lazily in a scrubby
field just on the other side of the fence. Near the car a huge iguana startled him from twenty feet away as it suddenly rose up on its tail, its head
higher than Condley's waist, and then scurried into the underbrush.

"I hate those fuckers," said the sailor, watching the iguana disappear. "It's like hitting a big, fat alligator when you run over them."

"Then don't run over them," said Condley dryly, as he climbed into
the rear seat of the staff car.

"Not much else to do out here. Hitting a horse really fucks up your
car." He held out a hand, shaking Condley's. "Mr. Condley, right? My
name's Alfred E. Newman. Petty Officer, Third Class. No shit, that's
really my name. I have two very fucked-up and cynical parents."

The sailor was maybe nineteen years old. He seemed oddly happy to
be greeting them. He solicitously closed the car doors for Condley and
Muir as they settled into the rear seats. Then he eased into the driver's
seat and started the engine.

"Where to?" he said. And then he laughed, as if at himself. "That
was a joke."

Condley grinned. "Did you hear the one about the American sailor stuck in the middle of the Australian desert?"

"That's not a joke," said the sailor. And then he and Condley laughed together.

The staff car slowly made its way down the dirt trail, finally leaving the airport and turning onto a two-lane paved road that led to Exmouth. "This is Professor Hanson Muir," said Condley to Alfred E. Newman. "He's a scientist. An anthropologist, actually."

"Well, everybody's got to be something," said Newman, giving Muir a grudging nod in the rearview mirror.

"How many American military are stationed up here?" asked Condley.

"It's classified, sir," said the sailor, becoming suddenly official. "I'm not allowed to tell you. We have a joint communications facility with the Aussie Navy. The town itself sort of feeds off us. If you look hard at the map and think submarines, you know why we're here. The Indian Ocean ends just to our north, funneling naval traffic all the way down from the Asian mainland so that it has to cruise between Australia and the Indonesian Islands. I mean, you've got the Straits of Malacca up there at the end of the Malaysian peninsula, and down here, unless you want to go all the way around the west coast of Australia toward Antarctica, you have to pass us. So if they're transiting east to west or west to east, no matter where they start and no matter where they end up, they pass through this bottleneck."

"So you watch them," said Condley.

"Mostly we listen." The sailor shrugged, retreating into his Navy-regulation pose. "Sorry, that's all I can really say. It's classified."

"Lovely place," said Muir sarcastically, looking out the window at the persistent scrub that surrounded them. "A marvel of tranquillity."

"Best skin diving in the world," said the sailor. "But if you don't swim, forget it. Take a jog every now and then. Learn to like Foster's. Sit around, waiting for your weekend every month or so in Perth trying to get laid."

The road curved, and the blistered little town appeared suddenly to their front. Except for them, the road was completely empty of traffic, as if the entire little town went indoors during the day to escape the baking heat. Muir was all business now, his briefcase open on his lap, studying a map and looking out the windows for landmarks.

"Well, at least we know why he left home," said the professor.

Condley chuckled. "Yeah, some sailor probably snaked his girl."

"Oh, no," protested the sailor as they began to pass blocks of weary-looking, dilapidated shacks. "Don't date the townies. Unless you want to get married, that is. The dads out here shoot to kill."

"There it is," said Muir, checking the map on his lap and then pointing out the window toward an old one-story cinder-block building. A small sign was posted in its yard:

JOSEPH McHENRY, JOSEPH McHENRY, JR.
DENTAL SERVICES

"Objective number one," announced Muir. "Pull in there, would you, Alfred?"

It was just past noon. If there had been any patients that morning they were gone, leaving no indicators of their presence. Inside the office door a tall, balding man in a white medical coat was standing behind a scarred wooden desk, next to an old-style black telephone. Several file cabinets filled the space behind the desk. One of the cabinet drawers was open. The man was next to the drawer, holding a pile of well-worn manila folders. He looked up from the folders as Condley and Muir entered his office, his parched gray eyes peering at them over the top of a pair of reading glasses that were halfway down his nose.

Condley stepped toward him. "Doctor McHenry?"

"Junior," he said, his voice brick-dry. "My father died five years ago." He paused, evidently remembering the sign outside. "Never got around to changing the sign. It doesn't matter. He was retired before that, actually. People here know who I am."

"I'm Brandon Condley. This is Professor Hanson Muir."

"Not hard to figure that out." McHenry gestured toward a second pile of folders on his desk. "I've been looking all morning and I can't find a thing." He caught Muir's exasperation. "I warned you when we spoke on the phone, Professor. The man left here thirty years ago."

"Nothing?" said Muir.

"Nothing at all. We're not exactly the government, you know. Keeping archives on dead people isn't what we get paid to do. I'm a digger and a filler and an extractor. If you want braces, go to Perth. Not that anyone around here worries about crooked teeth."

Muir frowned, frustrated and weary. Condley stood next to him, deciding to fill the awkward silence. "Do you remember treating him?"

"I remember my father treating him," said McHenry, softening a bit. "I wasn't through dental school yet. But I knew him. He was quite a bit younger than I. Totally wild, even by western Australian standards. And of course I remember when he disappeared. It was big news around here. The whole thing killed his mother."

"His dad?"

"Drank himself to death. It would've happened anyway. Mathew's antics might have hurried it along a bit, that's all." McHenry raised his eyebrows, anticipating the next question. "Nobody else. No brothers or sisters. God only knows where his parents were before they drifted here. Or maybe they even met here, I don't know. We don't ask about things like that. If people tell us, then fine."

Condley and Muir stared quietly at each other, their minds working furiously. Muir tapped the folders he was carrying, as if for inspiration. "Do you know Doctor Kenneth T. Hasler?"

"He'll be able to help you," said McHenry, brightening a bit. "Not that he can verify any dental work, but he did know Mathew pretty well." McHenry chuckled, old memories filling his fleshy face. "A regular patient, he was. The boy did know how to brawl."

———

DOCTOR HASLER WAS waiting for them. As the car pulled into the small parking area in front of his combination house and office building, the small, wiry white-haired old man walked out of the front door and hobbled toward them, leaning on a cane. He wore thick glasses and hearing aids. His head was tilted to the side as he searched their faces. Moving instinctively to Condley, he held out a trembling, liver-spotted hand.

"You're in charge," he warbled, shaking Condley's hand. And then he pointed at Hanson Muir. "And he's the scientist. I'm very glad you've come, actually. Follow me inside, boys."

Doctor Hasler's office was in the front area of his home. He led them through it, past a desk area and a well-lit examination room, and then into a surprisingly well-furnished living room. Hundreds of books filled a floor-to-ceiling wooden bookcase that covered an entire wall. A new Japanese air conditioner whirred quietly from near the ceiling. They followed him to a sitting area, falling into lush leather chairs as he took his favorite place on an old leather couch. A wall just across from Condley was filled with pictures and military citations from World War Two.

Hanson Muir sighed happily, at home in these surroundings, basking in the cool breath of the air conditioner. He dropped his folder onto the sturdy mahogany table in front of the chairs.

"Thank you for seeing us, Doctor."

"Thank you for coming," said the old man. "I've been wanting to put this to rest for a very long time."

Muir glanced quickly at Condley, surprised at the intensity of Doctor Hasler's response. "So you knew Mathew Larkin, did you?"

"Yes," said Hasler, his head bouncing slightly from the same tremor that caused his hands to shake. "Yes. Quite well."

"Unfortunately, there are no dental records here, so we're going to have to try and match up what little evidence we have from his skeletal remains."

"What happened to him?" asked the doctor, his opaque eyes intense behind the glasses. "How did he die?"

Muir seemed to balk at the question, so Condley leaned forward in his chair, speaking quietly to the old man. "If these remains are actually those of Mathew Larkin, he was murdered."

"How?" asked Hasler. "By whom? Why? That is, if you don't mind. Excuse me, but I'd very much like to know."

Condley cleared his throat, somewhat nervous under the doctor's steady stare. "The matter is still under investigation, sir. It shames me to say it, but it appears he was killed by an American deserter while both of them were in a remote area with the Viet Cong. From what I can personally tell, I think the guy wanted Larkin's passport as a way to leave the country."

The old man shook his head sadly from side to side, as if the incident had happened only yesterday. "I knew something like this would happen to him. Something violent and unpredictable. He was so wild and yet so wide-eyed. So trusting in his own odd little way."

Professor Muir took several pages from the folder, including photographs of the remains and his own detailed drawings of the key areas that had provided him evidence. He scanned them as he spoke. "Doctor, we strongly suspect that the remains we recovered were those of Mathew Larkin, but obviously we need to clarify that. From my examination I can confirm that this was a man in his early twenties, about five foot nine inches tall, with brown hair." He looked over at the doctor, looking for any refutation and finding none. "We don't have much to go on other than that. I did find evidence of repeated trauma to the joint area of his right shoulder—right here—and also several areas in the neck and upper vertebrae that indicate an unusual amount of trauma in that skeletal region for a man so young. Look at this area here."

Muir handed the pages to Doctor Hasler. The old man stared at them for several minutes before handing them back, as if he was looking for secret answers of his own.

"It's Mathew." The old man's face was filled with grief and yet seemed softened by the knowledge of discovery. "Of course it is. I can't tell you how many times I set the boy's shoulder. And the teeth. Odd, but I remember his fillings. Very good teeth. And the neck trauma. Yes. He was a fighter, you know. Inside and outside the ring. An absolute terror." Hasler smiled softly now, remembering. "I loved to watch him fight. He never knew that."

"So you feel positive about this identification?"

"I have no doubt."

"You can write a letter of certification for us?"

"Of course." Hasler's mind seemed to wander. "He didn't have to go to Viet Nam," said the old man, glancing for a moment at the wall that contained his own war mementos. "The Australian Army had pulled out of there by the time he finished school, you know. But he had that passion in him. He had a reach that was too great for this little town in this desolate region. I was very proud, watching him take up photography the way he did. He was quite a talented young man. There wasn't much else he could have done around here, particularly in his circumstances. The camera was his way out. Once he realized he could turn it into a ticket to Sydney, it was all over. And from Sydney it was on to Viet Nam. The boy was quite talented."

Hasler rose from the couch with effort and made his way to a well-polished mahogany bureau. Opening a drawer, he took out a thick folder and brought it back to the table. His hands trembling, he worked carefully to place a dozen eight-by-ten photos on the table. There in black and white were a series of action shots that Mathew Larkin had captured during his time in Viet Nam, street scenes and battlefield moments that were so vivid they made Condley himself shudder with memories.

"He was good," said Condley quietly.

"No, he was brilliant," said the old man. "If he had survived he could have been world-famous. I'm sure that's why he took that unfortunate, secret assignment. To get something no one else had ever captured on film. To become famous. To push the limits and prevail. It's a shame, I tell you. A sad, abominable shame."

The old man looked up from the pictures, an odd pain in his weathered, ancient face, and nodded to Condley. "You're in charge. Are you going to send us his remains for a proper burial?"

"We don't know quite what to do about that," answered Condley. "We'll be in touch with your government, I suppose. We were just told by Doctor McHenry that all his family members are dead."

"Then I will tell you the truth," said Doctor Hasler. He took a deep breath, looking at the photographs on his table and shaking his head with a primal and eternal sorrow. "I am the young lad's father. And it would mean more to me than you will ever know if you would arrange to send him home. Can you please, please do that?"

CHAPTER TWENTY-THREE

Sai Gon

AS THE METER taxi neared the center of the city, Condley saw a succession of familiar red banners strung above the streets, dozens of them, going on for block after block, with yellow letters proclaiming the anniversary of some obscure event in the history of the revolution that few remembered other than the government officials who had ordered the painting and the hanging of the signs. Billboards had been erected along favorite street corners, showing shadowed images of Ho Chi Minh and other communist heroes, splattered with hammers and sickles and red stars, all blending in the figure of a fighting soldier with a fist high in the air, the signs announcing in bold letters filled with exclamation points that nothing was more beautiful or more precious than the nation's independence and freedom.

Independence and freedom. *Doc lap va tu do*. Ho Chi Minh's rallying cry, pasted on billboards in the town that bore his name, most of whose citizens had wished with all their hearts to be liberated *from* him, not by him. Yes, thought Condley, millions had died with that slogan on their lips. And how painfully predictable that most of the progress gained since their victory had come from the efforts of those who learned to work around Uncle Ho's system rather than through it. Yes, he thought, the people of Sai Gon were still stronger than the sloganeers.

No matter. Coming back to Sai Gon was always like coming home, and a part of him rejoiced as he watched the hazy, fecund center of District One unfold before him. The chaotic madness of the traffic, horns beeping and motorbikes whining. The old, mostly French landmarks, chapels and fountains and government buildings amid the ugly, reaching new construction, their peeling paint and mildewed corners marking the city's and thus the nation's historic journey. The street-side vendors with their postcard stands and cigarette boxes and little trays of food, sitting in lawn chairs behind their stalls as their children slept next to them on the sidewalks or played along the street. The odors, up from the street, in from the buildings, windblown from the river, all mixing together. The music, whining from the windows. The beggars and the hustlers, their eyes adrenalized, ever searching. The *cyclo* drivers, lazing in their cabs at every street corner, always waiting.

They reached the Rex Hotel, dropping off an exhausted Hanson Muir, who had decided to remain in Sai Gon while Condley went to Moscow, rather than returning to Hawaii. As the Rex's bellboys unloaded Muir's baggage, Condley waved to several familiar faces among the *cyclo* drivers in the park across the street, an unspoken signal to let Dzung know he had returned. The meter taxi then dropped him off at the Vien Dong Hotel, where he checked back into his room, collected and read his mail, then showered and put on a change of clothes.

Back outside a half hour later, he was surprised that Dzung was not waiting for him at his usual post under the shade tree just across the street from the hotel. He stood in front of the hotel for several minutes, chatting with the doorman, watching and waiting for Dzung. And then finally he began to walk toward the Rex.

He had walked less than a block when he saw Dzung pedaling toward him in the busy street, as always leaning gracefully side to side as he powered his *cyclo* in the midst of a stream of motorbikes and cars. Condley waved, catching Dzung's eye, a small thrill filling his heart at the sight of his friend, just as it always did whenever he first returned to Sai Gon.

Dzung sat high in the seat and braked his *cyclo*, holding his right arm out and looking behind him to make sure he was not rear-ended by a careless Honda or a speeding taxi. Then he pulled onto the curb where Condley stood waiting for him. He managed a small smile, but Condley immediately saw the fresh lines that marred his friend's face and the apprehension in his eyes.

"I was looking for you!" said Condley, climbing onto the seat of Dzung's *cyclo. "Dzung khoe khong?"* he asked as he always did, wanting to know if his friend was doing well.

"*Da, khong khoe,* Cong Ly," said Dzung, losing his forced smile and looking far off into an unknown horizon. It was the first time Dzung had ever said that he was not well. "My baby, he die already."

"I'm very sorry." Condley studied Dzung's face for a moment, trying to read the depths of his sorrow. "Is there anything I can do?"

"*Khong,*" said Dzung immediately, snapping his head as if the very question had the impact of a stun gun. "Thank you very much, Cong Ly, but it is all taken care of." He forced a smile back onto his face, pointing toward the road. "Where we go today, Cong Ly?"

"Are you sure?" asked Condley, still searching his friend's face for clues. "Do you need money? Is your family all right?"

"No problem, Cong Ly." Dzung fidgeted a bit, staring out at the road. "Everything copacetic," he said, using a slang phrase from their shared, long-ago war. "Only I am very sad. *Buon qua.*" He worked up another smile. "So where we go?"

It was Sunday. The government offices were closed, but Condley had business to discuss. "We go to Colonel Pham's house." He gave Dzung a quick look, remembering the resistance of a few weeks before when he had first made that decision, but saw no sign of it now.

"*Duoc,*" said Dzung simply, his face expressionless again. And in seconds they were in the midst of a heavy flow of traffic.

The mingling of the traffic and his own exertion seemed to calm Dzung. After a few blocks he tapped Condley on a shoulder, leaning forward just as he had done so many thousand times before. His voice was lighter now, almost teasing.

"Colonel Pham. You love his daughter, Cong Ly?"

"*Chua,*" said Condley. "I don't even know her very well."

"Good," said Dzung, suddenly becoming emphatic. "Cong Ly, you are my friend so I should tell you. I saw her only last night at the Rex. She was with another man. He took her to the roof for drinks. And then they went dancing. They seemed very close, like lovers."

"*Da, biet roi. Nguoi Phap,*" said Condley flatly, as if stating an historical fact. *That Frenchman again.*

"So you know!" answered Dzung, the sweat now soaking his T-shirt as he pedaled. "He is very rich. He had a limo driver."

"Yes, I know," said Condley. "A very rich man. He sells perfume."

"*Nuoc hoa?*" asked Dzung, incredulous at the thought. "Those little bottles? They can make you rich?"

"It's very expensive just to smell nice. Women become addicted. Don't ask me why. One little bottle of French perfume can cost more than a hundred bottles of beer."

Dzung nodded judiciously. "So, Cong Ly, you should sell some perfume. Or maybe find another woman to love."

"Don't worry!" laughed Condley. "She is very beautiful, but this is not a problem for me. He has the money, so he has the burden of making her happy. When she gets bored with him, maybe she can make me happy."

"Maybe she no good, Cong Ly."

"No, she is good, Dzung. She plays the hand God dealt her."

"Playing with her hands? I don't understand."

"*Dao Phat,*" said Condley. *Karma.* "After all the bad times, wouldn't you like to have nice things?"

Dzung sat high in his seat for a moment, looking all around him in the traffic to see if someone might overhear him. He tried to swallow the words back down, but he could not control them anymore. Then he leaned forward again, his face near Condley's ear. "I would like to be free," he finally said, almost whispering.

His simple words went through Condley like a lance, for he had spoken the unspeakable word, penetrated the airy, accepting facade of his culture, asked for the impossible. Condley sat quietly in the *cyclo*'s chair as they turned from Hai Ba Trung onto the dense traffic of Dien Bien Phu Street, not knowing how to respond to such directness. "I'm trying to help you have a better life," he finally managed to say. "I'm buying that car, Dzung. When your license is approved you'll have a real job. We'll make good money. Partners."

Dzung's face tightened with its own burden, the dread that had not left him since his first day at the shooting range with Manh. His eyes became intense, staring at the back of Condley's head and imagining what it would look like if a bullet broke it apart. Was that what Manh wanted him to do? And despite his promise, could he really do it? He had things to say, but he could not bring himself to mouth the words. If he began he would be unable to stop, and if he said too much it would be all over. At least with his silence he still had options. Finally he compromised, muttering an avoidance. "Viet Nam no good for you, Cong Ly. No good. Maybe you should leave."

"*Thuong Viet Nam*," said Condley with a quiet passion, staring out at the broiling, chaotic streets. *I love Viet Nam.* "*Thuong Viet Nam nhieu qua.*" *I love Viet Nam too much.*

"No, Cong Ly. Too much trouble here. Just leave."

"I have work to do, Dzung. You know that."

"You do that work for a very long time. Maybe you go home, let somebody else do it now."

"Home?" Condley chuckled, looking around him. "Maybe the Vien Dong is my home."

"No, Cong Ly. I am sorry to say this, but you are not Vietnamese. Viet Nam will never be your home."

Condley gave him a strange glance now. "You're always asking me to stay."

They had left Dien Bien Phu and were maneuvering slowly through broken streets and dead-end corridors, heading for Colonel Pham's villa. Dzung removed his baseball cap and pushed his face into one shoulder and then the other, wiping sweat as he pedaled. He knew he had already said too much, and he did not want these thoughts on Condley's mind as he met with the colonel. For if the colonel heard any part of them, who knew how they might be later communicated to Manh?

"You are my good friend. I only want you to be happy, Cong Ly. And sometimes I think Viet Nam is not a happy place."

They had reached Colonel Pham's villa. Condley stepped down from the *cyclo* and stood for a moment, looking deeply into Dzung's face. Tragedy rested on it, as visible as the sweat that now poured down its hollows, gathering in Dzung's already soaked T-shirt.

"Please tell your wife I am very sorry about your baby."

"*Cam on*, Cong Ly," said Dzung. And at that instant he knew he was safe, for Condley in his unending empathy had taken his words as nothing more than simple grief. "I wait here?"

Condley looked over the villa wall toward the house. Mrs. Pham was waving to him from her doorway. "Come back in an hour," he said to Dzung. "If I'm not outside the gate waiting for you, just keep going."

She met him near the gate. Her gray-streaked hair was pulled back into a bun and she wore no makeup. She was in her house clothes: flowing black silk slacks and a black, collarless tunic. But despite her casual dress she was openly delighted to see him. She smiled warmly through her blackened teeth, taking his right hand in both of hers and pulling him gently toward the house.

"*Chao Ong,* Cong Ly," she said, speaking only Vietnamese. "You haven't visited us for so long! Where have you been?"

"*Chao Ba Tho,*" he answered, following her into the house and shifting completely to Vietnamese as well. "I'm very sorry, but I have been constantly on the road. First, in Quang Nam with your husband. Then Hawaii. And after that, Australia. I returned only this morning."

"Too busy!" They had entered the house and reached the dim-lit sitting room. She offered him a chair at their greeting table, pulling it out for him. "All for business?"

"Yes," he said, taking the seat and suddenly sensing that Van had something to do with her question. "Only for business."

"You work too hard, Cong Ly. You must find some time for relaxation now that you are back." She left it at that, but her face held a knowing look. "May I get you some tea?"

"Thank you."

"Van is upstairs," she said as she walked out of the room. "I will get her for you."

Her announcement jolted him, a sudden reminder that he had two differing relationships inside their home, each of which might threaten the other if handled poorly. It was urgent that he meet with Colonel Pham and that he keep the older man's confidence. And yet Mrs. Pham was right to think that his unannounced arrival at their home on a Sunday would have been motivated more by her daughter's beauty than the need to talk business with her husband.

Within seconds he heard shuffling feet and a quick, whispering exchange in the hallway, just around the corner where the family altar stood. He turned toward the noise and saw Colonel Pham walking into the greeting room. Condley stood to greet him, but the colonel motioned him back into his seat with both hands.

"No! No, sit, Cong Ly. You are my guest."

The hard little man slapped him on one shoulder, a delighted smile on his face, and took a seat on the other side of the table. "Van is getting dressed," he said, as if excusing his own presence. "But I have a little bit of news. Do you have time for a short discussion before she comes?"

"Of course," said Condley, relieved to be taking the colonel's cue. "In fact, I have some news for you as well."

"Good."

The colonel leaned over the table and took Condley's hand for a moment in both of his, a gesture of affection. Mrs. Pham appeared briefly, leaving a small tray on the table with a pot of tea and two ceramic cups. Colonel Pham began pouring the tea. "I do not like Monsieur Petain very much," he said with an openly worried nod, switching to heavily slurred English for the first time since Condley had met him. And then he switched back to Vietnamese. "I believe he is using my daughter."

The colonel's directness made Condley uneasy, as if he himself were being asked to find a solution. "I don't know anything about that, Colonel."

"She is spoiled, yes, but she is a good girl. Very emotional. She leads with her heart and not her head. She is too young to be living in his world. Not in years, but in experience. She is very naive, Cong Ly. It is all too sudden a change, from the simplicities of the revolution to his night-clubs and designer clothes and limousines. She wants nice things. She sees them on the television and in the magazines that come from France and America. Petain tantalizes her with these things. But she does not understand the price she might have to pay to get them."

"She is a good person," said Condley lamely, uncertain of where the canny colonel was taking him. "A very beautiful woman."

"She told me about your evening after we all went to temple." Colonel Pham raised a hand, as if there were no need for apology or explanation. "It opened her eyes, Cong Ly. I wish to thank you for that. We are Buddhists, as you know. We are not controlled by such an exact formula as your own Ten Commandments. Instead, we must look inside ourselves to find what is good and what is not. If she had . . . been intimate . . . with you that night, I would not have liked it. But if she had truly struggled with it and determined that it was for the good, I cannot say that it would have been wrong."

Condley watched the colonel quietly, stunned by his directness. Finally he shrugged nervously. "I appreciate your insight, Colonel. But as you know, nothing happened between us."

"I thank you for that. She is, as I have said, very naive. And at this moment more than a little bit confused by her freedom."

Condley shrugged again, with a casualness that he did not feel, wishing to move on. "We are all confused, Colonel. It is a very confusing time."

"All kinds of freedom can be confusing, yes?" Colonel Pham nodded, done with his little lecture. "I wanted to report to you that your trip to Quang Nam was most successful," he said, raising his teacup as if delivering a toast. "The People's Committee was very impressed with the way you conducted your business. There will be more cooperation if you need it."

Condley lifted his own teacup as if returning the toast. He knew immediately that the five-thousand-dollar rental fee had been properly distributed, with some of it no doubt going to Colonel Pham himself. "That is good news, Colonel. And I appreciate very much your precious advice."

The colonel sipped his tea, leaning toward Condley and speaking softly. "I want also to tell you that I passed the name of this man Deville to people whom I trust in our government. They did a thorough check for us in Ha Noi. Very quietly but very thorough. We have nothing on the man. Nothing."

"You mean, your government knows nothing about what happened to him after he killed Mathew Larkin?"

"Mathew Larkin?" said Colonel Pham, his brow furrowing behind the thick glasses. "Who is Mathew Larkin?"

"He was an Australian photographer who was on a secret assignment with your side. We believe Deville killed him. It was his remains that we found in Ninh Phuoc, wearing Deville's dog tags."

"Not a soldier?" said the colonel, seemingly amazed.

"Not even an American."

"You are making my head spin," said the colonel, a smile masking his embarrassment. "I will ask if they know anything about this man Mathew Larkin in Ha Noi. But anyway, Cong Ly, we know nothing about this man Deville. Nothing at all."

"We know he was in the Que Son Mountains in June 1969, Colonel.

And we know that his dog tags mysteriously appeared on the body of Mathew Larkin in 1971, in the same area. And that Mathew Larkin's hand was cut off, in the same fashion that another victim of Deville's was mutilated in Long Binh in 1967. So we do know something about Deville."

"You know something," corrected the colonel. "I am saying we do not." He hedged, finishing his tea and reaching for the teapot. "If he was in the mountains, maybe he went there by himself. Maybe he was hiding. Maybe he was helping a local militia without our knowledge. As you saw, the mountain people are very independent. But he was not working for us."

"Then how did he reach the Que Son Mountains from Sai Gon?" The question was so obvious that it embarrassed Condley to ask it. "There was no free movement back there during the war, Colonel. He had to be escorted, probably at night, just as Mathew Larkin was escorted. This wasn't exactly a resort area."

"Many strange and unexplainable things happened in the war, Cong Ly." The colonel sighed heavily, as if wearying of this conversation. But he was holding his ground, and Condley knew immediately that there would be no deviation from the story he had been given by his government. "Since you know all these other things, maybe you can find the answer to that question as well. We cannot be responsible for the movements of Americans in our country thirty years ago."

"But if we gain some information and need to find an answer, you are still willing to help?"

"*Why are you so obsessed with this?*" The colonel's suddenly impatient question was a veiled accusation, no doubt the echo of conversations that had already taken place among his government contemporaries.

"Because it's my job," said Condley, working to contain his emotions as he held the colonel's stare. He finished his own tea, setting the cup gingerly onto the table. "And because he killed two of my men."

The colonel watched him silently, then waved a small hand in the air. "Okay, Cong Ly. Yes, of course I will still help you. I promised you that, as long as you will be reasonable." He paused, thinking. "And what about the skull of Nguyen My Den?"

"We identified him through his dental records," said Condley. "He was a deserter. Alphonse no-middle-name Smith. I hope you will be pleased to know that we have decided against publicizing anything else about his . . . other conduct. Our official statement will only say that he left his military post and was never heard from again."

Colonel Pham nodded, relieved by this news. "Then you are being reasonable. Ha Noi will be very glad to hear this. It will be most helpful in the relationship between our countries."

"But I still need your help with Deville."

"Because you have been careful with Nguyen My Den, it will be possible for me to continue to help you."

Condley slowly poured himself more tea, deliberately avoiding the colonel's eyes. "Our government has information about a Russian soldier who says he was in the Que Son Mountains during the war."

"A Russian soldier?" Pham seemed genuinely confused. "Where is this Russian?"

"He's in Moscow. I want to talk to him. I want you to come with me."

Colonel Pham eyed him closely for several seconds, sitting very still, his mind working. "Cong Ly, I like you very much, and so I am giving you some good advice. You must be more careful from now on. You are making many people in my government very nervous."

"Why?"

"I don't understand your question."

"Why should they be nervous, Colonel?"

"You are not the State Department," said the colonel immediately, as if regurgitating a recent conversation. "You are supposed to be finding the bones of soldiers lost on the battlefield during the war. It is not your job to be rewriting history or gaining some personal revenge, and it is not my job to help you do that. And I must tell you, Cong Ly, it causes people to wonder about your true motivations in coming back to this country. About whether you truly want to help improve relations between your country and Viet Nam. And even whether finding bones is your . . . true occupation."

Condley thought about that for a moment. "That's fair," he finally said, shrugging his agreement. "So let me put it this way, Colonel. I'm going to Moscow to meet with a former Russian soldier who says he was in the Que Son Mountains during the war. I am going, do you understand? The day after tomorrow. It has already been decided. And for the very reasons you just gave me, I believe it would be in the interest of your government to have you come along as a witness to this meeting. In fact, I will allow you to interpret for me, since I don't speak Russian. And I am comfortable with you providing a complete report to your government about everything that is said in that meeting."

"What is this man's name?"

Condley grinned mischievously. "No way, Colonel. I don't want my man disappearing on me before I even get there."

Colonel Pham laughed knowingly. "You are very smart, Cong Ly. And I know that you do love Viet Nam, so there is no malice in your heart. I will ask Ha Noi if I can accompany you."

"Thank you, Colonel. I have nothing to hide. I am only looking for the truth."

"The truth about what, Cong Ly? The truth can be very evasive. Or sometimes it can be different to different people, depending on whose eyes are seeing it."

"Then let's keep it simple," said Condley, swilling the final half inch of his tea in the little cup. "The truth about Deville. Not who he was, or why he did what he did. But what he did, and where he went after he did it."

The colonel shrugged deliberately, growing restless in his chair. "As I said, we know nothing about that, and to be very honest, my government has no interest in it either. This man was never a prisoner of war. He was never listed as missing in action. And he never worked for our side. I will ask Ha Noi about going to Moscow because I value your friendship, but this is all beyond our normal jurisdiction."

He checked his watch and rose from his chair, a deliberate gesture meant to end their conversation. "My daughter is waiting to see you, I think? Let me see what is taking her so long."

Van spoke from outside the room. "I'm here, Father."

"All right," said Colonel Pham, formally shaking Condley's hand. "Then I will say good-bye, Cong Ly."

Condley turned to see Van enter the room as if on cue, just as the colonel left it. Her knowing grin as she neared him told him immediately that she had indeed been waiting for her father to be done. Standing to greet her, he could not stop his eyes from lingering on her flowing cascade of hair and the smooth skin of her neck and the way her white spandex T-shirt hugged so closely to the contours of her body. She caught the journey of his eyes and smiled deliciously, followed by an open laugh.

"I think you like this shirt? Francois bought it for me in Paris."

She was barely a foot away from him now, happily flirting, and despite the logic that worked against such thoughts it was all he could do to keep himself from pulling her into him. "Francois has excellent taste," he finally managed to say.

She shrugged dismissively. "Yes, but sometimes I think he is dressing me up as if I were a doll."

She turned slowly and took the chair in which her father had just sat. Watching him sit down, she leaned back in the chair, smiling to him again and crossing her legs, the fabric of her black designer slacks tight along her thighs and hips.

"Did you miss me, Cong Ly?"

"Not even 'hello'?"

"Okay," she laughed, her face lighting up. "Hello! Did you miss me?"

"Actually I heard you've been busy. My sources tell me you were all over Sai Gon in a limo last night."

"I told you, that was only Francois," she said, waving a hand into the air and then touching her new clothes as if presenting them to Condley as evidence. "He won't drive in the Sai Gon traffic. It makes him nervous. And he won't ride on my Honda. So he always takes a limo. And besides, he is in love with me already!"

"It was 'only Francois'? You're acting very French," he said, laughing at her sudden look of indignation.

"It's fun to go places with Francois," she countered. "Why should I lie about such things? But I am very happy to be Vietnamese." She gave him an open, challenging smile. "And you have been waiting only for me, Cong Ly? Is that what you're saying?"

He could hear her parents talking softly in the other room. For a moment he concentrated, trying to understand their conversation. She watched him intuitively, not losing her smile.

"She is asking my father if we are going out," said Van. "If we are staying she thinks she should begin making some dinner."

Condley found himself chuckling softly, mostly at himself. He could not help but feel somewhat leery of the welcome he was receiving, and yet he was undeniably seduced by it as well. Something had changed since the last time he had seen her, either in Van's relationship with Francois Petain or in her feelings about Condley himself. From her parents' warmth toward him and the knowledge of her intimate activities that was evident in the colonel's words, it was even possible that in the intricate, Vietnamese way, a family decision had been reached and he had become the front-runner in a race that he had not even consciously entered.

"I'm not used to being treated so nice," he finally teased, working to shift his focus from the careful dialogue with her father to her breezy and openly inviting charm.

She smiled confidently, lifting her perfectly sculpted chin and looking out the window toward the front gate. "Do you want to have dinner with my parents or do you want to go away with me?"

"Where do you want to go?"

"To dinner." Her eyes grew musky with what seemed to be a memory. "But before that—someplace. A place I go to dream." She gave him a hopeful smile. "You told me something last time. A secret from your heart. I want to show you something from mine."

"Is it far?"

"What do you care? We're not on a *cyclo*." She stood, looking down at him, her hands on her hips, overwhelming him with nothing more than her raw, natural beauty. "Let's go."

He suddenly grinned, rising from his chair and now standing over her. "Your bike?" he asked.

"I drive," she laughed. "You would get me killed."

Sitting behind her on the bike, he immediately put his arms around her waist. As she pulled out onto the alleyway he gently squeezed her to him, warning himself all the while that he should not dare to like her and that she was not yet equipped, as her father himself had said, to understand the implications of the very forces she was putting into motion. Then her soft hair fluttered in his face as the motorbike sped forward, air-brushing all such thoughts away.

Making a turn, she dropped one hand onto his leg and patted it for a moment just above the knee.

"I did miss you," she said, surprising him with her words.

The motorbike left the winding back roads and reached Dien Bien Phu Street. He saw Dzung just off the curb on one corner, lazing in his *cyclo* as he waited for his assigned hour to pass. When she turned onto Dien Bien Phu they came very close to Dzung. Condley called to him as they passed.

"*Di ve nha,*" he said. *Go home.*

"*Da, di.*" Dzung waved casually to Condley as the motorbike gained the main road, leaving him behind.

She turned left onto Nguyen Van Troi Street, and he knew where she was heading. After fighting thick traffic for a few miles, they angled off to the right, past large billboard signs and an old concrete bunker left over from the French days. A tollgate met them in the center of a widened road. She paid five thousand *dong* at the busy gate, and in minutes they were outside the terminal of the Tan Son Nhat airport.

Throngs of cars and taxis lined the street and parking areas around the terminal. Hundreds of travelers flowed into and out of the building. Behind the terminal they could see a huge Boeing 747 parked on the runway. An international flight had just landed. Shuttle buses were hauling passengers from the tarmac to the terminal, captained by smiling young women in pink or blue *ao dais*.

"Here," she said, looking longingly at the terminal building where the travelers ebbed and flowed. "This is my dream."

"It's only an airline terminal," he said, thinking she was joking.

"To you it is an airline terminal," she said quietly, her eyes lost in the endless possibilities that rose into the sky with every departing flight. "You can come and go whenever you want. Where do you come from? Where do you go when you leave? Do you know what this airport is like to someone who doesn't know the answer to those questions? Japan or America might really be the moon. That's what it's like when you do not know."

Her dream was his normality, and for the first time he saw the bustle of the airport from her eyes. Dzung's struggle was to survive; that he understood. But hers was different; it was to live. How many times had he passed through those doors, on his way into and out of Viet Nam, thinking of nothing more than the foul taste in his mouth and the sleep he had lost on the plane?

"Maybe you could work for Viet Nam Airlines," he said weakly.

"It's too late," she said with a genuine, muted sadness. "There is so much competition for those jobs, Cong Ly. I think it is the hardest job to get in all of Viet Nam. I tried three years ago, but they stopped most of their hiring when the economy went bad. If I had known Chinese I could have had a chance. But Chinese is so hard. I could not pass the test. And now I am twenty-six. Too old."

Twenty-six and too old. The longing in her eyes was palpable, as was the reality of her fading dreams. "Maybe when things get better you could work for a business that travels overseas," he said.

"Maybe," she said, still straddling her motorbike. "Someday." She turned to him, her face far older than it had been a half hour before in the front room of her father's house. "You come and go, Cong Ly, and you think nothing of it. You're going tomorrow or the day after, I know. I heard you talking to my father. I want to go. Not to Russia, but just to go! I want to know what is on the other side. I hear the stories. And I dream. There is nothing wrong with that, Cong Ly. I want that dream."

At that moment he wanted more than anything to take her into his arms and promise her that somehow she could have her dream, as simple and yet impossible as it was. But he had nothing to offer her. He did not know her, not in that way, and he did not wish to become merely the agent of her fantasies. And so he sat silently on the rear of her little Honda, watching the giant plane unload its cargo, and retreated into his own unending memories.

She remained quiet for a long time, staring at the energy of people coming and going and then back to his face, as if waiting for him to offer a solution. Her silent charisma was urgent and demanding, just as when she had waited outside the hotel that first night as though he would kiss her if she only watched him long enough. And then she suddenly turned away from him and gunned her motorbike.

"I know a good restaurant," she said over her shoulder as she powered into the traffic. "On Dong Khoi Street, near the river. Do you like fish?"

CHAPTER TWENTY-FOUR

Moscow

THE AIRCRAFT MADE its way through what seemed like a never-ending night. The cabin lights were out. Every now and then a sleepy flight attendant passed them in the aisle, offering water or juice. And under the glow of a reading light Colonel Pham matched Condley scotch for scotch, waxing nostalgic for his "student" days in Moscow a quarter century before.

"The first time I went to Moscow, it took me a month to get there," he recalled, as always speaking in Vietnamese. "I left by train from Ha Noi, traveling north through China and then to Vladivostok, where I changed to a Soviet railroad line. And then west, west, forever west. It took two weeks, day and night, just to cross Siberia. No food on the train, only what my wife had packed for me before I left Ha Noi. No blankets, no bed. I have never been so cold, shivering on that train, looking out at the dark, empty tundra and wondering if this was what all of Russia except Moscow itself would look like. Or maybe even Moscow! I had seen a few pictures of the city, but I don't need to tell you, Cong Ly, that pictures lie if governments want them to."

He drained the last half inch of scotch from his plastic cup, his face warm with memories. He was wearing an old gray sweater that he had saved for all those years after coming home. The sweater stank of mothballs. "But Moscow was so beautiful. And its people were so warm. I know that most Americans will never truly like Russians, Cong Ly, and also the other way around. To the Vietnamese you are both like jealous suitors, wishing to be understood. Both cultures are so strong, and yet so completely different. Power in Russia has always come from the top, even before communism. The people are used to it. In fact, they expect it. But my impression of power in America is that each individual feels he is powerful and believes he has the right always to resist those at the top."

Colonel Pham looked at Condley. "Your Scottish and Irish family, yes? As you say, always fighting. Sometimes in a war, but even when there is no war. Maybe fighting their own government, or when the government is calm maybe just fighting each other. Such people are impossible to rule completely from the top."

"Like the Vietnamese," grinned Condley, sipping on his own scotch. "Fighting and golf, right, Colonel?"

The colonel nodded, as always enjoying these little exchanges that showed he understood Americans. "Very good, Cong Ly. Very clever. But you are right. Our present system pretends to adore the Soviet model, but it knows it must adjust. The Vietnamese do not like being ruled from the top either, so maybe we are a little bit like the Americans. Someday there will come a different style of government."

"A dangerous thing for a communist official to say." Condley was taken aback by the colonel's bluntness.

"We are speaking conceptually, of course," demurred the colonel. "And we are not presently inside Viet Nam, so it is easier to talk about such things." He hedged carefully. "What we cannot have in Viet Nam is a collapse of authority. You see, Cong Ly, this is where we are very different from the Americans. We cannot function with protests in the street. We do not like being ruled from the top, but we are not yet capable of that sort of democracy. We cannot function at all in those circumstances, because there is no anchor in our culture beyond our loyalty to family. We are a very competitive and sometimes a very violent people. We do not like those at the top telling us what to do, but it is important to have strong leaders at the top telling certain factions what not to do. Without that we would have total chaos."

"So you're a little bit like the Americans," said Condley. "But every now and then you need a commissar to kick ass and take names."

"Yes," admitted the colonel with a small shrug. "I could lie to you, Cong Ly, or I could say it more nicely. But that is the way I feel."

The plane began losing altitude as the pilot began his descent into Moscow. Colonel Pham lifted up the window panel, looking outside. Dawn was beginning to lighten the far horizon. The colonel's taut frame held the excitement of a child as he peered outside the window.

"Why have you never been to Russia before?" he asked Condley.

"I think they called it the Cold War," said Condley dryly.

"No spy missions to Moscow?"

"Actually, this is my first."

Colonel Pham smiled amusedly, watching Condley's face with the knowing, intricate scrutiny that was his trademark. "Your first spy mission to Moscow, with a communist colonel as your interpreter. It's a funny time we live in, yes?"

Condley laughed. "Whatever it takes, Colonel. I'm just glad to have you as my tour guide."

"Then I will admit something to you," said Colonel Pham, a look approaching shyness coming over his weathered, aging face. "I have watched you so many times in Viet Nam, and I understand you, Cong Ly. No, I even appreciate you. Because I love Moscow with the same hopeless passion that you must feel for Sai Gon."

The pilot announced that the plane was entering its final descent. Colonel Pham folded the blanket that had been on his lap. "I am very anxious to see Russia again, Cong Ly, and I thank you for this invitation, whether or not we make any progress on your case. The Soviet Union was our big brother, you know that, not only politically but economically. They were giving our country billions of dollars every year. To be honest with you, we were certain that someday the Soviet Union would defeat the United States and that communism would be the dominant political force in the world. We were stunned when the Soviet Union ceased to exist. Even now, I cannot imagine it. And so I am very interested to visit Moscow and see for myself what this has meant."

"The country is having hard times, Colonel."

"I know that, yes, and I feel terribly about it in my heart," said

Pham. "But the people of Russia have always struggled. That is why I love them. Everything is always against them. They struggle so fiercely and yet they never stop singing."

"Or drinking."

"Sometimes," shrugged the colonel. "It is impossible, the way so many of them drink their vodka."

The plane made a turn and dawn revealed the city just below them. Colonel Pham's face softened and his eyes went faraway as he surveyed the long rows of apartments and the churches with their onion roofs and the river itself, clogged with ice. *"Nha thu Nhi,"* said the colonel softly. *My second home.*

───────────

SKIP ROGERS WAVED to them as they stepped from the terminal building, immediately driving up in a black Lincoln Continental with diplomatic license plates. Stopping the car, he jumped out of the driver's side and went to the trunk, opening it. He was a kinetic man with bright eyes and round cheeks. Looking at his tweedy plumpness, Condley had a hard time picturing the CIA agent as a former Marine.

But Rogers's deep baritone voice removed all doubt on that question. "Condley, right?" he said, with the flat, give-a-shit cynicism that somehow recalled fierce drill sergeants and long forced marches in the heat. "I think we have a mutual friend in Hawaii."

"Nice guess."

Rogers grinned, reaching into the trunk and pulling out a thick overcoat, then throwing it to Condley. "Hey, I'm a spook, that's my job." He reached inside the trunk again and tossed Condley a fur-covered hat. "Not to mention that you're the only passenger walking out of the terminal still dressed for the tropics, with a Vietnamese sidekick who's already wearing an overcoat."

"Colonel Pham spent many years in Russia," said Condley.

"So I've heard." Rogers openly scrutinized the bundled, fur-hatted Colonel Pham and for a moment squinched his nose. "He smells like my grandmother's attic."

"Try storing a fur hat in Sai Gon," chuckled Condley.

Rogers took Pham's suitcase and put it into the trunk of the staff car, then opened the right rear car door for the colonel, who nodded to him and climbed inside. Shutting the car door, the CIA agent spoke indirectly to Condley. "Interesting file on him. I can tell you about it later."

"You can tell me in the car," said Condley. "His English is no good."

"That's not what his file says," said Rogers, giving the colonel a grin and a little wave. "He speaks great English. At least he used to."

Condley had reached him. He quickly extended his hand. "Skip Rogers, by the way. You can call me Mister Rogers. And like they say, welcome to my neighborhood."

"General Duncan tells me you were a Marine," said Condley, tossing his own bag inside the trunk.

"Thirty pounds ago," joked Rogers, slamming the trunk closed and putting both hands over a growing belly. "I was in operational intelligence. First Skivvy Divvy, Camp Pendleton. Had a few, shall we say, interesting moments in the Gulf War. Got bored after that. Went to language school, signed up with a different team, and here I am."

"Still doing operational intelligence," joked Condley.

"Different targets, different rules," said the peripatetic Rogers, pointing to the passenger-side front door to indicate where he wanted Condley to sit. "Interesting targets. And my rules. I like that."

Rogers climbed in and started the car. The tires barked as he put the car into gear and headed away from the terminal. His clipped, frenetic style created an aura of control. He was, decided Condley, the kind of man who did things and who could be relied upon.

As they drove toward the heart of the city, Rogers pushed a folder across the front seat, giving it to Condley. He purposely gave the colonel a knowing look in his rearview mirror as he spoke. "Everything you need is in this folder. No problem, it's sanitized. Colonel Pham should obviously expect that I would provide you with this information, so don't worry about sharing it with him. In fact, I wouldn't be surprised at all if he decides to go for a long walk this afternoon all by himself. You know, a nostalgic little tour to reacquaint himself with the city. And with certain of his . . . friends, shall we say, who are still residing here. That's fine too. Just don't show him these materials until he's back from his walk and you're ready to go after your target. Otherwise, your target might somehow disappear."

"An excellent point," said Condley dryly. "One that I have already shared with the colonel."

"Obviously you're not new to this," said Rogers, his eyes constantly in motion as he drove. "So you also know I can't go with you. I don't want to cause an international incident if the guy decides to claim that some American intelligence agent is trying to mark him. Could get me thrown out of the country, and I'm having too much fun right now to leave. If you want to make him on your own, as a citizen searching for historical information, that's fine. There's no blow-back if he refuses to cooperate. But you're really on your own. This is your show, not mine. No noise, Mr. Condley. Please. The last thing either of us wants is for our favorite Marine Corps general to be standing with his heels locked in front of some bow-tied White House weenie."

"That would be General Delivery?" grinned Condley, flicking his eyes toward Pham.

"No, General Background," laughed Rogers. He tapped the folder as he drove. "But everything you need is in there. Everything. Whoever put this together"—he looked in the mirror at Colonel Pham, having issued a disclaimer in case their conversation was indeed passed on to Russian intelligence—"has got the guy down to what time he goes to the bathroom, and how many times he farts."

"You're a good man," said Condley.

"The general passed on your story after he read the back brief about my little shopping trip to the Arabat," said Rogers. His eyes never stopped moving, flitting from the road in front of them to the occupants of nearby cars and then to the colonel's face in the rearview mirror. "I'm doing this out of respect, Mister Condley. For you and your Marines."

———————

NEAR RED SQUARE the car slowed in front of a glorious old hotel. Watching the uniformed doormen and the glowing chandeliers inside, Condley's eyes lit up.

"You can't afford it," laughed Rogers as the car turned a corner and stopped in front of a clearly seedy, second-rate establishment. He halted the car in front of a worn walkway that led up a wide set of stairs to the entrance of the Kamchatka Hotel.

Rogers jumped out, meeting them at the car's trunk, where they unloaded the luggage. Colonel Pham had said nothing since leaving the airport terminal. He picked up his bag, watching Rogers with his ever-discerning eyes, and finally reached out and shook the agent's hand.

"Nice to meet you," he said in heavily accented English.

"See?" said Rogers as he shook the colonel's hand. "I told you he spoke English."

"Only a little," admitted the colonel with a small, embarrassed grin. "Too long ago I learned."

Condley lingered at the car with Rogers as Pham headed into the hotel. He tapped the folder, then shook Rogers's hand.

"Thanks for the ride."

"I'll bet 'only a little,'" said Rogers cynically, giving the colonel a quick look.

"He's all right," said Condley. "No matter what I say inside Viet Nam I assume somebody's listening anyway."

"Ask him about Sasha," said Rogers.

"Who's Sasha?"

Rogers grinned, nodding toward the colonel. "Ask him."

"You're pretty good," Condley grinned back. "In fact, I would hate to have you on my ass in Sai Gon."

"From you, sir, that is the ultimate compliment," said Rogers. "So don't get lost on the subway."

"I've got a perfectly trained guide," said Condley.

"Better trained than you even know." Rogers waved good-bye. "You're on your own, Mister Condley. It's not a good idea for you to call me again while you're here. Whatever you find, just pass it on through General Duncan."

Condley called to Rogers as the CIA agent climbed into his car. "Hey, Rogers!" As Rogers turned toward him, Condley gave him a crisp Marine Corps salute. "*Semper fi,* Mac."

Rogers smiled, obviously moved by Condley's gesture. "Marines never salute when they're in the field, Lieutenant. You know that." He waved again, then shut the car door. And in a moment he was gone.

CHAPTER TWENTY-FIVE

THE KAMCHATKA HOTEL was a dump by any standards. Cluttered and dusty, the old hotel was run by haggard employees who looked as though they never changed their clothes or even slept. Its lobby was filled with dozens of oddly clothed foreigners of all stripes, as if this were the official gathering place for visitors to Moscow from Africa, southern Asia, and the Middle East. So far as Condley could tell, he was the only American at the hotel. Thinking about that, he decided that Skip Rogers had probably put him and Pham there deliberately, to reinforce the notion that they were not diplomatic guests of the American Embassy in case their little adventure somehow went sour.

After a thin breakfast of weak tea, hard-boiled eggs, processed meat, and toast, Condley napped for several hours in his heavy-curtained, dust-filled little room. As he slept on a narrow bed against a wood-paneled wall, he was awakened periodically by a rhythmic pounding on the wall from the adjoining room, accompanied by strange, guttural noises. Finally he realized that a hooker was entertaining a series of clients only inches from where he lay.

He gave up on sleep, moving to the small desk in the room and pulling out the folder Rogers had left him. The folder included not only a thorough analysis of Anatolie Petrushinsky's military career, current living habits, and personal history, but also a detailed script regarding where, when, and how best to approach the former Soviet soldier. Rogers was good, he thought again. Very, very good.

He had arranged to meet Colonel Pham in the lobby for lunch. Walking downstairs into the huge, expansive lobby, he was surprised to see the colonel walking into the hotel on the arm of a young Eurasian woman. She was smiling happily, pointing here and there as she walked with the colonel, clearly enthralled by his presence. Her physical makeup was a wild, almost slapdash mix of Russian and Vietnamese— reddish hair over Asian eyes on a pale face that was wide and heavy-cheeked, a small, squat body that nonetheless carried itself on powerful Slavic legs.

Finally the colonel noticed Condley. He nudged the young woman, pointing excitedly, and walked quickly to Condley, all the while chattering to her in Russian. His face was beaming with pride.

"My youngest daughter," he said. "This is Sasha."

"I thought Van was your youngest daughter," said Condley.

"Van is my youngest *Vietnamese* daughter," answered Pham, looking oddly at Condley, as if the distinction should have been self-evident. "Sasha is the youngest of *all* my daughters."

The young woman giggled delightedly, taking a step forward and offering her hand to Condley. She held his hand for a long moment, staring deeply into his eyes. Then she spoke a seductive, teasing sentence in Russian that caused the usually stoic colonel to burst into uncontrolled laughter.

"She says, you must marry her sister Van. Then maybe we can all come to America and live together with family-reunification green cards."

"Let me check out the regulations on that for you," teased a stunned but recovering Condley. "When we get back I'll call Maria."

"Who is Maria?" asked the colonel.

"My immigration expert."

Condley looked at the girl with an almost morbid fascination. The colonel piercingly read his expression and grew serious again. "Her mother is dead now," he said. "But while I was in Russia she was my . . .

vo be," he said, using the Vietnamese expression that meant a "lesser wife," a title honored and accepted in the Vietnamese culture. "I was here by myself and so it was proper that I have another wife. Sasha's mother accepted this reality. So did Van's mother. There is no shame. No problem."

"You must have missed her very much," said Condley.

Pham nodded, speaking to Condley with a rare, deep emotion. "So, Cong Ly, now you know why I understand you. And yes, why I accept your emotions for my daughter Van. I lived in Moscow for five years, just as you lived in Sai Gon during the war. When I returned to Viet Nam I left behind people that I loved. I had to accept that I probably would never see them again. It took nothing away from my feelings for my family in Viet Nam or for my country, but I am forever torn in two. I am richer for it. But I will never be fully whole. Like you, Cong Ly. Never whole."

Condley alternated his gaze from the happily smiling young woman to the serious gaze on the face of the man he once thought he fully understood. "You haven't seen her for—"

"Twenty years," said the colonel. "That does not mean I don't love her. I send her money every month. Not much, but she is my daughter. My wife approves. Family, Cong Ly. Very simple but very complicated."

Colonel Pham checked his watch. "What time do you want to leave tonight for our . . . obligation?"

"Seven o'clock," said Condley.

The colonel smiled, putting an arm on Sasha's shoulder. "So you don't mind if I leave you until then?"

"See you at seven, Colonel."

Condley stood silently as Colonel Pham exited the hotel's front door with his daughter on his arm. Yes, behind those forty-year-old industrial-strength glasses and that rabbit-skin hat that stank of mothballs was a man less different from himself than he had ever fully imagined. Finally he chuckled, muttering to himself, "Well, that wasn't in Skip Rogers's folder."

And then he went to lunch.

CHAPTER TWENTY-SIX

A HUGE REPAIR truck was parked incongruously at the edge of Red Square where they entered it, apparently broken down and abandoned for the evening by its crew. Passing it, Condley noticed a muddy old military hat hanging loosely where the gas cap used to be. The Square itself was fairy-tale gorgeous with its colorful spires and ancient buildings, all lit up with spotlights in the crisp night air. They walked briskly through it, gawking like tourists on their way to the subway. Condley shivered uncontrollably as they walked, the flaps of his fur cap down over his ears and his gloved hands pushed deep inside his overcoat. It had been decades since he had experienced winter, and Moscow in January was belly-whimpering cold.

He had shown Colonel Pham the map that Skip Rogers left inside his folder, and the old Viet Cong soldier had immediately taken charge of their hapless little patrol. On the far side of Red Square they reached the subway platform and marched down the steps toward the trains. They passed grand statues and walls covered with mosaic murals, all depicting heroic, muscled workers engaged in the never-ending struggle against—*what?* thought Condley, thinking of the decades since the murals had been done. Capitalism? Corruption? Or who knew, maybe in the end, communism itself? No matter, he decided. They were beautiful and if nothing else had provided someone with a job.

The train was nearly empty. They did not speak to each other as Colonel Pham counted the stops. The colonel sat expressionless, glancing now and then at the map and then outside, as if navigating. Condley stared straight ahead, rehearsing over and over in his mind the possibilities of the encounter to come, wrapped in an intensity that resembled the last moments before a combat mission.

Finally the colonel stood, nodding to him and walking to the subway door. The subway halted and Condley silently followed him onto the platform.

As they climbed the steps, the bone-biting, wintry darkness hit them as if they were forcing themselves through a wall. At the top of the steps Condley discovered they were in a residential neighborhood whose nearly treeless streets were crowded with mammoth, dimly lit apartment buildings. The streetlights were out, and even the occasional cars that passed them in this section of the city drove only with their parking lights on. The darkness and the cold and his own electric anticipation made Condley's limbs shake uncontrollably.

Oddly, Colonel Pham seemed completely unaffected by the weather, at home in the cold, greeting it with the same nonchalance as he did the steaming heat and rains of his favorite golf course in Sai Gon. He took a few deep breaths, gaining his bearings in the dark, then pointed toward a set of buildings far away, across an open field.

"Over there," he said, and began walking.

They walked for fifteen minutes, neither of them saying a word as they trudged across treeless, empty fields and little-traveled streets. As they walked, Condley's body generated some much-needed heat, and by the time they reached the huge apartment complex his limbs had ceased their shaking. Each building of the complex was huge and boxy, consisting of hundreds of units, as unimaginatively designed as a penitentiary.

Colonel Pham studied the buildings from the road that bordered them, then finally nodded, choosing one and heading toward it.

"This one," he said, tapping Skip Rogers's map. "I know, I know."

Inside the dim-lit building, the air was damp and very cold. A large pile of stinking trash sat just inside the door, bottles and garbage spilling from the usual trash room into the doorway itself. Down the hallway the colonel found a metal-plated elevator and pushed the button, summoning it. The elevator light did not go on. Condley started shivering again as they waited for the elevator to descend. After a few minutes they finally realized that it wasn't going to come.

The colonel pointed to a set of stairs and resolutely began climbing them, with Condley close behind. When they reached the fifth floor the colonel stepped carefully into the darkened hallway. He peered for a long moment down the corridor and then at the nearest apartment numbers to get his bearings. Deciding, he pointed to his left and began walking again. After a few steps his pace slowed considerably, as if he were a hunter on the prowl. Finally he stopped, turning back to Condley and pointing just ahead.

"Right there," he whispered.

Condley checked his watch. It was ten minutes to nine. They were ahead of Skip Rogers's schedule by ten minutes but were well within the boundaries of the CIA agent's suggested time frame. It was important, Rogers had written, to arrive at the apartment after Anatolie Petrushinsky had returned from his daily sojourns but before he drank himself to sleep.

They stood silently for a moment in front of the iron-plated door. The colonel took a deep breath, gathering himself. Then he gave off a little shrug and knocked loudly on the door.

All was silent on the other side of the door. They waited for a full minute, staring nervously at each other. Then the colonel knocked loudly again. Several more seconds passed. They heard a shuffling and after that a scratching on the door itself, as if someone was undoing an inside lock. And finally came a deep, slurred voice, speaking in indecipherable Russian, its tone filled with suspicion.

As he listened to the words, the colonel's face became filled with the same electric tension as Condley's. He took another deep breath and answered in Russian, his own voice rich and surprisingly deep and his tone warmly upbeat. The only words Condley recognized were *comrade Anatolie Petrushinsky* and *Viet Nam*.

Another pause, as if the man on the other side of the door was measuring the validity of the colonel's response against the possibility that he was being somehow tricked. Another question from the unknown voice,

Condley able to decipher only *Viet Nam* from the words that drifted through the door. And the colonel giving a long, emotional response, seeming to alternate between pleading and scolding.

Then, with a clarity that shocked Condley as deeply as if he had grabbed on to an exposed electrical wire, the voice behind the door began speaking Vietnamese. "My friend," the deep voice intoned, suddenly devoid of the rich, slurring Russian tones, "if you have truly come from Viet Nam to see me, speak Vietnamese and tell me why."

The colonel and Condley smiled to each other, neither hiding his sudden and overwhelming excitement. Then the colonel turned back to the door, as if speaking to the giant curtain that hid the Wizard of Oz.

"I was a soldier in our common cause for many years, and after that I lived in your country for five years, studying the way of the future," said Pham, now in Vietnamese. "I bring you the greetings of my government. I bring you our thanks for all of your assistance to us, both during and after our glorious war of liberation. I bring you the fond memories still carried in the hearts of many of our people. And finally I bring you a request for help, on a difficult matter that might only be solved with your assistance."

"You need my help?"

"Yes. It is very important. Anatolie Petrushinsky, the people of Viet Nam are once more asking you to assist them."

Another long pause, and then a low sound from the other side of the door, so heartfelt that it was almost primeval. *"Anatolie nho' Viet Nam nhieu qua!"* Anatolie misses Viet Nam too much.

"Da," smiled the colonel, moved by the comment but also knowing he had broken through Petrushinsky's barriers. *"Viet Nam cung nho' Anatolie!"* Viet Nam misses Anatolie too.

The door swung slowly open. Petrushinsky filled it on the other side, mildly drunk, large and gray, wearing a rumpled black sweater and gray wool trousers. His sagging, wrinkled face was permanently burnt from the cold, streaked with tears. Reaching out with his enormous arms, he embraced Colonel Pham, pulling the little man off the ground as he kissed him three times, cheek to cheek.

"Welcome, my little friend," he said in Vietnamese, choking on his sobs as he spoke. "It has been too long, too long!" Releasing the colonel from his massive grasp, he noticed Condley standing with him in the dark hallway. "He is not a Russian," he said with renewed suspicion.

"No," said the colonel. "But you must trust me, Anatolie. All of us are now working for a common good."

Condley stepped forward, offering his hand and speaking in Vietnamese. "I am an American. I was on the other side," he said. "But that was a long time ago, Anatolie Petrushinsky. Colonel Pham and I are now coworkers inside Viet Nam. We wish to make peace and we need your help."

"You were an American soldier?"

"I was a Marine."

"But you fought?"

"Yes," said Condley, steadily holding Petrushinsky's eyes. "In fact, I may even have fought you." Petrushinsky remained silent, and so he continued. "Quang Nam Province. The Que Son Mountains. In 1969?"

"I was not there in 1969. Not in Quang Nam."

"In 1971?"

"Perhaps. But we were only observers," said Petrushinsky carefully, now looking skeptically from Condley to Colonel Pham.

"He is a good man," reassured Colonel Pham. "My friend. I have observed him for years. Ha Noi has allowed me to travel with him. So, Anatolie, we must talk. It is very important."

Petrushinsky suddenly began to cough, continuing heavily for several seconds. Then, as if using reverse logic, he pulled out a cigarette and lit it, all the while studying the two men with a mix of suspicion and longing. "Quang Nam?" he finally said, nodding to Condley.

"Quang Nam," said Condley. "Que Son, 1969. And other places, other years."

Petrushinsky gestured with one huge arm toward the interior of his apartment. "At least you are a fellow soldier. And you are with my Vietnamese friend. So I welcome you inside my home."

Inside the apartment Petrushinsky took another long drag on his cigarette and showed them into his living room. "This is where I live. This is where I remember what my life was like when I had a life. So, please, sit down."

Following Skip Rogers's instructions, Condley had brought Petrushinsky the finest bottle of vodka available at the hotel. He handed it to him as he entered the small living room.

"To thank you for your hospitality," he said. "And in hopes that we might become friends."

The former soldier's eyes widened with pleasure as he examined the label. "Ah, very good! Very good vodka!" He raised the bottle to Condley and Pham, walking from the room. "So, I think we should have a drink. I will be right back."

The living room was furnished with a thin metal reading lamp, a small cloth couch, and two stuffed chairs. On one wall was a large bookshelf, and it was evident that, despite his recent hard times, Petrushinsky was an avid reader. A hundred books lined the shelves, and a half dozen others were stacked on the coffee table in front of the couch. But Condley's eyes were immediately drawn to a shelf table behind the couch, against another wall, where three miniature models of Vietnamese village homes had been carefully constructed.

Condley and Colonel Pham walked together to the dollhouse-size models, studying them with vast appreciation. Someone, perhaps Petrushinsky himself, had created a small hamlet in the living room. The models were intricately done, from the thatch roofs of the homes to the mud walkways surrounding them to the water buffalo pens that adjoined them off to the side. Tiny toy waterbulls were in the pens and in the fields behind the houses. Miniature Vietnamese villagers sat in the homes, washed at the wells, and rode atop the waterbulls.

"Very good," commented the colonel, pointing at the models. *"Mien trung,"* he said. *Central Viet Nam.*

"Yes, *mien trung,*" said Petrushinsky, appearing behind them as he reentered the living room. He was carrying a small tray with three full glasses of vodka. "It took me more than a year to build them. But it is the way I am able to remember. When I look at them, sometimes I feel as though I am there again."

The burly Russian carefully set the tray on the coffee table, pushing a few books out of the way to do so. Then he put one hand on his heart and made a fist with the other, a gesture of solidarity with the colonel. "Viet Nam! Viet Nam! I have been many places in my life. Germany. Poland. Cuba. Yes, even Afghanistan. But in my heart, Colonel, I have never left Viet Nam!"

He handed each of them a tall glass filled to the brim with Condley's vodka. Then he raised his own glass into the air, his haggard face wretched with emotion. "I make a toast to you, Colonel. To my friend and my ally. And to our victory, because we did win, did we not? To Viet Nam!"

Colonel Pham raised his own glass. "To our liberation, yes? *Doc lap va tu do!* And to Russia! And to all our Soviet friends!"

Condley continued to hold his glass, declining to drink, watching the two men as each drained half of the vodka from his own glass. The colonel's capacity for vodka was another little surprise. Finally they lowered their glasses, revealing reddened, suddenly cheerful faces. They were blissful in their shared ritual, living for that moment in a past that did not include him. Indeed, in a past where he had been the very object of their joined efforts. And yet undeniably a past whose boastful victories had long since disappeared.

Finally they turned to him, looking at him as if he were a voyeur intruding on their intimacy. And in a way he was. "Ah," muttered Pham, raising his glass to Condley and searching for words that would somehow include Condley as well. "And to the future. With new friends."

Condley finally raised his glass, forcing a smile. "Yes. To new friends. Because you may have won, but then you lost, didn't you? And we may have lost, but then we won. Didn't we?"

"You are too clever," said Petrushinsky darkly.

"Perhaps, but I am only speaking the truth," said Condley, still holding his glass up near his eyes. "You're gone. We're back. And we're not going to go away. And if you think about it, we're pretty good people to have around. Ask the colonel."

Pham watched Condley for a moment, then nodded to Petrushinsky. "We know him," said the colonel. "Sometimes he boasts too much, but we like him. This is not a bad thing."

"Well, I don't know him," resisted the Russian, still frowning darkly. "And so far I do not like him. But he did bring the vodka. So I will drink with him." And the former soldier drained his glass.

The ceremonies over, Petrushinsky gestured to his two chairs, taking a seat on his couch. "I thank you for the vodka, Mr. Condley. So now we must talk." He watched them closely as they took their seats, his face flushed and his eyes cloudy from that night's ration of vodka, much of which had been taken even before they arrived. "Colonel Pham, my friend, you said that I could help you. What is it that you want from me?"

"We are trying to find an American who was with you in the Que Son Mountains," said the colonel. "I think you would remember him."

"There were many westerners in the mountains," hedged Petrushinsky. "They drifted in, they drifted out. Our comrades had taken several German nurses and doctors from a hospital near An Hoa in 1969 and kept them for several years. There were a few American prisoners of war captured during the fighting on the ground who were being held in caves. Now and then a journalist. And a few others who worked with us." He hedged again, looking quickly at Condley. "Or with you, that is, Colonel Pham. As I said, I was merely an observer who offered . . . advice, from time to time."

"He worked with you," said Condley. "Salt and Pepper. A black man and a white man. We're looking for the white man."

Petrushinsky stared at him for a long time, as if measuring his own knowledge against his fears of betraying former comrades. "There was one we did not like," he said carefully. "A very bad man. We did not know what to do with him."

"And an Australian," said Condley, pushing the issue before Petrushinsky caught himself and changed his mind. "A photographer."

"The twins," said Petrushinsky immediately, his face alive with memories. "The good twin and the evil twin."

"The twins?" Condley leaned forward, not letting Petrushinsky think.

"They looked alike. We used to tease the photographer. His name was"—Petrushinsky searched his mind, his eyes faraway—"like the bird. I don't know English. I'm sorry."

"Larkin."

"Lark, like the bird. Yes," said Petrushinsky. "The happy bird. And the American's name was like the devil. Good and evil twins. They looked alike. The devil was bigger than the lark, but not by much. He studied the lark, all the time. Not like a friend. Like a book."

"What do you mean, like a book?"

"Like a book," said Petrushinsky, suddenly recalcitrant. "How do you study a book? All the little details. Why are you asking me these things? Of what use is it?"

"We think the devil killed the lark," said Colonel Pham quietly, as if mediating between the two. "We would like to solve this matter."

"It would not surprise me," said Petrushinsky delicately, toying with his vodka glass and for some reason avoiding both of their eyes. "They disappeared. We were told that the lark was taking the devil back to Sai Gon, but neither of them was seen again. And why would the devil want to go to Sai Gon? The Americans were looking for him. What if they caught him?"

Something tugged at Condley's emotions, as irritating as the dreams that had not let General Duncan drop the matter when he first read the message traffic regarding Deville. Something odd, but inarticulable. A piece that was obvious, and yet was missing. Or perhaps it was merely Petrushinsky's flushed and avoiding face. "Did you know the lark?" he finally managed to ask.

"Of course I knew the lark," said Petrushinsky.

A sudden light went off in Condley's brain, giving him a moment of awesome, frightening clarity. *How could that be?* "Did he ever take a picture of you?"

Petrushinsky froze. He watched Condley carefully, as though a gun were suddenly being pointed at his head. Condley's own pulse quickened, filling his veins with a rush of adrenaline. And finally Condley pressed forward, not wishing to give the former Soviet soldier more time to think. "If he took a picture of you, and if that picture was published in the world's newspapers, wouldn't that have compromised what you were doing?"

"I don't understand," said Petrushinsky, fighting off the vodka.

"According to your government there were no Soviet soldiers in Viet Nam. So what would the picture say about that lie? And what about the devil? Did the lark take a picture of him too? He did, didn't he? Perhaps even without permission? And what would that picture say? A Russian soldier—or maybe a lot of Russian soldiers—and at least one American deserter working with the Viet Cong in the Que Son Mountains? Not only in Viet Nam but in South Viet Nam? This would have been important news if it was documented with a photograph. Huge. It would have been displayed in every newspaper on earth. Maybe the lark was going to become the most famous photographer in the world. What do you think about that, Anatolie? Is that why the lark was killed? Because he had the evidence? And because even if you took away his cameras, he knew the truth?"

"This was a long time ago," said Petrushinsky, leaning back against his couch. "It was a war. A very important war. A war we won, I will remind you."

"And so the lark became expendable, for the importance of the war."

"He made mistakes. He was not supposed to see us. We were in another camp. But one day he wandered along the trails and he found us. And then he was not supposed to photograph us. He betrayed his hosts. He became uncontrollable."

"And so you killed him."

"No, we wouldn't have done that as long as he was with us. But once he became uncontrollable, he had to stay with us as a captive until the war was over. That was his only alternative, unless he wanted to resist that fate and die." The former Soviet soldier's face was now wild with uncertainty. "But it was the devil who killed him. The lark wanted to escape. The devil studied him, studied him, and then one day told him he would help him return to Sai Gon. They left at night, as if escaping. But I know the devil killed him."

"Where did the devil go?"

"To Sai Gon? I don't know. We never saw him again."

"Where did the lark want to go?"

"I don't understand you," said Petrushinsky.

"When he thought he was escaping. Where did he want to go?"

"I have had enough of your questions," said Petrushinsky, suddenly weary of Condley's probing. "It is time for you to leave my home."

Colonel Pham, flushed with his vodka, had also been ambushed by the direction Condley's questions had taken. He burped slightly, studying Condley's insistent, incandescent eyes, and then surprised him by supporting him. "Anatolie Petrushinsky," said the colonel. "You are not in trouble. You will not be questioned again. Your own government does not know we are talking to you. And anyway, it was the old government that set such policies into motion. This is a matter only of history to the Russian people, but in Viet Nam it is important to our future."

"Your new future," slurred the drunken Petrushinsky. "Without your Russian friends? With the Americans who are not going away?"

"We will never forget our Russian friends," insisted the colonel. "You will return someday also, I am sure of it. But please. You must trust me and answer the question."

"What is the question that you wish me to answer?" asked

Petrushinsky quietly, with an almost tragic helplessness. "Now I am confused. Tell me exactly what you want me to answer, and I will try. And then you must leave me alone with my little dollhouses and my memories. Viet Nam is gone for me, like my parents in their graves. I am growing old now. The rest of it is too much to contemplate."

"The lark," said Condley. "The photographer who had to die. If things had gone all right for him, when he finished with his story in the mountains, where did he want to go?"

"To see his girlfriend." Petrushinsky grew dark again, his face filled with jealousy and with the memory of a moment that would never be offered to him again. "That was why he tried to escape. Always he was talking about her, rubbing her beauty in our faces as we sat isolated in the mountains. I used to say to him that anyone can buy a whore in Bangkok."

"Bangkok?"

"Yes," said Petrushinsky, his face blanketed with green-eyed memories. "He was always boasting. Every month he flew in from Sai Gon to be with her. Every month, for a week! So what? He was such a naive fool. What about the rest of the month? What did he think she was doing for the other three weeks?"

"He flew in to Bangkok every month?"

"Yes, yes! I saw his passport. It was filled with immigration stamps."

———————

THE VISIT WITH Petrushinsky had for some reason deeply shaken Colonel Pham. He was quiet as they made their way across the frostbitten fields toward the subway stop, not with the silent, warlike tension of their journey toward Petrushinsky's apartment, but with an introspective gloom. He teetered now and then as they walked, still flush from the vodka, looking up at Condley from time to time as if questioning himself for this relationship and indeed for their very journey.

"I know you do not like them, but they were good people," he finally said as they neared the subway.

Condley was shaking again, his face numb from the cold. "I have no opinion, Colonel."

"Then you might respect mine." They reached the subway and walked together down the steps. "What are you going to do now, Cong Ly?"

"I'm going to Bangkok."

"Please keep this man from getting into trouble. He loves Viet Nam just as you do, and he has given enough."

"No one will know, Colonel."

They reached the platform. It was very late and they were the only people there. Pham studied his face for a very long time. "You are a good man, I think. And this devil, I can see how he hurt you. But don't be stupid. Bad things happen in wars. And this war is over."

"Almost," said Condley, holding the colonel's gaze.

They could hear the train approaching, and then they saw a light, far off inside the tunnel. "I will stay in Moscow for a while longer, Cong Ly. It has been a very long time, and it may be my last visit."

The train reached the platform and they climbed in, taking seats across from each other. Condley nodded, indicating that he understood. And they did not speak to each other again until they said good night at the hotel.

CHAPTER TWENTY-SEVEN

Sai Gon

"CONG LY," SHE was saying, again and again. "Cong Ly. Are you awake?" And then a lilting, nervous laugh. "Cong Ly, it's me! Wake up!"

He lay in his bed, clutching the phone to his ear, trying to do just that. So many time zones over such a short period of time, so many airports, so many flights, so many questions, and so many odd, unfulfilling answers. Six hours of sleep beginning in the middle of a Sai Gon afternoon and here he was, helplessly groggy, and yet happy that she was so rudely awakening him.

It was just after ten o'clock. The sky outside his window was pitch-black. The motorbikes serenaded him like an unending stream of two-hundred-pound mosquitoes, whining insistently as they came and went along the street below. He had been dreaming about his mother, the dream itself almost a memory, filled with the warmth in her still-young eyes as she combed his hair just before sending him off to his very first day of school. How many decades ago?

Oh, Brandon, I swear to God in heaven on high, you are gonna be some kind of lady-killer when you grow up. It's all over, honey-pie. They are not gonna be able to keep their hands off of you.

When the telephone awakened him he had felt an immediate, over-whelming sense of sadness. He had abandoned his mother, indeed his entire family, for this odd and unproductive life. He had never decided to. It had simply happened, one tragedy and one failure at a time, until he no longer had a place to come home to without having to explain it all, and it would have taken forever to explain. His father had died while he was on a security detail for an oil company in a remote section of Indonesia. He missed the funeral and had yet to visit the grave. He had not visited his mother in ten years. He called her now and then when he was in Hawaii, holding stilted and disjointed conversations about her tulips and her dogs, but the same reasons that had kept him in Asia after the war somehow prevented him from going home.

Okay, where would we begin? Long time no see. So here's how this disaster happened. I fell in love with a woman and kept killing bad guys so that I could stay with her, I mean everybody needs a job, and finally they killed her because I was too good at my job, and then I killed them back for her until the killing ended, more or less, and when that was over what was I supposed to do, come home and apply for a job at the Chamber of Commerce?

In the dream his mother was calling to him and now it was Van on the telephone calling to him, or maybe it had been Van all along as he struggled to awaken, rather than the voice of his mother in a dream. But when he finally came out of his stupor all he could say was—

"I'm sorry."

She laughed at that. "What are you talking about? Are you awake?"

And now he was, finally, fully awake. He sat up in his bed, sur-rounded by the overwhelming darkness and the whining of the motor-bikes below, and realized that he was indeed back in Sai Gon. At least for a day or two.

"Van?"

She laughed again, and yet he heard a nervous edge in her voice. "Who else did you think it was? Should I be worried that you asked me that?"

He shook his head, snapping his brain into gear, and finally chuck-led. "I was dreaming about my mother."

"That is a good sign," she said almost happily. "Your mother visit-ing you in a dream just as I am calling you. A very good sign."

Her voice was hollow, as if it were coming from the bottom of a well, and he knew she was talking on a cell phone. Dishes clattered near her, or perhaps it was glasses clinking in an idle toast. People were laughing. Mixed with the intimacy of her conversation, all these public signals disappointed him, making him feel somehow violated, as if he were on display. She was calling him and talking about his mother and his dreams, for the enjoyment or even the approval of—whom?

"And how is the grand merchant of aromas?" he said dryly.

"Who?"

"The Perfume Prince?"

"How is he?"

"Yes, my faithful friend Francois?"

"Why do you think I'm calling?" she said, immediately switching from English to Vietnamese. "No good. I want you to come and get me."

"Where are you?"

"I'm at the East Wind, Rain. It is a nightclub. Do you know this place? Only a five minute walk from your hotel!"

"Then why don't you just come on over here?"

"No!" she said emphatically, still speaking Vietnamese, as if all of this were their secret. "For me to walk away alone would be . . . *mat mat*," she indicated, meaning that she would lose face. "You must rescue me, Brandon. I promise you, there is a good reason for this. Let me choose to leave him openly, to his face, so his friends will understand that he has lost. Please? I am waiting for you. Take me away from here."

"What's happened?"

"I will tell you later."

"No promises, Van."

"Just come get me. Please."

"And no fights," said Condley carefully, rubbing the sleep away from his face with the back of one hand.

"A fight? Francois, with you?" She laughed. "Oh, that is very funny."

A SUDDEN, LAZY rain began to splash the streets. He walked along dark, wet sidewalks toward the East Wind, Rain, thinking about her last words on the telephone. He was not afraid to face down Francois, and yet he knew that the very thought of a physical confrontation between them was absurd. Francois might mock him and certainly would find ways to subtly ridicule him, but the impeccably manicured Frenchman would never risk his ego in a fight. Especially a fight over a woman.

No fights. Van had misunderstood him. What he wanted to avoid was an ugly, public scene between Van and Francois, with him ending up as the moral equivalent of a getaway car. There was a note of urgency in Van's voice that he had never heard before. And he knew that asking Van to control her emotions was about as sensible as begging a bird not to fly.

The East Wind, Rain was one of several upscale nightclubs that had recently sprung up in Sai Gon, catering to foreigners on expense accounts and younger, well-connected Vietnamese with a penchant for western frills. Condley avoided such places, seeing them as cesspools of the corruption that had invaded the higher reaches of Sai Gon's business economy. An evening's bar tab could feed and clothe a family of four in the provinces for a year. Drugs were quietly available for the asking, from old standbys like opium to the most modern western imports such as Ecstasy, which had swept through the upper levels of Sai Gon like an invisible typhoon. Cell phones, designer clothes, and MTV music were the standard fare, with the old notions of dress and ritual courtesy seen as marks of a failed past. And despite the government's public ranting against corruption and "westernization," most of the Vietnamese regulars at such clubs were the sons and daughters of communist officials who had pulled strings to send them overseas for schooling or to find them jobs with foreign corporations.

The westerners were no better. The East Wind, Rain was the watering hole for an ever-changing group of young professionals who saw themselves alternatively as financial pioneers in Viet Nam to strike it rich or Conradesque adventurers seeking to live on the fringe. They had come to Sai Gon from Britain, Australia, the Netherlands, France, the United States. They paid four dollars for a beer, eight dollars for a hamburger, and left large tips for some of the most beautiful waitresses in the world. They sat for hours in groups of four and six in the vast, muraled, pastel-orange nightclub, trading boasts and fantasies as clouds of cigarette smoke invaded their lungs and raucous music attacked their eardrums.

They were ever cheerful. Their faces were creamy and luminescent in the glow of glittering chandeliers. The latest music videos from the rock and rap factories of Los Angeles and New York echoed from quadraphonic speakers mounted on the ceiling. They traded hip snippets of Vietnamese street slang. They laughed together at that day's examples of government and worker stupidity. One or two might even have dared to spend a week or so in the provinces or an evening on the seamy side of Sai Gon.

And it all had a sickly ring to it, a false resonance that reminded Condley of too many foreign correspondents posted to Sai Gon during the war. They could count months and even years spent in Viet Nam. They had written reams about Viet Nam. And yet few of them had ever known much about what happened outside the bars and tennis courts of Sai Gon.

He sweated inside an old blue poncho, even as the rain pelted it. His hair and shoes were wet. He knew that such disarray would cause him to be stared at and even mocked when he reached the East Wind, Rain. And in a way he was glad. He did not belong there, nor did he want to.

The rain stopped, just as suddenly as it had begun. He took off the poncho, shaking water from it and folding it as he walked. As he neared the club, a rat as big as a cat ran across the top of its sign, hopped onto a windowsill, and then disappeared into the night.

It was chaotic, circuslike outside the club. A steady stream of people came and went, moving into and out of taxis and limousines, a few arriving on motorbikes that they parked just across the street. On the sidewalk and in the street the evening shift of hustlers was back at work, pushing, chasing, pleading. Like starving goldfish in an aquarium, they were waiting to be fed.

A little boy with slicked-back hair in designer blue jeans and a Disney World T-shirt was carrying a wooden box, hawking shoeshines in urgent, gutter English. A hunchbacked young woman with sad eyes and arthritic fingers shyly waved a package of old black and white photographs. A thirtyish man dragged useless legs behind him as he hobbled on wooden crutches, trying to sell packs of gum. A young man wearing a Chicago Cubs baseball hat marched briskly in front of the restaurant, holding an array of foreign English- and French-language newspapers. Two suborning little girls in identical red wide-brimmed hats formed a tag team, offering cigarette lighters and foreign cigarettes from similar foldout cases.

Near the door a ferretlike man with a drooping mustache approached him from the shadows of a nearby building, where a dozen *cyclo* drivers and hustlers lazed. The thirtyish hustler was smiling with a too-easy familiarity, as if searching for a tawdry camaraderie. He wore a long-sleeve, silk-flowered shirt, and a large hoop earring in his left ear. A gold bracelet drooped from his wrist as he reached out and tried to touch Condley's shoulder.

"You want blow?" the man asked. "Very good, number-one reefer."

"Khong can," said Condley. *I don't need it.* He pushed away the man's arm, having surprised him by answering in Vietnamese.

"Oh," said the hustler, recovering quickly and himself switching to Vietnamese, offering opium instead. *"Anh muon a-phien khong?"*

"Fuck you," answered Condley, reaching for the door.

"You want fuck?" The hustler laughed mockingly, joined by his nearby friends. He called again as Condley pushed open the door. "I got very good taxi girl for you, number-one good time, no problem!"

Walking inside the club, Condley immediately noticed Francois Petain, dressed in a gray suit and a red silk tie, at a corner table near the rear of the room. The soft-featured Frenchman was holding court before a half dozen people, his large hands waving grandly in the air as he entertained them with a story. Van sat next to him, wearing a tantalizing black sheath dress. She was smiling, seemingly dazzled by his narrative, as if she had never made the phone call that had roused Condley from his sleep.

It was clear that this was Petain's show and that the others, who were laughing hilariously, were enjoying it immensely. The table was cluttered with a stack of Heineken, Foster's, and Tiger beer cans, as well as Perrier and Orangina bottles and a half dozen empty wineglasses. Van noticed Condley first. Petain, following her gaze, stood up and waved, surprising him with an open smile.

"Ah, *Monsieur* Bone Picker has arrived."

Condley sauntered to the table, glancing quickly at Van for clues. She looked at him and then away, her arms folded across her stomach and her face stiff, as if she had suddenly become catatonic, paralyzed by either fear or indecision. He grudgingly shook the Frenchman's hand. "The merchant of aromas. The seller of smells. Are you staying rich?"

"Of course I am staying rich!" Petain glanced mischievously to the others at the table, as if sharing a secret. "People will pay millions just to smell a certain way. Amazing, yes? But true. It's like Coca-Cola. Why does anyone need to drink fizzy brown water with sugar in it? And yet they are happy to pay billions. A few drops of perfume and my customers feel like royalty."

"What a service you're providing!"

"Yes, I know," said Petain with a false sigh. "I think I am the Mother Teresa of the upper classes, saving countless lives from emptiness and ennui." He examined Condley's dampened clothes. "You are well-dressed, as always." The entire table chuckled, as if on cue.

"Just my little way of showing how much I respect you, Francois. But I can always change my clothes. And you will never stop being a jackass."

Petain smiled, raising his eyebrows as if enjoying the exchange. "As I said before, it is a pity that you become so emotional." He gave a little shrug, looking at the others at the table as if Condley were hopeless. "Please," he said, motioning to a nearby waitress. "Have a seat and join us."

"I'll stand."

"And you are finding not so many bones in Russia, I hear?"

Condley glanced quickly again at Van. She looked away, as if dismissing his unspoken allegation. "No bones in Russia," he said. "Only Colonel Pham's little family reunion."

"Quite a family, yes? And so it is with the Vietnamese. They did not ask for it. The world simply came to them. Russia, France, America, China, Japan—what is it that draws them here? So many different people with their memories, no? It is a very complicated country, Viet Nam." Petain waved his long fingers into the air. "Whatever you want you will find, as long as you are willing to look for it. And as long as you are willing to pay the price for finding it. And if you do not want to see it? Poof! It isn't here."

"And what you see are customers," muttered Condley.

"No, I see only beauty," smiled the Frenchman. "The rest of it I do not want or need."

The waitress brought a chair. She was startlingly beautiful and was wearing a black sheath dress that stopped just below her thighs, not unlike the dress Van herself was wearing. Her long hair shimmered under the glow of the chandeliers and fell across her face when she pushed the chair into the table. Petain casually brushed her hair from her eyes with his fingers, an act of deliberate ownership. And then he slowly pressed a twenty-*franc* note into her hand, thanking her for her trouble.

"*Merci,* my dear." He turned to Condley as she disappeared. "You should really sit with us."

"I'm on my way out the door, actually."

Petain nodded toward the departing waitress. "Would you like to bring that girl with you? It could be arranged."

"I can personally guarantee that she is an immensely pleasurable experience," said a round-faced, balding man sitting just across from Petain, whose accent Condley recognized as British. The others at the table laughed, except for Van, whose eyes were now avoiding Condley's.

"She's what we call a semipro," said another, whose accent marked him as Australian. "You know, it's not her job, but she has a certain talent and doesn't mind having a go at it. And I'd say her jewelry is pretty good evidence of her competence."

"For the right financial incentive," chuckled Petain. "And there you have it, no? The foundations of a capitalist economy, boiled down to the ultimate microcosm. Money and pleasure in a black silk dress."

They laughed some more, congratulating Petain on his wit. As they laughed, Condley studied Van's avoiding face. "A black silk dress. Kind of like yours, Van?"

"Do you like it?" teased Petain. "I bought it for her."

"You mean you bought her with it."

"Why have you never learned to accept the reality of your environment, *Monsieur* Bone Picker? Why must every fact of life become an argument?"

Condley stood nakedly before their laughing eyes, unshaven and ill-dressed, suddenly so weary of it all that he no longer even had a good retort. "Because I've seen it all before. And I know how it's going to end." He gave Van one final look and then turned to leave.

"Cong Ly, wait!"

She was standing at the table next to Petain, looking around the room, biting her lower lip. Her head was high in the air, as if she was measuring her chances without its false but glorious ambience, or perhaps taking it all in for one final time. Deciding, she glanced for a moment at Francois Petain, and then nodded to Condley.

"I'm going with you."

"Of course she is," said Petain, holding his amused grin and nodding to his friends as if the moment had been preordained. "These things must inevitably end, you know?"

"I am the one who is leaving. It was not your decision, Francois." She bit her words off, throwing them at him like knives as she moved slowly past the cluttered chairs and stood next to Condley.

"Ah, melodrama!" chuckled Petain. "She is like you in that sense, is she not? Too filled with emotion. The two of you together will be a disaster."

"I'm not here to replace you, Francois. She just needed a ride." Condley took her hand, uncertain of where the moment was leading him but instinctively wanting to protect her. "See you later."

"You can keep the dress, Van," said Petain. "It looks very nice on you. Too bad about the rest of it."

She began tugging Condley's arm, pulling him toward the door. "Good-bye," she said, not looking back at Petain.

The waitress had returned with a new round of drinks. Petain put an arm around her waist, pulling her to him. He called to them as they left. "With your emotions, the two of you will wear each other out within a week."

THE HUSTLERS AND the hawkers called lewdly to them as they left the East Wind, Rain. It began to rain again, light, pulsing breaths of it, as if a garden hose were twirling from high above. Without speaking, he put his poncho over her bare shoulders and squeezed it around her until it covered her. She grabbed his right arm in both of hers as they walked and put her head on his shoulder. After a few more steps he looked down at her face. She was walking with her eyes closed, letting him guide her to wherever it was that he wanted to go. He touched her cheek with his fingers. Finally she opened her eyes and looked up at him with a tragic confusion.

"In Viet Nam it takes a long time for someone to say they are in love. But then they are in love. *Yeu,* I mean, not *thuong.* The kind of love that is forever. I think in the western countries they start out saying they are in love. And then they try to decide if it is true. So it is a different word in another language. Love and love, but different. Isn't that true, Cong Ly?"

"What happened?"

"*Khong co sao.* Never mind. Thank you for coming."

"You don't want to tell me?"

"I am ashamed to tell you." She looked away and then back at him again. "All right, I will tell you. He offered me to his friend. For an evening. *For an evening, Cong Ly!*"

"Forget it, Van. It's over."

She was crying. "You know my culture. What am I going to do? I've been with a foreigner. A rich man! People know this. Now I will be laughed at. And maybe worse."

"You shouldn't be thinking of that right now. You left with your dignity in place. That's important."

She pulled him more tightly to her, clutching his arm as if it were a life preserver, saying nothing. A *cyclo* passed them, creaking slowly by, and then a string of motorbikes. Her tears mixed with the rain, and then they stopped.

"So," she finally said as they walked along the dark, wet sidewalk. "Are we together now?"

Her nearness, the strength of her grasp, and even the very warmth of her body were overwhelming. It was not logical to think that they could ever find happiness together. But he could not stop himself from wanting to fall inside this moment and keep it, at least until it ended.

"No," he finally answered, nonetheless pulling her into him as they walked. "Not a good idea, Van." But finally he stopped in the darkness, with the rain falling on them and the motorbikes beeping at them from the roadway, and kissed her for a very long time.

In minutes they reached the Vien Dong Hotel. Standing outside the door, she looked directly into his eyes. Her tears were gone. There was a strength in the firmness of her lips. "Take me to your room."

"No."

"I know you want to make love to me, Cong Ly. I knew it the first time I met you."

"Let me say this as a friend, Van. You have to be careful with yourself. You can't jump from one man to another."

"I decided to leave Francois weeks ago. But I wanted to wait until you came back."

How many women had he been with since Mai died? He could not even count. But it had never been complicated. "I need to call you a taxi."

"Later."

She held him silently as the elevator ascended, pressing her head into his chest. They made love for hours on his rumpled bed, and then she fell asleep in his arms. As the motorbikes began whining underneath his window and the sky began to gray with the first hint of dawn, she awakened, grabbing his wrist and staring unbelievingly at the dials on his watch.

"Oh, this is very bad. Now I will have to tell my mother!"

"Should I come with you?"

"And then what?"

She sat on the edge of the bed, watching him. As she looked down, her hair fell forward, resting on her high, rounded breasts. She ran a finger along old shrapnel scars that still pocked and gouged his legs.

"What is happening to me?" she said. "I'm very afraid. Are you going to leave me?"

"I can't leave you, Van. We aren't even together." He saw the hurt in her eyes and took a few strands of her hair into his fingers, gently pulling until she had turned her face toward him. "This is why I didn't want to make love to you. I like you too much."

"You like me too much? Then why don't you want to love me?"

"You're too young."

"No, Cong Ly! In Viet Nam, I am almost too old!"

She was right about that. In Viet Nam, women were usually married by their early twenties. "Okay, I said that wrong. You haven't seen enough. You've been through a great deal with Francois, and you need to calm down before you decide to be in love with anyone else."

"Maybe we will be in love?"

"Maybe," he said. "But not yet."

"That was honest," she said. "So I don't feel bad."

He watched her for what seemed to be a long time. She avoided his eyes, her fingers still playing along the edges of his scars. Finally something broke inside him, so real that he almost heard it.

"No promises?"

She gave him a little smile, as if accepting a truce. "No promises."

"Would you like to go to Bangkok?"

She looked at him as if he had offered up a dream. "Of course!"

"Can you get a visa?"

She had obviously thought about visas many times before. "I know

a man at a government travel agency. A friend of the family. It is difficult, you know, because of the political situation. Almost no one can
travel outside the country unless they are part of a political group. But
there are ways. My father is trusted, so that would help. And it will cost
me a hundred dollars. Under the table, you understand? But, yes, it is
possible to get a visa."

"Can you get a visa today?"

She smiled impishly, her face filled with an unfathomable excitement. "Do you have an extra hundred dollars?"

"Yes," said Condley, shaking his head and forcing himself out of
bed. "But you'll have to move quickly. Be the first person in line at your
friend's office. The flight leaves at three o'clock this afternoon."

CHAPTER TWENTY-EIGHT

DZUNG PEDALED SLOWLY in the early-morning traffic, wiping the sleep out of his eyes. He was following the new routine created by Manh, a daily journey past the Interior Ministry building before he headed to the Rex Hotel. If Manh was standing at his window in Room 212, looking down at the street, it meant that Dzung was needed on that day for further training, and so he would stop and go inside. If Manh was not in the window, Dzung would continue on to the Rex.

Nearing the building, Dzung felt a small relief when he saw that the window in Room 212 was empty. But as he pedaled past, he saw Manh waiting for him on the curb just outside. "So, Dzung!" called Manh. "Over here, over here!"

Manh seemed electric, his eyes filled with excitement. A cigarette dangled from the corner of his mouth. His head was cocked to one side, just as he always imagined the gangsters in the old movies held theirs. His arms were folded across his chest. He was leaning against a white, unmarked van. And now he put both arms up into the air, as if the force of this gesture was itself stopping Dzung's *cyclo*.

Dzung slowed his *cyclo* and then halted next to Manh. Watching the Interior Ministry agent with an intuition honed by decades of sub-servience, he felt suddenly breathless. Manh was bouncing on the toes of his pretty leather shoes, as if ready to spring into action. A line was being crossed. A time had come. A moment had arrived. Something was going to happen.

"Get into the van," said Manh, sliding open the side door.

"What about my *cyclo*?"

"We will take care of your *cyclo*. Get inside. Hurry up!"

Dzung climbed from his *cyclo* and crawled into the van, moving to a rear seat. Manh followed immediately, sliding the door closed behind him and taking the seat just in front of him. By the time the driver had put the van into gear, a young man had run from the Interior Ministry building and jumped onto the seat of Dzung's *cyclo*, then pedaled it away. Dzung watched forlornly as the van pulled out into the traffic and the young man disappeared with his *cyclo*. The young man was wearing well-pressed slacks and leather shoes. He was not a *cyclo* driver.

"Where is he going with my *cyclo*?" he asked quietly.

"I told you, don't worry about the *cyclo*," said Manh, leaning back in the seat and peering out the window. "Would you rather that we left it on the street?"

"No. But where are you taking me?"

"Calm down, mister big-time soldier. I thought you had nerves of steel."

"My nerves are fine. But my brain is very curious, Manh."

"We are taking you someplace," said Manh carefully. "And if you succeed in what we are asking you to do, we will return you to this place. And then you will be reunited with your precious *cyclo*."

"What about my family?"

"They will be told that you have been detained for interrogation in a remote location." Manh shrugged. "A routine political matter."

Dzung thought about all this as the van made its way north and west along the crowded streets. He had fired off thousands of rounds of ammunition in the past several weeks, always using the same pistol. His training under Manh's direction had been exact. After the first week on the firing range, they had moved to a cluttered, darkened warehouse building. Day after day, Dzung had been required to run quickly toward a wide array of different targets in the dark, through debris and knee-high obstacles, and then empty a full magazine into each target from very close range. The magazine was emptied the same way each time— two bullets to the heart, three to the head, two more to the heart. The targets and the obstacles had varied, but his approach and escape had always been the same. After firing a full magazine he would immediately conceal his weapon inside his clothing, race for a short distance away from the target, and then begin walking slowly, as if he were just appearing at the scene.

He knew what this was all about. It was no mystery what Manh was preparing him to do.

"And what are my chances of being reunited with my precious *cyclo* after I perform this service?" he asked dryly, staring at Manh's relaxed frame from behind him.

"I thought you hated your life, mister *cyclo* driver."

"Oh, no," smiled Dzung, fighting back the nervousness that was now causing even his fingers to tingle. "It is a wonderful existence. Fresh air. Plenty of exercise. Interesting people. And when I take a vacation, I can park my *cyclo* free of charge in front of the Interior Ministry building."

As Dzung spoke he noticed the van's driver looking quickly at him through the rearview mirror, a silent, threatening reproach that prodded Manh himself into action. "Careful with your disrespect, Dzung."

"But that was not disrespect," grinned Dzung. "I was expressing my gratitude for all the benefits the revolution has brought me."

"I am warning you—"

"Yes, I know," answered Dzung. "My files."

Manh shook his head, as if Dzung himself was hopeless. "I actually like you, Dzung. But you are too careless with your own safety."

Dzung looked out the window, vainly searching faces among the stream of the motorbikers and *cyclo* drivers who were looking into the van as they passed. "That is an odd way to put it, Manh. You've given me a gun. You want me to use it, for the good of the revolution. I may not survive. And then you tell me I am too careless with my own safety."

"Enough," warned Manh, lighting a fresh cigarette as he held it at the bottom of two fingers near the palm. His eyes were on the mirror as the driver looked back at them with disapproval, and his face had grown suddenly hard. "I am serious about this. We have developed a . . . certain way of talking to each other, which might cause you great difficulty in the coming few hours if you continue to use it. No more silly talk. You may think you are protected from retaliation because we need you to perform this service, but you should remember that there is life on the other side of what you are about to do. Assuming you do it successfully, that is. And that life will be just like this life, Dzung. So these are your choices: fail in your task, in which case you will not survive. Or carry out your task, in which case you still belong to us."

"Those are really not such different choices," shrugged Dzung, feeling somehow emboldened by their very futility. "Fast death or slow death. But I will succeed. For the good of the revolution, right, Manh?"

Manh finally waved a hand into the air, looking out the window and dismissing him. "Be careful, Dzung. I am serious. We will not forget."

District Three faded behind them, as did the busy markets of Cho Lon. Dzung lost his bearings as the van twisted and turned along the crowded streets. Finally they reached a walled compound that covered an entire city block. Barbed wire ran along the top of the walls. Sentry boxes manned by hard-faced soldiers sat atop the walls at every corner and on both sides of the double iron gate, as if they had reached a prison.

"My new home?" teased Dzung as the gates slowly opened, allowing the van inside.

"You're not that lucky," snorted Manh, grinding out his latest cigarette on the van's metal floor. The van halted, and the Interior Ministry agent slid the door open, jumping outside. He pointed to Dzung, his demeanor and his voice having lost all hint of familiarity.

"Okay, out."

Dzung stepped out, finding himself at the entrance to yet another bleak, yellow-plaster building built by the French nearly a century before. He followed Manh up a short flight of worn, rounded steps and then inside. The air was clammy, heavy with moldy Asian odors, similar to the stairways in the Interior Ministry building itself. Manh brought him down a long, dimly lit corridor and then into a side room. The room was stark and empty, its walls painted blue. A picture of Ho Chi Minh hung on one wall, above a wooden bench. Except for the bench, the only furniture in the room was a small table in the center and two small wooden chairs that seemed to have been built for schoolchildren. A floor-length mirror was on another wall. Next to the mirror was an internal door that led, no doubt, into another room.

Manh closed the outer door behind them and nudged Dzung until they were standing before the mirror.

"I want you to see what you look like," said Manh. "Have you seen yourself before, Dzung?"

"Not in a long time," Dzung answered. "Only my face in a small mirror. Sometimes my reflection on a hotel window. And Cong Ly took a picture of me last year for Tet. I saw that."

"A picture is tiny," said Manh. "Take a look at yourself."

Dzung moved slowly to the mirror and stood before it for a long time. His hair shot raggedly out from underneath his worn baseball cap. His thin arms dangled from his stretched and faded T-shirt. His fingernails were cracked and dirty. His legs looked like pencils at the bottom of his rolled trousers. His sandaled feet were wide, callused, and dirty, their toenails blackened. He moved closer, examining the gaps between his stained teeth and the lines that creased his face and neck. He did not like what he saw, but he was not surprised.

"Why do you want me to look at myself?"

"Because I am going to change you," said Manh. "Come with me."

For two hours Manh led Dzung from room to room inside the ancient, mysterious building. In one room a barber waited for him and skillfully cut his hair. In another room a technician brushed and expertly cleaned his teeth, while another clipped and manicured his nails. He was then brought to a shower room, where he dropped his old clothes and scrubbed himself for a long time, taking his first hot shower in more than twenty-five years.

After he dried himself he was issued a set of snow-white underwear. Once he put on the underwear he was brought into another room, where a frowning, stylishly dressed young woman awaited him. Without saying a word to him, she meticulously blow-dried his hair, rubbing gel into it and styling it for him. She went into a closet and brought out a new, tropical, worsted olive-colored suit, a pair of patterned silk socks, and a pair of brown leather shoes. As he put on the trousers, socks, and shoes, she went back to the closet, bringing out a handful of ties and several shirts. Holding the ties against the suit and looking at his face, she finally chose a blue and gold rep pattern and matched the tie to a sky-blue shirt. He had never knotted a tie before, and so she did that for him, tying it and slipping it around his neck, showing him just how to fold the collar over the tie and how to pinch the knot at the bottom once the tie was tightened around the neck.

And finally Manh brought him back to the first room he had entered, walking him in front of the mirror again.

"Now look," said Manh as he lit his thirtieth cigarette of the day, a devilish grin slashing across his face. "Who do you see?"

"I see Dzung," he said.

"No, you don't," said Manh. "Look again."

He moved closer to the mirror, looking more closely. Staring back at him was a sleek, handsome powerhouse, an entrepreneurial giant, the kind of man he could never have dreamed of conversing with on the sidewalk, much less luring into his *cyclo*.

"I see a *hai ngoai*," said Dzung quietly, using the term that identified the overseas Vietnamese who lived in Australia, France, or America.

"You see Nguyen Le Trong," said Manh. As he spoke, a thin, frazzled man entered the room, carrying a camera. Manh nudged Dzung and pointed toward one of the dull blue walls. "Stand over there with your back to the wall. Hurry up!"

As Dzung stood against the wall, the man took two pictures of him and then quickly left the room. Watching him leave, Dzung shrugged his shoulders absently. "Who is Nguyen Le Trong?"

"You are Nguyen Le Trong," answered Manh. "Listen to me. You have only a few hours to memorize this and fully understand it. It was impossible to tell you earlier because, quite frankly, it would have been too dangerous to tell you before you were completely under our control. You are Nguyen Le Trong. You were born on March 23, 1949, in a small village in Thua Thien Province. Your father was a doctor. You moved to Hue at an early age. You served in a few innocuous logistics positions during the war but mostly studied economics at Hue University. You are now a businessman—"

"A businessman?" grinned Dzung, looking again at himself in the mirror. "I must make a lot of money."

"You're supposed to be nervous!" grimaced Manh, watching Dzung preen before the mirror.

"Me, or Nguyen Le Trong?"

"You, Dzung!" Manh watched him for another second and then relaxed into silent laughter himself. "You do have nerves of steel, don't you? I see we picked the right man."

"Tell me more about this business," said Dzung, running his hands over the material of his suit.

The photographer walked back into the room, handing Manh a small, bulky envelope, and then left. Manh opened the package, nodding his head approvingly as he flipped through several pages. Then he held it up for Dzung to see.

"This is your passport. As you will be able to see, you have been to Thailand many, many times."

"To Thailand?" breathed Dzung, staring at the small booklet. "What have I done there?"

"Business," said Manh.

"What kind of business?"

"Rice," answered Manh. "We are the third-largest exporter of rice in the world, you know."

"We export rice while our children starve?"

"Cease talking like that," said Manh. "You are not living in District Four. You are an exporter." He handed Dzung the passport. "This is not a forged document, Trong. Please note that from now on I will call you Trong. But this is not a forged document. It is an official government passport. The only thing that is inaccurate is your identity."

"What are we doing?" asked Dzung.

"We are going to Thailand," said Manh. "There is a flight that leaves at three o'clock this afternoon."

"To sell rice?" asked Dzung sarcastically.

"To sell rice," said Manh.

"What time does my limo pick me up?"

Manh laughed, folding his arms and looking proudly at his creation. "You learn quickly, don't you, Trong?"

Dzung preened for another moment at the mirror, turning this way and that, amazed at his own transformation. "Maybe I like this idea of selling rice."

It was an idle comment, but as Manh watched the newly converted Dzung's face he saw a power emanating from those simple words. And it made him very uncomfortable.

———

THE WALKWAY OUTSIDE the Tan Son Nhat airport terminal was jammed with travelers, cab drivers, family members, hawkers, hookers, and thieves, all waiting anxiously to greet passengers on the flight that had just arrived from Bangkok. They stood three-deep along a roped corri-

dor that allowed the new arrivals to exit from the terminal's glass doorways, holding flowers or signs, their eyes filled with anticipation. They
peered wistfully inside the terminal through the windows, as if all of the
outside world were a jail and the terminal building itself were an envi-
able node of freedom. They pulsed with an undeniable energy, an excitement so palpable that it crackled among them like static electricity.

And nothing that had happened to him in the last quarter century
amazed Dzung so completely as when the thick crowd parted upon seeing him approach, allowing him to walk untouched into the terminal. In
the usual tradition of Sai Gon he had expected to be jostled, pickpock-
eted, suborned, and even insulted. But when he stepped out of the government van in his olive suit with his leather carrying bag and his
swept-back hair and walked resolutely toward the terminal doors, the
mass of people parted before him. His elegance stunned many of them
into silence. There was envy in many of their eyes, curiosity in others,
but in all of them he saw an eerie, undeniable respect.

When he reached the terminal door, Manh came up from behind
him, opening it for him. The Interior Ministry agent was grinning with
delight. "Allow me, Mister Trong."

At the business-class section of the ticket counter, Manh brought
their passports to the front of the line. Immediately a Viet Nam Airlines
employee left the counter and personally escorted them through security,
and then through Customs, where they were waved into the departure
lounge without inspection. Dzung remained silent, following Manh,
having little idea of where he was and no idea of where he was going.

In the departure lounge hundreds of people milled about, most of
them foreigners at the end of their Viet Nam adventure. Dzung strolled
among the backpackers and the sport-shirted tourists, marveling at their
easy opulence, wondering how many of them he might have implored to
ride for an hour on his *cyclo* for a dollar, only a dollar, a fraction of what
they now were throwing away on beer and peanuts as they whiled away
the minutes before the flight that would take them to their next few days
of frolic.

Manh guided him to the business-class lounge, where a half dozen
other passengers were already waiting. In the small room he sat for a
half hour on a cushy sofa, watching television for the first time since the
war's end. A cute young woman in a blue *ao dai* spoiled him with defer-
ential smiles, offering him napkins and food. He ordered a bottle of

orange juice, then two bags of cashew nuts, and finally three slices of papaya.

Another escort from Viet Nam Airlines greeted them in the business-class lounge. Ever smiling, ever gracious, she guided them past the long lines and around the X-ray machines, taking them to a small bus that drove them onto the runway, directly to the waiting aircraft. They climbed the flight ladder and took their seats in the front row of the business-class section. They were the first people to board the aircraft. The flight attendants greeted them as royalty, knowing they were on a special travel assignment from the government.

Dzung took off his jacket, folding it carefully and stowing it with his bag in the overhead compartment, and then settled into his seat. A flight attendant brought him a glass of juice and that day's edition of *Tuoi Tre*. It was almost impossible to comprehend that a mere seven hours before, he had been pedaling his *cyclo* in the dust and fumes of District One, on his way to work at the Rex Hotel.

As he was reading the newspaper, the rest of the flight began to board the aircraft. Soon he heard a familiar voice. Then he heard another familiar voice, and finally that of a woman talking to the other two. He sat, stunned, his heart pounding uncontrollably for the first time that day. Looking carefully from behind the newspaper, he fought back a moment of stark terror.

Condley, Van, and Hanson Muir stood only a few feet away from him, waiting for the passengers in front of them to take their seats. Condley and Van were standing very close together. Hanson Muir was just behind them, carrying a too-large hanging bag and grumbling good-naturedly.

"I am in a state of extreme depression, Brandon, and it is only fair that you also be in a state of extreme depression. Back in the States they have a show called *Sesame Street*. They teach us all about sharing. Sharing is a good thing. So if you can't share your good fortune with me, at least I'm going to make a point of sharing my depression with you. Do you understand my concept? And will you two please stop it?"

"I told you, Professor. As soon as we get to Bangkok I'll get you a bubble bath and a massage."

"My wife wouldn't like that."

"How do you know? Has she ever had one?"

Van laughed lightly, a hand moving casually along Condley's arm. Dzung weakened for a moment, allowing himself to scrutinize her face. It was the closest he had ever been to her. An emotion rolled through his belly, somewhere between jealousy and concern.

Condley picked up his look. With a sudden protectiveness he turned toward Dzung and stared menacingly back at him, squinting his eyes just for a moment, as if in recognition. Shaken, Dzung quickly returned to his newspaper. Condley looked at him curiously for another moment, as if considering a thought and then dismissing it. And then the three moved on toward their seats in the rear of the aircraft.

Dzung looked over at Manh. The Interior Ministry agent was smiling grandly, a look of complete victory on his face.

"So you see, Mister Trong. You are a different man."

Dzung clung to the newspaper, shifting uneasily in his seat. "This business of exporting rice is becoming very complicated."

"Perhaps. But it has its rewards."

He glanced at the carry-on bag that Manh had kept on his lap. "Did you bring the gun?"

"Of course I brought the gun."

"What will happen on the other end?"

"The same thing that happened here," said Manh simply. "We will be met by Thai officials and Vietnamese diplomatic staff, who will escort us through Customs. A driver will take us to the Vietnamese Embassy. We will stay at the embassy."

"Where am I going to . . . sell my rice?"

"Wherever I decide," said Manh, putting his carry-on bag under his seat and then buckling his seat belt.

"Why is Cong Ly on this plane?"

"Who? We don't know such a man." Manh picked up his own copy of *Tuoi Tre*. "Enjoy your flight, Mister Trong. There will be a meal when we take off. You are the kind of man who appreciates a good glass of wine."

"I have never had a good glass of wine."

"Actually, you have had many good glasses of wine. You make this trip frequently. Check your passport. And you always have wine with your meal when we fly to Bangkok."

"Bangkok is crowded?" asked Dzung gamely, trying to picture their destination. "Like Sai Gon?"

"More buildings," answered Manh. "Very nice hotels. But the traffic is terrible."

Dzung felt suddenly weary. "I think I will take a nap on the plane."

"A good idea," said Manh, turning to his copy of *Tuoi Tre*. "We will have a lot of work to do when we reach Bangkok."

CHAPTER TWENTY-NINE

Bangkok

"OH, CONG LY. This is the most beautiful thing I have ever seen."

She was on the terrace just outside the fifth-floor hotel room, looking stunning in a black bikini that he had bought for her after their arrival the day before. She had awakened at dawn and spent an hour in the swimming pool while he showered and shaved. Now she stood, one hand on the railing, her chin raised into a gentle morning wind. She closed her eyes for a moment as if she were in the middle of a glorious dream. The wind lifted her long hair, sending it fluttering behind her shoulders so that she looked bold and innocent and free, like an island girl catching her first glimpse of civilization. Watching her, he descended into a flash of mawkishness. For at that moment she, and not the view before her, was the most beautiful thing that he had ever seen.

He joined her on the terrace, carrying a cup of room-service coffee. They were staying in a corner suite, so that one side of the terrace looked out on the ancient Chao Phraya River while the other was directly above the Riverside Hotel's elegant courtyard. The wind blew in from the river, pungent with the smells of lilies, gasoline, and musk. The Riverside was a nice enough hotel, and from their room they had a splendid view. But for Van, who had never before been out of Viet Nam, it was as massively ostentatious as the palace at Versailles.

On the river a caravan of five barges laden with tons of rice cut slowly through the chalky water, pulled along by a creaky old steamer. A family sat on the steamer's fantail, eating breakfast as that day's laundry flapped above their heads like circus pennants. Little boats cut up and down the river, powered by long-stemmed outboard motors. At the dock just below them, the Riverside Hotel's ferry was loading up for its fifteen-minute journey upriver to the famed Oriental pier. And all along the river, as far as they could see, clusters of tall, modern buildings jutted up against a crisp blue sky.

"Welcome to paradise," he said dryly, standing next to her. "The river is polluted, and there's so much chlorine in the swimming pool that it will flake your skin."

"But look at the buildings and the boats and the temples!" she said. "They are glorious, Cong Ly. New and shiny, so modern! And the people seem so happy, not like Viet Nam!"

He put a hand on her shoulder, amused. "I think you should give it at least another day."

One day in Bangkok had created in Van's mind a fanciful, even poetic vision of another world. Despite its dirt and traffic, the city's pleasures and promises had grabbed her like a vise from the moment she exited the aircraft. "I don't ever want to leave this place."

He chuckled cynically. "And she hasn't even seen Hong Kong."

"Is it better?"

"That depends on what you're looking for. It's thick with buildings, crammed with people. But they live far better." His arm swept before him in an arc as he spoke. "If this were Hong Kong we would be looking out at the harbor into the sea. Ships of all sizes. Mountains over there. Narrow streets packed with shops that make Bangkok look like—like a starving stepsister."

Her eyes were transfixed with the magic of these new and sudden possibilities. "Then I want to go there too. Let's go!"

"You would need a new visa."

"I could get one! You could pay the bribe at the Vietnamese embassy here, Cong Ly! Everything is possible with the bribe. *Ca phe ca phao!*"

He shook his head. "Not very likely. Anyway, I don't want to go to

Hong Kong. I don't even want to be in Bangkok any longer than I have to. I have a job to do, Van."

She gave him a look that bordered on amazement. "You would rather be in Viet Nam than here, I think?"

"Actually, yes."

"Why?"

He laughed. The Why thing again. "Why do fools fall in love?"

"I don't understand you."

"In a world of five billion people, what makes two people develop the chemistry that causes them to single each other out and fall in love, Van?"

"I don't know." She watched him carefully, as if he were asking a trick question. "Why do they?"

"I don't know either." He waved to her, leaving the terrace. "And I don't know why I'd rather be in Viet Nam. I only know it's true."

HANSON MUIR AND Paul Archer were waiting for him at a table in the Riverside Garden Café. The large café was crowded with western tourists of all ages and stripes, from a few sassy young American backpackers to a large group of loudly dressed older Germans who obviously were part of a tour. A uniformed flight crew from Air New Zealand milled among the tourists, catching a quick meal before a bus took them to the airport.

Muir stood and waved as Condley entered the café. Plates and bowls from a huge buffet breakfast lay scattered on the table in front of him and Archer. Condley teased the ample scientist as he took a chair at the table.

"Getting your money's worth, huh, Professor?"

"A simple but ample meal, Brandon. I was famished! After the usual spy-infested omelettes of the Rex Hotel, not to mention weeks of airline food, I'm beginning to wonder if this isn't simply a plot to make me lose weight."

"The Brandon Condley Diet," joked Condley. "Keep the boy on the road." He rolled his eyes slightly, looking at Muir's bright-orange shirt. "You just can't get rid of that luau fashion statement, can you?"

Muir waved a huge arm into the air. "I'm perfectly at home here, Brandon. Look around you."

"Yeah, all those I-went-to-Asia shirts hurt my eyes. It's like they all stole the same tablecloth." Condley pointed, sharing a quiet chuckle with Paul Archer. The fortyish, graying CIA agent had shown up in a coat and tie. "Now, look here, Professor. This is the way a self-respecting government employee dresses in Bangkok." He had not yet met Archer, and now he extended his hand. "Brandon Condley."

"Take a look at yourself, Brandon," said Muir as the two shook hands, pointing to Condley's casual sport shirt and blue jeans. Then he caught himself. "I know, I know. I won't even finish that thought. So this is Paul Archer, from the American Embassy."

"Your reputation precedes you, Mister Condley," grinned Archer. "I'm told you've spent a bit of time over on this side."

"I was a knuckle-dragger for a while," said Condley. "Up-country and in Laos, mostly. Did some corporate security work after that. I had a few friends around here, but there was never much to do around Bangkok except get laid." He thought about that. "Not that I have ever been opposed to getting laid."

Archer laughed. "Like I said, your reputation precedes you."

"If you didn't see it with your own eyes, it's a lie!" bantered Condley.

"Plausible deniability. That's exactly what they predicted you'd say," quipped the CIA agent.

Hanson Muir gestured to a manila folder lying on one edge of the table. "Mister Archer did a very thorough job going over the materials we faxed him, but I'm afraid he doesn't have much to tell us."

"Are you the station chief?" asked Condley.

"No, but I'm a lawyer as well as a"—Archer looked briefly around at the other tables—"State Department employee. And I do a lot of work with Interpol."

"According to a fax I received from a friend of mine at Cinc Pac, your colleague in Moscow, Skip Rogers, seemed to believe you could help us," said Condley, keeping things deliberately vague.

"I'd like to, but there's only so much I can do off-line," said Archer, shrugging hopelessly. "I looked at your stuff and had a few quiet talks with some of our longtime Asia hands, but that's it. And if we're talking about the official position of the embassy, there's really not much that we can do on this at all. Let me explain. Realistically, you've got a set of military charges that are now thirty-four years old—one for murder, and another for desertion after the murder. There's no statute of limitations on either of these two crimes. Murder because it's a capital offense. Desertion because it's continuous, meaning that the crime doesn't end until the desertion does. But I would emphasize that these are military charges, at least at this point, under the Uniform Code of Military Justice. In addition, they're very old and we have no suspect. We don't even have a set of regular criminal charges from a host nation. First, South Viet Nam doesn't exist anymore, and second, we never allowed the South Vietnamese government to prosecute our military people anyway."

"What about the murder of an Australian national in 1971?" Condley asked idly.

"Get me an indictment," said Archer. "We do have strong circumstantial evidence, given the dog tags and the severed hand, but you guys haven't even officially shared this information with our own government, much less made it public. If I had something of that sort that was official, I could put it into the international system. But even then . . ."

Archer shrugged, not finishing the sentence. Condley reached across the table into a bread basket, stealing one of Muir's muffins. "We sent you that fax three days ago, Paul. I expected to walk in here and put the cuffs on Deville this morning."

"Cuffing him would be the easy part," Archer replied. "If he's alive, that is. And in Bangkok. And discoverable."

"I think he's here," insisted Condley. "If he's still alive."

"Is there a basis for that thought?" asked Archer.

"Invincible optimism."

"Optimism is commendable but a rather fragile reed to lean on when it comes to invoking the powers of government." Archer gestured toward the manila folder that Muir had brought to the breakfast table. "Your materials are interesting. No, let me say that they are fascinating. But they don't establish anything. And I mean nothing at all. What do we know about this man as it connects to Bangkok? All we have is an assumption that he would have escaped from Sai Gon—if he ever did make it from central Viet Nam back to Sai Gon—by using Mathew Larkin's passport. And a further assumption that he would have come to Bangkok because a flight to Bangkok would raise the least amount of suspicion, given the visa stamps that were in the passport. Or at least that some drunken Russian veteran claims were in there. We don't know for sure that this man Deville ever escaped from Viet Nam. We don't know for sure that he came here. We don't know that he would have stayed here or anywhere else in Thailand if he did come. We have no fingerprints that match his, although that's a long shot in a place like Thailand, anyway. And to be blunt, thirty years leaves us a pretty cold trail. No, let me change that estimate. A pretty dead trail."

Condley continued to chew slowly on Hanson Muir's lost muffin, holding Archer's gaze. "So, tell me some good news."

"Well, the Redskins are favored in the Super Bowl," panned Archer. "And oil just went down to twenty-five dollars a barrel."

"Twenty-five dollars? No kidding? Remind me to adjust my portfolio." Condley took an empty cup and poured some hot coffee from a pot the waiter had left on the table. "Let me tell you why I'm optimistic. And you're right, we don't really know much of anything, at least past the point where our man killed Larkin and stole his identity. But we do know he did that. He left his dog tags around Larkin's neck and he cut off his hand. There's no question there."

"Fine," said Hanson Muir, nudging Condley along as if he were the moderator on a panel discussion. "We do know that, Brandon. So tell Mister Archer why you are optimistic. Although *optimism* is a rather odd term to use when one contemplates the implications of your happy mood."

"Put yourself in this guy's shoes," said Condley. "You've been on the run inside Viet Nam for four years, doing everything you can to keep from being caught by the American authorities. You killed a guy in cold blood over a blown drug deal before you went AWOL. You rendered aid and comfort to the enemy, probably in order to survive. And you killed another guy in cold blood so you could steal his identity and finally get the hell out of the war zone. Once you're out of the war zone, the last thing you're going to do is take the kind of risk that will cause you to be recognized by western authorities. What are your priorities? Not getting caught, that's your first and maybe only priority. No airports, no crossing the border into new countries, and no getting into any trouble where western police or diplomats are going to be called upon for assistance. Not only that, but you've been in the jungle or on the run for four years. You want to unwind. In other words, you're going to burrow in and hide for a while. Celebrate your escape, learn the new terrain, choose how you're going to operate in it."

"You stay in Bangkok," said Muir.

"You definitely stay in Bangkok. Particularly in the early seventies, when there is still a steady stream of American GIs flying in and out of Bangkok from Viet Nam for R and R, not to mention the Air Force weenies who are in and out of here all the time from their bases at U Tapao and U Dorn. Unplugged young Americans in Bangkok aren't anything unusual. You can float along the edges of the underworld, live for almost nothing, and nobody pays you any never-mind."

Archer nodded slowly, again and again, alternating his look from Condley to Muir. "Logical," he said. "Actually, more than logical. Visceral. I would have to agree with your instincts. But unfortunately, the fact that he was very likely here thirty years ago still means nothing when it comes to how I conduct my work."

"So you're saying there's nothing you can do?" asked Muir. From his expression, Condley sensed that the professor was actually relieved, as if the entire journey might now, thankfully, be over and he could return to his quiet world of skeletons and DNA.

"I respect you gentlemen, please understand me. But it's almost like you're on more of an archaeological dig than a criminal investigation. I've got my hands full with real-life problems."

Archer checked his watch. "Traffic is a fire-breathing dragon in this city." Reaching into his briefcase, he pulled out a small black leather folder and opened it, taking out two business cards. He stood, handing one to each of them. "In any event, happy hunting, gentlemen. And if you find somebody to charge with a crime, I'm only a heartbeat away."

Hanson Muir watched as Archer walked away from them, disappearing into the lobby. "Traffic is a fire-breathing dragon," he mimicked. "What an absurd metaphor. Traffic is a broadly based condition, like fire ants or the flu. How can something that happens all over a city be a dragon?" He glanced over to Condley. "I guess we've run out of luck, Brandon."

"Wrong. I know this city pretty well," said Condley.

"Yes, and you never saw Deville in it, did you?"

"I didn't say I knew everybody in it."

"So what are we going to do, start going door to door? Let's see, at six million people, at a rate of perhaps—shall we say ten doors an hour, and working eight hours a day—and figuring that an average of four people live in each home, that means 1.5 million homes." Muir's brows furrowed as his mind calculated furiously. "Okay, I'd say, just under two hundred thousand days, which means, let's see . . . we could have this wrapped up in about five hundred years. Depending, of course, on the population growth in the meantime."

"No," said Condley. "We call Ted Simolzak."

"Great," groused Muir. "He can cover half the houses and we'll be finished in two hundred fifty years." He watched Condley for a moment. "Who is Ted Simolzak?"

"He's a private dick out here. I've known him forever. Came here from California toward the end of the war after he finished his time in the Air Force. Fell in love with the place and never left. He knows everybody, and he knows just about everything *about* everybody. He's the reigning encyclopedia of the city when it comes to expats. We did some things together in the late seventies and early eighties. Maybe even the late eighties."

"Maybe even the nineties," grinned an obviously envious Muir.

"Maybe the early nineties."

"Probably some pretty beautiful things?"

"Stop drooling, Professor. In fact, some very beautiful things. Simolzak throws a hell of a party."

"Yes, but you've brought your own party with you," said Hanson Muir with exaggerated propriety.

"Oh, I'll bring my party to his party. But you need to see his party." Condley became serious. "If Deville left any tracks at all in this city, Simolzak will know where and how to follow them."

"So you're telling me I can't go home yet?"

"You can go home whenever you want."

"I know that." Muir sighed. "Brandon, if you knew about Simolzak, why did you let me contact Archer?"

"Archer could have been helpful, but I've been out here long enough to know that something's holding him back. Probably internal politics inside the embassy, if I had to guess. But he'll still be useful, Professor. If the embassy gets any third-party reports from out in town, he'll be our fire wall. They've been briefed in on what we're up to, more or less. I didn't mention General Duncan's name, but they know that we have support at some level at Cinc Pac, which should slow them down. So even if Archer doesn't help us directly, he'll keep them from filing a bunch of diplomatic cables asking what the hell we're doing."

"You do know Bangkok," nodded an impressed Muir.

"Yes, I do," agreed Condley, rising from his seat.

"So we won't see Archer again?" asked Muir as they headed toward the restaurant door.

"If we call, he'll come," said Condley. "But they've basically kissed us off for now. They've got their hands full with other problems, and they think we're on a hopeless ghost chase. So they'll leave us alone."

CHAPTER THIRTY

TED SIMOLZAK WAS a man of routines. He worked out with weights and on a treadmill every morning at the Oriental Hotel's exercise club. He kept meticulously regular work hours, operating a successful business as a private investigator from an office with two secretaries who made detailed lists of his calls and carefully filed his correspondence. He lunched every noon at the Royal Yacht Club, methodically rotating his guests to ensure continuing access to information and power. He kept no less than two and no more than three young Thai girlfriends, even now that he had passed the age of fifty, always treating the women well, even mentoring them in their professional desires, but never allowing any of them close enough for a truly serious relationship. In late afternoons he liked to treat his favorite clients and sources to tea or drinks at the Regent Hotel, where he had become a semifamous regular in the luxurious outer lobby.

And almost every evening he drove for nearly an hour through the choked traffic of Sukhumvit Road until he reached one narrow *soy*, or side street, passing the ubiquitous roadside food stalls with their running

kids and yapping dogs, the clutter of cars and motorbikes, and the
clutches of smiling bar girls, and dined at the Cezanne, his personal club.
The Cezanne catered mostly to American expatriates. Its ambience was
the closest to family life that Simolzak ever cared to come. It had a regular coterie of customers, Americans whose professions ran the gamut
from oil rigger to spy to corporate executive. It had a constant core of
beautiful young Thai hostesses, women of taste who were technically
not prostitutes but who would go out or home with a man if they liked
him. It was, of course, mandatory that a woman's host "pay the bar,"
buying her from the bar's owner for the night, and then recompense her
for her time. But a prostitute didn't have a choice, while the women in
places like Cezanne's did, making them more like independent contrac-
tors than actual whores.

It was seven o'clock. Simolzak sat back in his chair at one of the
Cezanne's ground-floor tables, drinking his beer and smiling, surrounded by an atmosphere of thick smoke and loud American music.
Behind him at the bar, two dozen well-dressed American and Thai men
had gathered, sharing drinks and jokes, debating the merits of that
night's activities. A young woman half Simolzak's age was massaging his
back and cooing to him over the music and loud conversation. Her nickname was Sapphire. She was sultry and happy and beautiful. She wore a
tight black bodysuit and blue jeans, an outfit that could have come from
a page in a top fashion magazine.

"Zak, you pay the bar, you pay the bar," Sapphire was urging. "I
want to be with you tonight. You need a beer, let me get you one more
beer."

As Sapphire cooed to him and pressed her fingers into his massive
upper back, another girl came over and helped Simolzak light a fresh
cigar. She was shorter and had a round, wide-mouthed face. Although
she was very pretty, the other girls had named her Frog. Simolzak joked
with Sapphire and Frog as he pointed to the empty seats he had arranged
around the small table.

"Later, ladies. Maybe I'll pay the bar for *both* of you. But first we're
going to have a party! In fact, here comes Father Mike right now."

"Oh, Father Mike," said Sapphire with genuine reverence. "He
speak too-good Thai."

Sapphire stopped rubbing Simolzak's back and stood straight up,
placing her palms together just underneath her chin, the Buddhist

symbol of peace. The small, frail priest walked from the doorway to their table, wearing an unobtrusive short-sleeve pullover that barely showed his priest's collar. He smiled, returning Sapphire's gesture, dipping his chin until it touched the top of his joined hands, and greeted her sweetly in her native tongue.

Simolzak gestured grandly to one of the empty seats. "Father Mike, you're good to join us. Sapphire, get the father a beer, would you?"

"Well, I'll take just one," said Father Mike, a phrase Simolzak knew the old priest would continue to repeat with every new round of drinks.

Father Mike had come to Thailand's mountains nearly thirty years before, as a Redemptorist missionary. For the past twenty years he had ministered to Bangkok's few and desperately poor Christians, most of whom slaughtered hogs and lived in the ramshackle slums of Klong Toey. The bald, devout missionary was a wily provenance of Christ's message. To smooth his way with the predominantly Buddhist Thais, he mixed his message with their own cultural symbols. He did not discourage his parishioners from setting up shrines similar to those in Buddhist homes, with a statue of Christ instead of Buddha at the center, on which they left fruit and flower offerings and burned their joss sticks. And Father Mike matched the raucous American expatriate community drink for drink, curse for curse, so long as they allowed him his moment of ministry.

The beers arrived. Simolzak and Father Mike toasted each other and drank Singha from the bottle.

"So, whose party is it?" asked Father Mike.

Simolzak puffed on his cigar. "Well, it's a double blessing, Father. Sal Marino's back from jail, and Brandon Condley's back from . . . hell, I guess. Viet Nam."

"I doubt that Brandon Condley will ever be back from Viet Nam," shrugged Father Mike. "And may the Lord bless Sal, because he needs our help and understanding." A teasing gleam shone in Father Mike's eyes. "Will they be working with you, then?"

"No, Father. But I think they might find each other's company useful for the evening."

"Well, Sal does know where all the bodies are. And I heard that Brandon has been digging them up for the past few years."

"Exactly," smiled Simolzak. "Brandon is looking for somebody. And Sal is the man to ask."

"And what has this got to do with you and me, Theodore?"

"Brandon needs Sal's help, but as you will recall, they've never exactly been the best of friends." Simolzak watched the door, anticipating their arrivals. He put an arm on Father Mike's thin shoulder. "I may need your mediation if things get out of hand."

"Me?" Father Mike laughed lightly. "And which of them believes in God?" He watched Simolzak shrewdly. "And speaking of God, I ought to urge you to come to confession. I haven't seen you in a while."

"I became a Buddhist."

"Didn't we all, then?"

The door opened quickly, as if it were being kicked in. They turned to see Sal Marino standing just inside the room, dressed in baggy slacks and a too-tight T-shirt. He was a small, wiry man, dark and nervous. His face was etched and hardened, and his long hair was streaked with gray. His hooded eyes scanned the club for dangerous faces, shadowed threats. Finding none, he nodded to the two men, walking slowly to the table. He nodded again to Simolzak, then peered for a moment at Father Mike, and finally extended a thin, hesitant hand.

"I remember you."

"Kind of you to say so," answered Father Mike. "And how was Japan?"

"Cold and damp."

"And what were you doing there?" teased Father Mike knowingly.

Simolzak interrupted, gesturing toward a seat. "Welcome back, Sal. I'll order you a beer."

Marino slowly took the seat, now squinting at Father Mike as if he'd been deeply insulted. "I was running whores, but I lost my license. So I got myself an office in Fuchu Prison and made paper bags."

"Well," said Father Mike, knowing what Marino was saying but deliberately ignoring it, "you must be one of a very few Americans who've been able to do business successfully inside Japan."

"I could make about forty bags on a good day, depending on how cold my cell was," shrugged Marino. "When it was colder, my fingers got kind of stiff so I had to move slower. When it was warmer and I felt good, sometimes I could hit fifty."

"Forty bags a day," nodded Father Mike. "A lot of bags."

"I figure I made about twenty-five thousand bags. Think about that, Father. I personally reached out and touched twenty-five thousand

Japanese, in less than two years. Consumers. People with careers and educations. And I didn't even have to leave my . . . office."

"And how did you come to this good fortune?" asked Father Mike.

"I lost a fight with an Okinawan cop. I thought he'd be easy. I mean, I had two keys of marijuana on me and I knew I was toast, so I thought I'd take him out with a quick punch and run off into the alley. But as soon as I pulled my fist back, the little bastard walloped my chest with a *henbo* stick, then floored me with a quick *uchi taoshi*. Right in the fucking throat. I couldn't move. Thought I was going to be a quadriplegic the rest of my life."

"Tough little bastard, indeed," nodded Father Mike.

"Kicked my ass. One raised fist, then a crushed windpipe and two years in solitary on *Candid Camera* in an unheated cell. And all because of a few lousy keys of marijuana."

"Totally inconsiderate," said Father Mike.

"Fucking camera on me all the time!" said Marino. "They caught me beating off one afternoon and added two weeks to my sentence."

"I'd have settled for a few Hail Marys," said Father Mike.

"They didn't bother me when I was running whores. That was illegal in Japan too, but they didn't care. I had a great deal going on. American women on Okinawa. Lots of them there. Military, school-teachers, even wives. The rice dicks would pay up to a thousand dollars a trick just to spend time with an American. They really loved the blondes. Put some blond wash on the girl's hair if they needed it, teach them how to give a man a bubble bath, and send them off on an adventure in some of Okinawa's best hotels with the safest, cleanest customers on earth. I'll tell you, Father, it was a win-win-win situation. Everybody was happy. Especially me."

"So why did you get into the marijuana business, Sal?"

Marino shrugged. "I got lazy. I started to think I was a business genius. And I started thinking that Okinawa's cops were like Bangkok's."

"Bad assumption," grunted Simolzak, waving to Sapphire, reminding her of their beers.

"It didn't take me long to notice there weren't any drugs in Japan. And I knew where to get them. All these years in Bangkok, you know. Seemed like a pretty straight business proposition."

Simolzak laughed comfortably. "Maybe you forgot that the Japanese are pretty brilliant businessmen themselves? If it was a simple matter of supply and demand, don't you think the Japanese would already have solved it?"

"Gee, Simolzak, where were you when I needed you?" grunted Marino. "That's what's fucked up about Japan. Sex is sex, but drugs are jail."

Sapphire approached with a tray of beers. As Father Mike nodded his gratitude to her, his face hardened slightly. "So that's what you are these days," he said, never losing his serenity. "A bag man, is it?"

Marino laughed at Father Mike and spat onto the floor. "Save it, Father. If you don't shut up I'll drink your beer, I mean it."

"Well," interrupted Simolzak, deciding to end the standoff. "We just thought we'd have a little dinner to welcome Sal back. And maybe do a little business."

"Business," said Marino, immediately growing suspicious. "You never said anything about business."

Marino looked up from his side of the table and saw that virtually every man in the club had now grown silent and was looking his way. He flinched nervously but then also noticed that Simolzak, and even Father Mike, were also staring, not at him but past him, toward the door. He turned around in his chair, following their eyes.

Van filled the doorway, staring back at them, a smiling vision of black and white. Her black hair fell in piles along her shoulders and down her back. Her dark eyes rested comfortably on the room before her, measuring them all seemingly without emotion. She had taken Condley shopping that afternoon and now wore a white silk pantsuit and carried a black patterned Gucci bag. Even the Thai women of Cezanne's stared at her in admiration or unmuted envy. Their tired litany of false worship and passion-for-hire seemed as tinny as the go-go drums on the club's stereo as Van slowly walked to the table, followed by Brandon Condley and Hanson Muir.

"Vietnamese," whistled Simolzak with a devouring look. "My God. I haven't seen anything like that in years." He stood, taking her hand and giving her his chair. Van sat slowly, with deliberate grace, as he then scrambled to a nearby table and retrieved another chair. For a moment she was silent, as if gathering herself. Then she nodded to Father Mike.

"How are you? My name is Van."

"Well, I must say," answered Father Mike, rising to take her hand, "you look like an angel, come upon us from above. Nice to meet you, dear."

Simolzak spoke softly, dropping reality on the table like a hand grenade. "And you remember Brandon Condley, Sal?"

Marino spun quickly, finally recognizing Condley. "I'm out of here," he said, rising to leave.

"The hell you are," said Simolzak with a sudden fierceness, standing up and slamming Marino back into his chair. Marino stood again. Simolzak slammed him down again.

"Stay in that chair."

Marino tried again. "Get your fucking hands off me!"

Simolzak slammed him down yet again, now holding him there. "Brandon needs to talk to you."

"I said, get your hands off me, mung ball."

Marino was reaching for an ankle holster. Simolzak smoothly chopped the smaller man's wrist with a fist and took his pistol away from him. "Oh, you've been in jail too long, Sal. You've got to be faster than that."

"Give me my gun, fucker," growled Marino.

The larger and stronger Simolzak easily restrained him, slamming him one more time into his chair. "Salvatore, I'm buying you dinner tonight. You should at least be polite."

Marino sat very still in the chair, breathing heavily, his eyes staring vapidly forward, reflecting his defeat. The other club patrons, used to such occasional disruptions, went back to their drinks and conversation. Van, who had backed herself against the wall, readjusted her chair, sitting next to Marino without looking at him. She smiled uncertainly to Father Mike, who had not even moved his elbows from the table during the entire altercation.

Father Mike winked to Van. "Relax, my dear. This is normal. And it is a delight to meet you." And now he stood, taking Condley's hand in both of his. "Brandon, Brandon. I've prayed for you every day." He glanced mischievously down at Van. "And perhaps God has been listening after all."

"She's just a friend, Father." Condley caught Simolzak giving Van another look. "A very *good* friend, by the way."

"Brandon is famous for the quality of his very good friends," beamed Simolzak, reaching out and touching Van on a knee. "I'm Ted."

"You can call him *con trau,*" said Condley, causing Van to laugh.

"What does that mean?" asked Simolzak.

"You forgot your Vietnamese," said Condley. "It means water buffalo."

"Okay, *con trau!*" Van leaned across the table and took his hand. "I think Cong Ly is saying you are strong and kind, like the waterbull!"

"I meant ugly," said Condley.

"No, he's not ugly!" teased Van. "He's very handsome!"

"I'll go with strong and kind," said Simolzak. He then turned to Marino. "Okay, Sal, this is very simple. Brandon wanted a little reunion."

"*Jesus,*" said Marino, turning his head toward the door like a dog ready to bolt. "Sorry my *daughter* isn't here."

Condley shrugged as if protesting his innocence. "That was a long time ago, Sal."

"Yeah, and I haven't seen her since."

"So," said Father Mike, his small hands around another beer and his face wrinkled in a teasing smile. "Sal has approached the obligations of fatherhood in the same upstanding manner as he has the duties of citizenship."

"Father, get over it." Marino again glanced at the door. "Don't tell me about being a bad citizen. I served my country in a time of war."

"What've you done lately, Sal?" Father Mike turned to Van with mock seriousness. "He's not always this bad, dear. Once I actually saw him help a little lady out of the traffic. Of course, he then stole her purse."

"I never did that," answered Marino. "And why don't you give Condley one of your little lectures, huh? Tells my own daughter that I slept with other men. My own daughter, who I hadn't seen in nearly twenty years."

"Well, you didn't have any problem with it before she came," shrugged Condley. "Some of them for money."

"So I needed money!" Marino turned to Father Mike, as if for support. "And then he sleeps with my daughter!"

"Sal," sighed Condley. "She asked me to. Tell him, Father. It's a sin to turn away an attractive woman when she asks you."

"I'll have to look that one up, Brandon," said the priest wearily. "Are we talking about the King James version, here?"

Marino glanced at Condley, then looked malevolently at Simolzak, muttering under his breath, "You happy?"

"I'm always happy." Simolzak raised his shoulders in a helpless shrug, trying to calm Marino down. "Just take the meeting, Sal. Or you're going to have to listen to Father Mike all night."

Condley leaned across the table toward Marino, speaking quietly. "I need to find somebody, and you're maybe the only guy who would know. Sal, I know we've had our problems. But you were a good soldier. That means a lot to me. This guy was an asshole. He killed another soldier. He deserted. He fought for the other side for years, killing a couple of my Marines along the way. Then he killed an Australian photographer to steal his passport and his identity. And I think he's here." Marino was weakening, he could tell. "His name is Deville. Theodore Deville. If anybody would have a take on him, you would. That's it. No hidden agenda. No paybacks."

Marino's face was a mask, but his eyes flitted quickly around the club, taking note of who was near them. "I don't know anybody like that."

"Meet with me privately."

"Don't ever bother me again?"

Condley smiled coolly. "You'll never see me again."

"All right, let's go."

Marino began to rise, but Simolzak read something in his eyes and slammed him back into his chair again. "Uh-uh," said Simolzak.

"I'm going to *meet* with him, goddamn it!" Marino snapped, on the verge of violence. "Simolzak, you got my gun. You embarrassed me in front of all these people. The next time you push me down, this whole place is going to blow up."

"All right," said Simolzak, sensing also that Marino had reached his limit. "I respect that. Let's do business, Sal. If you walk out that door and don't meet with Brandon, I lose five thousand bucks. I'll say that again: five thousand dollars. I'll make you an offer. You go upstairs and meet with him, I'll give you a thousand out of my five. Consultant fee."

For the first time that evening, Hanson Muir spoke, looking up from his half-drained beer with mild astonishment. "Brandon, the last time you gave somebody five thousand dollars you ended up with a skull for a urinal."

"Everything in Bangkok has a price, Professor," said Condley flatly.

"Whatever happened to friends helping friends?" said Muir.

"Exactly," announced Simolzak. "Sal is a dangerous person, plus he was very difficult to locate. If Brandon were a normal client this would cost twice as much." He leaned toward Marino now. "A thousand bucks, and you'll never have to deal with Condley again. Hell, Sal, it sounds like you just beat everybody at the table."

"Maybe I did." Sal Marino rose and actually pulled back Condley's chair for him. His lined face carried a small, victorious smile, as if he had convinced himself that this was indeed his own idea. "All right, Condley. Let's go upstairs."

"OKAY, CONDLEY—"

"—You can call me Brandon."

"Fuck you." Marino nervously surveyed Condley from across a dining table in a small room usually reserved for private dinners. He had brought a king-size bottle of Singha beer, courtesy of a celebrative Ted Simolzak. He began again.

"Anyway, you got your meeting. And I got a, uh, separate engagement later tonight. So what's up?"

"I want to ask you a question—" said Condley.

"—the five-thousand-dollar question," quipped Marino, interrupting him.

Condley took a photograph from the large manila envelope he had been carrying and laid it onto the table.

"This is Theodore Deville. Or at least this was what he looked like thirty-five years ago when he joined the Army. Five years after that picture was taken he escaped from Viet Nam and came to Bangkok."

"That's about when *I* escaped from Viet Nam and came to Bangkok," said Marino cavalierly. "That fucking shithole. I've never been so glad to get out of a place in my life."

"No, Sal," said Condley patiently. "He really did escape. He was wanted on charges of murder and desertion. It took him four years to get out of the country."

Condley dropped another photograph onto the table, this one of Mathew Larkin. "He looked a lot like this guy, and that's why he killed him. Murder number two, at least. Took his passport, which was filled with exit visas to Thailand. I think he came here. I think he's been here ever since."

Condley watched Marino's face carefully as the con man studied the two photographs. No visible reaction. Finally Marino looked up at Condley. "So what's the five-thousand-dollar question? I've got to go."

"Well, if I ask it you're going to leave. So let's just talk for a while."

"That wasn't in the contract."

"How do you know? You didn't read it." Condley peered intently at Marino's face, looking for the slightest gesture. "He had what's called a signature when he killed people. He cut off a hand. Don't ask me why."

"Maybe he's a hand collector." Marino's eyes smoked for one quick moment as if he was remembering something, even though he was pretending to blow the whole thing off. "You know, like some people collect seashells, and others collect stamps. Hands."

"Maybe you knew somebody who looked like that. Or maybe you heard of somebody around here who got his hand collected."

"Is that your question?"

"I was just thinking out loud."

Marino pulled on his beer, avoiding Condley's eyes. He checked his watch. Condley leaned across the table. "I really want to find him, Sal. He killed two of my people."

"Simolzak's after your girl." Marino smirked, taking another long pull from his Singha. "It's so fucking clear."

"What makes you think so?"

"So I guess that's your question?" Marino laughed, pointing at Condley and starting to rise from the chair.

"Sal, if you start for that door I'm going to beat the fuck out of you."

"You got no right to say that to me. I'm a free man."

"I'm paying five thousand dollars for this conversation, and I'll decide when it's over. Now, sit back down."

Marino watched him carefully, measuring his intentions, and then sat back down in the chair. "I've known you for a long time, Condley. And I've never seen you so worked up."

"By the way, she's not my girl. I mean, not seriously." Condley watched him for a moment, then grew quiet. "Look, I am sorry about your daughter. I wanted to say that for a long time."

"She already knew, actually." Marino recovered, warming a bit. "But you didn't have to sleep with her."

"That's different. She asked me!"

"All right, all right, she did. That's done, okay? Over, like history. I don't want to talk about it." Marino stared at the photographs for a long time. "You got any more?"

Condley pulled out another one, dropping it onto the table. "This is a computer enhancement. A guess as to what he would look like today."

Marino's eyes smoldered again, just for a second. He looked up to Condley and then back at the photograph. Finally he took a deep breath, as if daring himself. "I want to give you some serious advice, Brandon."

"Brandon, huh? This must be *seriously* serious."

"You've survived too long to be this fucking naive, man. Don't be talking about this to anybody else. Not out loud, like you just did in the club down there."

Watching Marino's dark face and his skittish, bouncing eyes, a sudden reality settled over Condley, as scary as a heart attack. Perhaps the time zones and the jet lag had indeed numbed his logic. Perhaps he had forgotten that asking a question about a murderer in Australia or Moscow was quite different from asking about one in Bangkok. Especially if—

"He's here."

"You got a pen?"

"A pen?"

"What part of *pen* don't you understand?"

Condley took out a pen and handed it to Marino. The hustler looked darkly around the room, as if for cameras. Then he wrote something on the back of one of the pictures and walked toward the door.

"Where are you going?"

"Stay away from me, man. I'm not kidding. I can't see you again."

Marino walked out of the room, slamming the door behind him.

———————

Marino ignored the others as he walked downstairs into the main room of the club. Muir, Van, Simolzak, and Father Mike were finishing a dinner of seafood, vegetables, and rice. Father Mike appeared quite drunk, on the verge of sleep. His head bobbed up as Marino approached, and he gave the hustler a hopeful smile. "And did we reach a sense of peace?"

"Give me my gun," said Marino, taking his pistol back from Simolzak. He jammed the weapon back inside his ankle holster and headed for the door.

Simolzak called after him. "I owe you some money, Sal."

"Mail it," said Marino, not even turning back around. He pulled the door with one quick motion and was gone.

"Mister Personality," said Simolzak, shrugging as he turned back to the others at the table. "I don't even have an address."

Condley appeared, pointing at Simolzak's plate, his face masked with a small, forced smile. "Can I still order some dinner?"

"Of course," said Simolzak, urging Sapphire off to the kitchen.

"Was he rude to you?" asked Father Mike.

"He has . . . issues," said Condley, taking a chair. Then he hedged, inwardly disturbed by Marino's cold warning. "But he wasn't much help."

Simolzak had moved his chair very close to Van's, his face now animated with an unconcealed glow. Muir caught Condley's attention and secretly raised his eyebrows, looking at the two.

"Ted was telling me about the mountains near Chiang Mai," said Van with a look that was swimming with anticipation. "And the beaches at Phu Ket. He says that we should go to Phu Ket. Have you been to Phu Ket, Cong Ly?"

"Yeah, I've been to Phu Ket."

"And he travels to Hong Kong once a month. Your city! Looking out onto the bay instead of the river, with all the boats. And the little streets filled with shops. Just like you told me, remember?"

"Yes, I remember," said Condley.

"He is a good friend, isn't he? And he has a wonderful life, doesn't he, Cong Ly?"

"A great friend. Time to go," said Condley, standing up and pulling on the back of Van's chair.

"I thought you were hungry," protested Van.

"Sorry, Van," said Hanson Muir, picking up on Condley's intentions. "I have to call Hawaii. It's very important."

"I'll call you tomorrow!" said Simolzak, waving good-bye to them as they neared the door. He was looking at Condley, but it was Van who smiled delightedly and waved back.

"Yes!" she said. "Good night!"

Van held back, walking behind them as they reached the street, oblivious to the danger of their mission, caught up in the romance of the roadside stalls and playful antics that surrounded them. Muir nudged him, speaking quietly. "Didn't you say he was a friend?"

"This is Bangkok, Professor. If it's not nailed down you can steal it, and if she's not in the rack with you she's fair game."

"How was Marino?"

"Scary. Very scary."

Condley held on tightly to the manila envelope as they walked silently down dark streets looking for a cab, suddenly worried that he might lose it, or that someone might burst from the shadows and steal it. But he had already memorized the name Marino had so nervously written on the back of one photograph.

Andrew Brandywine.

CHAPTER THIRTY-ONE

ON THE DARKENED street outside the Vietnamese Embassy, Manh flagged down a *tuk tuk,* a small three-wheeled motor-driven rickshaw, then expertly negotiated a fare of forty *baht* for the driver to take them to Patpong. Dzung was an ungainly afterthought to Manh's commanding presence, standing awkwardly next to him on the curb as they searched for a *tuk tuk* and then sitting stiffly in its cab as the driver motored them madly along the crowded streets.

The late-night air was damp and gamy, like someone else's breath. Dzung found the rush of traffic intimidating, even after the crowded roads of Sai Gon. Everything in Bangkok was bigger and faster. The streets were filled with *tuk tuks,* cars, buses, and trucks instead of the *cyclos,* bicycles, motorbikes, and the less frequent cars of Sai Gon. He stared out at the massiveness of Bangkok through Rip Van Winkle eyes, unable to fully comprehend the fullness and sophistication that surrounded him.

The very size and unfamiliarity of Bangkok made Dzung for the first time deeply afraid of what Manh was going to ask him to do, not in the sense of whether it was right but of whether he could carry out his task at all. Seeing Condley on the plane had chilled him. He was shocked to look up into the eyes of his American friend and amazed when Condley did not recognize him. But mostly he was stunned at himself. His first reaction had not been a fear for Condley's safety but rather an over-whelming relief that he and Manh had not been caught in their little game.

Since that moment he had tortured himself with questions. Why had he not cared? Was it the fear of being embarrassed on the airplane and hauled back into Sai Gon with an uncertain ending in sight, probably indeed a visit to a remote interrogation facility in order to "cleanse" his reentry to the *cyclo* routes of District One? Was it the thrill of this odd freedom that had been given him, filled with the electric falsity of dis-guises, double names, and the chance to become again, if only for one terrible moment, a man of action? Or had Manh subtly reached a point inside him that he never thought would be surrendered, making him once again what the Interior Ministry official would call a "true Vietnamese," willing to kill and even possibly to die for the survival of— what? This government? This system? Or maybe the country itself?

Finally he decided that he did not really care at all. He was free— even if that meant actually being kept on Manh's leash—for a short time in a city that he had never thought he would see, sleeping on a good bed, eating good food, and wearing real shoes. At some point the freedom would end and he would be called upon to perform an act of violence, and there was no guarantee of what would happen to him after that. But how was that any different than combat had been? He had never hated the North Vietnamese soldiers he fought on the battlefield during the war. He was called upon to kill, and he had killed. And what had been his reward back then? Respite from the battlefield for a while, hot meals for a while, a bunk in a barracks for a while, the chance to see his family for a while. There was no difference here.

He ran a hand through his perfectly styled hair and then looked down at the bright blue golf shirt and tan silk trousers that had become his latest costume, replete with white Nike walking shoes. "I'm not used to riding in the cab!" he said to Manh, pointing forward to the *tuk tuk* driver.

"I'm very sorry, Mister Trong," joked Manh. "But we were unable to arrange for your limo tonight."

"What is Patpong?" he asked.

"Patpong is what we hope will never happen to Sai Gon," answered Manh. "Nothing but bars, strip clubs, and prostitutes."

"And Sai Gon is so different?" gibed Dzung. "Or maybe you're saying that you hope they can keep the strip clubs out?"

"Be careful," warned Manh, his voice firm but his smile indicating he was only half serious.

"As a rice exporter it is important that I be able to make such observations," chided Dzung. "In order to improve the quality of the revolution. So Manh, I will be honest. There are far too many prostitutes in Sai Gon. At night when I work, the streets are filled with them. Maybe if we built a few more strip clubs they would be finding happier work."

"Enough social policy," commanded Manh, cupping a cigarette from the wind in the open cab as he lit it. "We are heading to Patpong for a very serious purpose."

"To stare at the bodies of naked Thai women," nodded Dzung.

"We will do that, but that is not our purpose."

"To make love to them, for the good of the revolution."

"Mister Trong, you amaze me with your lack of respect."

"It's what happens when you make a little money," said Dzung, staring wide-eyed out at the mass of traffic and the sky-high urban sprawl that surrounded them.

"No," said Manh, dragging deeply on his cigarette and smiling mysteriously to Dzung. "Our purpose is more singular. Tonight we must turn you into a Thai."

"A Thai!" Dzung smiled, nodding his enthusiasm at the concept. "So how long have I been a Thai?"

"Not actually to be a Thai," said Manh, shouting over the noise of a large truck that was passing them on the thickly traveled street. "Just to be so comfortable that no Thai would notice you or remember that you walked past them in the dark."

"A fish among their fish."

"Yes," nodded Manh. "Like that! A guerrilla in their midst."

They reached Patpong. Manh tossed his cigarette into the street, paid the driver, and they began to saunter slowly along Bangkok's most famous evening entertainment district. The streets, which were closed to traffic at night, were jammed shoulder to shoulder with revelers of every race and nationality, including a surprising number of Thais themselves. Stalls lined the middle of the streets, selling everything from rip-off jewelry to fake designer clothes to pirated music and films. On the curb was a mix of establishments catering to people of the night: open-air bars where customers stood before large-screen TVs showing the fanatically popular Thai kickboxing matches, raucous strip clubs whose music pounded into the night air like jackhammers, and small hotels awaiting that evening's ration of customers who rotated into and out of the strip joints.

It took Dzung less than half a block to relax into the crowd. "Give me a cigarette," he said to Manh.

"Anything you say, all-powerful Mister Trong."

They stopped walking. Dzung lit the cigarette off Manh's match, a few apologetic tourists bumping into them as they passed. And then they began walking again. The doors of a strip joint opened. Four drunken westerners stumbled into the street. The music from the club was very loud. Dzung stopped again, staring through the doorway at a half dozen young Thai women dancing naked on an elevated stage.

Every time you go away, the music blared as the naked women twisted on the stage. *You take a piece of me with you . . .*

"Let's go in there," said Dzung.

"I don't have the money," said Manh simply. "And neither do you."

"The rice business is not as profitable as I thought," grinned Dzung.

"AIDS is a very big problem in this city," warned Manh. "You don't want to die like that."

Dzung watched Manh carefully. It was a chance to test the Interior Ministry agent's intentions without confronting him directly. "If I knew I was going to live, I would worry about AIDS. But if I am going to die in Bangkok, I should at least be rewarded with a woman for one night."

Manh put a hand on Dzung's shoulder. Anyone watching them would have believed they were close, longtime friends. "We are great soldiers."

"We?" asked Dzung, a hint of irony in his eyes.

"The Vietnamese. Great soldiers, Mister Trong. So you're not going to die in Bangkok. As long as you do your duty."

"I already promised you that, Manh."

"You have a rich man's haircut," teased Manh, flipping his fingers for a moment at the front of Dzung's newly styled coiffure. "Maybe if we stand at one of these bars for a while, an American woman would pick you up."

"Do we have money for the bar?" asked Dzung.

"No."

Dzung grinned, knowing he'd been had. "So I guess we keep on walking." He gave Manh another shrewd, measuring look. "What are you going to do with me when we get back to Sai Gon?"

"*When* we get back," nodded Manh. "I like that. That's a very good attitude, Mister Trong."

"Is there an answer?"

Manh shrugged casually. "It will all depend."

"On how much rice I sell?"

"On how well you sell your rice."

"Then I will sell it very well, Manh."

They were reaching the end of Patpong. Manh checked his watch, turning around to stroll back through the district one more time. He put his hand on Dzung's shoulder again.

"I know that," he said.

CHAPTER THIRTY-TWO

"THAT WILL BE Paul Archer," said Condley with a casual certainty.

Hanson Muir settled back into the large wicker chair. "And how do you know, oh mighty sleuth?"

"He's the only guy in Bangkok who would be wearing a pair of old leather-heeled Florsheim shoes."

Muir listened to the approach of heels clicking on the marble tiles of the hotel lobby. They were sitting at a table in the Elephant Bar. It was eleven in the morning and they were alone in the bar, which was closed. But that was the reason Condley had asked Archer to meet them there.

"It could be a woman in high heels," reasoned Muir.

"No, Professor, a woman in high heels walks faster—*click click click,* you know, because she's up on her toes. It's a man."

"Bets," said Muir.

"You buy beer tonight."

"Only if we go back to the Cezanne."

Condley grinned indulgently. "You liked that place."

"Frog was a very sweet little woman." Muir caught himself. "Okay, I liked her. But only as a friend. Somebody to talk to, you understand."

"A window into the culture, so to speak," said Condley.

"Precisely," said the professor. "An anthropological discovery."

"Someone to be studied close-up, as it were."

"Brandon, you know I'm all talk."

Archer turned in to the bar, dressed in his usual suit and tie, looking frazzled and carrying his briefcase. Condley exultantly turned to Muir. "I win."

"So you're telling me I have to go back to that bar tonight?"

"If you pay."

"Better leave Van back here at the hotel," winked Muir. "Your friend Simolzak plays a very fast hand."

The two men stood, greeting Archer. From the stiffness of his expression and the abrupt manner in which he shook their hands, it was clear that the CIA agent was not very happy to be seeing them. He nodded curtly to them, taking a chair at the table and immediately putting his briefcase on his lap. He avoided their eyes as he opened it.

"Sorry to be late, gentlemen. It took me an hour to get here in the traffic."

"We could have saved you a trip. I told you I'd come to the embassy."

"Mister Condley, what I definitely do not need right now is for you to show up at the embassy. You're on your own here, I emphasized that yesterday."

"Whoa," said Condley, surprised at Archer's tone. "Easy, there. I just asked for some help."

"Sorry," said Archer. "You've made things a little tense over at the embassy right now."

"Me?" said Condley, folding his hands below his chin and peering studiously at the CIA agent. "Or Andrew Brandywine?"

"A very poetic name," nodded Hanson Muir. "Andy. Brandy. Wine. In fact, it sounds totally made up to me."

Archer pulled out a folder and put his briefcase on the floor. He had a sour look on his face, as if he'd just finished a glass of buttermilk. He held the folder close to his chest, as if he were playing a poker hand, flipping through a sheaf of pages, grimacing here and there, and then finally looked back up at Condley.

"We know a good deal about what he does. But we don't know very much at all about who he is."

"You fill in my blanks and I'll fill in yours," said Condley.

Archer took in a deep breath, measuring Condley. Either he was under specific orders regarding the matter of Andrew Brandywine or he somehow had decided over the past day that Condley represented a way of doing things that repulsed him. Or maybe both. "First, I want you to understand a few things," he warned. "And I'm very serious about this, Mister Condley. We have limitations on what we can do on foreign soil. We are not the world's policemen. It is not within our power to solve every problem, criminal or otherwise, that is brought to our attention. When a host government wants our assistance, we can provide it. Sometimes, that is. Within the boundaries of law and policy. And sometimes a host government will assist us if we ask for help. If it fits their own national interest, that is. But there are a lot of things that go on in this world that are beyond our ability to control. Are we in agreement here?"

Condley looked at Muir, and then back to Paul Archer. "I don't know what the fuck you're talking about."

"Yes, you do," said Archer. "That's what makes me leery of sharing this information with you. You do know what I'm talking about. You've operated out here, Condley, so don't play stupid on me. Shit happens all the time, and if it doesn't directly affect American interests we're limited to watching it. That's all, watching it. Unless we're asked to play. And we decidedly have not been asked to play in this one."

"I was going to leave you out of this," said Condley lightly. "But we got something specific, so I thought I'd let you play."

"It's not funny," said Archer.

"I know. It's a terrible dilemma. Feel better for telling me?"

"Actually, I do."

"Ready to continue?"

"No, but I have a lunch back at the embassy, so we may as well get on with it."

"An honest answer," said Condley. "I appreciate that, Paul."

Archer gave a quick look around the bar, ensuring that they were alone. "The ambassador has asked me to inform you that this briefing is classified secret. Any divulgence of the information I provide you can result in your being prosecuted for a felony. Do you gentlemen understand that?"

"Of course we do," answered Condley. "So, Andrew Brandywine?"

"Apparently an Australian national," said Archer, flipping through a page or two of his notes. "I'm still working on that."

He looked up at Condley, his face again tight with an undefined anxiety, and pulled a map from his folder, laying it on the table. "All right, I don't know why they gave me the authority to tell you this, but here's the deal. For years the Thais have turned their backs on what I guess we'd have to call a drug highway that runs through their country, connecting opium grown in Burma—or, what the hell, Myanmar, I guess we call it now—to export outlets in Viet Nam."

Archer began running his hand over the map as he spoke. "The Burmese end of it has been run by a couple of warlords just off the western border of Thailand. Generally in this area, right here. They grow it, harvest it, and process it into heroin in their own labs. Very sophisticated operation. They then transport it through Thailand and turn it over to the Vietnamese side right here in Bangkok."

"How do they transport it?" interrupted Condley.

"Trucks," shrugged Archer. "At night."

"Avoid the rush hour," said Muir. "Sort of like UPS."

"Exactly like UPS," said Archer, returning to the map. "The Vietnamese pick it up in Bangkok, shoot along the highway across the Cambodian border and then down to Sai Gon, keep some of it for their trouble, and ship the rest out of Sai Gon Harbor to parts unknown."

"Load and reload?" asked Condley.

"No load or reload. They swap the trucks on every trip, two trucks each direction," said Archer. "The Burmese drivers get out of the loaded trucks, the Vietnamese drivers pay for the load and get in. The Vietnamese drivers take the new load of heroin into Viet Nam, the Burmese take the money and the empty trucks back to, whatever they call it, Myanmar, and the beat goes on. It all happens pretty fast, in the middle of the night."

"Why don't you stop it?" Muir, incredulous, asked the question.

"Lots of payoffs inside the Thai government and among some very powerful families," said Archer immediately. "Some pretty important people involved. Same in Viet Nam. This isn't an action that's actually supported by either government, but some highly influential people have been getting rich off it. Megarich. The official position of the Thai government is that it isn't happening at all. And their quiet position to us is that it doesn't really concern them directly, so they'd rather not get into a brawl with the Burmese on one side of them and the Vietnamese on the other. Kind of like airspace, except it's roads. The stuff isn't grown here, and it isn't sold here. It just passes through."

"Not to mention that stopping it would, shall we say, reduce the revenues of certain, as you called them, pretty important people?" quipped Muir.

"So Brandywine is involved," said Condley.

"He's the purser on the runs." Archer squirmed in his chair, his face buried again in the notes of his folder. "The money guy. He makes the deals and he runs the exchanges."

"What do you know about him? Tell me everything."

Archer watched Condley nervously. "I know what you're thinking, but you can't do this. It will blow up in all our faces. We can't stop you but we can't help you either, Mister Condley."

"I'm not asking for help. I just want some information."

"These guys are well-trained and well-armed. You don't have a prayer. I'm not kidding you."

"Brandon," said Muir. "Listen to him. He's a very realistic man."

"I want to know about Brandywine," said Condley. "A very good source told me this is our guy Deville. You know Sal Marino?"

"Sal Marino?" Archer shook his head dismissively. "We've followed Sal for a long time. How do you think he got busted in Japan? Not your most credible witness in a trial."

"I've known him for twenty years," said Condley. "I even—uh, dated his daughter at one point. He'd never bullshit me about something like this."

"But what do you know about him and Brandywine?" Archer had become intense, with the demeanor of a defense counsel. "For all we know, your friend Marino is playing off a grudge. Maybe Brandywine crossed him up over something. Maybe he thinks Brandywine got him thrown into jail in the Japan deal. He could be setting us all up, Mister Condley. He isn't too happy with our own drug-enforcement people, and he'd be laughing his rear end off if we bumbled around and embarrassed the American drug effort here. A true Sal Marino moment, setting off two enemies against each other."

Condley grunted, folding his arms in disgust. "No wonder you guys never solve shit around here."

"We put Sal Marino away."

"Now, there's a major victory. A true kingpin."

Archer took a deep breath, looking again inside his folder. "Okay. All right. Brandywine is a rather mysterious fellow. I don't think we even have a picture of him. According to local lore, he's been living in the mountains west of Chiang Mai for decades. He's got his own army up there. Apparently he fought and killed his way up through the ranks of the drug business, so to speak. He's the Svengali of the Vietnamese connection. He set it up, he runs the show, he pays the bills, and he keeps the money."

"How often do they run the trucks?"

"Once a week. They've never been challenged, so it's a clockwork operation." Archer rubbed his temples. "I hate to say this, but the next drop-off is probably tonight."

"Where?"

"Klong Toey." Archer sighed now, as if defeated. "Okay, here's how it works. Every night in Klong Toey they slaughter around three thousand hogs for the Bangkok market. Thai pork is famous."

Condley gave Archer a knowing grin. "I sold a few hogs there back in the late seventies. When I worked security for the Black Diamond Food Group."

"You do get around, Mister Condley," said Archer, recognizing the company as an old CIA front. He loosened up a bit. "Take any goats to Iran?"

"Lots of goats. A nasty place, Iran."

"Right. Okay. Then you know they kill the hogs in Klong Toey at night, because there's no refrigeration. It's cooler then, and they can deliver the meat to the shops and restaurants at first light. A lot of hogs are raised in the west. So the Burmese trucks bring in hogs from Chiang Mai along with their heroin. It makes the trucks less conspicuous when they're heading into Bangkok, just in case some dumb police officer who hasn't gotten the word stops them on the highway. And once the trucks are switched at Klong Toey, it's not unusual to see empty trucks heading back toward Chiang Mai in the morning. Same with the Vietnamese trucks. They bring in a load of hogs that they pick up after they cross the Cambodian border. After they're slaughtered they drop off the meat in Bangkok—legitimate business, there—and hit the road. Bring back a load of stereos and TVs in the trucks with the heroin."

"Two truckloads of heroin a week." Condley let out a low whistle. "Very serious money, even if you're just taking a payoff."

"Millions," agreed Archer. "I couldn't even put a number on it."

"Pigs!" exclaimed an amazed Muir. "A brilliant idea, actually. What policeman in his right mind would want to search a truck filled with stinking, stomping, screaming hogs?"

"Exactly," shrugged Archer. He straightened his tie, a signal that he was finished. "Look. I've given you what I know. But I've also done my best to warn you. If you try to pull off something stupid, you're not only going to get killed, you're going to embarrass the government of the United States of America."

"And how would that happen, Paul?" asked Condley, weary of the CIA agent's persistent nervousness. "All you have to do is deny that you knew what I was up to. Tell them that my track record indicates I was down in Klong Toey trying to fuck a pig."

"We'll definitely do that," said Archer, closing his briefcase and standing. "Seriously, Mister Condley, I'd suggest that your most logical course of action would be to rethink your whole involvement here. Give us some time. If we can establish that Brandywine is indeed this man Deville, and if you can get us something more concrete regarding his past criminal activities, we've got a case."

"And he'll be laughing his ass off, living up in the mountains of Nepal," said Condley. "Or maybe Uzbekistan. I've heard it's no problem getting a visa to go there."

"You don't really need a visa to get into Uzbekistan. It's a pretty porous border, mostly with people trying to get out."

"Hey, he got the joke."

Archer hesitated, then said it anyway. "We could arrange for the Thai police to arrest you, you know. Just take you out of the marketplace for a few days."

Condley measured Archer's nervous eyes and the way he was squeezing and relaxing his hands, and he finally understood the CIA agent's reluctance to help. "You do that and I'll have to tell the press all about this little classified briefing and how the American government has been sitting on its ass while certain of its friends have grown rich on heroin payoffs."

"That could get you killed." Archer thought about it for a moment, and then shrugged. "But then again, if you do something stupid tonight, that will get you killed too. So either way I've done my duty." He waved perfunctorily and turned away. "Don't say you weren't warned, Condley."

Condley called to him as Archer neared the doorway. "Worried about your career, are you?"

No answer. Archer's leather heels clicked more and more faintly as he walked along the lobby, heading for the hotel's front door.

"So, you win on the leather heels," smiled Muir. "Florsheims. What an ear you have, Brandon."

"I used to own a pair. A very characteristic sound."

"I guess that means I buy the Singha at the Cezanne tonight?"

"Nice try, Professor," said Condley. "Frog will have to wait. Tonight we go to Klong Toey."

"I knew that, actually." And then Muir's eyes went horrifically wide. "Brandon, it isn't the war."

"What do you mean?"

"You finding Deville," said Muir.

"Yeah, it is."

"No, listen to me. Why are the Vietnamese so nervous about what you're doing? You heard what Archer said. Some very powerful people in all three of these countries have been involved. So it isn't the war, not to them. Somebody in the Vietnamese government knows about this. And they're protecting the people who are running drugs with Deville."

Condley grunted, unimpressed. "It may be drugs to them, but it's the war to me."

CHAPTER THIRTY-THREE

VAN WAS NOT in the room when he returned. Somehow it did not surprise him. He walked quickly through it onto the terrace, trying at first to convince himself that she might have gone swimming. The pool in the courtyard just below their window was filled with lazing tourists, but she was not among them. Back inside the room, he noticed that none of her clothes were laying out near the still-unmade bed, where they had been when he went down for breakfast with Hanson Muir.

So she was gone. It did hurt, but he quickly accepted it, even telling himself that it was for the best.

He went to the closet and then the bathroom, deciding to compare what she had left behind with what she might have taken with her. Her side of the closet was empty. She had brought so little to Bangkok that it had fit inside one small cloth bag, anyway. Over the past two days she had taken him on a minor shopping spree, but still that had amounted only to a couple of changes of clothes. Nice clothes, to be sure. Van was a woman of surprisingly good taste and decidedly large appetites. But they were all gone, as was the swimming suit.

The only thing of any value that she left behind was in the bathroom. On the counter next to the sink, just in front of the ceiling-high mirror, was a bottle of Francois Petain's perfume. Looking at the bottle of perfume, Condley started laughing, despite himself. Van did have a wicked sense of humor, even when she was laughing at herself.

A sealed hotel envelope with his name on the outside was underneath the perfume bottle, as if the perfume had been left as a gift. Opening the envelope, he saw that she had written him a letter in her careful schoolgirl scrawl, switching back and forth between English and Vietnamese. *What do I have?* she asked him in the note. *I am smart, I know, but so are others who have a better education. I can work hard, but doing what? For who, and where? I do have my beauty, though. When I compare myself to other people, I know that is my strongest weapon. But only for a short while, Cong Ly. You do not like this, but my beauty is my business! It is my college degree! It is all I have, and if I cannot find a good life while I still have my beauty I will have nothing! Or should I ignore the power of my beauty and grow old in Viet Nam, remembering that once a rich man loved me, and once another man took me for a week to see Bangkok?*

And you, Cong Ly. I do think I could have loved you. But you love Viet Nam more than you could ever love a woman.

Someone knocked on the door. He opened it to see Hanson Muir in the hallway, looking like a sumo wrestler in a white terry-cloth robe.

"I heard you laughing."

"I'm having a great time."

"Glad to hear it. Since you're going to make me work tonight, I thought I'd take a dip in the pool and then nap for a while. Is that okay?"

"Good idea, Professor."

Muir caught Condley's ironic smile and poked his head nosily into the room. "Where's Van?"

"Looks like she split."

"Then why were you laughing?"

"Because I was starting to take myself too seriously."

Muir stuttered a few times, trying to say something meaningful, the nurturing mundanity of his own life not having equipped him to understand how Condley might be feeling at that moment. "That's a terribly ungrateful thing for her to do," he finally managed to say.

"Not really," shrugged Condley. "It took guts, actually. She saw the brass ring and she grabbed it." He walked into the bathroom and retrieved the bottle of perfume, ceremoniously handing it to Muir. "Here, Professor. A present for your wife, from Francois Petain."

Muir took it, daring now to smile. *"Tigress,"* he said, reading the label. "Whooee. It must make you go wild, huh, Brandon? I'm almost afraid to let my wife put some of this on." He gave Condley a concerned look. "Are you all right? What are you going to do?"

"About Van?" He shrugged. "Nothing for now. I've got a lot of things to worry about before tonight. She doesn't even make the top five."

Muir pocketed the perfume. "Do you need my help?"

"Go take your nap, Professor."

THE DOORMAN AT the hotel told him that a large white man about his age had picked Van up about an hour before. The man seemed to have been an American, spoke pretty good Thai, and had arrived in a chauffeur-driven black BMW. Simolzak was not in his office when Condley called, and he decided not to leave a message. He knew where his old friend lived.

As the hotel ferry made its way upriver he sat alone on the fantail, leaning grandly back against the seat cushions with his arms spread wide on either side of him. Just above his head, a large Thai flag flapped lazily in the dank and gentle wind. The sun beat heavily against his face and arms, hot as a lightbulb. He ignored the dozens of nearby tourists. He had absolutely nothing in common with them. They were zoo-kept, sitting with their sun hats and their street maps along the canopied side rails of the boat, pointing and chattering as if the fifteen-minute ride to the Oriental Hotel's dock were somehow a grand Asian adventure. And he was certifiably wild, country-bred and jungle-trained, as untamable as a mountain lion.

The ferry churned against the wavelets and his mind floated above him to a place that neared nirvana, asking him when he would finally cease all this incessant struggling. The river surrounded him, timeless, deep, and powerful, its current no different than when he had first seen it or even when Rudyard Kipling had sat on the grand old Oriental Hotel's veranda more than a century before and penned his poetry.

> *Ship me somewheres east of Suez, where the best is*
> *   like the worst,*
> *Where there aren't no Ten Commandments an' a*
> *   man can raise a thirst;*
> *For the temple-bells are callin', an' it's there that I*
> *   would be—*
> *By the old Moulmein Pagoda, looking lazy at the sea.*

The ancient Chao Phraya's currents were the same and yet everything else about it had become vastly different, as had he in the decades since he had first come to Bangkok. The ferry made its way slowly past hotels and sky-high apartment buildings, making him think of all the changes in his own life since that first moment, just after he had left Viet Nam, raw with anger over the loss of a war and forever scarred by the death of a woman he had truly loved. A woman who had just as truly loved him. Yes, that was different. *Yeu,* as Van would have put it, not *thuong.* An unending, lifetime love.

The simpler, cleaner journey that the river had taken before the tall buildings and the factories had come to Bangkok was now forever gone. And so was the volatile but nonetheless simple life that he himself had led. Gone, the time of good and bad, right and wrong that drowned itself in blood, leaving lost visions of life and death but mostly death and more death. In its place, the enemies and allies that his returning years had squeezed together until there simply was no difference, leaving only friends. Gone, the innocence that had forever died with Mai, the marriage and babies that did not happen. In its place, surrounding him, the promises that took one turn around the track and always came back as lies.

He missed the river's unpolluted beauty, in the days when the *klongs* that fed into it were open and healthy, dotted with fleets of small boats and floating markets rather than covered over with concrete and turned into sewers. He missed the simple thatch homes that once lined its banks and the time when smiling women could lean over from their houseboats and dip their cook pans into it without coming up with a bowlful of mud and disease. He missed it all, as deeply as he missed what life might have brought him had fate dealt him a different hand.

Or maybe it was just the thought that Van had split, even though he knew that running away was her own best shot. And the knowledge that before the evening ended he himself might end up dead.

———————

HE TOOK A *tuk tuk* from the Oriental Pier to Sukhumvit, not even haggling with the surprised driver when he asked for the outrageous price of four hundred *baht*. It took an hour in the thick, impossible traffic. At the major intersections the policemen stood on boxes, wearing white gloves and gas masks, twin metaphors for the modern Thais. The Thais were a beautiful and gentle people who loved fine things; hence the cops in clean white gloves. And the gas masks were a sign that their leap into prosperity had rewarded them, Pandora-like, with a set of imported ills that they in their innocence had not been able to anticipate. Intransigent traffic. Air that choked the lungs. And the persistent, unending whirlwind of AIDS.

Simolzak had lived on a quiet, tree-lined *soy* in Sukhumvit for more than twenty years. Condley stopped the *tuk tuk* a block from the house, not wanting the lawn-mowerlike engine to signal his arrival. The yard in front of the narrow, two-story house held its very own jungle of overgrown tropical plants. Simolzak let the yard grow wild on purpose, to mask the teak-filled splendor of the home itself.

The BMW was parked in the narrow driveway that ran along the side of the house. Condley waved casually to Simolzak's driver, who sat dozing in the car. The driver, who also functioned as Simolzak's bodyguard, recognized him immediately and waved back absently. As he passed the driver, both men raised their hands prayerlike underneath their chins in the Buddhist greeting of peace.

He knew the front door would be locked, and he knew that the back door would not be. That was just Simolzak's way. Deliveries were often made to the back door, where Simolzak also kept a smaller office in case clients needed to meet him at his home on short notice.

He walked around to the rear of the home and silently tested the doorknob, then pushed the door open without a sound. Simolzak's back porch was cluttered with floor-to-ceiling shelves that held stacks of files from cases he had pursued over the years. A bundle of new mail was on the floor. The door that led into the main part of his house was wide open, and Condley moved through it with the quiet grace of a panther on the prowl.

He could hear them upstairs. Simolzak was talking throatily to her, hoarse whispers and urgent little laughs. She was screaming high in her throat, not words, just screams, in persistent, uncontrollable pants that came again and again and again.

They did not see him standing in the doorway as she romped on top of Simolzak's huge frame, straddling him with her hands on his chest, her back arched and her breasts flailing wildly in the air. Her back was to him and her long hair swung from side to side as if accentuating the abandonment of her screams. And then finally Simolzak noticed him.

"Brandon," he said, clutching the top of her thighs in an effort to slow her down. "Oh, Jesus!"

"Hi, guys."

She rolled from Simolzak's belly and clutched a sheet around her shoulders, crouching on her knees on the mattress. She was still panting heavily. Her eyes were wild and her hair was a sweaty tangle that stuck to her face and neck. She started looking from Simolzak to Condley and back again, as if waiting for one or the other to rescue her from her dilemma.

Simolzak sat up in the bed, slowly pulling a part of the sheet over his crotch. His eyes were glued to Condley's, looking for clues. Condley leaned against the doorway, holding Simolzak's gaze. Both men were fighters, and both knew the other would fight or die if the wrong words were said.

"I can explain this," Simolzak finally said.

"Look—" started Condley.

"No! Don't say anything, Cong Ly!" Van cut him off, raising two fists full of sheets up to her chin, not waiting for the inevitable to play out. "I'm not going back to Sai Gon!"

"She called me," said Simolzak. "She asked me. Is that any different than Sal Marino's daughter asking you?"

Despite himself, Condley started chuckling softly. "Keep the girl," he said. "I need your gun."

Simolzak glanced tensely down toward the floor. Condley knew there would be a pistol underneath the bed. "Can I trust you if I give it to you?" he asked.

"Can I trust you if you reach for it?" said Condley.

"Brandon! Of course you can. We've been friends for a very long time. The last thing I want to do is kill you."

"Then you can trust me."

Slowly, Simolzak reached under the bed, pulling out a new nine-millimeter Glock. "It's loaded, Brandon," he said. "There's an extra magazine in my desk, plus a box of ammo."

"Give it to me." As Simolzak started forward, Condley pointed quickly at him, a warning. "Turn it around so the barrel is toward you." Simolzak turned the weapon around, giving it to Condley handle-first, then lay back on the bed.

Condley checked the pistol, pushing the slide back to make sure it was loaded. Then he pointed it at Simolzak. "Get up. You owe me five thousand dollars."

"Now, wait a minute, Brandon! That was a fee!"

"Fuck your fucking fee, get me the money!"

Simolzak stood warily, starting to dress, but Condley moved toward him. "No clothes, no pit stops. Hands in the air. Move it!"

Simolzak moved slowly from the bedroom and down the stairs, naked, with his hands above his head. "This is unethical, Brandon. That was a deal."

"Let's just say I'm giving you a reciprocal charge for transporting a woman from Sai Gon."

Simolzak reached his desk and began opening a drawer. Condley nudged him away, making him step back, ensuring that a second weapon was not inside. He took out the extra magazine for the pistol, as well as a box of ammunition. An envelope containing cash was also in the drawer. Condley tossed it to Simolzak.

"Five thousand. Count it out."

Simolzak grumbled as he counted out the hundred-dollar bills. "I already sent Marino his thousand."

"Write it off," said Condley. "Business loss."

"That pistol is worth at least five hundred dollars."

"I'll get it back to you."

"I'm not sure you'll be that lucky, Brandon."

"You'll have to take that risk."

They watched each other carefully as Simolzak reached out with the wad of bills, lest the larger man try to wrestle the gun out of Condley's hand. Condley pocketed the bills, never taking his eyes off Simolzak. And then he backed slowly out of the room.

As Condley reached the back door, Simolzak dropped his arms, standing huge and naked in the inner doorway. And finally he gave Condley a smile and a wave.

"Are we still friends?"

"Shit, yes," said Condley.

"Be careful, Brandon."

Condley raised his head, as if looking upstairs. "She's a sweet girl, Ted. Don't fuck her up."

"How'd we ever end up this way?" asked Simolzak.

"Hey, man. It's called Bangkok."

Condley waved back to his old friend. He opened the door, beginning to leave. And as he left they both were laughing.

CHAPTER THIRTY-FOUR

THEY LEFT THE Vietnamese Embassy just after lunch, dressed as laborers in old T-shirts and plain cotton slacks, each carrying a beaten knapsack under his shoulder, and walked for more than two hours under the afternoon sun. Manh decided that Dzung should wear his new walking shoes instead of sandals and had taken them into the basement of the embassy the night before and dyed them black.

As they walked, the ever-meticulous Manh stopped Dzung every few blocks to quiz him on key landmarks so that he could remember them later in the confusion and the dark. He had demanded that a dinner of rice and boiled chicken be made in the embassy kitchen and put in the knapsacks for each of them, lest food from the roadside stalls cause a sudden diarrhea that might abort their mission. The knapsacks also held a liter of bottled water, a change of clothes, and, in Dzung's, his loaded Heckler & Koch P7 pistol.

Manh had personally loaded the bullets into the pistol, wearing plastic gloves and carefully wiping down each bullet, as well as the casings. Dzung could not understand why the Interior Ministry agent went to all the trouble with the bullets. No registry held his fingerprints. Perhaps, he reasoned, it was simply Manh's fascination with old movies. Or perhaps Manh thought that such a sophisticated approach would steer investigators away from a Vietnamese suspect once they found the sanitized casings. Or maybe, shrugged Dzung, there was a new form of science that could pick up his body identification from oils left on the bullets and beam the information up into a satellite and then cause the satellite to instantly make him glow so that the police could come and pick him up. Who knew? Whatever it was, it wouldn't work. He had not touched any of the bullets.

They walked south for a long time, toward the distant, curving Chao Phraya River. After an hour the city slowly began to change. After a few more blocks they entered a neighborhood that seemed to have been built only yesterday, perhaps by using waste materials from old construction sites. The few people on the streets walked listlessly under the scorching sun, viewing Dzung and Manh with little interest. Others sat motionless under outdoor stalls, some numb from opium and others merely enduring the heat.

"It smells worse than District Four," said Dzung, looking around them at a mass of ramshackle, open-air houses made of plywood and loose tin set along mud pathways.

"That's because there are no hogs in District Four," said Manh.

"Yes, another benefit of the revolution," said Dzung. "That it protects my family from having to eat such meat."

Manh ignored him, having become deeply intense in this new environment. He pointed in front of them, where four open-air slaughter pens marked the center of another clearing. "They kill them there."

A dozen huge hogs squealed and cowered in one concrete pen, early arrivals for that night's slaughter. A muscular, bare-chested young man with tattoos on both his thighs stood in the dirt at the center of the pen, hacking away at the carcass of one hog that had died early from the heat. Concrete gutters ran along the edges of each of the pens. Much of the blood and debris from the daily slaughter would be washed down the gutters to the river, a block below them. Even now the gutters buzzed with flies, stinking horribly with pools of stagnant water from the killings of the night before.

Just off to their left, on a powder-dry half acre turned into a playground, a dozen little children pretended to chase an uninterested dog. A shirtless man walked toward them along a mud pathway. His muscles were young and hard, but his face was devastated with wrinkles. His eyes were so red that they appeared to be burned by fire. A naked boy ran happily toward him from the little plot of dirt. The man grabbed his young son in his arms, turned him upside down, and put the boy's penis in his mouth.

Dzung walked a few steps further, uneasy in these raw surroundings. "What do they call this place?"

"They call it Klong Toey," said Manh, enjoying his status as an expert travel guide. "We are at the very end of the district, in what is called the slaughterhouse section. The river is down there, on the other side of these buildings."

It was four o'clock. Even as they walked, the trucks began arriving, one at a time, bringing the hugest hogs Dzung had ever seen to the concrete pens. Young men with hard bellies and shattered faces and wild tattoos were waiting for the hogs. They quickly unloaded each truckload at the pens' open gates and shuttled the hogs inside. Soon the slaughter would begin, and it would last all night.

"So, this is the place where I will . . . sell my rice," said Dzung, watching Manh's face for clues as he spoke.

"Yes," said Manh simply. "But we still have preparations to make. Nothing can go wrong. We will get only one chance."

"I know that," said Dzung. "You've told me a thousand times." He checked Manh's face again. "Where?"

"There, I think," said Manh, pointing to the road just before them, where two open-bedded trucks were now waiting to unload their hogs. He stopped on the road, squinting at the trucks for a moment. "Think of yourself right here, Mister Trong. In the dark. Think hard! Get your bearings." He looked at Dzung, his dark eyes searingly alive, then began walking toward a narrow path that bordered one of the concrete gutters. "Now down here. Follow me!"

Dzung caught up with him and began following him down the dirt path. *Cong Ly? Here?* "Who?" he asked.

"Whoever I tell you to," said Manh. "You must not think of a person, Mister Trong. You must keep your mind totally clear of that. You will be shooting a target, that is all. It has no face, no name. You cannot afford to personalize this mission. You will shoot only when I tell you to, and only the person I tell you to shoot."

"Tonight?" asked Dzung. The path dropped slightly, and through the little slum of makeshift hooches he saw the wide, churning river.

"Tonight, I am fairly sure," said Manh. "But there is a possibility that he may not be here tonight."

"If he is not here, what do we do?"

"We come back another night."

Dzung smiled hopefully. "So, we would have to wait here in Bangkok until our target makes himself available?"

"He will be here tonight," said Manh.

"For sure?"

"Not for sure. But you should count on it."

"No," said Dzung, "I think I will not count on it."

He watched Manh carefully, torn between the hope that the moment might indeed never come and the sure knowledge that if it did he would carry out his duty. There was indeed no other option in this place of dust and hogs, unless he wished to die himself. And wasn't that the essence of combat anyway, to kill so that you yourself might live?

They were very near the river. Manh scolded him. "Why are you saying that to me?"

Dzung forced a grin, making light of it. "He should take his time, Manh. We could go to Patpong again. And in the end he will only die anyway."

They reached the river. Manh stopped, looking curiously back at Dzung. "You are the calmest man I have ever worked with."

"I've done this many times before," said Dzung. "So stop worrying."

"Not this," said Manh.

"No, but this is easier than combat." Dzung shrugged at Manh's surprised expression. "Here I will be in control. I will have a target and after I finish with my target I can leave. Do you know how long combat lasts? You can never leave. Combat lasts forever."

"If you make even one small mistake you will be dead."

"So you care about that, Manh? That I might die?"

"If you die, I will never have known you," Manh said flatly. "I will have disappeared. You have no identification papers with you. Your fingerprints are not recorded. Your pistol will be traced to the old West German Army." He smiled, pleased with himself, looking out at the river as he spoke. "From your stylish haircut, maybe they will think you are a Vietnamese who came to Bangkok from America."

"Yes," agreed Dzung. "I know all that. But you do care? That I might die, I mean?"

Manh turned back to Dzung for a long moment, saying nothing. Then he put a hand on Dzung's shoulder. "Why do you think I am preparing you so thoroughly? From the moment you shoot your target, our mission is a success. The rest of it is taking care of you."

"I am surprised at myself, but I believe you," said Dzung.

"I told you the night your baby died that I would take care of you."

"No," corrected Dzung. "You said you would take care of my family. No matter what happened to me."

"Well, I will take care of you," Manh said, his face slowly working into a warning grin. "But if you screw things up, it will be my duty to disappear."

The river was so brown at this turn that it seemed thick, like a turbulent current of gravy. The concrete gutters from the slaughter pens made neat little rows, their troughs ending just inside the water along its banks. They saw an old man slowly bathing, standing thigh-deep a hundred feet downstream from the gutters. He was wearing brown shorts and was rubbing a rag over his body. His chest and stomach were covered with a rash, no doubt from the bacteria in the river that he thought was cleansing him.

"So, the plan. After you hit your target you run down the path to the river," instructed Manh. "And then you throw the pistol, as hard as you can throw it, toward the other side. They would never dredge this river. How could they? Just throw it hard, and then run back upriver. Upriver, remember. Along the bank. Make a triangle in your mind. A hundred meters upriver, then cut to your right, and you will be at the park where the man kissed the little boy's penis. I will meet you in the park, and we will walk slowly back to the embassy. If I am not in the park, don't wait for me. At the slightest suspicion I will go back to the embassy by myself and wait for you there. If that happens, you must remember the landmarks. Do not try to talk with anyone. Do not let anyone clearly see your face. Do you have any questions, Mister Trong?"

"Why did he kiss the little boy's penis?" wondered Dzung.

"I do not know," said Manh. And then he shook his head, amazed at Dzung's serenity.

They made their way back up the dirt path to the concrete pens. The trucks were now lined up six deep, and the killing had begun. Hogs were screeching and howling with an almost human sound as the muscular men tied them down and hacked them up.

Just across the street from the slaughter pens, a very old woman sat on a wooden platform inside an open-air home, smoking a cigarette. Near her, a kitten cuddled up against a sleeping rabbit, and a gray ferret slithered snakelike in and out of the raised boards that made up her floor. The woman was looking toward the pens where the hogs were being killed as if it were a TV soap opera.

Manh took out a booklet and approached her, forcing his hands prayerfully underneath his chin and speaking a few sentences in Thai. She shrugged and then nodded, pointing to a corner of her shack. And then she went back to watching her evening show.

"She says we can eat here if we like," said Manh, walking into the shack and taking a seat on the floor. "I don't know what she's looking at. She seems to have very bad cataracts."

"So she won't remember us?" asked Dzung cautiously, watching her face as he sat near Manh.

"What does that matter?" shrugged Manh. He opened up his pack and took out the boiled chicken and rice they had cooked in the embassy kitchen. "Shoot what you're told to shoot, Mister Trong. As long as none of their people get hurt, they won't care at all."

CHAPTER THIRTY-FIVE

HANSON MUIR WAS waiting for Condley at a table on the back terrace of the Oriental Hotel, idly nursing a beer as he looked longingly at a firmly built German woman in a string bikini who was sunbathing at the edge of the nearby swimming pool. Sharing a drink and a snack at the Oriental had been Condley's idea. It seemed a nice way to kick things off, sitting next to the river under the smiling eyes of doting young waitresses who fawned over their every move, in the shadow of the grand hotel that had been there long before they were born and would still be there long after they were gone. The Oriental was expensive but Condley had recaptured his money, so at that moment expensive appealed to him. He took great delight in the idea of paying the bill with a wad of Ted Simolzak's cash.

"You should buy her a lemonade," said Condley, following the professor's gaze as he took his seat.

"We don't have time for that, do we?"

Condley checked his watch, eyeing Muir. "It depends on how fast you work."

"Dreadfully slow," chuckled Muir, patting his ample stomach with one hand. "You think in terms of minutes, Brandon, and I measure things in terms of centuries."

"Better hold the lemonade."

"Did you find Van?"

Condley beamed, raising his shirt slightly and tapping the pistol so that Muir could see. "I traded her for a Glock."

"Simolzak?"

"Sort of," said Condley. "Or I should say, for now. It could have been anybody. She wanted out."

"Sorry about that, Brandon."

"We've got more important things to think about."

Professor Muir's beer had sweated a little pool of water on the outdoor table. He twirled it, looking far upstream toward the setting sun. "Archer called. Sal Marino's dead."

Condley grunted, as if he was not surprised. "How many hands did he have when they found him?"

"One, actually." Muir's eyes were wide, and his face was lit with apprehension. Finally he could hold it back no more. "Is that all you have to say about this? The man is dead, Brandon. This was a rather prompt response, don't you think? I just met him last night. He's dead and his hand is gone. I doubt we have many copycat killers out there who know what we're after. So what does this tell us?"

"It means Mister Deville is in town," said Condley, "and evidently he's pissed."

"How would he know you met with Marino?"

"We don't know what he knew, and we don't know why he did it."

"Of course we do! Brandon, don't play games with me, not when we're about to try to—apprehend this man."

Condley's eyes had gone molten, as if there was so much burning inside him that his brain had turned lava-hot. "It already happened, okay? What can we do about it? Let the Thai police figure that out. We don't have the time."

Muir looked worriedly around the terrace, as if he might see Deville creeping toward him at that very moment. "Archer says he can't imagine them going through with the delivery tonight."

"Sure they will. He's already launched the job. The Vietnamese trucks had to leave Sai Gon yesterday in order to get here tonight. He knows we work for the government, and he knows governments are slow. And around here they're either bought off or deliberately looking the other way."

"Don't you have any thoughts about your friend Sal?" Muir said nothing else, just sitting at the table, staring upriver into the fading pink sun and twirling his beer.

"Focus your mind, Professor. If you want the truth, it's obvious. He killed Marino to scare us."

"Well, it worked with me."

"Why? Didn't you think this was real before?" Condley watched the gentle scientist for another moment and melted a bit. After all, this was his calling, his way of life, not Muir's. "You can always wait for me here. Or just go back to the hotel."

Muir twirled his beer some more, staring at the bottle as he worked his mouth into little grimaces. "Obviously, I am tempted by that thought."

"You've got nothing to gain by going down there. And no offense, but you'd probably be in the way."

Muir thought about it some more and then looked up at Condley. "We've been through a lot together, Brandon." He smiled self-consciously. "I guess that sounds like a cliché, but I'm oddly proud of it, sick as it might seem. And if I didn't come tonight, I'd feel like I was abandoning you. You need someone to look out for you, whether you'll admit it or not."

"Sounds like a plan," said Condley, reaching his hand across the table.

Muir took his hand, shaking it firmly. "Actually, I'm counting on you to indeed have some kind of a plan."

"I do," said Condley, smiling grimly. "My plan is to see their plan, and then improvise."

Muir rolled his eyes, then sighed deeply. "Are there any . . . shall we say, specifics to this idea?"

"Four trucks," said Condley. "Two driven by Vietnamese, two driven by Burmese. A white guy taking a payoff. And drivers trading places."

"A white guy with a gun."

"There'll be more than one gun. So maybe I can use your eyes."

"I could be your spotter."

"We could always try to shake Simolzak down for another pistol," teased Condley.

Muir shrugged, pretending seriousness. "I think the moment has passed on that one, unless you brought another girl."

"Have you ever fired a gun, Professor?"

"Actually, I used to own a BB gun. They came in handy in Indiana. I was twelve at the time."

"Not good enough."

"I knew that." Muir suddenly chuckled, as if the whole thing were so ludicrous that it was logical. "Oh, all right, I will be your squire. Lead on, fair knight. And I shall follow."

It was growing dark. Condley drained his beer and checked his watch. "Then let's go."

Muir took a deep breath. His eyes moved this way and that, avoiding Condley's. "Can I go to the men's room first?"

Condley laughed, rising from his chair. "I'll go with you. This is probably going to take a while."

WHEN THEY LEFT the hotel Condley walked down to the nearby Oriental Pier, where he flagged a boat taxi rather than taking a *tuk tuk* or a cab to Klong Toey. From this part of Bangkok the river was far faster than the choked roads.

The two men sat on low seats near the waterline in the long, slim boat, its outboard motor whining and the warm, musky water of the river splashing against their faces. The bright lights and gaudy hotels of new Bangkok slipped quickly past them as they sped down the river. A bridge flashed overhead, choked with evening traffic. The river bent slowly around a turn. And soon the boat's driver had beached them up against the darkened shoreline near the shacks and concrete gutters of the slaughterhouse. They landed only yards from where Manh and Dzung had stood a few hours before.

"Amphibious assault," joked Condley quietly as he helped the lumbering Muir out of the boat. Then the boat taxi sped away, and they were alone. It was pitch-black. Nothing moved around them. Uphill they could hear the woeful screams of dying hogs.

Muir's face shined from the glow of a distant light, his terror palpable. "Don't get too far away from me, Brandon."

"Stay right behind me." Condley pointed toward the noise. "It's not far. Walk slowly and don't talk. If somebody sees us, pretend you're bored. We're going up this hill."

"Bored?" asked Muir, breathlessly following Condley. *"Bored?"*

"Like maybe you're here to buy some meat."

Condley knew Klong Toey. When he first came to Bangkok after the war, he had run the security detail for an American company that, among other things, owned several farms near Chiang Mai. The company, a part of which was a CIA front, had raised hogs and goats. The goats, with Condley escorting them, were usually sold to Iran and were shipped along with hidden weapons to assist the clandestine forces of the recently ousted Shah. The hogs, along with Condley, most often came to Klong Toey. A lot had changed in Iran since then. But despite all of Thailand's advances, very little had changed in Klong Toey, especially in the slaughterhouse section.

The gutter next to them on the dirt path was pulsing and splashing with a runoff that was rolling slowly downhill toward the river. Its rich aromas surrounded them as they crept up the hill, filling their nostrils and attacking their lungs.

"What is that?" whispered Muir, pointing to the gutter.

"Hog blood," said Condley. "And guts. Mixed with water."

"I stood in it when I got off the boat!" said Muir disgustedly.

"You sure did," muttered Condley, his eyes fixed piercingly to his front. They were nearing the slaughter pens, and in front of them the road was lined with trucks. Behind him he heard the professor retch. He kept going. This was not the time to baby-sit a sick scientist.

As he moved slowly up the path he reached underneath his shirt, testing his grip on his pistol. He did not want to walk into the open with the pistol in his hand lest someone, even a worker, see it and attempt to disarm him or kill him. Instead, he had placed the Glock inside the belt just over his right hip, so that he could draw it and fire it in one smooth motion. The extra magazine was in his left pocket, as were enough bullets for a reload.

Your fucking ammo better work, Simolzak.

Muir shuffled close behind him, done with his puking. The dirt path ended and the slaughter pens were suddenly before him, filled with the sickening sights and screams of hogs being killed, hacked into sections, and dressed for the market. As he walked along the edges of the pens he saw them in the floodlit street: four trucks with identical company markings and green sideboards near the front of a long line of vehicles, moving slowly into place at the slaughterhouse gates so that their hogs could be off-loaded into the waiting pens. The drivers and passengers in the front two trucks were clearly Vietnamese. The drivers and passengers in the third and fourth trucks were Burmese. Also in the fourth truck was a brooding, dark-faced Caucasian.

"He's early," said Condley quietly to Muir as well as to himself, his whole body going electric with goose bumps. "If we'd taken a taxi we'd have missed the son of a bitch."

The trucks halted. The men on the passenger sides got out first, jogging to the rear of the trucks and dropping the tailgates so that the Thai workers could begin unloading the hogs. As the hogs were being unloaded, the drivers and the Caucasian also left the trucks, nine men gathering in a small circle, conversing with an idle familiarity as they waited for the hogs to be slaughtered, dressed, and packed back into their trucks.

Condley watched them intently as he moved slowly toward a concrete wall off to his right that made the outer boundary of the nearest slaughter pen. The Caucasian was thick and heavily muscled. His head was shaved to the scalp, and his round face was gashed with a long, full mustache. For a moment Condley stutter-stepped, unsure of himself. He could not be certain that this was the computer-enhanced face of Deville that he had studied for so many hours. Deville had not been so bulkily built. The face should have been squarer. Or maybe it was just that the computer enhancement had given Deville hair. Lots of hair.

"Professor, get inside that slaughter pen."

Muir's voice came from behind him. "With the hogs? You've got to be kidding!"

One of the Vietnamese men took a package out of his truck cab and walked back to their little group, handing it to the Caucasian man. The package was about the size of a briefcase and was wrapped in brown paper. The Caucasian man took it, holding it in both his hands. It all seemed to be happening too quickly, but with the Caucasian man's hands full and with the others so distracted, there could be no better time. And if he did not act now, there might not be another time.

Condley leapt inside the slaughter pen. The concrete wall was waist-high in front of him. He drew the Glock from under his shirt and started to aim. But then he stopped. A lot of trucks came through the slaughter-house district. A lot of packages passed back and forth. Even a few Caucasian men made it there with the trucks from time to time. Condley himself had done so in another life.

He was ready to kill this man. But before he did, he wanted to know.

"Deville!" He screamed it as loudly as he could. His voice echoed off the nearby trucks, above the screams of the dying animals and the sounds of machetes hacking through pork and bones. The Caucasian man dropped the packet, looking toward him and racing for the cover of a nearby truck. And Condley knew that he was right.

He fired Simolzak's Glock but was unfamiliar with its trigger pull. The round went low, causing him to curse as it whacked into the truck. Behind him, Hanson Muir was screaming, scrambling to get his body over the wall and inside the slaughter pen. The men in front of him were pressed against the trucks, calling to one another and drawing weapons. He thought he could take all of them if he had to, but most of all he wanted Deville. The asshole's head appeared and he aimed again, this time squeezing the trigger with a slow, deliberate pressure.

He didn't get the round off. Without warning, a burst of fire came at him from further to his left. He turned toward it, stunned. A second round, a third, steadily pulled from a rifle. He spun to the ground, still cradling his pistol as a bullet tore into his shoulder. Another round and Muir dropped just beside him, holding a ripped thigh.

"Brandonnnnn!"

"Okay, goddamn it, they brought *five* fucking trucks," he muttered to no one in particular, huddling against the wall.

"Didn't you say you knew how to *improvise?*" screamed Muir, looking up at him and then over at a pen full of squealing, stampeding hogs.

He quickly checked his shoulder. Lucky hit, on the outside, not much in the muscle at all. The shoulder was bleeding, but he still could move the joint. Slowly he knelt, trying to look forward again.

ON THE OTHER side of the street, inside the nearly blind old woman's hooch, Manh and Dzung lay flat on the wooden slats that made the floor. After they had eaten, Manh had reached into his pack and ordered Dzung to slip black pajamas over his working clothes. They had sat quietly for two hours after that, watching the trucks move slowly past the slaughter pens, Manh's electric eyes counting, calculating, waiting for some magical chimera that would cause him to send Dzung into action.

When Condley screamed Deville's name, Dzung had immediately recognized his voice. He had looked quickly to Manh, taking deep breaths to burn up some of the adrenaline that exploded inside his veins. The Interior Ministry official had merely nodded, as if agreeing that it was indeed Condley. Dzung clutched his pistol, crouching. It was going to happen, whatever it was. And then it would, at least, finally be over.

The nine men from the four trucks now stood on the road just in front of them. They were all looking the other way, toward Condley, leaning into the trucks and using them as barricades. Four of them, including the large white man, were firing pistols in the direction of the slaughter pens. Off to their right Dzung could see another man behind a different truck, shooting slowly and carefully with a military carbine, as if he were a sniper. No firing was coming from the slaughter pen where Condley had fallen.

Maybe he is already dead. Maybe I won't have to kill him.

Manh took a deep breath and then slapped Dzung on his back. "Now it happens!" he said fiercely, his face wild with determination. He pointed toward the trucks.

"The white man!"

Dzung had already crouched, ready to burst across the narrow road. He turned quickly to Manh. "*That* white man?"

"With the mustache. At the truck. *Go!*"

Dzung bolted from the hooch, running wildly, fired by the reality that there were five guns in front of him, that he had only seven shots in his pistol, and that Manh had trained him repeatedly to kill only one man. One man. Seven shots. Two to the chest, three to the head, two back to the chest. *Shoot only the man I tell you to shoot.*

Bullshit.

They were only thirty feet away, and they were looking toward the slaughter pens. He held his fire until he was within five feet of his target, then put a bullet quickly into the back of his head. The other three with pistols were less than twenty feet away. He turned to the right, quickly shooting the single man on that side, and then rolled behind one truck bed, standing up and putting two bullets apiece into the other two on his left. One in the chest, one in the head.

He had one bullet left. The men who were not shooting before were scrambling in the dirt road, trying to find the weapons that the others had dropped. Two trucks down from him, the sniper with the rifle had turned around toward him and had a bead. Dzung had enough time to raise the pistol and fire a shot that careened off the truck, near the sniper's head, causing the man to cringe for a second.

And then he was out of ammunition.

He was in the middle of the road and had to run across it, past the slaughter pens and down the dirt trail to the river. The sniper had a free shot, and the sniper was good. Dzung crouched between two trucks, preparing to sprint for his very life, and then three shots suddenly exploded in front of him. They crossed him, left to right. He looked quickly at the far truck and saw the sniper fall.

He had no more time to think. He bolted across the road, heading for the dirt path. And as he passed the slaughter pen he saw Condley leaning against its concrete wall. Condley was bleeding from his left shoulder and grimacing, his eyes wild with anger and pain. But seeing Dzung, he held his Glock in the air as if in victory and gave Dzung a thumbs-up with his left hand as the *cyclo* driver raced down the dark path toward the river.

INSIDE THE PEN, the slaughterhouse workers had raced away, taking refuge from the gun battle behind the far walls. More than twenty huge hogs were trampling the flesh of hog-tied and already-killed animals, grouping in one corner until a few of them would suddenly bolt and squirm, causing them to again rush madly until they reached a new hiding place. Muir lay against one wall, holding his bleeding leg, seemingly more fearful of the hogs than of the battle on the road.

Condley still leaned against the front wall, his pistol at the ready, watching to see if the other five men would open fire. But these were the drivers, and they seemed bent on escape. Instead of shooting back at him, they had quickly moved into the trucks and were starting the engines. One of the Burmese drivers had picked up the package and thrown it into his cab. Condley did not care. He wanted them to go. What he had come for was lying dead on the dirt road before him. He had no quarrel with them, and he did not want to fight another war over the contents of their cargo.

Then the other Burmese driver ran to Deville's body and started to drag it by the belt toward his truck. Condley fired a round through the driver's windshield, warning him, and another at his feet. The driver dropped the body, then put both of his hands into the air and ran wildly to his truck. Within seconds, the five trucks churned out of line, running over the bodies they left behind as they quickly made their way out of Klong Toey.

He sagged against the wall. It was over. All of it. The danger and the evil both were gone, and with them the anger. He was bleeding, but it was good blood, spilled in a just cause. A sense of peace passed over him, like the stroking of a large and gentle hand. For the first time in his memory, Condley felt content with himself. It occurred to him at that moment that now would be a good time to go home. If he actually had a home.

The hogs grew quiet. There was a dreadful hush, and then the people of Klong Toey slowly started howling. Condley stared cautiously around him amid the whines of little children and old women that were emanating from the nearby houses, testing the certainty of his victory. Then he stood at the wall, remaining for several seconds, almost inviting someone to kill him. No gunfire. And finally he walked slowly toward a corner of the slaughter pen where several hogs were cowering, causing them to squeal anew.

"Brandon, what are you doing?" asked a wheezing Hanson Muir.

Without answering, he picked up a machete that one slaughterhouse worker had abandoned in the dirt when the gunfight broke out. Then he slowly climbed over the slaughter pen wall and walked toward the bodies that littered the dust-filled street.

"Head shots," he muttered, moving from one body to another and seeing the results of Dzung's few seconds of work. "Look at that! The fucking guy was a pro."

The body of the Caucasian man was lying facedown in the road. Three sets of truck tracks had squashed it from hips to ankles. Condley stood over it for a moment, taking deep breaths to control his seething fury. Then he grabbed it at the shoulders, turning it over so that he could see Deville's face. Dzung's bullet had exited just below the left eye, but other than that small hole, the face was smooth and oddly unlined. Life after Viet Nam had apparently treated Mr. Deville pretty well, despite his venal journeys.

"Hello, Salt," he finally managed to say. "Marines are like elephants. We forget nothing." And then he took off the dead man's left hand with one smashing blow of the machete.

He dropped the machete and picked up the hand by its thumb, a slick angry nausea growing within him. Inside the makeshift house just behind the man's carcass he found an old green knapsack. He did not know it, but he had just put Theodore Deville's hand into the pack that Dzung had left behind.

Muir had managed to stand and was leaning against the wall of the slaughter pen, testing his leg. He watched with amazed eyes as Condley walked back across the street and dropped the knapsack on the wall. And then he spoke quietly, in the careful tones of a nervously empathetic counselor.

"And just what compelled you to do that, Brandon?"

"I thought you'd want a set of fingerprints."

"That's very kind, actually." Muir looked down the dirt path toward the river. "Who was that man?"

"He looked Vietnamese," said Condley.

"Where did he possibly come from?"

"I have no idea, Professor. But the boy could shoot."

MANH HAD PREPARED him well. Dzung jogged easily down the dirt path, familiar with its bumps and contours from the afternoon's visit. At the riverbank he heaved the pistol with all his might into the muddy river. No one would ever find it in the turgid waters and the hog-drenched mud. Then he turned upriver, measuring his steps until he had gone as close to a hundred meters as he could estimate. At that point, as an afterthought, he removed his black pajamas, wadding them into a tight ball and then wading into the river, placing them underwater inside a thick bed of water hyacinths so that they would not float downstream. He then made his way uphill along another dirt trail until he reached the road.

It surprised him that the slaughterhouse district seemed to have quickly regained its calm. Far down the road he could see people gathered in front of the slaughter pens where the gunfight had taken place, but the trucks were again moving and the hogs were squealing as the workers again stood in the pens, hacking them up for food. The vacant lot where the man had kissed the little boy's penis was just across the street. He walked slowly to it and then stood for a moment, waiting. But he did not see Manh.

He is angry at me because I killed so many soldiers.

Yes, soldiers, he thought insistently, because that was what he had done. He had again been ordered into battle and he had again survived. And like so many times before, his commanding officer's orders had to be revised on the battlefield. Manh would have to understand that.

And then a cold thought chilled him. Maybe Manh had prepared him falsely on that one point, deliberately setting him up to die. The thought worked on him as he made his way toward the Vietnamese Embassy, checkpoint by checkpoint, just as Manh had taught him. Maybe all of Manh's careful preparation was itself a ruse, designed to gain his confidence so that he would not fail in the actual attack. Maybe when he returned to the embassy the Thai police would be waiting for him, alerted by Manh himself that a Vietnamese national had perpetrated a heinous crime. For what did Manh, whose own father had died on the other side, owe a former enemy soldier from District Four?

Another thought visited him as he walked along Bangkok's dark streets. He was free. He did not have to go back, either to the embassy or to Viet Nam. He could simply keep walking, or turn around and head in another direction, and never be found again. He could learn the language, find work, move to America or Australia, sleep in a bed, wear real shoes.

But after he had thought about such dreams for another block, he knew that they were pure fantasy. Manh had it right. He was as predictable as the rains. He wanted nothing more just then than to go back to Sai Gon, to somehow find where they had taken his *cyclo* and reclaim it so that he could pedal home to his family again.

Manh was waiting for him at the last checkpoint, two blocks from the embassy. The agent surprised him, stepping out from an alley and suddenly walking beside him. Manh's face was still bright with amazement as he put an arm around his shoulder.

"So, Mister Trong. You sold your rice very well. And more importantly, you came back!"

"Yes, Manh," said Dzung. His earlier anger flashed, as if a release valve inside his usual serenity had blown. "So why did you tell me to shoot only one person, and only the person you said? Tell me the truth,

Manh. It doesn't matter anymore. Did you want me to be killed by the others?"

"I will tell you the truth," said Manh simply as they walked. "There are not usually this many guns. My intelligence report was not complete. I did not even know that the man would be on the other side of the road and would shoot at them. It totally surprised me."

"It was Cong Ly."

"I swear to you," said Manh. "We did not think he would find the target so quickly. We wanted to kill the target before Cong Ly could convince other people to capture it. It was important that the target die before it could talk."

"You and Cong Ly were after the same man?"

"For him it was a man," shrugged Manh. "For us it was a target."

"Who was it?"

"You are not allowed to know. And you must never ask again." Manh looked at him with genuine awe. "I did not think you would be able to do that. I have never seen such shooting."

Dzung relaxed for the first time. He began to feel sleepy, as if his feet were dragging behind him on the pavement. "I told you I was born to do this."

"I know," said Manh, lighting a cigarette as they walked.

"My files," joked Dzung.

Manh nodded cerebrally. "Of course."

"So, another thing?"

"Yes?" said Manh.

"How did my side lose the war?"

Manh laughed. He ceremoniously held his cigarette up in the air in the odd place that he always kept it, at the bottom of two fingers. "We are on the same side now, Mister Trong. The war is over."

"Maybe for you and me," said Dzung, thinking about what awaited him on his return to Sai Gon. "But for the others, I don't think so. Not yet."

They walked silently for a while. The Vietnamese Embassy was just in front of them. "We go back tomorrow," said Manh. "In case something goes wrong in Klong Toey, I don't want anyone to see you in Bangkok."

It was bothering him. He deserved to know. He watched Manh's face carefully. "As long as I am still Mister Trong, I have the right to ask. Who did I kill, Manh?"

"It does not matter who you killed," said Manh. "You killed who you were supposed to."

"That's not good enough. Tell me. Who was it?"

Manh grunted. The question was beyond his authority to answer. "I cannot tell you, and again I must warn you. Do not ask me that, and do not mention anything about this mission when you are back in Sai Gon. To anyone. I am serious. It never happened, do you understand? But you should not feel bad. It was like killing the devil."

The embassy was very near. Dzung knew he would never have another chance to discuss it. "The devil was trying to kill Cong Ly?"

"Yes," said Manh.

Dzung nodded. They were at the embassy steps. If all went well, he would soon have a good meal and a long sleep on a real bed.

"Then I was on the right side," he finally said. "And that is good enough for me."

———

THE GUNFIGHT HAD become irrelevant in a matter of minutes. No one offered to help Condley and Muir, and no one asked them any questions about what had happened. At some point, perhaps tomorrow, the police would arrive and questions would be asked. But for now, it was simply another night in Klong Toey.

Condley eased Muir over the low wall of the slaughter pen, and they moved slowly across the street, finding a place to rest on the wooden slats that made the old lady's floor. The rats came out, scurrying from beneath the raised slats and heading toward the river. The drivers of other trucks had dragged the five dead bodies out of the road, making a litter pile not far from where Condley and Muir now sat.

Neither was badly shot. The sniper either had an awkward firing angle from behind his truck or had rushed himself after Condley's ear-shattering scream. Condley took off his T-shirt and ripped it, fashioning a battle dressing that he pulled tightly over the wound in Muir's thigh. He then folded another piece into a square and pressed it hard into his shoulder, holding it there in an attempt to stanch the bleeding.

"What now, oh master improviser?" asked the professor. His shoes stank of river mud and hog guts, and his face was wet with sweat as he fought against the pain of his wound.

"Now comes Father Mike," said Condley, nodding toward the rear of the line of trucks.

From the moment he was shot he had known that Father Mike would find him. The only question was whether the priest would bandage him or bury him. Father Mike's ministry was in Klong Toey. Nothing in the district went past him. And here the frail priest came, half jogging along the dirt road, his hands fussing with each other just above his waist as if he were counting beads on an imaginary rosary. His eyes went this way and that, searching, until he saw the bodies in the road. He stopped, looking down at them and shaking his head. And then behind the bodies he finally saw Condley.

"Brandon, is that you?" Father Mike crossed himself as he approached the bodies. "They're all dead, are they?"

"I've been waiting for you, Father."

Father Mike knelt next to Condley, examining his wound. "What have you gotten yourself into now?"

"I found the guy who killed my Marines. Remember?" The rest of it was too complicated. Condley thought about it and came up with some shorthand. "He murdered Sal Marino this morning."

Father Mike crossed himself again, closing his eyes. "May the Lord bless Sal and keep him." He looked at Condley. "And you decided to kill him in return, did you?"

"No, I didn't kill him," said Condley dismissively. "Father, I need to get out of here. There are some well-connected people who are going to be upset about those bodies over there. And the Thai police can be extremely weird."

"An astute observation," nodded Father Mike. "If you're in line for some form of retaliation, I don't think it would be healthy for you to be spending the night in a Bangkok jail cell."

"Not to mention that I need very badly to catch a plane tomorrow."

Hanson Muir groaned unbelievingly. "I need a doctor, Brandon, not an airplane."

"Trust me, Professor. An infected leg is better than a dead brain."

Father Mike tested the bandage on Muir's thigh. Muir winced when the priest pushed on his wound, and then groaned, fainting. "If you didn't kill him, then this man did?" asked Father Mike.

"No," said Condley, chuckling at the absurdity of that thought. "It was pretty messy. Look around you, Father. Look at us. There were a lot of guns."

"I understand," said Father Mike, probing Muir's wound again. "But most of them seem to have been pointed at you. So, who? Who killed him?"

"I don't know, I really don't. The guy came from nowhere, and he took off when he was done. I only shot one man. Because he was trying to shoot the man who saved me."

"Only one?"

"Only one." He could not stop himself from laughing. "I tried to shoot the white guy but I missed. Then this deadeye dinger showed up. What a show, I'm not kidding."

"Brandon, Brandon," sighed Father Mike. "There's always something, isn't there? I think you were simply born to be shot at." The priest began humming softly as he worked on Muir. "It's not a bad wound. And you seem fine. So what do you need?"

"You didn't see us here, Father." Father Mike watched him carefully, his soft face going stubborn in the shadows. "In fact, you've got to get us out of here before somebody else does see us."

"Are you asking me to lie?"

"Actually, yes."

"It would be on my conscience. I will have to think about that." It didn't take long. Father Mike stood, helping Condley to his feet. "All right. If we can wake your friend up, he will be easier to assist."

Muir slowly awakened. Together they helped the professor to his feet. Condley strapped the knapsack containing Deville's severed hand over his shoulder. Then the two men braced Muir between them and walked along the street, heading toward Father Mike's mission house.

The small priest lectured Condley as they walked. "You must understand that I cannot allow you to stay inside my mission. There are careful lines that must be drawn here, Brandon. I can honor my vows by administering first aid to you, so I will dress your wounds. But then you must leave. If the police ask me to identify you, I will decline. I am comfortable with that. I am a priest, not an identifier of criminals. Not an agent for the police. Any police. But if I wish to remain morally and legally neutral, I cannot harbor you in my chapel either."

"Fine," said Condley through gritted teeth. "Then do you think God will allow you to call me a fucking cab?"

"It would be unfair to make a cab driver a potential aider and abettor of a crime," said Father Mike judiciously. "Not to mention a witness to your escape." He delicately dropped a key chain into Condley's pocket. "If you're strong enough to drive, Brandon, my best recommendation is that you should steal my car."

"I'll leave it at the Oriental pier," said Brandon.

"No, take it back to your hotel."

"I didn't commit a crime, Father. Remember that if we don't see each other again?"

"I believe you," said Father Mike, allowing himself a small grin. "And I assume there won't be a problem if I pick up my car tomorrow morning?"

"I'll leave your key with the valet. And you don't even need to worry about a tip."

Inside the medical office of his mission, Father Mike carefully cleaned and dressed their wounds. Afterward, he went to a closet where he kept several boxes of clothes sent to the people of Klong Toey from parishioners in the United States, finding Condley a shirt and Hanson Muir a pair of baggy sweatpants. On the way out, he located an old cane and gave it to the professor, who was recovering nicely now that his leg was properly wrapped. And then he led them back outside.

Far down the road, the trucks were still lining up before the slaughter pens, and no police were yet in sight. They reached Father Mike's Honda and he opened up the passenger-side door, helping Hanson Muir into the seat.

"There'll be a gun in the trunk when you pick up the car," said Condley, opening the door on the driver's side. "Give it back to Ted Simolzak."

Father Mike sighed wearily. "Are you saying Ted Simolzak is involved in this too?"

Condley tossed the knapsack containing Deville's hand and now also the Glock into the backseat. "Not unless they take fingerprints off the casings from the bullets I shot," he said. And then he laughed softly, remembering. "But I think he's got an airtight alibi."

"At the Cezanne, is he?"

"I doubt it," said Condley, easing himself into the driver's seat. "I made him a trade for the use of his pistol, Father. He's probably got his hands full with that right now."

"I won't ask," smiled Father Mike as Condley closed the door and started the Honda's engine.

"Don't, Father," said Condley. He put his hands prayerfully together underneath his chin, everybody's Bangkok good-bye. "It would only disappoint you."

Then he waved and pulled out from the narrow driveway, turning onto the road.

CHAPTER THIRTY-SIX

The Bangkok Post

Shoot-out in Klong Toey Kills Five

Rival Drug Gangs Clash

In a scene reminiscent of the infamous gunfight at the OK Corral, five men were shot dead last night in a shoot-out that took place in full view of residents and workers in the slaughterhouse section of Klong Toey. The five victims included two Vietnamese, two Burmese, and a Caucasian man who has yet to be identified. They were apparently members of a drug gang believed to be responsible for the death yesterday morning of Salvatore Marino, an American expatriate who had just returned from serving a sentence in Japan for running drugs in that country.

Witnesses say that the gunfight broke out when the five men, as well as several other members of their operation, were waiting for a cargo of hogs to be slaughtered and returned to their trucks. Mr. Marino had been found dead earlier in the day, with his left hand forcibly amputated, and the killers last night cut off the hand of one of the victims in seeming retaliation.

Witnesses claim that there were at least three attackers, all of whom escaped, although one may have been wounded. Local hospitals are being asked to report visits by anyone with suspicious gunshot wounds. Although the killings took place near the slaughterhouse pens of Klong Toey, police investigators claim that the killings were "almost definitely" drug related, due to the obvious connection with Mr. Marino's murder. "It is a puzzle to us, but this was the work of professional hit men, and they certainly wouldn't be killing each other over pigs," said one police spokesman, who asked to remain nameless. The investigation will continue, he said, "until we have brought all sides to justice."

CHAPTER THIRTY-SEVEN

The Honolulu Advertiser

Deserter's Remains Recovered

Bangkok Shoot-out Yields Odd Results

One of the victims in a recent gang-related shooting in the slums of Bangkok was identified today as Theodore Deville, a U.S. Army deserter from the Viet Nam War.

Dr. Hanson Muir of the Central Identification Labs, Hawaii (CILHI), which is responsible for the identification of remains of U.S. servicemen, issued a formal statement this morning indicating that the lab has "positively identified" the remains based on fingerprints obtained from the crime scene. Deville, who disappeared from an Army base near Sai Gon in late 1967, had been charged with murder as well as several drug-related offenses at the time he deserted from the Army. "Apparently, this individual made his way to Thailand in the massive confusion that attended the war itself," speculated Dr. Muir. "And from the indications we have received from Thai authorities, he must have continued his earlier endeavors in the drug trade."

Dr. Muir further indicated that a preliminary check shows there are no known family members who could be contacted regarding the recovery of Deville's remains. "It is truly an odd ending to a tragic war," said Muir. "And we are happy to return to our business of identifying the remains of American heroes who were lost on the battlefield."

CHAPTER THIRTY-EIGHT

Sai Gon

"CONG LY! CONG LY!"

He could hear them calling even as he left the packed shops and the sidewalk vendors of Le Thanh Ton Street and turned in to the park. He had been lost in thought, celebrating as he always did the fading memories in this special heart of old Sai Gon. He loved the old landmarks, and as he walked toward them he had been worrying that they might soon disappear. In front of him was the ornate, yellow and white government building erected empires ago by the French, and over its shoulder he could barely see the red spires of the Duc Ba Chapel. The moonlike old Opera House was far off to his left. Tall hotels and office buildings were shooting up all over Sai Gon, many of them ugly and egregious, and soon these relics would be lost among them, like quaint houseboats in a modern shipyard.

But as long as the landmarks remained, there would be memories. And it was important that they remain, he thought again, for Sai Gon would be nothing but a broiling, rain-swept city without the haunting reminders of its past.

"Cong Ly! Over here!"

He walked across the grassy little park toward the Rex Hotel, just as he had done so many hundred times before. He waved gladly to them as they left their *cyclos* to greet him, passing under the garish statue of Ho Chi Minh, pushing his way through the sea of vendors, hustlers, and gawkers, ignoring the oddly dressed foreign tourists, until he was standing in their midst on the street corner across from the front doors of the Rex. And it was as if he was truly coming home.

"*Lau qua,* Cong Ly, *lau qua!* Maybe one month already! Where have you been for so long?"

"*Da, bi thuong, phai di nha thuong My,*" he said cockily, for in this world wounds were to be bragged about. *Wounded. American hospital.* It might have been the war itself as he pulled up his shirt and flashed his newest scar. "A gunfight in Bangkok."

"A gunfight!" They laughed and pointed and gawked, no strangers to wounds and scars. "*Rat tiec!* But you look strong now, so that is good!"

It struck him at that moment that he had now known these striving, uncomplaining men for more than five years. How could that be? he thought. Where had those years gone, and what had they gained him other than a bone over here and a friend over there? And then he smiled, secretly satisfied with that summation. Bones that were dug up and given an honored burial, bringing solace to forever-grieving relatives. Friends who had given him a strange but powerful sense of peace, so that he might finally bury the furious anger that had sent him out of orbit, into his own space journey for so long.

Or maybe he was just happy to be back.

They surrounded him in their worn clothes and old baseball caps, smiling through wrinkling faces, piercing eyes, and broken teeth, teasing and chattering as they touched his newest scar and celebrated his return. Dzung was not among them at that moment, but Condley was not surprised. It was not yet noon, and Dzung often worked late into the night.

It was as if all of them were shouting to him at once, elbowing each other and smiling with their peculiarly Vietnamese mix of flattery and shrewd ambition. "Hey, you take me, Cong Ly, this time you take me!"

"Maybe someday," he laughed. "Each one of you, someday!" He spoke to all of them, as a group. It was the same message and he had no need to single out one driver. "You tell Dzung I'm back in Sai Gon, okay? Tell him to come to the Vien Dong Hotel."

Luong, the driver who had taken Hanson Muir to District Four, stepped forward, hiding secret thoughts behind a wickedly careful smile. "Oh, Cong Ly. Dzung, he don't work here anymore. So you take me now?"

"Where is he?"

Luong ceased his pidgin English, switching to Vietnamese. "They took him off the street one day and brought him to Xuan Loc Prison," said Luong as the others nodded. "They interrogated him for many days. He was afraid to tell us everything, because if he speaks too much they will come and put him back in jail. But much of the questioning was about you, Cong Ly. They wanted to know everything about you. Where you go, what you think, who you see. But Dzung, he is your good friend. And he convinced them that you are not a dangerous man, I think."

"Why do you think that?" asked Condley, his insides roiling at the thought of his friend being back in prison.

"Okay, I show you."

Luong looked at the others, as if they now could reveal their little secret. He took a business card from his pocket and handed it to Condley:

World's best limo driver
Sai Gon 887-4135

Luong smiled slyly, again looking at the others as Condley read the card. "So, Cong Ly, you don't like the limo, I know that! Cong Ly, you never take the limo! Dzung, he gone! So now you let me be your *cyclo* driver. I will do very good job for you. No problem, anything you want. And maybe in five years you can sponsor me for limo business too?"

"Give me that card," laughed Condley, taking it from Luong's falsely protesting hand and walking back toward the hotel.

———————

TWO HOURS LATER, Dzung pulled up in front of the Vien Dong Hotel in his new Toyota four-door limo. He smiled proudly as Condley exited the hotel and walked toward him. Dzung's hair was cut and neatly combed.

He was wearing a clean white shirt, pressed gray trousers, and black leather shoes. He stood just a bit awkwardly, his arms dangling as his American friend met him at the curb, still in the habit of presenting himself humbly for inspection. And then he gestured toward the car.

"So, where we go today, Cong Ly?"

Seeing Dzung in front of the new car with his clean clothes and scrubbed face, Condley was overcome with a sudden rush of emotion. He put an arm around Dzung's shoulders and hugged him to his chest.

"Very good car, yes?" laughed a faintly embarrassed Dzung.

"A very good car. How did this happen?"

"You," said Dzung simply. "They asked me many questions, Cong Ly, about why you pick me for your business. Why did you want a business in Sai Gon, and why did you want to work with me? I was a soldier from the wrong side. I have no family connections. I have no money. But I think you passed their test. They decided that they trust you. I do not know why."

Condley thought about that possibility. While in Hawaii he had argued strongly in support of Colonel Pham's request that Deville's wartime activities be omitted from the official statement announcing the identification of the turncoat's remains. He had at first resisted the idea but then decided that he owed that much to the former Viet Cong colonel. Without Pham he never would have been able to find Pepper's remains in the Que Son Mountains or to question Anatolie Petrushinsky in Moscow. The colonel's only request was that the story of Theodore Deville die with him. And what good would it have done to tell it now?

And perhaps, he thought, Dzung's limo business was his reward. "Maybe I know why," he answered, opening the right front car door.

"Maybe," said Dzung judiciously, suppressing his memories as he climbed into the driver's side and started the car's engine. "So, where we go, Cong Ly?"

Condley thought for a moment, looking out at the busy street, and then decided. "You know Sai Gon University?"

"*Dai Hoc Kinh Te*, you mean?"

"Take me there."

Dzung glanced at him with surprise, for he knew that *Dai Hoc Kinh Te,* the School of Economics, was where Mai had studied. "You don't go there, Cong Ly. I remember that."

"I go now."

"That girl who died?"

"It's time."

Dzung smiled, gladdened at the thought. "You're sure?"

"We go now."

"That is good, Cong Ly. It makes me very happy for you."

Dzung pulled into the traffic. The car was impressively new. Its interior smelled as though it had just been delivered from the showroom floor. A question gnawed at Condley as he watched Dzung drive. "How did you pay for the car?"

"I don't pay yet," said Dzung carefully, turning onto Hai Ba Trung Street. They stopped at a red light and he glanced briefly at Condley. "They tell me I can drive the car and pay for it from our business."

"A loan from the government?" asked Condley, amazed at the thought.

"They tell me that," answered Dzung.

"They don't have any money."

Dzung shrugged. "Maybe they do."

The light turned green and a swarm of motorbikes whined past them, weaving in and out of the traffic lanes. Dzung drove smoothly. The old Duc Ba Chapel was off to their left, as was the huge post office built at the same time by the French a century ago. Soon the limo would turn left onto Nguyen Thi Minh, near the grounds of the Reunification Palace and the Ministry of Foreign Affairs.

Dzung seemed to gather himself a bit as he drove, and now he looked at Condley again. "They move my family out to Song Be. I have a house now."

"Song Be?" Condley began to eye Dzung carefully. "All of this good luck, and I've been gone only a month?"

"No space to park a limo in District Four," said Dzung. "I must tell you the truth. I was worried when you made the business application. But now I think it was a smart thing to do, Cong Ly."

Another light. The palace itself was two blocks off to their left. In the park between them and the palace, dozens of Vietnamese sat languidly in the grass and on old benches, waiting to be interviewed inside the Ministry of Foreign Affairs so that they might emigrate to the United States. The locals called this area Reeducation Camp Park. Thousands of long-term reeducation camp survivors had sat on its benches over the past decade, waiting for the visas that would allow them to leave.

Dzung turned left onto Nguyen Thi Minh. The road was jammed with trucks, cars, bicycles, *cyclos,* and people walking. He moved very carefully in the traffic. Condley studied the former *cyclo* driver, as if trying to see him for the first time. He could not take his eyes off Dzung's haircut as his old friend maneuvered in the thick traffic. Dark flashes burst inside his memory, from guns that were trying to kill him. And then a silhouette in black pajamas, shooting with the precision of a trained assassin. *Could it have been?*

They turned right onto Pasteur Street and soon reached the low walls of the university. Dzung slowed the car, pulling over to the curb next to the gate that led into the grounds. "I wait here?"

"Five minutes."

Dzung smiled fondly, his eyes reading Condley's emotions. "Like going to temple?"

Condley looked off toward the double-decker buildings, his mind filled with unquenchable memories. "A little."

"This will be good for you, Cong Ly. Now all the ghosts will be gone."

Condley began to open the car door, and then suddenly stopped. He leaned toward Dzung in the car, giving him another curious look. "That was you in Bangkok, wasn't it?"

Dzung kept smiling, serene in the silent majesty of a courage that he knew could never be openly acknowledged. "You can't ask me that, Cong Ly. It would be very dangerous for my family."

Condley laughed, looking left and right along the street as if for spies. "I know, I know. And I will never ask again. But it was you."

"I think," said Dzung, shrugging enigmatically.

"I've never seen anybody shoot like that."

"And you save me, Cong Ly."

"Hey, that was an easy shot."

"And so now we have a good business," smiled Dzung. "And we keep our mouths shut."

"Partner," said Condley, extending his hand.

"Partner," laughed Dzung, taking it in both of his. "I drive the limo. You pay the bills."

"*Duoc,*" said Condley. Then he climbed from the limo and stood for a long moment on the sidewalk, facing the small yard and aging buildings of *Dai Hoc Kinh Te*. And finally he walked inside the grounds.

He had not visited the tiny, French-built university in all the years since Mai had died. Even the thought had been too painful, like staring too long into the sun or putting one's hand inside a flame. His life had changed inalterably on the first day that he watched her pass through this very gate, in her white *ao dai* with her hair flowing down her back and her schoolbooks tied in a strap and clutched against her chest. And it had changed again just as dramatically the last time he had walked out of it, following a memorial service held by her former classmates. Her family had watched him throughout that service, blaming him and yet unable to denounce him, for to publicly denounce him would have been to admit that Mai had loved him, and their only satisfaction was to keep that recognition from him as she disappeared into her grave and they faded from his life. But their unforgiving eyes had scarred him more deeply than any war wound.

Walking inside the gate, he found himself glad that he had come. So much had changed since he last stood on this spot. And yet as he looked around him, he found that on the surface almost everything inside the gates had remained the same. It wasn't the same, he knew it. But he knew also that one had to look closely and understand deeply to comprehend that it was different.

Classes had just ended. A sea of young women wearing the white *ao dais* that marked them as students poured out of the buildings, ready to leave the campus through the gate that he had just entered. They reached him and flowed endlessly past him, as if he were walking through a valley of flowers or a heaven crowded with young angels. They smiled curiously at him as they passed, amused at his silent, remembering stare, and then went back to their playful chatter, forgetting him in the instant it took to reach the gate. Their white *ao dais* were nunlike, and yet ineluctably inviting. Their long hair cascaded down their backs, marking the white silk of their identical dresses like necessary vestments. Their voices were musical as they laughed and teased in that difficult, tonal language that had over the long years become almost as normal to him as his own.

As the girls flowed through the gates he found that Mai was with him, laughing also, whispering her delight. He felt her buoyant presence. Yes, he decided, Mai was here, and she was happy. He had been in Viet Nam long enough to believe that such visits were possible.

And he sensed that Van had been right in the frantic note that she had left underneath Francois Petain's perfume bottle in the bathroom of the Riverside Hotel all those weeks or maybe lives ago. Not about herself; only time would tell with that. But about him. Now he was free. Someday he might even find a woman to love for a lifetime, *yeu* instead of *thuong*. There was still time for that. Van herself might return someday, wiser and more loving from her journey, and who knew what would happen if she did?

And yet what Van had said was inalterably true. He might love another woman, and he hoped that someday he would. But no woman could ever fully own his heart. Because he would always be in love with Viet Nam.

Viet Nam, Viet Nam. The whole land laughed at him with fresh delight every morning, winking playfully as it set out once again to betray him. It dangled its mysteries before him, puzzles that only deepened every time he tried to solve them. It embraced him so tightly that in a way he had become it, looking out at the rest of the world from inside its eyes as if he were Brer Rabbit, gummed up in the Tar Baby.

Viet Nam, Viet Nam. It had suborned him all those years ago like a wily beggar, luring him inside the tangle of its tragedies and stealing away his boyhood. It had wounded and punished him as he dared to believe he could change it. It had shown him that he could love and then relentlessly destroyed the very treasure it had offered him, finally driving him away as if he were a demonic madman. And after all the years in the wilderness it had welcomed him back again only to tease him, asking everything of him but giving nothing in return except his heart, the same heart it had once so cruelly stolen.

But despite it all he had remained, unable to end his passion for its jungles and its alleyways. Was that not a monumental sort of love?

Dzung was waiting for him at the curb, watching his movements with ever-careful eyes. His friend smiled shrewdly as Condley reached the car, having seen the right signs in his stride.

"So, she was with you, Cong Ly. The girl who died."

"You always know, don't you, Dzung?"

"About these things, I think."

Dzung's smile turned sentimental. His hands were cupped together in front of him and now he looked down at them. He opened them a bit and Condley saw that he was holding a small white pigeon. The bird looked this way and that as Dzung gently stroked its head with a finger.

"My father came to see me. He landed on the roof of the car!"

With a slow, uplifting motion, Dzung tossed the bird into the air. It fluttered a bit, finding its wings, and then flew away toward the school. For a long moment Dzung watched it, his hands remaining high in the air as if he were reaching for the sky.

"He went over the school, Cong Ly! A good sign."

"A very good sign," agreed Condley, watching the pigeon disappear.

Satisfied with this good fortune, they climbed into the car. Dzung grinned at him as he started the engine. "So, where we go now?"

Condley leaned back against the seat, enjoying its firmness and the fresh, new smells of the car's interior. He felt very, very free, and even slightly prosperous. Dzung pulled carefully into the traffic and then looked quickly over to him, his eyes asking for directions. Where did he want to go? Condley did not know and at that moment he did not even care.

"*Di dau, ma chang duoc,*" he finally said, drawing a quick laugh from his friend.

Anywhere we want.

ABOUT THE AUTHOR

JAMES WEBB has worked and traveled in Vietnam extensively since 1991. A graduate of the U.S. Naval Academy and the Georgetown Law Center, he was one of the most highly decorated Marines of the Vietnam War, receiving the Navy Cross, Silver Star, two Bronze Stars, and two Purple Hearts for his combat service. An attorney and Emmy Award–winning journalist, he has served as Secretary of the Navy, Assistant Secretary of Defense, and full committee counsel to the U.S. Congress. He lives in Virginia, where he has authored five critically acclaimed, best-selling novels, including *Fields of Fire*, the classic novel of the Vietnam War.